BLACKCOLLAR
THE
JUDAS SOLUTION

BY
TIMOTHY ZAHN

D0210111

BLACKCOLLAR: THE JUDAS SOLUTION

This is a work of fiction. All the characters and events portrayed in this book are fictional, and any resemblance to real people or incidents is purely coincidental.

A Baen Book Original

Baen Publishing Enterprises
P.O. Box 1403
Riverdale, NY 10471
www.baen.com

ISBN 10: 1-4165-5543-9
ISBN 13: 978-1-4165-5543-8

Cover art by David Mattingly

First Baen paperback printing, May 2008

Distributed by Simon & Schuster
1230 Avenue of the Americas
New York, NY 10020

Library of Congress Cataloging-in-Publication Data: 2006005329

Printed in the United States of America

10 9 8 7 6 5 4 3 2 1

BLACKCOLLAR
THE
JUDAS SOLUTION

PROLOGUE

A sprinkling of new snow had fallen overnight on the western slopes of the Bernese Oberland in central Switzerland, and Security Prefect Jamus Galway found himself squinting against the reflected early-morning sunlight as he walked down the transport's entry ramp. It had taken five months of slow and painstaking investigation, but at last the search was about to come to an end.

Maybe.

A young man was waiting for him at the bottom of the ramp, and even through slitted eyelids Galway could see the other's face go suddenly rigid as the prefect's escort appeared in the shuttle's hatchway behind him. It was the same reaction he'd encountered nearly everywhere he'd gone in the past five months, from the back streets of central Europe to the elite governmental centers of New Geneva. Even here on Earth, after thirty years of Ryqril rule over what had once been the proudly independent Terran Democratic Empire, the vast majority of TDE citizens had never seen a Ryq up close and personal.

Even fewer of those citizens had seen a *khassq*-class warrior like the one now striding down the ramp a pace behind him. Certainly fewer *living* citizens. Most people who found themselves facing a *khassq* didn't survive the encounter.

The young man had his expression under control again by the time Galway reached the bottom of the ramp. "Prefect Galway," he said formally. "I'm Security Lieutenant Albert Weissmann. Welcome to Interlaken."

"Thank you," Galway said, gesturing to his escort. "This is Taakh, *khassq*-class warrior of the Ryqril."

"Honored, Your Eminence," Weissmann said, bowing low. His voice, Galway noted with approval and mild surprise, was calm and steady.

Approval, because that was how one was supposed to face humanity's conquerors. Surprise, because if there was anyone on Earth right now who could inspire fear and trembling in those around him, it was Taakh. His well-muscled bulk topped Galway's own height by a good thirty centimeters, and even in the cold of central Europe he wore nothing above the waist except the elaborately tooled belt and baldric combination that indicated his rank and authority. Fastened to the belt at his right hip was a large laser pistol, while a wide-bladed short sword with carved hilt rode its sheath on his left. "I trust the region's been locked down?" Galway asked, looking around at the rows of neat homes and businesses stretched out beneath the towering mountains in the distance.

"Yes, sir, since two o'clock this morning," Weissmann confirmed.

Less than half an hour after Galway had sent out the order. "Excellent," he said.

"Thank you, sir," Weissmann said. "We take orders from New Geneva very seriously."

"Of course," Galway said, trying not to sound cynical. Neither Weissmann nor any of his people had any real choice in the matter, of course, any more than Galway himself did. All TDE Security officers, government employees, scientists, and top business people were routinely loyalty-conditioned by the Ryqril to be incapable of revolt, sedition, or even serious misbehavior. There was nothing Weissmann's people *could* do except take their orders seriously.

Still, there *was* a certain degree of slack in the conditioning. Galway knew a few of his own officers back on his homeworld of Plinry who never put in more than the bare minimum of effort required. If Weissmann's contingent was as dedicated and efficient as he claimed, perhaps the young officer had reason for pride after all.

"That's his house over there," Weissmann went on, pointing toward a light brown structure at the end of a row of modest homes a block away. His eyes flicked furtively to Taakh, shifted quickly away. "Will you want our assistance in taking him?"

"*Yae* rill take he," the Ryq rumbled before Galway could answer. "Yae hunans."

"As you command," Galway said, bowing his head in acknowledgment. Either the Ryq didn't want to get his own hands dirty with this one, or he wanted to see how Interlaken's human contingent handled themselves. Either was fine with Galway. "Your people are in position, Lieutenant?" he asked.

"Yes, sir," Weissmann said. "My thought was to send four men in through the back. We can cut through the garden fence and move in under cover of some small bushes—"

"Whoa, whoa," Galway interrupted. "Any reason we can't just try the front door?"

Weissmann seemed a little taken aback. "Uh . . . no, sir, I guess not." Lifting his hand over his head, he gave a series of hand signals. "Whenever you're ready, sir."

Galway gestured, and together he and Weissmann headed down the street, their boots making odd squeaking noises in the fresh snow. "New Geneva didn't say anything about the *khassq* being involved in this," Weissmann murmured, glancing furtively over his shoulder at the big, rubbery-skinned alien. "Should I have brought more men? I mean, so we would look more professional?"

"If we can take Herr Judas quietly, then by definition you brought enough men," Galway assured him.

Ahead, armed figures were emerging from concealment, converging silently on the target house. Apart from the standard paral-dart pistols each wore at his hip, Galway saw, their weaponry was a mixture of various types of flechette and pellet scatterguns. Yet another reason for Weissmann to feel nervous about Taakh's presence, though the hodgepodge equipment was hardly the lieutenant's fault. "Unusual name this man has, don't you think?" he commented.

"Yes, it is," Weissmann agreed distantly, his mind clearly concerned with his command's preparedness. "I don't think I've ever met anyone with such a surname."

"And for good reason," Galway agreed. "Note the pattern

here. First they gave us Allen Caine, obviously named for history's first murderer, and now here we have Karl Judas. The Resistance leaders aren't without a sense of ironic humor."

Weissmann snorted. "If you can call plotting to betray and destroy their own people humorous," he said darkly.

That was the loyalty-conditioning speaking, of course. Galway felt the same way, though a small part of his mind wondered if under other circumstances he might see things differently. "Every era has its share of malcontents," he reminded Weissmann. "This one's no different."

"Except that the Resistance has gone far beyond simple malcontentment," Weissmann countered. "I heard a rumor the other day that some of them actually tried to get into the old Aegis Mountain stronghold in Western North America this past summer."

"There was a team working in the Denver region, yes," Galway confirmed, wincing at the memory. "But they never got into the base, and I doubt they ever will."

"I hope not," Weissmann said, turning his head slightly to look back at Taakh. "There could be all sorts of weapons still in there. We certainly don't want them in Resistance hands."

"Agreed," Galway said. "And as to the concern you *haven't* yet voiced, Taakh's presence isn't a sign that the Ryqril are planning to set up shop here in Interlaken. He's with me, and he'll leave when I do."

"I see," Weissmann said, his carefully neutral voice not quite able to hide his relief. "Thank you, sir. I have to admit that . . . well, when they took most of our lasers away two months ago, I wondered if there was some sort of reorganization in the works."

"Not as far as I know," Galway said. "And it wasn't just you. I gather that most of the Security forces around the TDE have gone back to flechettes and slug weapons."

"I didn't know that," Weissmann said again, a frown in his voice. "Any idea why?"

Galway shrugged, trying to make the gesture look casual. The dark fact of the matter was that the Ryqril had lost three of their colony worlds to the advancing Chryselli forces over the past six months, and suddenly their long-standing space war had taken on a serious land component as well. With close-combat weapons in short supply, the Ryqril high command had ordered that the lasers be collected from their conquered worlds' security forces and rushed to the ground troops now fighting to push back the Chryselli beachheads.

But that was hardly something to be discussed with a junior officer in a remote sector. "Not really," he said.

A pair of Weissmann's men were in position at the front of the house by the time they arrived, crouching in flanking positions by the walkway as they trained their paral-dart pistols watchfully on the door. Others, Galway knew, would be guarding all the windows. "Shall I call for a ram?" Weissmann murmured.

Galway didn't bother to answer, but simply stepped up onto the small porch and rang the bell.

One of the flanking guards muttered something under his breath. Apparently, the polite approach hadn't occurred to any of them.

Or maybe they simply thought breaking down the door would look more professional in front of Taakh.

He rang the bell again. This time there was the click of a lock, and the door opened a crack. "Yes?" a disheveled young man asked, blinking sleep-heavy eyes as he finished tying a sash around his robe.

Galway smiled tightly. After five months, the search was indeed over. "Good morning, Herr Judas," he said, holding up his ID. "I'm Security Prefect Galway. May I come in?"

Judas looked pointedly at the guns aimed at him, then silently pulled the door fully open and stepped back out of the way. "You and your men wait here," Galway ordered Weissmann, and followed Judas inside.

The door opened into a plain but neat conversation room. "Am I in some sort of trouble?" Judas asked as he backed up to the middle of the room beside what appeared to be a handcrafted center table.

"That depends on your point of view," Galway said. Even the man's voice was the same. "I've come here to offer you an opportunity. Please; sit down."

Judas hesitated, then crossed to an upholstered comfort chair and sat down. The chair frame, too, appeared to be handmade. "Nice furniture," Galway commented as he took a double seat a quarter of the way around the center table from him. "Your work?"

"Yes, it's my hobby," Judas said. "What sort of opportunity?"

"The sort that can guarantee safety and security for you and your family for the rest of your lives," Galway said.

Judas snorted gently. "Sounds way too good to be true,"

he said. "Why don't we start by hearing what exactly this wonderful deal will cost me."

Galway leaned back in his chair, studying the man closely. The face and voice were perfect, but what he could see of the man's physique through his robe would definitely require some work. At least four months of it, he estimated, plus the other training the man would need.

Still, they had at least five more months before the rest of the operation would be ready. Plenty of time. "It'll cost six to eight months of your life," he said. "Under the circumstances, hardly worth mentioning."

"Oh, hardly," Judas agreed with the cynical smile of a man who's been offered a card from a magician's deck. "And what exactly would I be doing during those six to eight months?"

"A job only you can do," Galway said. "We want you to impersonate someone for us."

"What, I've got a twin brother walking around?"

"Actually, you have *two* twin brothers," Galway corrected, watching him closely. "Maybe more. You see, Herr Judas . . . you're a clone."

The other's smile vanished. "That's a lie," he said, his voice suddenly stiff.

It was, Galway knew, the correct reaction. But it was a little too quick, a little too practiced, a little too perfect. Judas had already known who and what he was. And there was only one place where he could have learned the truth. "I'm afraid it's your friends who've been lying to you," he said. "Not me."

"What friends?"

"Your contacts in the Resistance," Galway said gently. "The ones who've been grooming you since childhood for some special mission, then suddenly and inexplicably abandoned both you and the project a little over two years ago."

Judas was good, all right. His face barely registered the emotional shock he must surely be feeling at hearing supposedly secret parts of his life being calmly listed by a Security prefect. "I have no idea what you're talking about."

"Of course you don't," Galway agreed. "That's the other thing I'm offering: the chance to get a little of your own back in return for their shoddy treatment. Interested?"

"Why bother to ask?" Judas countered. "Fifteen days of loyalty-conditioning and I'll do whatever you want anyway."

Galway shrugged. He was certainly right on that score. "Personal ethics, I suppose," he said. "An effort to allow you a certain dignity in this."

"*False* dignity."

"Perhaps," Galway conceded. "And, for the record, the loyalty-conditioning will take a little longer than that. If we quit after the standard fifteen days, the psychor barriers your Resistance friends gave you might still leave some cracks in the wall. Nice try, though."

Judas grimaced. "Touché," he conceded. "Do I have time to dress and say good-bye to my wife and daughter?"

"Certainly," Galway said, gesturing toward the curved stairway leading to the second floor. "That was my other reason for not simply hauling you out of bed."

For a moment Judas studied Galway's face, perhaps

wondering if it was genuinely possible for a loyalty-conditioned puppet of the Ryqril and the collaborationist government to have a conscience. Galway had often wondered the same thing, and wondered now what Judas would conclude. "Thank you," the other said, standing up. "Give me fifteen minutes."

He was back in twelve, dressed for travel. "I didn't bother to pack anything," he said as Galway ushered him out into the cold morning air. "I assumed you wouldn't let me keep any personal items anyway."

"Quite right," Galway said. Taakh had moved up to join Weissmann at the end of the walk, and Judas's step faltered briefly as he caught sight of the big alien. But he recovered quickly and continued on. The two Security men flanking the door formed up behind them, paral-dart guns still held at the ready.

"Any trouble?" Weissmann asked as the group reached him.

"None," Galway said. "As soon as we're gone, you can lift the lockdown—"

And without warning, a pair of high-velocity flechettes whistled past his back and head.

"Cover!" he snapped, grabbing Judas's coat collar and hauling him toward the ground. With his other hand he yanked his own paral-dart gun from its holster, his eyes searching for the source of the attack.

"Corner!" Weissmann barked, his gun tracking that direction.

There were two of them, Galway saw, crouched low beside a pair of houses on opposite sides of the street, the muzzles of their long-barreled hunting rifles dipping as they corrected their aim. He swung his own gun toward them, knowing instinctively that neither he nor Weissmann would make it in time.

And in that single frozen heartbeat, Taakh moved.

He wasn't as fast as a blackcollar, a detached part of Galway's mind noted. Nor was he as graceful, and his movements didn't carry the same ultrarefined precision and elegance theirs did. But he was fast enough, and more than precise enough. One of his huge hands grabbed the nearest of Weissmann's Security men by the collar, pulling him on top of Judas and sending both men sprawling onto the ground. The bits of snow from their landing were still flying when there were two silent bursts of green light from the laser in the Ryq's other hand, and both attackers collapsed on top of their guns.

"You all right, Prefect?" Weissmann demanded. The rest of his men were on the move now, three hurrying toward the would-be assassins, the rest spreading out for a sweep of the area.

"I'm fine," Galway assured him, watching Judas and the Security man as they untangled themselves and stood up again. "Judas?"

"I'm all right," Judas said, his voice shaking. "What in hell was *that* all about?"

"You really don't know?" Galway countered.

Judas's hands paused in the act of brushing the snow off his chest. "What do you mean?"

"I mean that wasn't a rescue attempt," Galway said bluntly. "Not with just two men. Certainly not with two men armed with lethal weapons."

Judas looked over at the sprawled bodies, a sudden

tightness in his throat. "Are you saying they were trying to *kill* me?"

"Why not?" Galway said. "You're of no use to them anymore. They might as well make sure you're no use to us, either."

Which wasn't entirely true, he knew, a twinge of conscience tugging at him. The Resistance didn't have to actually kill Judas to make him useless for Galway's purposes. All they had to do was mark him somehow, either with a fresh scar or some minor but noticeable bit of muscle damage. The fact that the first shots had missed strongly implied that that was indeed what they'd been going for.

But jumping to the wrong conclusion would help cut Judas's last emotional connection to the Resistance. And it certainly wasn't Galway's job to rectify any faulty reasoning.

Taakh turned to Weissmann, his eyes flashing with anger. "Yae rill 'urn down the town," he ordered. "All o' it."

Weissmann's eyes widened. "Burn down—? But Your Eminence—"

"Dae yae kestion ne?" the Ryq snarled, lifting his laser warningly.

"No, Your Eminence, of course not," Weissmann said hastily. "But—"

"I don't think we need to destroy the town, Your Eminence," Galway jumped in, gesturing Weissmann to keep quiet. "We'll simply have Lieutenant Weissmann keep the area locked down for the next eight months."

Weissmann transferred his stunned expression to Galway. "Eight *months*?" he hissed.

"Yae rill 'e silent," Taakh ground out.

For a long moment no one spoke. Taakh gazed across the snow at the Security men as they examined the would-be assassins; and though Ryq expressions were nearly impossible for humans to read, Galway had no trouble seeing the conflict raging behind the alien's eyes. On the one hand, his pride demanded that he utterly obliterate the town that had dared to raise a fist against their Ryqril overlords.

But on the other hand, he also knew that the war was going badly, and that his people needed an influx of spirit and imagination and tactical skill.

They needed the blackcollars. And without Galway, they would never get them. "'Ery rell," Taakh said at last. "Yae rill seal the region. *Re* rill tell yae ren it rill 'e o'ened again."

Weissmann took a deep breath. "As you command, Your Eminence," he said.

Galway suppressed a grimace. So that was how the alien's pride was going to work itself out. He would allow Weissmann to seal the district as Galway had requested, cutting it off completely from the outside world. But it would be the Ryqril who would decide when that lockdown would be lifted. Until then, it would be the local government's job to figure out how to keep the people inside the ring area alive and fed.

But at least they would *be* alive. That was the important thing.

For another moment Taakh gazed at Weissmann, perhaps wondering if the humans were getting off too easily. Then, apparently dismissing the thought, he turned to Galway and gestured toward the transport with his laser. "Re rill go," he ordered.

"As you command, Your Eminence." Stepping to Judas's side, Galway took his arm. "Come on, Herr Judas," he said. "Time to go."

"Yes," Judas said, his eyes on the dead men in the snow. Men who'd once been his colleagues and allies. "Maybe even past time."

For a moment Sam Foxleigh lay in his narrow bed in the darkness, wrapped tightly in his blankets, wondering what had awakened him. The wind had picked up since he'd gone to bed, whistling cold and wet off the western slopes of the Rocky Mountains. Probably that was what it was, he decided; the wind tearing around the corners of this one-room shack that old Toby had built to hide out in so long ago.

Or maybe it was the dropping temperature. The fire in the wood-stove in the center of the cabin had burned down, with only glowing ashes visible through the slats of tempered glass in the cast-iron door.

He peered at the old wind-up clock sitting on the rough nightstand beside his bed. Just after two in the morning. If he didn't restock the fire, it would get a lot colder in here before it got any warmer.

With a sigh, he unwrapped himself from his blankets and swung his legs over the edge of the bed. He winced as his feet hit the cold wooden floor, winced even harder as he carefully put weight on his bad left leg. The leg, he'd told his rescuers down in the tiny community of Shelter Valley, that had been damaged when he parachuted out of his crippled fighter in the midst of Earth's last, futile defense against the Ryqril.

And the villagers, simple folk that they were, had swallowed the story whole.

Hobbling over to the stove, he popped open the door and fed in a few sticks and a small piece of log. The snows had come early this year, and he just hoped he had enough wood cut and stacked to make it until spring. Cutting wood in the dead of winter with a bad leg would be a great deal less than fun.

For a minute he stood at the stove, stirring the ashes with the poker until the sticks caught. Then, closing the door again, he limped over to the south-facing window and pushed aside the shade, feeling a soft breeze on his fingers from the small leaks around the glass. A quarter kilometer downslope, Shelter Valley was mostly dark, but he could see a couple of lights still burning. Insomniacs, probably, up reading or watching television.

Or perhaps someone was tending to the Ryqril sensor pylon.

He gazed down at the lights, old memories burning at his throat. He'd been up here with Toby when the Security men had come by with their offer to allow the villagers to stay if they would accept the pylon and handle its day-to-day upkeep. Toby's family had argued against it, but the rest of the twenty-odd families had decided they had no choice.

Foxleigh's own opinion, of course, hadn't even been part of the discussion. For that matter, neither had Toby's.

One of the lights blinked off, the darkness flowing in to fill the spot where it had been. Toby's family had offered to run a power line up here back when the old recluse was still alive, a power line and phone line both. But Toby would have none of it. The closest he would come to communication had been letting them rig up the multiple multicolored window shades over this particular window that he could use to signal whether he needed food or medical attention or—rarely—wanted some company.

He hadn't wanted company very often, that was for sure. Eventually, even his family had mostly given up coming here and left him to his chosen lifestyle.

And what had been good enough for Toby was good enough for Foxleigh. Distantly, he wondered how many of the people down in the village even knew that Toby was dead.

He lifted his eyes from the town, turning his attention to the southeast and the dark mass of Aegis Mountain framed against the faint haze of swirling clouds, glowing with the reflected lights of Denver and civilization so many kilometers beyond it. Once upon a time, that mountain had been mankind's last stronghold against the Ryqril invaders, a place full of grim men and women and weapons.

But the men and women had died or disappeared, and the weapons had gone silent, and the mountain had gone dark. The Ryqril had taken over the small town of Idaho Springs ten kilometers west of Aegis and set up a pleasant little enclave for themselves, with their ring of sensor pylons guarding against even the possibility of an air attack. The mountain itself they'd ignored entirely.

But a year and a half ago, that had abruptly changed. They'd set up a heavily armed camp by the main entrance at the north end of the mountain and had begun picking carefully at the compressed hull metal of the door, trying to avoid the deadly booby traps that had been built into it so long ago by the humans.

So far, they hadn't gotten through. But someone else had.

They'd been young looking, for the most part, young and scrappy and full of the energy Foxleigh himself had once possessed. He'd seen them from the cabin, several groups of them over the past few years, working like ants at some unknown project a kilometer beyond his east window. Their view of Shelter Valley itself—and vice versa—had been blocked by a low ridge, and it was doubtful they'd even known the village was there. It was for sure that the villagers themselves had never known about the visitors. For the first month or two they'd worked on the surface, and after that had simply hiked in with their equipment and disappeared somewhere, emerging days or even weeks later.

And then, all of a sudden, they'd stopped coming.

Over the next few months Foxleigh had occasionally toyed with the idea of going over there himself to see if he could figure out what in hell's name they'd been doing out on the back molar of nowhere. But given his bad leg, there was no guarantee he could manage such a trek on his own.

He'd just about decided that whatever they'd been doing was over and done with when, in the middle of last summer, the others had suddenly showed up. Not the original workers—not those kids—but someone else.

Blackcollars.

There'd been no doubt about it. He'd seen them as

clear as day with his compact little spotter telescope, and there'd been no mistaking the color and texture of the glimpses of flexarmor he'd seen beneath their outer clothing.

And with that, suddenly the whole thing had become clear.

He'd watched for days after the group had left, waiting for them to return, or for Resistance troops to arrive and reactivate the fortress under the distant brooding mountain.

But they never had. At least, not when he was watching.

He sighed, letting the shade fall back over the window. That had been five months ago, and now that it was winter he knew they wouldn't be back any time soon. Shelter Valley's sensor pylon was designed solely to watch for aircraft, but Security techs came by at irregular intervals, and fresh tracks in the snow leading nowhere would be a trail too obvious and too intriguing to ignore.

But maybe when spring came and the snow melted they'd be back.

He hobbled back to the stove. The sticks had mostly burned down, but the log had caught. That ought to bring the temperature in the cabin back to a decent level. Maybe once the weather turned nice again he would see about re-siding the whole place. Maybe add some insulation to the ceiling, too.

And while he worked he would keep an eye on the mountain.

CHAPTER 1

The breeze whistled gently through the forest glade, rustling through the tree branches and sending mottled patterns of light and shadow across the rolling, grassy ground. Behind the trees, the majestic peaks of Plinry's Greenheart Mountains could be seen, the last of the previous winter's snow still clinging to them.

The young man standing in the center of the glade couldn't appreciate the view, of course. For one thing, his close-fitting blindfold didn't allow through even a glimmer of the warm sunshine. For another, he had far more urgent matters on his mind than mountainside scenery.

On the opposite side of the glade, standing well out of the way beside a thick tree, Damon Lathe raised an arm, his hand tracing out a rapid-fire succession of hand signals. *Caine, Skyler: move in. Pattern two.*

Lifting his own arm, Allen Caine acknowledged the order. Then, feeling decidedly awkward in the thickly padded practice suit, he started across the glade. A third

21

of the way around the circle, Rafe Skyler, his normal hefty bulk looking grotesque in his own suit, did likewise.

The two men had covered perhaps three-quarters of the distance when the young man's head turned slightly, his right ear now pointing toward Caine. Caine froze in response, a flicker of sympathy rippling through him as the other moved his head back and forth a few degrees. It hadn't been all that long ago that Caine himself had been in Will Flynn's position, standing blind in the center of the circle and trying to sense his opponents' approach. And, at least in Caine's case, silently but roundly cursing the whole ridiculous exercise.

Around the circle, Skyler was still moving inward. He'd made it another two steps when Flynn's head turned again, this time in the big blackcollar's direction. Lifting his arms into combat stance, Caine started forward again.

And without warning, Flynn did a long slide-leap toward him, twisting his arms and torso around like a berserk corkscrew and sending a spinning kick sweeping straight toward Caine's head.

Even as Caine reflexively dropped into a crouch he saw that the kick was going to be short. A quick leap forward, a quick midsection punch and leg sweep before Flynn could finish his kick and get his leg back under him, and they'd get a chance to see how well the trainee could fight on his back.

Flynn's foot shot past above and in front of Caine's face, exactly where he'd anticipated it would go. Shoving off with his back foot, cocking his right fist for a punch, he leaped to the attack.

And staggered backward as a pair of somethings thudded hard into his ribs and upper thigh.

He looked down. Embedded halfway into the padding were a pair of black, eight-pointed *shuriken* throwing stars.

Flynn finished his kick and spun around toward Skyler, and Caine looked across the clearing at Lathe. The other gave him a tight smile and drew a line across his throat with his finger. It wasn't a standard blackcollar hand signal, but the meaning was clear.

For Caine, the game was over.

Grimacing, he nodded and backed up. Setting his personal pride on hold, he shifted to analysis mode and settled in to watch the rest of Flynn's test.

The exercise was over, and Caine had had time to get out of the suit and take a shower, when Lathe appeared at his room at the blackcollars' lodge. "So what did you think of Flynn's technique?" he asked as he came in, closing the door behind him.

"Odd but interesting," Caine said, studying the older man's lined face and gray-flecked goatee as he snagged a chair and pulled it over. Damon Lathe had been a commando commander—a comsquare—during the losing war against the Ryqril thirty years ago. Instead of continuing a guerrilla-style fight after Earth's defeat, though, as other blackcollar and special forces units had, he and the remnant of Plinry's blackcollars had chosen instead to pretend to settle down under the alien domination. For nearly three decades they'd played the role of bitter but demoralized veterans, allowing themselves just enough of the youth drug Idunine to let their outer appearances age normally while still maintaining their muscles and joints and stamina, nurturing their strength and hope against the chance that one day they'd find an opportunity to strike one final serious blow against the Ryqril overlords.

That opportunity had come two years ago, when Earth's Resistance leaders had discovered the key to five hidden war-era Nova-class warships and had sent Caine to the Plinry archives to dig out their exact location. The end result had been a reactivation of the Plinry blackcollars, and five new warships in the hands of the Resistance and their alien Chryselli allies.

Five ships hadn't made that much difference, of course, considering the vast fleets arrayed on both the Ryqril and Chryselli sides of the battlefront. But it had made enough. Two of the ships had gone directly to the Chryselli, while the three kept by the Resistance had been pressed into service transporting humans around the TDE, Resistance agents as well as ordinary travelers, breaking the travel monopoly hitherto held by Ryqril-loyal government and business people.

The Ryqril hadn't been happy about the loosening of their travel restrictions, but they'd accepted the new status quo with the recognition that it was the lesser of many possible evils. If the Resistance had tried using their Novas as military weapons, harassing Ryq bases in the TDE or trying to foment open rebellion, the aliens would have been forced to pull some of their own warships off the battlefront and hunt them down. That would have bought the Chryselli a brief respite at best and the TDE nothing at all. As long as the Novas functioned exclusively as passenger liners, even passenger liners for undesirables like Resistance agents, they weren't worth the risk and effort of destroying.

After all, the Ryqril probably reasoned, there was little a handful of zealots could do against their vast, loyalty-conditioned bureaucracy.

"'Interesting' wasn't exactly the word I was thinking," Lathe said dryly, bringing Caine's thoughts back to the present. "He nailed you good with that double *shuriken* throw."

"That he did," Caine conceded, suppressing his reflexive flicker of embarrassment. As Lathe had frequently mentioned, there was no place for pride or ego in this business. "I never even saw him draw them."

"It's a trick Mordecai taught him," Lathe said. "He draws the stars as he starts into the kick, one in each hand, then uses the momentum of the spin to throw them. He doesn't even have to bend his elbows, which means his arms are out ready to whip across the head of anyone who might have tried to move in on him during his spin."

Caine nodded. "I should have guessed it was one of Mordecai's moves."

"Actually, Mordecai usually uses his *nunchaku* as the second move instead of stars," Lathe said. "And at the moment, Flynn still misses almost as often as he connects. But he's improving."

"I'd definitely recommend he keep at it," Caine said. "It's a technique well worth developing."

"I agree." A shadow seemed to cross Lathe's face. "It's really a shame he'll never be a blackcollar."

"It's a shame about a lot of them," Caine said, an old

ache tugging at him. The drug called Backlash, given in a carefully prescribed regimen during training, permanently altered a person's neural biochemistry, doubling combat speed and reflexes and turning what would otherwise have been merely a superbly skilled martial artist into a uniquely lethal blackcollar.

It was a transformation Caine had wanted for himself ever since his first encounter with Lathe's team. His first choice of mission as a team commander, in fact, had been to take a small group of trainees back to Earth a year ago in hopes of locating the formula in the still intact Aegis Mountain stronghold in the mountains west of Denver. But they'd come up dry, at least on the Backlash formula.

What they *had* found in Aegis might ultimately prove to be even more significant in the long run. Still, for now, the bottom line was that neither Caine nor Flynn nor any of the other trainees had any chance of becoming true blackcollars. "Maybe someday," he said.

"Maybe," Lathe agreed. "By the way, did you hear that Galway was back?"

Caine lifted his eyebrows. "He's *back*? In one piece?"

"I'm rather surprised myself," Lathe said. "Even granted that none of what happened in Denver was his fault, I'd still expected the Ryqril to take out at least some of their frustrations on him."

"And if not the Ryqril, certainly whatever was left of Denver's Security hierarchy," Caine agreed, frowning. "Do we know whether or not he's resuming his position here?"

"Not yet," Lathe said. "Of course, from Earth's point of view, sentencing him to continue as Security Prefect of Plinry might be considered sufficient punishment in itself."

"We can hope," Caine said, and meant it. Loyalty-conditioned or not, Galway nevertheless genuinely cared about Plinry's citizens. After living under Assistant Security Prefect Hammerschmidt for most of the past year, Caine would be more than happy to have Galway back. "I wonder if he'll be inviting us to visit him in the Hub anytime soon."

Lathe shrugged. "If not, we may be able to arrange an appointment ourselves."

Caine smiled. The Hub, the section of Plinry's capital city, Capstone, where the government people lived and worked, cowered behind a tall, sensor-equipped wall guarded by armed loyalty-conditioned Security men whose main purpose was to keep out the general, non-loyalty-conditioned public.

But then, dealing with walls and guards was a blackcollar specialty. "Let's at least let him settle in first."

"And see if he's actually staying," Lathe agreed, standing up. "Anyway, Flynn should be about ready for his debriefing. You want to help Skyler run Pittman through his paces later?"

"Absolutely," Caine assured him. As far as he was concerned, if the formula for Backlash was ever discovered, Pittman would be right there in line with Flynn.

"Good," Lathe said. "I'll see you then."

Lathe was halfway down the wide lodge staircase when the tingler on his right wrist came to life, tapping out rapid-fire blackcollar code onto two sections of skin: *Lathe: Lepkowski calling; urgent.*

He slid two fingers beneath the sleeve of his black

flexarmor turtleneck shirt. *On my way*, he tapped back.

Hamner Lodge, located in one of the most picturesque areas of the Greenheart Mountains and convenient to Capstone, had once been a retreat for hunters, hikers, and other nature lovers. After the Ryqril Groundfire attack devastated the majority of the planet, the lodge had been largely abandoned. A few years after the TDE's surrender, the blackcollars had reopened it, using it as a place where the old embittered veterans could get together to relive the glory days.

Or so the Ryqril and Security forces had been led to believe. Once the enemy had come to that conclusion and serious surveillance had ended, the blackcollars had turned the lodge into a quiet headquarters, running secret combat training for some of Capstone's youth and slowly turning it into what they hoped would someday be a fully operational command center.

The communications room in the lodge's basement had been one of their first upgrades, despite the fact that at the time there had been no one out there for them to talk to. It had been as state-of-the-art as they could manage, with long-range transmitters, encryption systems, and—most importantly—overlapping bug-stomper systems to make sure no one was able to slip any eavesdropping devices into the room.

Chelsey Jensen was seated at the panel when Lathe arrived, his eyes shifting back and forth between the monitor displays. "How's the reception today?" Lathe asked as he closed the door behind him.

"I think we may have some ears to the door," Jensen

said, tapping one of the displays. "If we do, though, it's a very slick tap. The signal shows barely a whisker of perturbation."

"Doesn't sound like anything Hammerschmidt's got," Lathe commented, sitting down beside him. "Unless Galway brought some new equipment back with him."

Jensen shook his head. "There hasn't been enough time for them to set it up," he pointed out. "I'm guessing this is Ryqril stuff."

"Stolen from someone else, no doubt," Lathe murmured. "Probably the Chryselli."

"Could be," Jensen said. "If it was, they're taking a huge risk using it on Lepkowski. Most of the *Novak*'s upgrades are also Chryselli, which means there's a fair chance he's already nailed the tap."

"Could be," Lathe said, studying the other out of the corner of his eye. The *Novak*, one of the recovered TDE warships, had cost the life of Jensen's best friend, and even after nearly two years there was a discernable catch in his voice whenever he mentioned the *Novak*'s name. At such times his mood, which sometimes seemed to have settled into a permanent twilight, went a little darker. "Have you had any kickers from him?"

"Not yet," Jensen said. "Probably waiting until you were here."

"Let's find out." Picking up the microphone, Lathe keyed it on. "This is Lathe," he said. "Welcome back to Plinry, General."

"One of my very favorite spots in the whole universe," Lepkowski said dryly. "How've you been, Comsquare?"

"Bored out of my skull," Lathe said. *Very favorite*

spot/universe—kicker given; *out of my skull*—kicker acknowledged. The Ryqril were indeed tapping into the conversation, but Lepkowski didn't know whether or not they'd broken the current encryption. It was more or less what Lathe had expected. "Any interesting passengers to drop off?"

"No interesting passengers, but some very interesting information," Lepkowski said. "I'm told the Ryqril are in the process of setting up a tactical coordination center on Khala."

Lathe exchanged looks with Jensen. "How complete a center?"

"Very complete," Lepkowski said. "Full comm feeds and couriers from every unit in the sector, including a large chunk of the local battlefront. Full data analysis and assessment section. Full decision-making capabilities, including a permanent half circle of command-rank Ryqril there to make them."

"Interesting, indeed," Lathe murmured. "Why Khala? Wouldn't one of their own worlds do better?"

"Not necessarily," Lepkowski said. "For one thing, Khala's actually closer to that part of the battlefront than any of their own worlds. More importantly, I think they've finally tumbled to the fact that we and the Chryselli are genuine allies, and that it's not just a marriage of convenience."

"Even if it's mostly one-sided at the moment?"

"Even so. And since allies try very hard not to slaughter each other's civilians, putting the center on a captured TDE world actually makes it safer than it would be on one of theirs."

"Safer from the Chryselli, anyway," Jensen murmured.

"But *only* from the Chryselli," Lathe agreed. "How close is it to a sizeable human populace?"

"It's right on the edge of one," Lepkowski said. "It's at the western edge of the capital of Inkosi City, with the city on one side and scattered forest and farmland around the rest of it. You interested in taking a look?"

"Very much so," Lathe said. "What's our timeline look like?"

"I'll be heading to Shiloh as soon as I drop my passengers. After that, I'm swinging past Magna Graecia and Bullhead. That puts me back here in about six weeks."

"Good enough," Lathe said. "Any idea how far along the center is?"

"According to my source, the overall construction is complete and they've almost finished with the equipment setup," Lepkowski said. "If their ramp-up schedule parallels human patterns, I'm guessing they'll be fully operational in three to four weeks."

"Which means that in six weeks they'll still be settling in and working out the last kinks in their security system," Lathe concluded. "Perfect."

"If you think *that's* perfect, wait'll you hear this," Lepkowski said, some grim satisfaction creeping into his voice. "My source for all this is a fine upstanding Khalan citizen named Kieran Shaw." He paused dramatically. "*Tactor* Kieran Shaw."

Jensen muttered something startled-sounding under his breath. "A *tactor*?" Lathe echoed, feeling a little stunned himself. "I didn't know any senior officers had survived the war."

"He was wearing a blue-eyed dragonhead ring," Lepkowski said. "Unless you think he's just a comsquare who gave himself a promotion."

"Unlikely," Lathe said, looking down at the silvery dragonhead ring on his own right hand and the red stones of its eyes. "Has he got anyone with him?"

"He was a bit vague about that," Lepkowski said. "But that may have been because he didn't trust our comm connection. I'm guessing he's got at least a few other blackcollars hanging around you might be able to borrow for the occasion. Anyway, he said he'll have a contact on permanent duty at the Guardrail Tavern on Teardrop Road at the south end of Inkosi City whenever you want to make contact."

"Sounds good," Lathe said. "One more question. After you swing back by here is there any chance we could rendezvous with any of the other ships?"

"Let me check," Lepkowski said. "Yes, I could arrange to meet up with the *Defiant* at either Shiloh or Juniper. You expecting to be getting tired of my company?"

"Something like that," Lathe said. "I may also have another job for you."

"No problem," Lepkowski assured him. "Well, happy planning. I'll see you in six weeks."

Lathe gestured, and Jensen keyed off the comm. "You think it's a trap?" the other asked, leaning back in his chair.

"Awfully long way to lure us in just for a trap," Lathe pointed out, his mind racing. After all the waiting, this might finally be it. "You'd think they could come up with something a little closer to Plinry if all they wanted was to take us out."

"True," Jensen said. "Which doesn't answer my question, of course."

"Oh, I'm sure it *could* be a trap," Lathe said. "Especially with all of this coming right on the heels of Galway's return."

"Certainly an interesting coincidence," Jensen agreed. "So what's your probable scenario? We leave Denver's Security apparatus in a shambles, Galway gets caught in the middle, and he tries to save his own skin by coming up with some bait to dangle in front of us?"

"Actually, I was crediting the Ryqril with more brains than that," Lathe said. "Bearing in mind that Galway's probably the closest thing to a blackcollar expert they have available right now." He gestured toward the ceiling. "In fact, I'll lay you odds he's spent a lot of the past year on Khala."

"Helping make their tac center blackcollar-proof?"

"Why not?" Lathe countered. "Especially since there seems to be a blackcollar presence already there for them to guard against." He lifted an eyebrow. "Unless you think that's just part of the bait."

"All I know is that the Ryqril don't like guerrilla teams operating on their occupied worlds, blackcollars or anyone else," Jensen reminded him darkly. "If this alleged tactor has been doing any serious damage, they should have taken him out years ago."

"Unless he's been playing it quiet, like we did," Lathe suggested.

"Maybe," Jensen said. "Unfortunately, there's no way to know for sure this side of Khala."

"True." Lathe shook his head. "Rather ironic, you

know. All Galway ever wanted was to sit out here in the middle of nowhere and do whatever his loyalty-condition-ing would allow to keep the people of Plinry safe. Now, for good or bad, he's got the full attention of the Ryqril. So much for the quiet, self-effacing life."

Jensen's eyes were steady on him. "You're going to go for it, aren't you?"

Lathe shrugged. "I don't see how we can pass it up. A Ryq tac center's the next best thing to the high command's supreme situation room. If we can take it intact, they might as well just hand over that section of the front to the Chryselli."

"The key word being 'intact,'" Jensen reminded him. "And if Galway's been helping them, it's going to be that much harder."

"Calculated risk is what warfare's all about," Lathe said, getting to his feet. "Meanwhile, I've got a debriefing I'm late for. Would you do me a favor and go find Skyler and Mordecai and have them meet me in my room in an hour? I'd rather not put this out on the tingler just yet."

"Sure," Jensen said, his face settling into hard lines. "If you decide to go, I hereby request to be a part of the team."

So that he could die in a blaze of glory in combat against the Ryqril? "Don't worry," Lathe assured him quietly. "If this works out the way I think it will, there'll be plenty of work for all of us."

The voices fell silent, and the carrier signal closed down. "That's it, then," Galway said, exhaling quietly in relief. After all these months, stage one was finally complete.

Beside him, Taakh pointed a finger at the communications tech. "Yae rill decry't it at runce," he ordered.

"I'm not sure we can, Your Eminence," the tech said carefully. "This sounds like a Chryselli code, and I don't think—"

"Dae yae kestion ne?" Taakh cut him off.

"There's no need for a decryption," Galway spoke up quickly. "Lathe is going to go for it."

"Dae yae s'eak Chryselli encry'ts?" Taakh snapped, shifting his glare to Galway.

"No, Your Eminence, of course not," Galway said, standing his ground. "But I don't need to. I heard the tone of Lathe's voice. He's suspicious, but the possible gains are too tempting for him to pass up."

For a long moment the Ryq stared down his long, openmouthed snout at him. Then, deliberately, he turned back to the tech. "Yae rill decry't it at runce," he repeated.

The tech's mouth twitched. "As you command, Your Eminence," he said.

Taakh turned back to Galway. "How dae yae intend tae learn their 'lans?"

"Unfortunately, at this point we can't," Galway said. "Between their bug stompers and other countermeasures we're not going to get any kind of eavesdropping devices within five klicks of any of them."

"Then rhy is yaer spy not here?"

"It would have been too risky to put in the spy here in their own territory," Galway said. "There'll be time enough for the switch once they're on Khala and too busy to notice any small discrepancies in his behavior or mannerisms."

"Yae are 'ery certain."

Galway hid a grimace. No, he wasn't certain at all.

But it *had* to work. It wasn't just his own life hanging by a thread here, but also the safety of his world. Neither Taakh or anyone else had explicitly stated that Plinry would pay the price for any failures, but Galway knew how to read between the lines. "I understand these blackcollars, Your Eminence," he said as calmly as he could. "They *are* going to go to Khala; and when they do, we'll have the solution we're looking for."

"'Erha's,'" the Ryq said, clearly not convinced. But he had his orders, and for the moment, at least, Galway was in charge. "Rhat dae re dae next?"

Galway hunched his shoulders slightly. In many ways, this next step was the hardest of them all. "We wait."

Skyler and Mordecai listened in silence as Lathe laid out the situation. "So you think this is it?" Skyler asked when he'd finished.

"Yes, I do," Lathe said. "A tac center is the kind of prize that only comes around once a lifetime."

"Which means it's probably some kind of trap," Skyler said.

"Oh, without a doubt," Lathe agreed calmly. "The point is that this is exactly the sort of thing Galway would set up: challenging, yet ultimately possible."

"*If* Galway's the one in charge," Skyler warned. "You have any idea what kind of trap it is?"

"Not yet," Lathe said. "But I'm not sure it matters. It's an opportunity we can't afford to pass up."

"And Galway would know that," Skyler pointed out.

"But even assuming we can pull this off, it'll take more than a resounding victory on a place as far off as Khala."

"I know," Lathe agreed. "That's why while I'm on Khala, you'll be taking a team to Earth."

Skyler's eyes widened slightly, but he took it in stride. "Where?"

"Back to Denver," Lathe said. "By now Anne Silcox should have her new Phoenix organization up and running, and with the supplies of Whiplash we left them they should have the whole government and Security system riddled with moles. It'll be the perfect place to stage a major uprising."

"Especially with Aegis Mountain in the neighborhood," Skyler said thoughtfully. "I wonder if she's gone back in there since we left."

"Depends on how much she trusts her new recruits," Lathe said. "I don't think she'll push it, though, especially considering that Whiplash was about the only thing of value we found in there."

"At least, the only thing accessible," Skyler agreed with a grimace. "Hopefully Kanai hasn't let anyone try to bull their way through doomsdayed doors."

"You'll find out soon enough," Lathe said. "I want Mordecai, Spadafora, and Caine with me. You can have anyone else."

"You sure you don't want a bigger team?" Skyler asked, frowning.

"We *do* theoretically have this Tactor Shaw and his blackcollars to draw on," Lathe reminded him. "Besides, we're certainly not going to take the tac center with a massed blackcollar charge."

"Okay," Skyler said, clearly still not entirely convinced. "In that case, I'll take Hawking and O'Hara. And Jensen."

Lathe and Mordecai exchanged glances. "You sure you want Jensen?" Lathe asked.

"He's fine," Skyler said firmly. "He's just not yet over what happened on Argent, that's all."

"I understand that," Lathe said. "The fact remains that he's become a little . . . unpredictable."

"He's fine," Skyler said again. "Besides, he's got a lot of specialized skills that none of the rest of us have, not to mention being our best pilot. We may need him."

Lathe shrugged. "Okay, it's your call. In that case, are you sure you don't want a larger group yourself? We do have those new six-man drop pods."

"*I'll* theoretically have Kanai and Phoenix to draw on," Skyler said. "Besides, I don't want to leave Plinry any more undefended than it already is. If this works, the Ryq are likely to be very unhappy with us."

"There's that," Lathe agreed soberly. "We'll need to make sure we've got something in place before we go."

"I'll get Haven and De Vries to cover that," Skyler said. "But since you mention the six-man pods, let me go ahead and take Flynn, too."

"You want Pittman or Braune, too?" Lathe asked. "They know the area, at least a little."

"No, Flynn will do," Skyler said, looking innocently over at Mordecai. "If I can't have Mordecai, I can at least get his bag of bizarre tricks."

"There's nothing bizarre about any of them," Mordecai protested mildly. "It's all simple, clean combat technique."

Lathe suppressed a smile. If there were any two blackcollars in his group that were a study in contrasts, it was Skyler and Mordecai. Where Skyler was big, bluff, and pleasantly garrulous, Mordecai was small, wiry, and seldom spoke.

But when he did, he was usually worth listening to. "You've been very quiet, Mordecai. What do *you* think about all this?"

"I was just thinking about a possibility neither of you has mentioned," the smaller man said. "Namely that this could be nothing more than a ploy to split us up and send us charging off in all directions."

"To what end?" Skyler asked.

Mordecai shrugged. "They've tried twice to beat us as a group," he said. "Maybe they think breaking us into smaller chunks will help."

"If they do, they're going to be sorely disappointed," Skyler rumbled. "Even with Caine's trainees aboard we didn't exactly constitute a major assault force last year in Denver."

"I know," Mordecai said. "I'm just saying that if we do take this on, it may be the last mission for some of us."

"Maybe even for all of us," Lathe said quietly.

There was a moment of silence. "Well, no one promised we'd live forever," Skyler said at last. "I vote we go for it."

Mordecai half lifted a hand. "Agreed."

"Thank you," Lathe said, nodding to each in turn. "All right, we've got six weeks to prepare before Lepkowski and the *Novak* get back. Let's get started."

Six weeks later, to Galway's quiet relief, Lathe, Caine, and a group of blackcollars boarded a shuttle at the

Capstone 'port and headed into the sky to rendezvous with the massive Nova-class warship waiting for them. An hour later, the *Novak* left orbit and headed for the stars.

"Hor long?" Taakh asked as he and Galway watched the departure on the tracking monitor.

"About eight and a half days," Galway told him. "More, if Lepkowski has other stops to make along the way."

"Then it is tine to go," Taakh said. "Our Corsair rill take three and a hakh days. Re nust 'e there ren they arri'e."

"As you command, Your Eminence," Galway said with a sigh. After all the months he'd spent on Earth and Khala, first locating Judas and then overseeing his training, the past six weeks had seemed to fly by. Now, once again, he was going to have to leave his wife, his home, and his world.

He wondered if he would ever see any of them again.

CHAPTER 2

With a jolt of shattered bolts, the drop pod released itself from the descending shuttle, throwing the five men inside into instant freefall. "Oof!" Flynn grunted as he gripped the straps holding him to his section of wall.

"Steady," Skyler warned, eyeing the young man closely in the dim light. "It's supposed to feel this way."

"Yes, thank you," Flynn managed between clenched teeth. "I'm okay."

"First time's always the hardest," O'Hara said soothingly. "Just take it easy and breathe through your nose."

"I'm okay," Flynn repeated. "It just feels like—well, we *are* falling, aren't we?"

"That we are," Skyler confirmed, watching the softly glowing altitude gauge. Another thirty seconds, he estimated. "But not for much longer."

"After that it'll be time for fun with hang gliders and mountain air currents," Hawking put in.

"Just remember that without a chute slowdown we're going to be coming in a lot faster than usual when we

41

pop," Skyler warned. "The gliders are designed to take the extra speed and stress, but be ready."

"*I* just hope Reger hasn't upgraded his security system since the last time we were there," Hawking muttered. "Dropping in on the man uninvited could prove hazardous to our health."

"I thought you said you and Jensen installed the system," O'Hara said blandly. "How does one upgrade from perfection?"

"Good point," Hawking said dryly.

Skyler looked over at Jensen. But the other was gazing straight ahead, apparently lost in his own thoughts.

A light on the altimeter flashed red. "Get ready," Skyler ordered, getting a grip on the release as he watched the gauge. "Five seconds . . . three, two, *one.*"

He squeezed the release; and with a violent jerk and an upward rush of icy air, the drop pod's floor disintegrated. The wall sections came apart at the seams, flinging the five men attached to them into the night sky.

For a few seconds Skyler clung tightly to his straps, watching the stars and the dark ground tumble crazily around each other. Then, with a snap of spring-loaded connectors, the wings of his hang glider extended themselves from both sides of his pod wall section. There were a few more seconds of vertigo, and then the glider leveled itself and he found himself hanging beneath the stars and his own gray canopy, swooping through the frigid air.

He took a deep breath, sternly ordering his stomach and inner ear to behave themselves as he looked around. He'd warned the others to expect a rough ride, but even he hadn't been quite prepared for just how rough it had been.

But he could see four other dark silhouettes blacking out the stars. Apparently, they'd all come through it all right. "Report," he said into the mike curving around the side of his cheek.

One by one, the others checked in. "Good," Skyler said when they were finished. "Everyone turn due east—"

"Skyler?" Flynn cut in. "I think I've got a problem."

"What kind?" Skyler asked, frowning again at the other silhouettes. One of them was definitely dipping beneath the others.

"I'm not getting much lift," Flynn said. "I seem to be crabbing to the right, too."

"I see you," Hawking said. "Looks like your glider didn't completely deploy."

Skyler swallowed a curse. Five klicks over mountainous terrain was not the place for an equipment malfunction. "Can you get to him?" he asked.

"I've got him," Jensen put in before Hawking could answer. "Hold as level as you can, Flynn."

"Trying."

Across the distance, Skyler saw one of the silhouettes make a tight curve and head back toward the sinking glider. "What are you going to do?" he asked.

"I'll start with the whack-it-with-a-hammer approach," Jensen said. "If that doesn't work, we'll have to try something else."

The two gliders had come together now, merging into one oversized shadow far below the others. Across the night breeze, Skyler heard a dull *thud* as Jensen slammed his *nunchaku* into the glider rib connectors. "Well?" O'Hara asked.

"Nothing," Jensen said. There was another thud, then two more in rapid succession. "Not looking good," he said grimly. "I guess it's papoose time. Flynn, I'm going to come over you and hook us together."

"You're not going to get much distance that way," O'Hara warned.

"He's right," Flynn said. "How about just letting me go down the way I am? I think I've got enough lift to land safely, just not enough to make it all the way to Reger's. The rest of you can go make contact, I'll hike to the nearest road, and you can send someone back to pick me up."

"No," Jensen said firmly. "One man alone in unfamiliar wilderness is a recipe for trouble. I'll link up, get you landed, and we'll hike it together."

"But—"

"Make that an order, Flynn," Skyler cut him off. "Jensen?"

"Give me a second."

The two shadows came together, and Skyler held his breath. "Okay, that's it," Jensen reported. "Gliders are linked. You three go on ahead and contact Phoenix. We'll find our own way to Reger's."

Skyler grimaced. Splitting up three-two wasn't a whole lot better than Flynn's suggested four-one. But Lathe had them on a tight schedule, and he couldn't afford for all five of them to go for a long hike in the woods. "You have maps with you?"

"We've got maps, rations, and fighting gear," Jensen said, starting to sound a little impatient. "We'll be fine. Get out of here, will you?"

"We'll have Reger send someone out to find you,"

Skyler promised, turning his glider back toward the east. Their second drop over Earth, and the second time something had gone wrong. What *was* it about this place? "Hawking, O'Hara—let's go."

The three silhouettes receded rapidly into the eastern sky until they had become part of the blackness of the night. Flynn watched them go, trying to ignore the sinking feeling in his stomach. Even with Jensen along, this wasn't going to be fun.

It certainly wasn't the way things were supposed to have gone. Did all military missions have setbacks right out of the box this way?

"Flynn, are you turning south?"

Flynn snapped his attention back. They did seem to be making a lazy turn to the right. "No," he said, experimentally fiddling with his control bar. It seemed all right. "At least, not on purpose."

"Must be your broken wing," Jensen grunted, and Flynn winced as a series of jolts rippled through his glider. "Or else we've picked up a northerly crosscurrent."

Flynn peered off to the east, but the other three gliders were already lost to view. "Shouldn't we let Skyler know?"

"We're already out of range," Jensen said. "Besides, it's not like there's anything he can do about it."

Flynn grimaced. Terrific. "Ah, well," he said, trying to be philosophic about it. "They say long walks in the woods are very therapeutic."

"Yes, they do, don't they?" Jensen said, suddenly sounding thoughtful.

Flynn twisted his neck to look up, a complete waste of effort with the glider wing between him and Jensen. "Something?"

"It just occurred to me that, given we're heading south anyway, maybe we should see if we can get close enough to Aegis Mountain for a quick look."

"I thought there was a Ryqril base just outside the main entrance."

"There is," Jensen confirmed. "That's what I want to look at."

A sudden lump formed in Flynn's throat. "Oh. Uh . . . you think that's a good idea?"

"What, you worried about a simple little Ryqril base?" Jensen scoffed. "And it *is* only a little one."

"Has it got autotarget antiaircraft lasers on its walls?"

"A couple."

"In that case, yes, I'm worried," Flynn said.

"It'll be a quick look, just to see if they've abandoned the idea of breaking into the mountain," Jensen soothed. "We'll pop our heads over the ridge, pop them back down again, then go straight back to the nearest road and head for Reger's. Okay?"

"Sure, why not?" Flynn said with a sigh. He looked up at the wing arching over his head. "It's not like I'm driving or anything."

"That's the spirit," Jensen said approvingly, turning them toward the southwest. "Settle in, and enjoy the ride."

The three blackcollars had lost a lot of altitude while they'd been circling around trying to fix Flynn's glider. Now, as Skyler watched the tops of the mountains passing them on both sides, he realized they weren't going to make it.

Hawking had clearly come to the same conclusion. "Looks like we're in for something of a hike ourselves," he commented.

"Walking's good for you," Skyler said encouragingly, trying to hide his own misgivings. The territory west of Reger's estate was extremely rugged, and the only roads through it might well be watched by Security agents and other unfriendlies. Nothing they couldn't handle, but it would cost them valuable time.

"Skyler, look about ten degrees right," O'Hara said suddenly. "There's a very dim light about a third of the way up the mountain that's blinking its little heart out."

Skyler frowned into the darkness. There it was, as dim and sputtery as O'Hara had said.

But it wasn't just blinking at random. It was blinking in Morse code. "Can anyone read that?" he asked. "It's going too fast for me."

"Yeah, I've got it," Hawking said slowly. "But it's not making any sense. *Right hand—open, closed to fingertips, slide thumb—*" With a snort, he broke off. "Oh, isn't that cute?"

"What's cute?" O'Hara demanded.

"Our friend there on the mountainside," Hawking said. "He can't know what kind of encrypt we might have with us, and even if he did we sure as hell can't do much in the way of serious decoding from hang gliders. And he can't just say, 'Welcome, blackcollars,' either, because he knows we'll suspect a trap and avoid him like the plague. So what *does* he do?"

Skyler frowned; and then it clicked. "He Morses us a description of a blackcollar hand signal."

"Oh, for—" O'Hara snorted. "Must be the altitude. Low oxygen flow to the brain."

"That, or senility is hitting all of us early," Skyler agreed, watching the light repeat its message. The hand signal their unknown contact was describing was the third-tier configuration for *safe—come ahead*. Security agents might have observed and documented any number of the first- and even second-tier hand signals over the years, but a third-tier signal was something only another blackcollar should know. "What say we wander over and take a look?"

The light turned out to be coming from the window of a small cabin built against a rocky cliff face. An area about twenty meters square directly in front of the cabin had been cleared of trees and brush, perhaps with hang glider landings in mind. Skyler dropped neatly into the center of the clearing, Hawking and O'Hara going for the more problematic but better concealed forested areas to either side.

Skyler had just popped free of his harness when a floodlight suddenly blazed from a corner of the cabin's roof, bathing the whole landing area in light.

Instantly, he leaped to the side, snatching a *shuriken* from his belt and sending it spinning toward the light. But even before it hit the light winked out again. "Welcome back, Skyler," a voice said from behind him.

Skyler turned around. Behind the purple blob bouncing in front of his eyes, he saw a slim figure emerge from the woods at the far end of the landing field. "Kanai?" he asked.

"Yes," Lonato Kanai confirmed, coming up to Skyler and bowing from the waist. "Do I take it from your arrival that something interesting is about to happen?"

"We certainly hope so," Skyler said, lifting his hand and giving an all-clear signal to the others. "How did you know we were coming?"

"I didn't," Kanai said. "But when an off-world shuttle is due in, I spend the night either here or at one of our other cabins, watching for supply shipments." He smiled faintly. "Or, even more hopefully, for blackcollar drop pods."

"Must be lonely duty," Skyler commented as Hawking and O'Hara came up from both sides. "You remember Dawis Hawking from our last pass through the area. Commando Kelly O'Hara; Commando Lonato Kanai. One of the leaders of the Phoenix resistance group."

Kanai's lip twitched. "Formerly one of its leaders," he said quietly. "No longer."

Skyler frowned. "Is there a problem with Phoenix?"

"Perhaps it's only a difference of opinion," Kanai said evasively. "But come—I have a car ready. Load your packs in the trunk and I'll take you to see Reger."

"Thank you," Skyler said. Manx Reger, one of Denver's most powerful crime bosses, hadn't been particularly pleased the last time the Plinry blackcollars had come through his territory, their presence threatening to upset the comfortable status quo that existed between the various crime bosses who effectively ran the region. Still, when they'd left he'd been cautiously interested in Anne Silcox's plans to rebuild a Resistance cell in the area.

Skyler could only hope the man was still feeling charitable toward unannounced guests.

*   *   *

Dragging himself out of a deep sleep, General Avral Poirot, head of Security for Denver, got to the phone on the third ring. "Poirot," he said, his voice croaking a little with dry throat.

"Bailey, sir," Colonel Pytor Bailey's voice answered. "I think we may finally have Manx Reger."

The last wisps of sleep vanished from Poirot's brain. "Explain."

"We had a drop pod breech in the mountains west of Boulder about half an hour ago," Bailey said. "Same general location where Reger usually gets his Resistance deliveries."

Poirot scowled into the darkness. Reger had been getting those deliveries at irregular intervals for nearly a year now, ever since Lathe's blackcollar team had come roaring into town and assassinated retired North American Prefect Ivas Trendor.

Why a man of Reger's wealth and comfort had gotten involved with the Resistance was still a mystery. But involved he was, and Poirot knew it.

But knowing and proving were two different things, even with the lax standards of evidence the Ryqril overlords permitted in cases like this. So far they'd never been able to catch Reger with the goods, or to find any other tangible evidence that he was involved. "How does this particular drop give him to us?"

"Because this one's chutes didn't open," Bailey said. "Which means that instead of being packed and ready to be thrown onto a truck, whatever it was should be scattered fairly randomly across the landscape."

Poirot smiled grimly as he swung his legs out of bed. And scattered merchandise could take quite a while to collect back together. If they hurried, they might make it to Reger's place before the goods did. "Do we have any spotters in the area?"

"I've scrambled two from Boulder," Bailey said. "They're still en route to the drop area."

"Keep them high," Poirot warned. "I don't want them scaring away the scavengers."

"Yes, sir," Bailey said.

"And then grab a couple of unmarked cars and a strike team," Poirot added, pulling his uniform off the bedside rack. "You and I are going to be sitting with Mr. Reger in his conversation room when the merchandise arrives."

"There it is," Lathe said, pointing out one of the shuttle cargo bay's small portholes at the dark mass coming rapidly up toward them from below. "Ever been to a frontline world in the Ryqril-Chryselli war, Caine?"

"No," Caine said, a shiver running through him. Growing up in Central Europe, though, he'd seen the kind of warfare the Ryqril could unleash when they wanted to. Lathe and the others, stationed on Plinry, had seen far more of it. "Any idea how badly it's been mauled?"

"Lepkowski didn't mention anything in particular," Lathe said. "I imagine we'll find out soon enough. Spadafora?"

"All set," Tardy Spadafora confirmed, straightening from his check of the large winch bolted to the deck at the shuttle's stern. "You sure this thing's going to work?"

"We've done it in reverse," Lathe reminded them. "How much harder can it be going the other direction?"

"Yeah, that's one way to look at it," Spadafora said dryly. "Sounds remarkably like those classic last words, 'Hey, everyone—watch this.'"

"You're welcome to ride the shuttle the rest of the way to the spaceport if you'd prefer," Lathe offered.

Spadafora wrinkled his nose. "No, that's okay."

Above the aft hatchway, an amber light blinked on. "Here we go," Lathe said. "Everyone into position."

Mordecai and Spadafora maneuvered themselves around the sides of the winch, pausing along the way to fasten the safety lines on their parachute-style harnesses to rings welded to the bay walls. Caine moved up behind Mordecai and did the same, feeling awkward and clumsy in his multiple layers of clothing. Beneath his long, light-absorbing civilian-cut coat he wore shirt and slacks, beneath which was his flexarmor. Above the coat, adding another twenty kilos to his weight, was a backpack with extra weapons, clothing, and emergency rations.

"Once more into the breech, as the poet said," Lathe commented, his eyes on Caine as he moved into position behind Spadafora. "You all right?"

"Of course," Caine said, his pounding heart belying the confident words. He'd done drop-pod insertions twice now, both of them more or less successfully. He might have even enjoyed doing it a third time.

Leave it to Lathe to suddenly change the rules on him.

"Get ready," Lathe said. The light turned red— "Go."

Mordecai slapped the release, and the shuttle bay was suddenly filled with a swirling windstorm as the drop door swung down into its usual ramp configuration. Caine grabbed his safety line, struggling for balance as his legs were nearly swept out from under him. The deck shuddered; and suddenly, out the open back, he saw the drop pods that had been fastened to the shuttle's outer hull go tumbling into the night behind them. "Drop pods away," Mordecai announced, peering out into the darkness. "Attitude and trajectory look good."

Lathe nodded. "Four minutes."

"Four minutes," Spadafora repeated, kneeling down beside the winch and unreeling a few meters of slender cable fastened to a large and very wicked-looking barb-nosed harpoon. Unfastening the harpoon from its harness, he carried it to a launcher attached to the floor just in front of the drop door and loaded it in.

Caine gazed out at the churning slipstream, counting down the seconds to himself as he visualized the drop pods' path. They would be popping their chutes about now, he knew, slowing their descent toward the ground below. Another minute, and their onboard timers would trigger their controlled destruction, blowing open the floors and breaking their walls into sections, each of which would sprout wings and turn itself into a self-leveling hang glider.

It would look exactly like the last two times he and the blackcollars had clandestinely landed on Ryqril-controlled worlds. Just like Skyler and his team should be doing on Earth at this very moment, in fact.

Only here on Khala there wouldn't be any infiltrators riding those hang gliders, just eight sensor-realistic dummies strapped beneath the wide, gray-black wings.

Eight make-believe blackcollars, apparently intent on sneaking into Khala right under Security's collective nose.

And with luck, that would be where Security's collective nose would be pointing for the next half hour or so.

"Thirty seconds," Lathe called from beside the launcher.

Spadafora moved back into position on his side of the winch and got his secondary line in hand. Caine did the same, checking one last time to make sure his main safety cable wasn't near anything it could get caught or tangled on. Resettling his harness comfortably across his shoulders and thighs, he made sure his goggles and gas filter were securely in place. It was going to be like a hurricane when they hit the air out there.

"Here we go," Lathe said, flipping up a protective panel on the launcher and resting his gloved hand on the glowing red button beneath it. "Harpoon in five . . . three, two, *one*."

He pressed the button; and with a burst of compressed air the harpoon blasted out the open hatch. It disappeared downward into the night, the slender attached cable from the winch reeling out madly behind it.

Caine felt his hand curl into a fist. Theoretically, Lathe had picked a landing area that would be clear of people or livestock or homes or anything else that would be instantly killed or destroyed by the harpoon's impact. But mistakes sometimes happened, . . .

He had half expected the harpoon's impact to be transmitted along the cable into something he might feel. But he was still waiting when Lathe turned his head toward them. "It's down," he called. "Go."

And in a single smooth motion, Spadafora unliooked the safety line that fastened him to the shuttle wall, snapped the large carabiner ring of his secondary line around the unreeling cable, and leaped out into the night.

Lathe was right behind him, then Mordecai; and then it was Caine's turn. Setting his teeth firmly together, working the two cables as he'd practiced on the trip, he popped his first line from the wall, attached his second to the cable, and jumped.

For the first few dizzying seconds he actually slid *upward* with the momentum he'd been given by the shuttle's own forward motion. Then friction and air resistance and gravity dragged him to a halt, and a moment later he was sliding downward with increasing speed.

He gripped his line with one hand and waved the other against the air in an effort to keep himself facing the direction he was moving. The broken clouds overhead were blocking most of the starlight, but there was enough getting through to show the ground rushing up toward him.

He couldn't see the three blackcollars anywhere below him. Was that simply because of the light-absorbing coats they were all wearing? Or had their connection lines somehow failed, dropping them off the cable to their deaths? And if theirs had failed, wouldn't his likely do so as well? He took a deep breath, trying to stay calm.

And exhaled that breath in a huff as the ring above him suddenly seemed to catch, sending his feet swinging upward and his harness digging into his thighs as the deceleration dragged at him like a fighter-turn G-force. He caught a glimpse of figures on the ground beneath him, the urgently flashing purple marker lights at the rear of the harpoon—

And then, with welcome anticlimax, he slid to an almost gentle stop with his feet safely on the ground.

Lathe was already at his side. "Everyone clear," the comsquare ordered, grabbing Caine's upper arm in a steadying grip with one hand as he slashed a knife through the connecting line with the other. Spadafora, Caine saw, was standing beside the harpoon, his hand poised over an opened control cover. Half guiding, half dragging Caine a few steps away, Lathe gestured to Spadafora.

The other pressed the control; and with a sizzle of high-voltage current, the cable still unreeling from the distant shuttle evaporated in a puff of acerbic smoke.

"I guess you were right," Spadafora said. "It *isn't* any harder going down."

"What about the harpoon?" Caine asked, eyeing it dubiously. It had buried a good two-thirds of its length into the ground and didn't look like it was going to be coming out any time soon.

"We leave it," Lathe said, pulling off his goggles and battle-hood and stowing them in his coat pockets. "Besides, they'll figure it out anyway as soon as the hang gliders are down." He pointed south. "If we're on target, there should be a town about a klick down the hill."

"How big a town?" Caine asked.

"Big enough to have some cars lying around waiting to be borrowed," Lathe assured him.

"Plus a few public phones," Spadafora added.

"Right," Lathe agreed. "We'll want to contact Shaw as soon as possible, make sure he's ready to receive. I'll do that while you three find a car." He looked at his watch. "If we hurry, we should be in Inkosi City in a couple of hours."

"There they go," Khala Security Prefect Daov Haberdae said, nodding at the long-range telescope display. "Right on schedule."

"Yes," Galway murmured, frowning at the indistinct hang gliders as they sorted themselves out from the scattering wreckage of the shattered drop pods.

"Dae yae ha' ratchers on the gro'nd?" Taakh asked.

"We have watchers all over the area, Your Eminence," Haberdae assured him. "Whenever and wherever they come down, we'll have them covered."

"Excellent," Taakh said.

"I just hope Prefect Galway's right about them being of some use," Haberdae added under his breath. "I've got a lot of men and resources tied up in this."

With a supreme effort, Galway ignored him. Haberdae didn't like Galway's plan. He hadn't liked it right from the very beginning, and hadn't been at all shy about saying so. The fact that Taakh's support of the operation meant that neither Haberdae nor anyone else on Khala got a vote in the matter only made it worse.

And the Ryq hadn't been shy about making *that* clear, either. Nor, apparently, was he interested in starting now. "I ha' seen Lathe in action," Taakh said in response to Haberdae's quiet comment, taking a step closer to the prefect. "The 'lan *rill* rork."

Haberdae grimaced. "Yes, Your Eminence," he said, his voice neutral again. Loyalty-conditioning permitted a man to offer suggestions to a Ryqril, or in certain circumstances to even argue with them.

But no one argued with *khassq*-class warriors. Not if they wanted to stay alive.

"Looks like they're splitting into two groups, sir," one of the techs at the monitor panel spoke up.

"Yae ha' 'oth directions co'ered?"

"*Everything* is covered, Your Eminence," Haberdae said. His voice was properly respectful, but beneath it his patience was clearly strained. "From that altitude, they have a maximum range of maybe thirty kilometers. We've got fifty klicks covered, in every direction—"

"Something's wrong," Galway interrupted him, the back of his neck starting to tingle as he stared at the silhouettes of the hang gliders.

"There's nothing wrong," Haberdae growled. "My people *have* them covered."

"They're not there," Galway said, his vague apprehensions suddenly becoming certainty. "Those are decoys."

Haberdae turned to the control board. "Vaandar?" he demanded.

"Sensors clearly show a person hanging under each of those gliders," the tech assured him.

"The sensors are wrong," Galway insisted, swiveling to the communications section of his panel and keying a switch. "Because that's *all* they're doing—hanging. They're not controlling the gliders. Dispatch? Get me fifty men—"

"Hold it," Haberdae snapped, grabbing the armrest of Galway's chair and giving a yank that brought him rolling back from the board. "You already have all the men you're entitled to for this operation. You do *not* have authority to grab any more without my permission." He looked at Taakh. "Isn't that right, Your Eminence?" he added.

"The gliders aren't under control," Galway said, carefully pronouncing each word. "They're decoys. Lathe and the others got off somewhere else."

"Rhere?" Taakh demanded.

"Exactly," Haberdae seconded. "We've had the shuttle under surveillance the entire way."

"Except where it dipped into the Falkarie Mountain foothills," Galway reminded him. "There were a nearly two minutes where the sensors were blocked."

"And the ground observers had visual contact the whole time," Haberdae countered. "They would have seen any parachutes."

"Then they didn't use parachutes," Galway insisted. "Look, Prefect, I don't know how they did it. All I know is that they're not with those gliders."

"Ha' yae other e'idence?" Taakh asked.

Galway braced himself. "No evidence, Your Eminence. Just my experience with the way Lathe does things."

"Then 'Re'ect Ha'erdae is correct," the Ryq said. "Yae nay not rekest his other nen."

And there would be no appeal, Galway knew. Not with Taakh. "As you command, Your Eminence," he said. "In that case, may I be excused for a few minutes? The gliders won't land for at least another half hour, and I have some other matters to attend to."

Taakh inclined his head. "Yae nay go."

"Thank you," Galway said. Standing up, he headed for the door.

"Don't you touch my people," Haberdae warned.

"I wouldn't think of it," Galway assured him.

No, he wouldn't touch any of Haberdae's precious Security men, he thought grimly as the door sealed itself behind him. Not even the ones who were currently doing absolutely nothing except lounging around Inkosi City's main entry roads, as if Lathe would be foolish enough to enter a city along such obvious routes.

But then, Haberdae's Security men were hardly the only resources available. There was an entire government's worth of bureaucrats and tech workers scattered around the city, all of them loyalty-conditioned, none of them under Haberdae's legal jurisdiction. If Galway could get them out onto the streets and highways in the next half hour—*all* the streets, not just the obvious entry points—maybe they could spot the incoming blackcollars in time to get Judas and the special ops team in position to intercept them.

Picking up his pace, he hurried down the brightly lit corridor. With luck, maybe he could still pull this off.

CHAPTER 3

"So has anyone been inside the mountain since we left?" Skyler asked as they drove eastward along the winding road toward Reger's estate.

"Anne and I went in a couple of times in the first few months," Kanai said. "We wanted to see if there was any more information on Whiplash we might have missed earlier."

Skyler nodded, thinking of the irony of it all. The old Torch resistance organization had spent its last days in Aegis Mountain, working to develop a drug capable of breaking the hitherto unbreakable Ryqril loyalty-conditioning. And they'd succeeded, only to succumb to the residual chemical warfare contamination in the base before they'd even had a chance to use it. "Was there?"

"Not that we could find," Kanai said. "We were able to get a couple other sections of the base operational, though, complete with heat and power. We got one of the elevators running, too."

"I hope you didn't go near the main command level," Hawking warned.

"And risk bringing the entire mountain down on us?" Kanai snorted gently. "Give us a little more credit than that, Commando Hawking."

"I'm sure he was just asking," Skyler assured him. "But you haven't been inside lately?"

In the reflected glow of the headlights, Skyler saw Kanai's lips compress briefly. "As I say, we've had some differences of opinion. I'm mostly working with Reger these days."

"What kind of differences?" Skyler pressed.

"Perhaps it would be best if we wait until . . ."

He trailed off.

"What is it?" Skyler asked, looking out the windshield.

"That's the road to Reger's estate," Kanai said, pointing ahead to a road branching off to the right. "Those two houses on either side of the intersection have their porch lights on."

"And they shouldn't?" Skyler asked.

"All the houses on that road are owned by Reger's people," Kanai said. The car came up to the road, and he drove past without slowing. "The porch lights are never lit unless something's wrong."

"Any other ways in?" O'Hara asked.

"There's an access road along the west side of the estate," Hawking said. "It'll bring us right up to the sensor keyhole Jensen and I put in."

"Unless Reger's closed it up," Skyler said.

"I don't believe he has," Kanai said. "No one but a blackcollar would be able to sneak in along it anyway."

"Okay, get us back to that road," Skyler said. "You and Hawking know the system and grounds best—you'll go in through the keyhole. O'Hara and I will give you some lead time, then we'll come in the front door."

It took Kanai a few minutes by back street and other people's access roads to return them to the western edge of the Reger estate. Maneuvering the car around the worst of the potholes, he came to a halt a few meters from the outer fence, a simple-looking wire-mesh design, two meters tall, that probably looked like any number of other property-line fences in this part of the mountains. "Electrified, no doubt," O'Hara commented as the four blackcollars approached it.

"Yes, but not seriously," Hawking assured him. "Jensen cranked back most of the juice so that he could run pressure sensors along the top without the current blinding them."

"Another good reason to leave the fence alone," Skyler said, pulling on his battle-hood and gloves as the others followed suit. "O'Hara?"

O'Hara stepped to his side, and together they eased their way cautiously forward until they were about a meter from the fence. There was no obvious reaction from either the fence or the environs. Turning to face each other a meter apart, they settled into wide horse stances, knees bent, hands cupped thigh high in front of them. "Kanai?" Skyler said, looking back at the others.

Kanai nodded and started forward at a slow jog, picking up speed as he came. He reached Skyler and O'Hara and leaped forward and upward.

And as he did so, the two blackcollars caught the undersides of his boots in their cupped hands and pulled convulsively upward, hurling him toward the night sky. He flew to the top of the fence and did a neat high jumper's roll over the top, continuing the roll and twist and landing in a crouch on the other side.

Fifteen seconds later, Hawking was beside him. "You've got fifteen minutes to get through the grounds and check out the house," Skyler told them. "After that, O'Hara and I drive up to the front door like we owned the place."

"We'll be ready," Hawking promised. Touching Kanai on the shoulder, he gestured, and together they slipped away into the night.

"This is completely outrageous," Manx Reger growled, his eyes blazing as he glared at Poirot from the middle of the large overstuffed chair where the two Security men standing to his right and left had planted him. "It's also completely illegal."

"That's good, coming from a crime boss," Poirot countered. "Let me ask one more time: What's in the shipment your friends dropped tonight?"

"I have no idea what you're talking about," Reger said stiffly. "And as for being a crime boss, I deny that categorically."

"Of course you do." Poirot turned to the door as Bailey came into the room. "You have everyone?"

"I think so," Bailey said. "There were two more hiding in shielded guard holes. We've put everyone together in the dining room."

"Make sure they stay quiet," Poirot warned.

"We will," Bailey assured him. "I also heard from the spotters. They say a car's gone down the access road west of the estate and stopped by the fence there. Four men got out, and they think two of them must have gotten through the fence somewhere and come onto the grounds. Only two got back into the car, anyway."

Poirot scratched his cheek. Suspicious couriers checking out the estate before making their delivery? Or was it standard procedure to bypass the house and deliver the contraband to a hidden cache somewhere else on the grounds?

He looked at Reger, but the other's face wasn't giving anything away. "Put a couple of our plainclothes men outside," he told Bailey. "Tell them to keep out of the light. Maybe the sight of some roving guards will make our gate-crashers happier."

Bailey nodded and repeated the orders into his comm. "What about the two in the car?" he asked.

"Let them be," Poirot told him. "Sooner or later, I'm sure they'll come to see us."

"Five minutes," O'Hara said.

Skyler nodded. So far, whoever had taken over Reger's estate hadn't come to check out this car sitting on the road along the western fence. Either inattention or overconfidence, and either was likely to cost them. "I'm thinking we'll just go straight in, play stupid, and take it from there," he said.

"They may remember you," O'Hara pointed out. "And if Galway's been doing his job, they probably have a photo of me, as well."

"Which I'm guessing local Security will have long forgotten," Skyler said. "They've got enough faces from their own neighborhood to memorize."

"I suppose." O'Hara was silent a moment. "I wonder what this difference of opinion is that Kanai's having with Phoenix."

"Whatever it is, I don't like it," Skyler said. "A Resistance movement is no place for politics and disagreements."

"Not that that's ever stopped anyone," O'Hara pointed out.

"Which is why those groups fall apart so often once they finally win," Skyler said. "The last thing we want is for that to happen here."

"I'll bet they're fighting over what to do with the moles they've created in the political structure," O'Hara mused. "One of them probably wants to start making trouble now, while the other wants to wait until they get word to act. Or maybe there's a difference of opinion as to what targets to go after."

"Or they're fighting over Aegis Mountain," Skyler said. "There's got to be a lot of interesting stuff in the doomsdayed areas. One of them may be wanting to take the risk of trying to get those rooms open."

"Ouch," O'Hara murmured. "That would certainly make the Ryqril sit up and take notice."

"Not to mention everyone in the immediate area," Skyler agreed. "That immediate area possibly including much of Denver itself."

"Yeah." O'Hara checked his watch. "Time to go."

"Right." Skyler started the car and pulled onto the road again.

"Signal from the gate," Bailey reported. "The car's coming down the road, two males visible."

"Have the men at the gate pass them through," Poirot ordered. "Then they're to close up and follow them in. Two plainclothesmen from the house are to meet them as they come up, with a sniper out of sight in one of the front windows. Hopefully, they'll be smart enough not to make trouble."

"Yes, sir," Bailey said, repeating the orders. "Heading out now."

"And warn them not to identify themselves until after the men are out of the car," Poirot added. "As far as they're concerned, everything here is business as usual."

"Yes, sir," Bailey said, frowning as he pressed his comm earphone harder against his ear. "Sir, the team leader reports he can't raise the two men we sent outside earlier."

From somewhere out in the hallway came a soft thud. Poirot turned that direction, wondering in irritation which of his men was falling over his own feet—to see a black-clad figure walk casually into the room.

For a single, impossibly long heartbeat it didn't register. Then, with a rush of adrenaline, Poirot finally understood what was happening. "Alert!" he shouted as loudly as he could, grabbing for his holstered paral-dart pistol.

The two Security men standing behind Reger's chair were already in motion. It didn't do them a bit of good. The blackcollar had a pair of throwing stars cupped in his hand, and even as the guards tried to bring their own guns to bear he flipped the weapons into their throats. Both men toppled backward, one of them sending a cluster of darts harmlessly into the ceiling as he died.

"Don't," the blackcollar warned. He had his arm cocked over his shoulder, another throwing star in hand, aimed at Poirot and Bailey. "Hands away from your guns, please."

Poirot focused on the two dead guards. "Hands away," he ordered Bailey through clenched teeth as he lifted his own hands. "But you're too late," he added to the black-collar. "My men have already been alerted."

The other shrugged slightly. "We'll see."

Skyler had brought the car to a halt at the mansion's ornate front entryway, and the two men waiting at the door were striding toward the car when both of them abruptly twitched and went for their guns. "It's blown," Skyler snapped. Wrenching open his door, he dived out onto the ground.

He was just in time. Even as he hit the ground a cloud of paral-darts scattered off the car's roof with a nails-on-slate screech. Rolling back to his knees, he sent a pair of *shuriken* toward the nearest attacker.

The man ducked, but not quite far enough. One of the stars skimmed past his head, as the second buried itself in his right shoulder. He staggered with the impact, his next shot going wild. Skyler grabbed out one of his knives before the other could regain his balance and with a hard underhand throw sent it to bounce hilt first off the man's forehead. He went down, his gun flying from his hand, and lay still.

There was a flicker of movement from the mansion itself, and Skyler was slammed backward as a flechette slammed into his chest, turning his flexarmor momentarily rigid as it blocked the shot and distributed the impact over his entire body. He dived away from the car as the flexarmor relaxed, dodging in a roll-leap evasive maneuver, wishing he'd had time to put on his battle-hood as he searched the windows for the sniper. There was a second flicker from one of the first-floor windows, and he caught a glimpse of a figure standing there as a patch of pavement beside him erupted into splinters. Dodging again to the side, he grabbed another *shuriken* and hurled it toward the window, knowing the sniper was well out of range but hoping to brush him back until O'Hara could get to cover and get out his slingshot.

There was another flicker from the window; but this time the shot buried itself in a tree trunk five meters to Skyler's left. He pulled out another *shuriken*, wondering if the man could really have reacted that strongly to his first throw.

And even as his brain caught up with the fact that that there had been *two* men at the window, the tingler on his wrist came to life: *sniper down; house secure.*

Skyler huffed a sigh of relief. But there was no time to pause for congratulations. The two men who'd followed the car in from the gate were sprinting toward them now, one rapid-firing paral-dart bursts, the other laying down scattergun blasts as fast as he could work the pump.

They were still coming when the paral-dart gunner abruptly folded over his stomach and flopped onto the ground. His partner had just enough time to work the scattergun pump one last time, and then his head jerked hard and he, too, crumpled into a heap.

"You okay?" O'Hara called as he rose from the partial cover of the car, a third stone ready in his slingshot as he surveyed his work.

"I'm fine," Skyler assured him, looking up at the stars overhead. Paral-dart guns meant Security, and Security meant high-flying spotters. He wondered how much of the brief battle they'd seen. "Let's get inside."

Kanai was waiting inside the front door, and together they went back to the house's well-stocked library. Reger was seated in a large chair near the center, with a couple of bodies on the floor behind him and two uniformed Security officers posed stiffly against one wall. Standing watch over the whole thing was Hawking. "Any problems?" Skyler asked as they joined him.

Hawking shook his head. "Most of them were conveniently grouped in the dining room, standing guard over the house men. The roamers were a little more trouble, but not much."

"Good." Skyler turned to Reger. "Nice to see you again, Mr. Reger."

"The pleasure's all yours," Reger countered sourly. "Skyler, isn't it?"

"Yes," Skyler confirmed. He nodded toward the Security men. "Who are your friends?"

"*Nobody* in this room qualifies as a friend," Reger retorted. "What the *hell* are you doing here, anyway?"

"Making trouble," Skyler said, looking at the Security men. "And you are . . . ?"

"General Avral Poirot, Denver Chief of Security," the older man identified himself, his voice as stiff as his posture but calm and professional for all that. "This is Assistant Chief Colonel Pytor Bailey. I see tonight's drop was personnel, not equipment. My mistake."

"Mistakes happen," Skyler said. So even with their new

nonchuted drop pod's faster descent, Security had still spotted it. That was useful to know. He hoped Lathe's zip line insertion on Khala had worked out better. "So was this just a social visit?"

Poirot snorted. "Please, Commando. The very fact that you're in this room proves our suspicions of Reger and his Resistance connections were right."

Reger swore under his breath. "Oh, that's wonderful," he ground out. "Just wonderful. Thank you, Skyler, thank you so very much."

"A temporary problem only," Skyler assured him. "The general and colonel are about to graduate from the third type of person to the fourth."

"What?" Reger asked, frowning.

"Never mind," Skyler said. "Private joke. Would you be so kind as to show Hawking where you keep your Whiplash supply?"

Reger shook his head. "I don't have any."

"*None?*" Skyler asked. "I would have thought you'd be—"

"You thought wrong," Reger cut him off. "Phoenix has it all."

Skyler looked at Kanai, noting the hard set of the other's mouth. Part of the argument he was having with the organization? "Then I guess we'll have to go get it from them," he said, turning back to Poirot. "What are your spotters' orders, General?"

Poirot looked at the others, perhaps wondering if cooperation would violate his loyalty-conditioning. "They're to stay at high altitude and watch," he said. "Though of course they'll have heard my warning. They're probably trying to contact us right now, preparatory to calling in reinforcements." He raised his eyebrows. "If you'd like, I could get on the comm and send them away."

Skyler smiled cynically. "Of course you could."

"Really," Poirot assured him. "What's Whiplash?"

"Nothing you need concern yourself with just now," Skyler said, walking over to them. "Pleasant dreams." His hand snapped out to slam a punch behind Bailey's right ear and then backfist Poirot behind his left.

Both men dropped without even a gasp, Skyler catching Poirot beneath his arms as he fell. "Well, don't just stand there," he said, turning back to the others. "We'll take the Security cars—might as well listen in on what they're up to while we drive."

"Are we taking both men?" Kanai asked.

Skyler looked down at Bailey's crumpled form. He had no problem with giving Whiplash to both men, certainly, but blatantly kidnapping two senior Security officers might stir up more trouble than he really wanted just now. Besides, if Phoenix had been doing its job, they would have built up personality and operational profiles on all of Denver's Security officers, and it would be better to leave one of them here than to have the Ryqril bring in a complete unknown from Dallas or San Francisco to take over. "No, just the general," he told Kanai. "Get out there and see if you're going to have any trouble starting the cars."

"So that's it?" Reger growled. "You come into my house, bounce a bunch of Security men around, and then just *leave*?"

"You're welcome to join us," Skyler offered as he hoisted

Poirot up onto his shoulder. "If not, I'm sure you can explain this to the follow-up group."

"You leave me so much choice," Reger bit out as he reluctantly got to his feet. "Where do you propose we go?"

"Let's start with a place where we can keep General Poirot quiet and incommunicado," Skyler said. "I trust you and Kanai have some idea where Phoenix's safe houses are?"

Reger shot a look at Kanai. "Personally, I wouldn't trust anything those amateurs set up," he said. "But I have a couple places of my own that should work. Assuming we get there in one piece, then what?"

"Then we go look up Anne Silcox," Skyler said grimly. "And find out what the hell she and her group are doing."

Between the drag of the crosswinds and the weight of Flynn's glider still tethered beneath his, Jensen wasn't quite able to make it over the final row of hills he'd been aiming for. Instead, the two men landed on the northern slope of one of them, fifty meters below the crest.

It was just as well they hadn't gotten any farther.

"So that's Aegis Mountain," Flynn murmured from beside Jensen as they lay flat on their bellies at the top of the hill.

"That's the place," Jensen said, a prickly sensation crawling across his skin. At the bottom of their ridge, perhaps half a klick away, a wide highway wound its way through the mountains, disappearing around hills in both directions. Away to their left, on the far side of the highway, a black mountain with a wide metal doorway set into its base rose majestically against the night sky.

And filling most of the space between the road and mountain, nestled right up against the slope, were the lights and domed buildings and perimeter wall and huge sensor-controlled laser cannon of a full-scale Ryqril military base.

"Good thing we didn't have any more altitude," Flynn said. He was obviously trying to sound casual, but even in a whisper Jensen could hear the tension in his voice. "That base is bigger than I expected."

"I know," Jensen heard himself say. "It's bigger than *I* expected, too."

Out of the corner of his eye, he saw Flynn turn to face him. "What?"

Jensen nodded toward the base. "It's bigger than it was last year," he said. "A *lot* bigger. Come on, let's get out of here."

Carefully, they backed down the hill until they were well below the summit and out of range of both prying eyes and line-of-sight autotarget lasers. "You think they've gotten into the mountain?" Flynn whispered as they crouched together in the shadows at the base of a tall pine tree.

"I doubt it," Jensen said, playing the image of the encampment through his mind. "All the equipment I could see under the entrance overhang looked like heavy tunneling and metalwork machinery. That would suggest they're still trying to cut their way through the various doors. Besides, if they'd broken through I'd think they'd have flown a few flag officers in for the occasion, and I didn't see any of those sawtooth-edged rank banners flying anywhere." He grimaced. "But they sure seem to have decided to up their ante on the project."

Flynn was silent a moment. "Maybe they know about Whiplash," he suggested.

"And are hoping to find data about it?" Jensen shrugged. "Could be. Either that, or their war with the Chryselli is getting more desperate than we thought and they're looking for something—anything—to tilt the odds back in their favor."

"I suppose that qualifies as good news for our side," Flynn said doubtfully. "Provided they don't actually find some nice superweapon in there."

"If we'd had any superweapons, we sure as hell would have used them," Jensen pointed out, gazing up at the stars peeking through the pine tree's branches. "But it's all academic, because they're not going to get in."

"I hope you're right."

"We're going to make sure I'm right," Jensen said firmly, straightening up. "Come on."

"Where are we—?"

He broke off as Jensen's hand flicked warningly toward his mouth. There had been the sound of movement over to their left . . .

Jensen's *shuriken* pouch was in his left coat pocket. He drew one of the throwing stars with one hand as he signaled Flynn to stay put with the other. Shifting the *shuriken* to his right hand, he eased his way to the next tree over, and then the next, his senses stretched out in full combat mode. The sound came again—

And from around a clump of bushes, a Ryq stepped into view.

Jensen felt his breath freeze in his throat. Had their gliders been spotted? Or had he and Flynn tripped some defense sensors he'd missed?

But the Ryq didn't seem to be searching for anyone or anything. On the contrary, his pace and posture were almost casual, certainly not the intense look of a soldier searching for suspected intruders. A sentry, then, walking his assigned territory with the low-level watchfulness of a warrior who hadn't run into any trouble for weeks in a row and wasn't expecting any tonight.

Under other circumstances, Jensen would have been more than happy to stay out of the alien's evening entirely. Unfortunately for the Ryq, his meandering walk was taking him straight toward the tree where Flynn was crouching. Hefting the *shuriken* in his hand, Jensen did a quick check of the rest of the area.

And as the Ryq half turned to face his direction he hurled the weapon straight into the other's throat. With no sound except the muffled thud of his impact, the alien collapsed to the ground.

Flynn was standing over the body when Jensen got there, *nunchaku* at the ready. "I think he's dead," the boy whispered, his body trembling slightly with adrenaline reaction.

"He is," Jensen assured him as he pulled out the *shuriken* and returned it to his pouch. "They've obviously pushed their perimeter out farther than I expected. Help me get him back up the hill."

The Ryq was on the smallish side, as Ryq went. Nevertheless, it was no small task to lug his deadweight back up the hill overlooking the base. Making sure they themselves stayed low and out of sight, the two men eased the body over the top and let it roll down the steep slope into the darkness below. "That's not going to fool anyone for long," Flynn warned as they again eased their way back down their side of the hill. "As soon as they see that wound they'll know what happened."

"True, but having to haul the body out of there may buy us another hour or two," Jensen pointed out.

"Maybe," Flynn muttered. "Skyler just better get that car out here fast."

"Actually, I hope he doesn't," Jensen said. "Because we're not linking up with him and the others just yet."

"We're not?" Flynn asked cautiously.

"No," Jensen said. They reached the bottom of the hill; getting his bearings, he turned northwest. "We're heading for the back door into Aegis Mountain."

"To do what?"

"Like I told you," Jensen said, hearing the grim set to his voice. "To make sure the Ryqril don't get into the base. Quiet, now—there may be more sentries around."

"Colonel Bailey?" a voice called in the darkness. "Colonel?"

The darkness grew lighter, and Bailey opened his eyes to find a Security medic peering anxiously down at him. "How do you feel, sir?" the medic asked.

"How do you *think* I feel," Bailey growled. He started to lift his head, instantly thought better of it. "What happened? Who's in charge?"

"I am, sir," a young officer said, stepping into view from behind the kneeling medic. "Lieutenant Ramirez, from the Boulder Security office. I'm afraid they got away, Colonel, the assailants and Reger's people both." His lips compressed. "And they seem to have taken General Poirot with them."

"*What?*" Bailey snapped, ignoring the pain in his head as he forced himself into a sitting position. "Why didn't you stop them?"

"We didn't know until the ground team had penetrated the estate that the general had been taken," Ramirez said, his voice under rigid control. "All the spotters could see was that one of the escapees was carrying a bundle over his shoulder wrapped in a blanket."

"Why didn't they come down for a better look?"

"The general had ordered them previously to hold position," Ramirez said. "There was a shouted alert, but no new orders."

"That's because no one was available to give them," Bailey ground out. "Do you at least still have them under surveillance?"

Ramirez's cheek twitched. "Actually—"

"*Damn* it, all," Bailey snarled. "I want those pilots on report. Every one of them."

"It wasn't their fault," Ramirez said firmly. "The escapees had eight cars, and they set off a smoke bomb before sorting themselves out among the vehicles. They split up just outside Denver, and . . . well, there was a certain lack of coordination between the Denver and Boulder offices. By the time we'd sorted it out and had enough spotters in position, we'd lost three of the cars."

Bailey bit back another curse, a chill running through him. It was starting again, just like it had a year ago.

Comsquare Lathe and his blackcollars were on the move, and already two jumps ahead of them. "What about the cars you *haven't* lost?"

"Their occupants have gone to ground, but we have the various locations under surveillance," the lieutenant said, sounding a little more confident.

"Go in and get them," Bailey ordered. "Paral-darts only. I want them alive and able to talk."

"Yes, sir." The lieutenant pulled a comm from his belt. "This is Lieutenant Ramirez. All Operation Seven surveillance units: move in." He got acknowledgements and returned the comm to its holder. "Maybe we'll be lucky, sir, and General Poirot will be in one of those groups."

"We're never that lucky," Bailey growled, pushing himself to his feet. "Not with this group. Get away from me," he added tartly, pushing aside the medic's hand as the other tried to take his arm. "All right, here's the plan. Call Athena and have them pull all intel reports on suspected Resistance activity and personnel, including everything we've got on this Phoenix group we keep hearing rumors about. Put surveillance units on everyone whose name shows up in those reports. They're to watch and report, but not to take action without my order."

"Understood, sir," Ramirez said, his comm in hand again. "And then we should get you to a hospital."

"The hell with that," Bailey said, again fending off the medic's proffered hand. His head was starting to throb again, but he was damned if he was going to let that slow him down. Not with General Poirot in enemy hands. "They can fix me up on the ride back to Athena. Get me a car and driver—I want to be there before they start bringing in the prisoners."

"Yes, sir," Ramirez said.

"And after you get those surveillance units in place," Bailey added as he started toward the door, "get someone looking for everything we might have heard about something called *Whiplash*."

CHAPTER 4

"There—take the next left," Lathe said, pointing toward a rambling building off on the left side of the road, the only one in the area with its lights still on and cars parked in its lot. A faded sign over the door identified it as Hernando's Hideyhole. "I wonder if they're still serving."

"Definitely a proud member of the cheap dive association," Caine commented, eyeing the place dubiously as he turned their borrowed car toward it. "We weren't supposed to stop until we got to the Guardrail Tavern, though."

"It's called getting the lay of the land," Lathe assured him. "There's no way I would just drop in on someone like Shaw without testing the local water first. Mordecai, you're on backup."

"Right," Mordecai said. "You can drop me anywhere, Caine."

Caine pulled the car closer to the side of the road and slowed down. It was still rolling when Mordecai popped his door and hopped out, hitting the pavement in an easy jog and heading for the row of buildings down the street from their target tavern. "We going with the arms-smuggler routine again?" Caine asked as he pulled back to the middle of his lane.

"Might as well," Lathe said. "It's a convenient way to stir people up." He paused, and Caine could feel the comsquare's eyes on him. "You ready?"

Caine took a deep breath. "Let's do it."

Inside, the Hideyhole looked even less promising than it had from the outside. It was about a quarter full, with a clientele that ranged from the scruffy to the downright frightening. The conversational buzz faltered as Lathe, Caine, and Spadafora headed toward a four-person table near a partition leading into a currently unlit back room, and out of the corner of his eye Caine could see the occupants giving them a suspicious once-over. Across at the bar, a big man who looked nearly as disrespectable as the worst of the clientele murmured something to the bartender, then angled over toward their chosen table.

He reached it just as they were seating themselves. "Evening," he grunted. "Morning, rather. What'll you have?"

"Three glasses of your best beer," Lathe told him. "You still serving anything besides alcohol?"

"We got a few things on the menu," the man said. "Anything special you're looking for?"

"Depends," Lathe said, looking around the room. "What does everyone else around here like?"

"Whatever's hot at the moment," the waiter said, a subtle new edge to his voice. "You buying just for the three of you?"

"Actually, we're more on the selling end," Lathe said. "Party favors for the more sophisticated sort."

The other frowned. "Party favors?"

"Noisemakers," Lathe said. "Small fireworks. That sort of thing."

The nearest tables had gone quiet, their occupants listening to the conversation. "Don't have much cause to celebrate around here," the waiter said. "With that new base the snorks just put in across town, it's going to be even bets as to whether it'll be Security or a Chryselli raiding party who nails us first."

"And it's a wise man who'll be prepared for either," Lathe said. "Like they say, the one who dies with the most toys wins."

"But he still dies," the waiter countered. "We're lying low, friend. If you want to do elsewise, you're welcome to do it elsewhere."

"Understood," Lathe said calmly. "We'll have our drinks, and be on our way."

For a moment the waiter seemed to measure him. Then, with a curt nod, he turned and headed back toward the bar. "Off to call Security, you think?" Caine asked quietly.

"Actually, I don't think he is," Lathe said, his eyes following the waiter's progress. "We may be in the one criminal hangout in the entire TDE where the patrons really are just going to leave us alone."

"In that case—" Caine broke off as his tingler began tapping code into his skin: *two cars approaching; eight armored men.*

"Or maybe not," Lathe amended, his battle-hood and gloves already in hand. He lifted his other hand toward the bartender and the waiter, conversing again at the bar. "Excuse me, gentlemen," he called. "You have a back door out of here?"

The two men looked at Lathe, their eyes widening momentarily as they saw the distinctive blackcollar gear. "Yeah, there's a door through the back room there," the waiter said, pointing toward the darkened room.

"Thanks," Lathe said as he pulled out his slingshot and unfolded the wrist brace. "You might want to move everyone over to the walls. Spadafora?"

"Ready," Spadafora said as he pulled a handful of bright yellow pellets from his ammo pouch. He tossed two to Lathe and set one of the others into his slingshot's pouch. "Double volley, then I handle the rest?"

Lathe nodded. "Caine, go check out our back door."

"Right," Caine said, standing up as he finished pulling on his gloves. He headed toward the archway into the back room, noting that the bar's patrons were making a hasty but orderly retreat away from the center of the upcoming action.

He'd just reached the partition when the front door was flung open and two armored and helmeted figures walked purposefully into the bar. Behind their faceplates Caine could see their eyes darting back and forth, their paral-dart pistols swinging warningly around the room.

They'd made it three steps inside when Lathe and Spadafora lifted their slingshots and sent a pair of yellow pellets squarely into the intruders' faceplates.

No nonexplosive projectile could penetrate that plastic, Caine knew, certainly nothing propelled by human muscle. But unlike the blackcollars' regular slingshot rounds, these pellets weren't designed for destruction. Instead, they burst on impact, splattering the faceplates with a thick, instant-setting paint.

Whatever curses the Security men might have uttered were lost in the double shot they sent blindly in the direction the pellets had come from, one of the paral-dart clusters scattering off the top of Caine's battle-hood as he ducked into a low crouch. Lathe and Spadafora were already out of the line of fire, Spadafora moving to the right with another paint pellet in hand, Lathe moving left and forward and stowing his slingshot in favor of his *nunchaku*. Caine caught a glimpse of two more Security men crowding in behind their comrades as Lathe swung the flail into one of the blinded men's helmets, sending him staggering, and Spadafora threaded a shot neatly between the two front men into the faceplate of one of the newcomers.

Caine didn't wait to see any more. He slipped around the partition into the back room, his own *nunchaku* cocked and ready under his arm. The room's chairs were stacked neatly on top of the tables in preparation for cleaning, and the only light showing was a single panel glowing softly in the ceiling. Senses alert, he made his way between the tables to the rear exit. For a moment he paused there, listening, then eased the door open.

It opened into a deserted alley. Carefully, he leaned out and looked out.

And staggered back into the edge of the door as a cluster of paral-darts slammed into his face, most of them ricocheting from his goggles and hood but a few sinking into the exposed skin of his cheek.

He dropped his *nunchaku* as his face went instantly numb, his hand grabbing for the tingler on his wrist. But the drug in his bloodstream was too fast. Even as his fingers dug under the sleeve, both arms went dead. Half a second later his legs folded under him and he sprawled helplessly in the doorway, lying halfway out into the alley.

He'd landed with his face turned uselessly toward the bar's outside wall, but he could hear the running feet coming toward him. The footsteps came to a halt, and he was pulled the rest of the way through the door and turned onto his back. A half dozen hard faces were looking down at him, and out of the corner of his eye he saw a couple pairs of hands unfastening his coat and throwing it open. Other hands attacked the civilian clothing beneath the coat, unfastening it as well and deftly maneuvering the shirt and slacks off his paralyzed limbs and tossing the clothing to someone outside his field of view. They took his *nunchaku* and slingshot from their respective sheaths, removed the knives from his forearm and calf sheaths and the *shuriken* from their thigh and belt pouches, and took his tingler from his wrist. Then, clad only in his flexarmor and the undersuit beneath it, he was lifted and hurried down the alley in the direction from which the ambushers had come. There was the muffled sound of a vehicle door opening, and he was shoved unceremoniously into the back of some kind of van.

Waiting for him there was Prefect Jamus Galway.

"Caine," Galway said gravely as the door closed again behind him and the vehicle lurched forward. The prefect's face was strangely somber as he gazed down at his trophy, with no hint of triumph or even satisfaction that Caine could see. "My apologies for all this. If it makes it any easier, let me assure you that we have no intention of killing or even hurting Lathe and the others. They're far too valuable to us as they are."

Too valuable. To us. With his face still paralyzed, Caine couldn't reply. It was, he reflected, probably just as well.

The first Security man staggered and collapsed, the impact of Lathe's *nunchaku* penetrating his helmet to stun the skull and brain underneath. The comsquare brushed against the second blinded man as he fell, who responded by spinning that direction and firing another blast of paral-darts. Lathe ducked beneath the shot and swung his *nunchaku* into the back of other's leg, toppling him on top of his friend.

Two more men were charging in behind them. One had already been blinded, and as Lathe swung his *nunchaku* around in a half circle and cocked it again beneath his arm Spadafora sent a fourth paint pellet past his head to splatter over the other's faceplate. Lathe made a crouching leap over the tangled bodies of the first two attackers and slashed his *nunchaku* across the third Security man's gun arm, sending his weapon spinning off across the nearby tables, then slammed a kick to his stomach that folded him up and dropped him to the floor.

The fourth Security man was firing off random rounds, clearly in hopes of hitting *something*, when Lathe's *nunchaku* slammed across his yellow-coated faceplate with a force that flipped him halfway over before he hit the floor.

Two more Security men were charging through the

door, this pair already firing before they'd even made it inside. Lathe spun around to put his back to them, letting the salvos scatter off his flexarmor as he snatched out a pair of *shuriken*. His spin brought him back around to face them, and he hurled the stars hard into their kneepads.

Their guns wobbled off target as they fought for balance. Ducking beneath the weapons, Lathe took one of them down with his *nunchaku* and the other with a sweep and a heel-kick as he hit the floor.

He had just delivered a knockout blow with his *nunchaku* to the last man when his tingler came to life: *outside clear*. "Let's go," he called back to Spadafora. "Caine?"

There was no answer. "Caine!" Lathe called again, digging for his own tingler. *Caine?*

Outside, the reply came. *Coming around to front*.

Acknowledged, Lathe sent as he got to his feet and looked around. Aside from the downed Security men, everyone else in the bar seemed to have been untouched by the brief battle. "Sorry about the trouble," he said, nodding to the bartender and waiter.

There were two unmarked Security cars parked by the front of the building. Spadafora headed directly to the closest and pulled open the door, leaning halfway inside as he studied the interior. Mordecai was standing between the two cars, a *shuriken* ready in each hand, his head moving back and forth as he watched for trouble. Two more armored men lay sprawled unconscious at his feet. "Where's Caine?" Lathe asked him.

"Here," the younger man called as he came jogging into sight around the side of the building. "Sorry—I thought we were going out the back."

"Change of plans," Lathe said. "Spadafora?"

"Looks clear," the other called, still leaning into the car. "Not picking up any tracers, and I don't see any booby traps."

"Good enough," Lathe said. "Everyone in."

He got into the front passenger seat, the other two blackcollars climbing into the back, as Caine slid in behind the wheel and started the car. "Where to?" he asked as he pulled out onto the road again.

"Guardrail Tavern," Lathe told him. "*Now* we can go meet Tactor Shaw."

Tactor Kieran Shaw, chief of the Khala blackcollars, wasn't at all what Judas had expected.

Lathe and Spadafora certainly weren't huge men, but they were at least a bit bigger than average, with a calm but almost tangible presence that made them seem even larger. Mordecai, the smallest member of the Plinry contingent, was noticeably shorter than the other two, but he had even more of a sense of coiled-spring danger about him than the others. Even Caine, paralyzed on his back in an alley, had nevertheless managed somehow to maintain a sense of dignity during the brief time Judas had seen him back there behind the bar.

Shaw, completely bald and shorter even than Mordecai, seemed neither dangerous, charismatic, nor dignified. Considering this was a man who'd achieved the second-highest rank in the blackcollar hierarchy, it was a severe disappointment. "You certainly took your time getting here," he said almost peevishly as they were escorted into a windowless room in the electronics manufacturing plant where the Khala blackcollars had apparently set up shop. "You get lost? Or couldn't you wait until you got here to find yourself a drink?"

"We stopped by a bar on the west side to try to get the lay of the land," Lathe said. His voice was civil enough, but Judas could see in his face that he wasn't overly impressed by the man, either. "Trolling for Resistance or criminal elements is part of the standard procedure."

"For the record," Spadafora put in helpfully, "we never actually drank anything."

"For the *record*," Shaw said, his voice going a little fussier, "stirring up Security is always a bad idea. Especially when there's no reason for it. Considering the present situation, it was an extremely *bad* idea."

"Our presence here alone would have stirred them up," Lathe pointed out. "I doubt the incident at the bar changed things one way or the other."

"I'm glad you're so confident about that," Shaw said stiffly. "Which then leads us to point number two. Namely, what the hell are you doing here in the first place?"

"You told General Lepkowski—"

"I told Lepkowski about the Khorstron Tactical Center so that he could pass on the information to the Chryselli," Shaw cut him off. "I never intended for him to blab about it all over the TDE. I *especially* never intended for him to invite a bunch of wild cards to drop in and get in the way."

"I apologize for the misunderstanding," Lathe said, his voice starting to take on a little acid of its own. "The fact remains that we're here, and we're going to take the tac center. You can either help us or stay out of our way."

Shaw's eyes narrowed. It had probably been a long

time, Judas guessed, since anyone had talked to him that way. "Who do you think you're talking to, Comsquare?" he demanded. "I'm the senior blackcollar officer here. More than that, this is my world. *I* decide what happens or doesn't happen on Khala."

"Our branch of the TDE military no longer exists in any formal sense," Lathe countered. "Our ranks—and your authority—went with it."

Shaw snorted. "As I said: wild cards."

"Hardly." Lathe gestured toward Judas. "Caine here is a duly authorized representative of Earth's Resistance leaders. He's all the authority I need."

"Not on *my* world he isn't," Shaw insisted, giving Judas a quick and piercing look. "I make the decisions here."

"Fine," Lathe said. "So make a decision."

For a long moment the two men glared at each other in silence, and Judas held his breath. Everything here depended on Lathe having a free hand to plan and execute the blackcollars' infiltration of the Khorstron tac center. If Shaw hamstrung those efforts out of sheer pique, all of it would be for nothing.

To his relief, Shaw blinked first. "I'm willing to listen to reason," he said grudgingly. "Let's hear your plan."

"First, I need to know what we're up against," Lathe said. "I'll need complete maps of the city and the area around Khorstron, a vehicle we can use, and every relevant news report from the past two months that you can dig up."

"And a safe place to go to ground?"

"I assumed that was a given," Lathe said. "We'll catch a few hours of sleep, then maybe we can go someplace where we can get a look at the center. Can you arrange all that?"

"Of course," Shaw said. "*If* I so choose."

The corner of Lathe's lip tightened; Shaw responded with a placid smile. The big fish, Judas thought cynically, making it clear that others swam in his little pond solely at his pleasure. "And?" Lathe prompted.

Shaw gave it couple more seconds, then shrugged. "I'll get you a safe house and whatever maps and data we have on hand," he said.

"Thank you," Lathe said. "By the way, Lepkowski implied you might have a few other blackcollars on hand."

"More than just a few," Shaw said, his eyes glittering. "I have a full company."

Lathe's eyes widened. "A *company*?"

"Yes, indeed," Shaw said, clearly enjoying the moment. "Eight squads, twelve blackcollars each."

Judas felt his throat tighten. Nearly a *hundred* blackcollars? *Here?*

The big fish, he realized with a sinking feeling, was bigger than he'd expected. Possibly bigger than anyone had expected.

And suddenly, Galway's plan wasn't looking nearly so good anymore.

From the number of tight twists and turns the road had taken during the last half hour of the trip, Caine concluded they'd left Inkosi City and headed into the mountains, either back to the Falkarie range to the west where he and the others had landed or else into the somewhat gentler slopes of the Deerline Mountains to the south.

At last they came to a halt, and he was hauled through the back doors onto a rolling stretcher. They had come to a low, flat structure nestled among the trees, its design indicating it had started life as some kind of camouflaged military strongpoint. Caine caught a glimpse of the waist-high posts of a sensor ring a dozen meters out, but saw no other vehicles. A minute later he was rolled up a gentle slope and through a thick door into a small entryway room with an elevator beyond it. From the slightly musty smell he guessed the strongpoint had been out of service for at least a few years.

The perfect place to hide a captive whose friends didn't even know he was missing.

The elevator took them down two levels below ground, letting them out into a long corridor lined with numbered but otherwise unmarked doors. Halfway down the corridor was his new home, a small room equipped with a table, a set of bunk beds, a large and squishy-looking comfort chair, and a corner bathroom facility complete with toilet, sink, and shower stall.

A pair of burly Security men transferred him from the stretcher to the lower bunk. There, with considerable difficulty, they got his close-fitting flexarmor off him. When he was finally down to his padded undersuit, they stepped back to be replaced by a medic who gave him an injection in the side of his neck. A minute of uncomfortable tingling later, the paralyzing drug had been neutralized and his body returned to normal function again.

"How do you feel?" Galway's voice asked.

Caine turned his head. The prefect was standing a couple of steps inside the room, the two Security men flanking him watchfully with paral-dart guns ready in their hands. "Do you care?" Caine countered.

Galway's face didn't even twitch. "Yes," he said.

Lathe, Caine knew, had always believed that Galway wasn't just a loyalty-conditioned thug, but that he genuinely cared for the people the Ryqril had set him up to keep in check. Now, studying the prefect's expression, Caine decided the comsquare's assessment had indeed been correct. "I'm fine," he said. "I hope you're not going to try to convince me that you caught the others this easily."

Galway snorted. "Hardly," he said. "The last time I was part of a genuine blackcollar capture, we lost a lot of men and equipment in the process."

"Denver?"

"Argent," Galway corrected, a little dryly. "Denver hardly counts as genuine."

"I suppose not," Caine conceded. "So the others are all right?"

"They're alive, well, and free," Galway assured him.

"And blissfully unaware I'm no longer with them?"

Galway's forehead wrinkled slightly. "You caught all that, did you? Interesting."

"Not really," Caine said, silently cursing himself. He should have played stupid a little longer. Too late now. "I was lying right there when he started putting on my clothes."

"He wasn't supposed to let you see him."

"He was a little hard to miss," Caine said. "Where'd you find a set of flexarmor for him, anyway?"

"There was apparently an incident on Shiloh a few

months back," Galway said, still looking a little troubled. "Several sets of flexarmor became available."

Caine grimaced. "I don't think I want to know the details."

"Neither do I," Galway said. "I gather, then, that you've figured out what we're doing?"

"Enough of it," Caine said. "You went back to Earth and found another of the Alain Rienzi clones that the Resistance started growing in the expectation that the Rienzi family would stay in the Ryqril's good graces long enough for it to be worth impersonating him."

"Very good," Galway said. "The irony being that in this case, we're using one clone to impersonate another." He gestured toward Caine.

"Yes, that part was obvious, thank you," Caine growled. Over the past two years he'd mostly worked through his feelings at being a clone. But only mostly. "So what happens now? You loyalty-condition me and swap us out again?"

Galway shook his head. "Fortunately for you, that won't be necessary. Knowing Lathe, I'm expecting the timing here to be tight enough that there wouldn't be enough time for the conditioning. And frankly, considering you've had both Resistance psychor training *and* whatever mental tricks the blackcollars might have taught you, I'm not sure I'd trust you on your own no matter how long the Ryqril had to work on you."

"Thanks for the compliment," Caine said. "What do you mean by the timing being tight?"

"I'd have thought that was obvious," Galway said, eyeing him closely. "Lathe intends to break into the Khorstron Tactical Center. We intend to let him."

"What makes you think that's why we're here?" Caine countered, frowning. So the whole tac center thing had indeed been a trap, just as Lathe had surmised.

But they were going to let the blackcollars *in*?

"No, I'm sure you're just here to sample the local cuisine," Galway said, stepping back to the doorway. "At any rate, you can look forward to a few quiet days here, after which you'll be released." He hesitated. "I'll try to get the Ryqril to let you go back to Plinry."

"After the others are dead?"

"Hopefully, after the others are on their way elsewhere," Galway assured him. "We'll just have to see how this first test goes."

"'Test'"

"Perhaps I'll be able to tell you all about it someday," Galway said. "In the meantime, whatever hospitality I can offer is yours. Is there anything you'd like?"

"How about something to read?" Caine suggested. "The history and current events of this part of Khala, maybe. Some maps of Inkosi City and the environs would be nice, too."

Galway smiled faintly. "In case you're able to escape?"

"That's the primary duty of a prisoner of war," Caine reminded him. "Some actual clothing would be nice, too. It's rather chilly in here."

"The clothing's on the top bunk," Galway said, pointing above him. "As to the rest, I'll see what I can do."

"Thank you," Caine said. "Maybe some music, too." He looked around the bare room. "And some pictures and a carpet."

"It *is* rather grim, isn't it?" Galway agreed, looking

around as well. "It was a spotter strongpoint during the war, using radar and searchlights to target incoming Ryqril ships."

"With the Ryqril response to such targeting thus being drawn away from the more important military and civilian areas?"

"Exactly," Galway said. "I understand there was a whole semicircle of these expendable, more or less single-use facilities around Inkosi City."

"I guess the guys in this one were lucky."

"As lucky as anyone was afterwards," Galway said quietly, and Caine could see his throat tighten with memories. For a moment he seemed to gaze into the past, and then his expression cleared and he focused again on Caine. "At any rate, I'll leave orders about the music and reading material."

"Off to attend to more pressing matters?"

"The game continues," Galway said, stepping back into the corridor. "You, unfortunately, are now off the board. Good night."

He disappeared down the corridor. The two Security men backed out behind him, their eyes on Caine the whole time. The door closed with a solid-sounding thud, followed by an equally solid thud from the lock.

And Caine was alone.

Galway made sure the cell door was locked securely behind them. Then, leaving the two Security men behind on guard, he headed back to the elevator and the command/monitor room two floors up.

He saw no one else in the lower-level corridor, or in the

elevator, or in the ground-floor corridors. Not surprising, really. Haberdae had made it very clear that the Autumn-Three Strongpoint would be running a skeleton crew, with no more personnel than he himself judged to be absolutely essential for the care and guarding of their single prisoner.

Penny wise, the old saying whispered through Galway's mind. *Pound foolish*.

Haberdae was waiting in the command room, his arms folded across his chest as he stood behind the tech at the monitor bank, glaring at the three active screens that showed the inside of Caine's cell. Taakh stood off in one of the corners like a silent, brooding statue. "What's he doing?" Galway asked as he came into the room.

"So far, just looking around," the tech reported. "I can't tell whether or not he's spotted the cameras."

"He's certainly spotted two of them," Galway said, coming up beside Haberdae. "It'll be interesting to see if he disables them or simply tries to work around them as much as possible."

"I'm sure whatever he does will be fascinating," Haberdae growled. "In the meantime, if you can drag your mind back to the main business at hand, we have a potentially serious problem brewing. Your man Judas reports Lathe and the Khala blackcollars may be setting up for a turf war."

Galway frowned. "Over what?"

"What do you think?" Haberdae retorted. "Over the whole Khorstron operation. Our pompous little Tactor Shaw has apparently gotten his back up and seems to think that whatever is done here should be under *his* command."

There was an obvious comparison just begging to be made, but Galway had already resolved to be as diplomatic as possible while in Haberdae's jurisdiction. "What does Lathe say about it?" he asked instead.

"He seems inclined to fight," Haberdae said. "He invoked Caine's Earth-based authority and Shaw backed off a little. But he might still reconsider." He eyed Galway. "And if he does, he's got the manpower to back it up. According to Shaw, he has nearly a hundred blackcollars on call."

Galway stared at him. "Why didn't you tell me he had that kind of force available?"

"Because we didn't know," Haberdae countered. "Besides, what does it matter? As long as they get into Khorstron, why do we care how many of them it takes?"

"Because I don't want them going in like the Charge of the Light Brigade," Galway said. "I want Lathe to do the magic he does with small teams."

"Oh, relax," Haberdae said scornfully. "In my opinion, Shaw's blowing smoke. He might possibly have a hundred blackcollars on paper, but I doubt more than a few of them are in any shape to fight. If he can actually field even fifteen blackcollars, I'll be very surprised."

"You might be, at that," Galway said tartly. "Underestimating blackcollars is a dangerous game."

Haberdae lifted his eyebrows. "And you know this from personal experience?"

Galway took a deep breath. *As diplomatic as possible* . . . "Yes, I do," he said evenly. "Which is why I don't want to do it again."

Out of the corner of his eye, he saw Taakh shift position

slightly. "Enou'," the Ryq said. His voice was quiet, but there was no mistaking the tone of command behind it. "Yae rill not argue rith 'Re'ect Galray."

"My apologies, Your Eminence," Haberdae said, turning toward the Ryq and bowing slightly. His tone was subservient, but there was a hint of resentment beneath it that even his loyalty-conditioning couldn't entirely erase. "I will, of course, defer to Prefect Galway in all matters of strategy and tactics on this operation." He turned back to Galway. "What are your orders? Sir."

"We first need to make sure that Lathe will be the main planner on the Khorstron raid," Galway said, choosing to accept Haberdae's new deference as genuine, which both men knew perfectly well wasn't true. "I'd prefer Judas stay in the background, but if necessary he and Caine's Earth Resistance authority can be used to support Lathe's position. If that doesn't work, we may have to look for a way to take Shaw out of the equation."

"Or maybe we should just go ahead and do that now," Haberdae suggested.

Galway shook his head. "Tricky," he said. "*And* dangerous. We don't want to risk Lathe getting caught in the crossfire."

"It would still be worth working out some contingency plans," Haberdae pressed.

Galway sighed silently. "Fine. Go ahead."

"I'll get on it at once," Haberdae promised, heading for the door. "You coming?"

"Not yet," Galway said. "I want to watch Caine a while first."

Haberdae snorted under his breath. "I trust you realize

that keeping him alive is a complete waste of time and energy and manpower."

"I don't kill unnecessarily," Galway said stiffly.

Haberdae gave him a thin smile. "Of course not," he said. "Neither do I."

The clothing Galway had left him turned out to be a loose-fitting, long-sleeved jumpsuit and soft indoor boot-slippers, the whole outfit made of a thin, crepelike orange cloth. Caine got dressed, then spent the next hour exploring his cell, methodically going over every square centimeter. From the design and lack of built-in surveillance equipment, he guessed the room had begun life as crew quarters and not a prison. That meant retrofits, all of which proved easy enough to spot.

The most obvious were the tiny cameras. The first, concealed in one of the bunk bed supports facing the door, provided the hidden watchers with a view of the bathroom area and the door itself. The second, in the top of the shower enclosure, covered the bunk beds and the rest of that half of the room. There was also a smaller and much more subtly hidden camera in the room's far upper corner, probably a fish-eye lens that by itself could monitor nearly the entire room. Apparently, the plan was for him to congratulate himself on spotting the first two cameras and miss the third. There was also a single audio pickup.

His parallel search for something he could use to break out of his prison was somewhat less rewarding. The bunk bed frame was bolted to the wall with the kind of nonreversible screws that required a special tool to remove. The

mattress itself was soft and floppy, filled with some kind of
foam chips, with no internal springs or anything else he
could adapt as a weapon. The table was fastened to the
floor, while the comfort chair was far too large and heavy
to be of any use as a weapon—he could throw it once and
probably flatten whomever it landed on, but he would
never get a second shot with it before the rest of the
guards piled on top of him. The bunk's two blankets, while
thick enough to be effective at their task, were composed
of a flimsy cloth that would tear with very little effort,
making them useless as bonds or choke cords. The large
bathroom towel was made of a similar material.

The room's single door ran all the way to the ceiling,
preventing him from suspending himself out of sight
above it in the classic jungle-cat-drop position so beloved
by action melodramas. There was likewise no room to
hide beneath the lower bunk, and the shower enclosure
was completely transparent.

There was a click of the lock, and he turned as one of
his guards opened the door, a thick sheaf of paper in his
hands. "Here," he said, watching Caine warily as he
crouched down and set the stack on the floor just inside
the door. "Prefect Galway's compliments."

"What is it?" Caine asked, frowning at the papers.

"You asked for a book," the guard said. "There it is."
His eyes still on Caine, he grabbed the edge of the door
and pulled it closed again.

Caine crossed to the papers and picked them up,
mentally chalking up one more to Galway's credit. An
electronic book would have required an electronic reader,
whose inner workings Caine might have been able to

jury-rig into a weapon against the surveillance cameras. A standard bound book, on the other hand, could have been used as a throwing weapon. Instead, Galway had given him five hundred individual pages that couldn't be used for anything except reading material.

Or so he apparently thought.

Setting the rest of the sheaf of papers on the floor beside the comfort chair, he took the first page and tore off the upper two corners. Going to the shower enclosure, he moistened them with drops of liquid soap from the dispenser, then took them to the two obvious cameras and carefully pasted one over each of the lenses.

That left the third camera still intact, of course. But he was willing to play the game for now and pretend he hadn't spotted that one. If and when he was ready to make his move, its presence shouldn't matter.

He took the rest of the page and meticulously folded and refolded it until he had a narrow, stiff, ruler-shaped probe. Then, lugging the comfort chair over to the door, he sat down and began prodding carefully at the crack between the door and the frame. It was late and he was tired, but it would look odd if he didn't put at least a little effort into freeing himself.

There was no way such a flimsy probe could actually spring the lock, of course, and he could imagine the secret watchers having a good laugh at the would-be blackcollar's pathetic would-be escape attempt.

They were welcome to their amusement. Playing with the lock this way gave him a perfect excuse to press his ear against the metal wall and to listen to the noises conducted through it. The first step, Lathe always said, was to scout

out the territory and to learn the unique rhythms of people and movement and equipment.

Working industriously with his folded paper, Caine settled in to begin learning the rhythms of his new home.

"General?" the officer at the *Novak's* comm station called. "Passenger section reports the shuttle has returned."

"Acknowledged," Lepkowski said, turning away from the bridge canopy and his contemplation of the darkened world turning beneath him. "What's current status on Security communications down there?"

"Still low-level, sir," the officer said. "Aside from that one thirty-minute spike, it's all been very quiet down there."

That spike most likely being when Security realized that the drop pods had carried only hang-gliding dummies. If things had gone according to plan, Lathe and the others should have been safely to Inkosi City by then, possibly even at Shaw's place and under the Khala blackcollars' protection.

If things *hadn't* gone according to plan, they might already be dead.

With an effort, he shook away the thought. They were in danger, certainly. Every military operation, no matter how carefully planned, carried risks. But he'd known these men a long time. If anyone could pull this off, it was them.

And meanwhile, he had more important things to do than worry. Squaring his shoulders, he stepped up behind the helmsman. "Change of plans, Lieutenant," he said, pulling a magnecoded card from his tunic pocket. "Here's our new course setting."

"Yes, sir," the other said, frowning slightly as he took the card and plugged it into the reader. "It'll take us about three days," he said, peering at the display. "That'll run us nearly a week off schedule, plus whatever time we spend there."

"The passengers will get over it," Lepkowski assured him.

The other smiled faintly. "Yes, sir. Helm stands ready."

"On our way, then," Lepkowski said. "Full power; flank speed as soon as she'll take it."

"Yes, sir."

Ponderously, the *Novak* began to pull itself out of orbit; and as it did so, Lepkowski gave the planet below one final look. Everything was going well down there, he told himself firmly. Of course it was.

CHAPTER 5

"Silcox's building is just around the corner," Reger said, pointing through the windshield at the next intersecting street. "Second from the corner on the right. You can see it over the row of houses here."

"I see it," Skyler said, leaning forward to look past Kanai's shoulder as he adjusted his goggles over his battle-hood. The building was relatively short, four stories tall, with only the top visible above the two-story duplexes lining the street they were driving on.

He shifted his attention back to the street itself, searching for other traffic. But aside from rows of parked cars along both curbs, no other vehicles were in sight. "Hawking?"

"All set," Hawking confirmed, sealing the last fastener at the neck of his borrowed general's uniform. "Did you want us to do a drive-by first?"

"Better not," Skyler said, getting a grip on the door handle. "A Security general shouldn't have to search for his stakeouts. Kanai?"

"Ready," the other blackcollar said.

"Okay, Reger, slow down," Skyler ordered. There were a pair of parked vans coming up that would be ideal. "Kanai . . . *go*."

Together, they wrenched open their doors and jumped from the slowly moving car, hitting the ground jogging. Kanai ducked between the vans, with Skyler right behind him. They waited there until Reger had made a leisurely turn around the corner, then stole across the lawn between the two duplexes, coming to a halt in the shadow of a stubby tree a dozen meters from the side of Anne's building.

Besides being short, the building was also relatively narrow, at least compared to the other apartment houses in the neighborhood. There were only two apartments per floor, Kanai had told them, with Anne's on the third floor east, the opposite side from their current position. The building had interior hallways, a staircase at each end of the building, and a single door front and rear on the first floor. Security's observers would probably be watching both those doors, of course.

Unfortunately for them, there were other ways into a building besides the doors. Especially a building like this one, whose exterior walls were composed of an alternating pattern of brick and rough-cut stone.

It took thirty seconds to fasten their plastic crampons onto their gloves and boots. Through the decorative bushes in the building's front yard Skyler could see Reger's car pulled alongside one of the other parked cars, with the newly minted General Hawking conversing inaudibly with the driver. The Security car's other occupant had gotten out and was standing by the curb, watching the conversation across the car's roof with his back to the building he was supposed to be guarding.

There was a tingling from Skyler's wrist: *two men watching front, one in back, west side unwatched.*

Skyler nodded to himself. Ideally, Security should have set up a fourth man to watch the west side, to prevent precisely what he and Kanai were about to attempt. Apparently, they'd decided it wasn't worth the extra effort.

Others in Phoenix also under surveillance, Hawking's signal continued.

Skyler grimaced. Or else they simply hadn't had the manpower to spare for a tighter net. They were reacting to Poirot's disappearance faster than he'd expected.

Too late to worry about that now. Kanai had already crossed the lawn, a silent shadow against the dark grass, and had started up the side of the building, his crampons hooking onto the edges of the bricks and stone as he climbed the wall. Keeping his attention on the building's rear, Skyler followed. He made it, apparently unobserved, and started up.

It took just over a minute for them to reach the third floor. Another minute and Kanai had one of the windows open and had slipped inside. Skyler glanced at the street, to see that Reger and Hawking had finished their conversation and were driving away, then climbed in behind him.

He found himself in a large but narrow conversation room packed with mismatched furniture and scattered groups of toys. There were no nightlights, but enough streetlight was seeping in around the curtains for them to find a clear path through the maze. Kanai unlocked the front door and slipped out into the hallway. Skyler paused long enough to tape a flat over the latch bolt so that the door wouldn't lock, then followed.

Anne's lock was a pick proof electronic job, but Kanai obviously had the code. He got it open and the two of them went inside, emerging into a mirror image of the conversation room they'd just left, only without the toys.

"Which way to the bedroom?" Skyler whispered as he closed the door behind him.

"Don't worry about it," Kanai advised, turning to face the rear of the room. "Relax, Anne. It's Kanai and Skyler."

"*Skyler?*" Anne's voice came. A small accent light flicked on, and Skyler saw the young woman crouched beside an overstuffed couch, a short-barreled pellet scattergun pointed their direction. "*Rafe* Skyler?"

"The one and only," Skyler confirmed, pulling off his goggles and battle-hood for her inspection. "Nice to see you again, Anne."

"I wish I could say the same," Anne said, lowering the scattergun a few degrees. "What are you doing here?"

"Getting you out," Skyler told her. "Go get dressed. Quickly."

"Don't be insane," she growled. "Security's already seven-eighths convinced I'm part of Phoenix—they check on me at least twice a week. If I disappear, they'll know for sure."

"They're not looking for proof tonight," Skyler said grimly. "Just bodies. Warm or otherwise."

"And not just yours," Kanai added. "Some of your associates are also being watched."

Anne's throat tightened visibly. "What kind of hornets' nest have you stirred up this time?"

"Maybe the last one we'll ever need," Skyler said. "Now go get dressed. And bring all the Whiplash you have."

Her lips compressed briefly. Then, with a curt nod, she turned and disappeared into the rear of the apartment.

"Exit strategy?" Kanai asked.

"Back the way we came," Skyler said, crossing the living room to the front windows. "I blocked the other apartment door open to let us get in." Pressing himself against the wall, he pushed the curtains aside a couple of centimeters. The Security car, he saw, was still parked where it had been when Reger and Hawking drove off.

Only the two passengers were no longer inside.

"Damn," he muttered, slipping his fingers up his sleeve to his tingler. *Front Security gone from car; front door exit; stand by for backup.*

Acknowledged.

"And there's bound to be backup on the way," Kanai murmured as he headed for the front door.

"Undoubtedly," Skyler agreed. "Any ideas?"

"I'll head back the way we came." Pausing at the door, Kanai put on his gas filter and sealed the battle-hood's flaps against it, covering the last bit of exposed skin. "Maybe I can draw their attention."

Skyler nodded. "Watch yourself."

"I will. You sure you don't want to use the back door instead of the front?"

"No, I figure they'll expect us to go out the back," Skyler told him. "Besides, there's that lovely Security car out front, just waiting to be borrowed or disabled. Anne! Shake a leg in there."

"I'm ready," Anne said, emerging from the bedroom. She was dressed all in black, with a dark kerchief tied around her hair and a small gray backpack slung over one shoulder. Her gloved hands still held the scattergun. "They're coming?"

"Any minute now," Skyler said, stepping to her side and nodding to Kanai. "Go."

Carefully, the other eased the front door open a crack. For a moment he stood motionlessly, then looked back at Skyler and jabbed two fingers toward the stairway at the front end of the hallway.

Skyler nodded acknowledgment and gestured across the corridor. Kanai nodded back and slipped out into the hall. "Wait here," Skyler murmured to Anne as he got his own gas filter in place and stepped to the door.

They were coming, all right: two sets of stealthy footsteps coming up the stairs. Pulling a pair of throwing knives from their forearm sheaths, Skyler stepped into the corridor and moved forward to intercept. By the time the first Security man poked his head into view, he was in position.

The would-be assailant had just enough time to gape before Skyler's knife bounced hilt first off his forehead, sending him toppling backward into his partner two steps farther down. The impact sent the pair rolling and tumbling in a confused mass the rest of the way to the next landing down. Skyler followed, retrieving his knife and giving the second man a quick chop behind the ear to make sure he stayed put. Hoping the rest of the tenants would have the sense to ignore the sudden commotion and stay inside their apartments, he eased an eye over the railing.

And ducked back reflexively as a withering hail of paral-darts shot up from the stairway below, scattering off his flexarmor and goggles and filter.

The backup had arrived.

He snatched out a *shuriken* and sent it blindly over the railing to give the unseen shooters below something to think about. *Attack in progress; front steps*, he sent urgently with his tingler. The paral-dart barrage continued without pause; from the angles and rhythm he estimated there were at least three shooters. *Minimum of three attackers; pinned on second floor landing.*

He had sent two more *shuriken* through the paral-dart salvos before Hawking's response came: *On my way; attackers gathering in rear.*

So he had been right to pick the front door. *Kanai: Can you engage rear forces?*

Affirmative, Kanai replied. *Pickup in front?*

Pickup in front, Hawking confirmed. *Ready.*

Slipping his knives back into their sheaths, Skyler pulled out his *nunchaku*. *Hawking: Go*. Grimacing to himself, he put one hand on the railing and vaulted over the side.

It was a risky stunt, with the downside options about evenly split between breaking his ankle or breaking his neck. But he avoided both potential disasters, swinging his body in just enough to miss the lower railing and managing to land solidly in the center of one of the steps instead of hitting the edge. There were actually four Security men there, as it turned out, all in riot gear, all clearly startled by his unexpected appearance. One of them managed to twist his gun around and get a shot off at point-blank range before Skyler's side kick sent him flying down the steps into the next man. Two double swings with his *nunchaku* took out the other two.

"Skyler?" Hawking's voice called from below.

"Clear," Skyler called back. "You?"

"Front clear," Hawking confirmed. "But that could change."

"On our way," Skyler said. "See if you can start the car out there. If you can't, disable it."

"Right."

Skyler started back up, but he'd only made it to the next turn when he met Anne coming down. "I told you to wait," he said.

"I did," she said, stepping over one of the unconscious men. "You're making a real mess of my building."

"They can take it out of my deposit," Skyler said, taking her arm as he exchanged his *nunchaku* for a pair of *shuriken*. "Stay close."

The front door was clear, as Hawking had promised, with four more armored Security men sprawled across the grass. They headed outside, Skyler pressing Anne close to his side to give her as much protection he could.

They were halfway to the street when there was a motion around the corner of the building to their right. He snapped his arm up into throwing position, targeting the figure with his eyes—

"It's me," Kanai called softly. "Rear is neutralized."

"Good," Skyler called back, lowering the *shuriken*.

Hawking had the car door open now, and he and Anne hurried toward it.

And were nearly knocked to the ground as a flechette slammed hard into Skyler's chest.

"Down!" Kanai shouted, hurling a *shuriken* in the direction the shot had come from. Wrapping his arms around Anne, Skyler rolled them both onto the grass, turning over to put his back to the concealed gunner. A second shot caromed off his shoulder as they fell, the impact spread out to a tolerable level as the flexarmor went momentarily rigid. Another pair of shots slammed into his back, and he heard a whisper of branches as Kanai sent another *shuriken* toward the unseen gunner.

From the street came a sudden squealing of tires. Skyler turned his head part way around in time to see the Security car jump the curb and roar across the grass. The sniper got off two more rounds, both aimed at this new and clearly unanticipated threat; and then Hawking rammed the car into a short decorative hedgerow. Even before the vehicle had come to a complete halt he was out the door, *nunchaku* flailing. He paused and glanced around, shifting his *nunchaku* to his left hand—

Clear, Skyler's tingler signaled. *Reger coming—everyone to street.*

"Come on," Skyler grunted to Anne, hauling himself to his feet and pulling her up beside him. "Hurry."

They reached the street just as Reger brought their car to a screeching halt. Skyler opened the rear door and half helped, half threw Anne into the backseat. Kanai was already on the far side of the car, diving in on Anne's left as Skyler climbed in on her right. "Stay down," Skyler ordered, pushing her head toward her lap and resting his arm across her back and head as partial protection. Ahead, Hawking had pulled the Security car back onto the street and was signaling the others to pass him. "Reger—go."

The other needed no encouragement. He peeled away, the engine protesting as he gunned it for all it was worth. They shot past Hawking, and Skyler looked back to see him pull in behind them, accelerating hard to catch up.

"Haven't done anything like this since I was a kid," Reger commented. His voice was a little strained, but Skyler had the odd feeling that he was rather enjoying himself. "Where to?"

"We'll change cars at the first cache point," Skyler told him, taking his arm away from Anne's back. She straightened up, pulling off her bandana and rubbing her shoulder where she'd landed when she and Skyler had hit the ground. "Ditto at the second. If all seems clear, we'll head back to the safe house."

"And then what?" Anne asked.

Skyler smiled grimly. "We have a little surprise for you."

In the intermittent glow of the streetlights he saw her eyes narrow. "I don't like surprises," she warned.

"You'll like this one," he assured her.

She leaned back in her seat and resumed rubbing her shoulder. "Yeah," she muttered. "Maybe."

The reports coming from the field were confused and incomplete. But the essence came through with painful clarity.

Anne Silcox, the number one person on Security's list

of probable Phoenix members, had escaped. And she'd done it with the help of the newly arrived blackcollars.

"Have all other units move in immediately," Bailey ordered the communications officer. "Have them pick up everyone they can and bring them here."

"Yes, sir." Raising his mike, the operator began issuing orders.

Bailey leaned back in his seat, gingerly kneading the swollen area beneath his ear. First Poirot, now Silcox. What the *hell* were they up to?

"Sir?" Lieutenant Ramirez said tentatively at his side.

Bailey had completely forgotten the man was there. "Yes, Lieutenant, you can return to Boulder if you'd like," he said. "Thank you for your prompt assistance at Reger's house."

"Actually, sir, I was hoping for your permission to stay here and help out," Ramirez said. "My men can certainly handle a mountain search without me being right there with them. If you can use my help, that is."

"Right now, I can use all the help I can get, Lieutenant," Bailey said candidly. "Thank you."

"My pleasure, sir," Ramirez said. "What I was going to say, though, was that it'll be at least an hour before any of the prisoners get here. It might be a good time to go up to the infirmary and have your injuries looked at."

"I suppose you're right," Bailey agreed reluctantly. There was certainly little he could do down here right now. "Fine. You stay here—if there are any updates, feed them to me right away."

"Yes, sir," Ramirez said.

Bailey glowered at the map of the Denver area spread

across the wall. "And make damn sure all the prisoners are stripped and searched before they're brought inside the Athena perimeter," he added. "Reger's men as well as the Phoenix people. We're not going to be caught like *that* again."

Between the car changes and the carefully circuitous route, it took over an hour for them to reach the safe house. "How's the patient?" Skyler asked as O'Hara opened the door and let them in.

"Still sleeping," O'Hara said. "I gave him another shot half an hour ago, just to be on the safe side. This our girl?"

Anne bristled. "Our *girl*?"

"He's sixty years old, Anne," Skyler reminded her dryly. "To him, anyone under fifty is a kid. Yes, this is Anne Silcox. Anne, this is Commando Kelly O'Hara, our reigning master of diplomacy."

"Sorry," O'Hara said. "Nice to meet you."

"Likewise," Anne said. She gave O'Hara a pointed once-over, then turned back to Skyler. "All right, we're here. What's this big surprise?"

"Come and see," Skyler said, gesturing her toward the conversation room. Reluctantly, he thought, she let him lead her there, the rest of the group trooping along behind them.

He'd expected to get a good reaction. He wasn't disappointed. "God in heaven," she breathed, her eyes goggling as she stared at the man sprawled on the couch. "That's *General Poirot*. What's *he* doing here?"

"He thought you were getting a new shipment and decided it would look good on his record if he was in on the snatch personally," Reger told her. "Got a little more than he bargained for."

"I told you you'd like it," Skyler added.

"You think so?" she demanded. "Do you have any *idea* the kind of manhunt they must have going out there right now? No wonder they tried to grab me and the others."

"What others?" O'Hara asked.

"The rest of Phoenix," Anne said, glaring at Skyler. "I made a couple of calls while you were clearing the stairs, trying to warn them. Rob—that's my second in command— said they'd already surrounded his house. I wonder now if *any* of them got out."

"We'll get them back," Skyler promised. "But first things first. Get the Whiplash out and let's get Poirot turned."

Anne sighed. "You really don't understand, do you?"

"Understand what?"

"I can pump all the Whiplash in him that you want," Anne said quietly. "But it won't do any good."

Skyler felt his stomach tighten. "What are you talking about?" he demanded. "We tested the stuff when we were here a year ago. It *works*."

"I didn't say it didn't work," she retorted, her voice suddenly bitter. "I said it wouldn't do any good. We've quietly kidnapped and treated over a dozen loyalty-conditioned government workers in the past eight months. Not a single one of them is interested in joining us."

Skyler looked over at Kanai, standing silently against the wall. "Kanai?" he invited. "You want to jump into this?"

"She's right, as far as she goes," he conceded. "All

those we've tried it on have gone straight back to their jobs."

"We can't get *anything* from them?" Skyler asked. "If not cooperation, at least some information?"

"There are a couple who occasionally slip us a little something," Anne said. "But only a little, and it's never anything really useful."

"Of course, none of them has access to anything really high up anyway," Kanai added. "But that doesn't mean we shouldn't keep trying."

"Until when?" Anne countered. "Until we get to someone who'll blow the whistle on us with his superiors instead of cowering in his cubicle trying desperately to pretend nothing's happened to him? If you think Security's interested in us *now*, just wait till you see what happens *then*."

"Seems to me that Security's reaction is kind of moot at this point," Hawking offered.

"Yes, thanks to you," Anne said, glaring at Skyler again. "What in the *world* did you think—?"

"You know," Reger interrupted, "maybe we should sit down, nice and quiet, and take this from the top. Skyler can start it off by telling us where Lathe's lurking and what he's up to this time."

"Actually, Lathe isn't here," Skyler said. "He got invited to Khala to break into a Ryq tac center."

Anne blinked. "He got *what*?"

"Let's sit down," Reger repeated, more firmly this time. "Discuss this like civilized men and women."

Anne snorted. But she stalked over to a chair beside Poirot's couch and dropped into it. "Fine," she said. "I'm sitting."

"Thank you," Reger said, pulling up a chair to the other side of the couch and sitting down. "You were saying, Skyler?"

"We got word that the Ryqril were building a new tac coordination center on Khala," Skyler said, pulling up a third chair equidistant from Anne and Reger and signaling O'Hara, Hawking, and Kanai to remain standing on guard. "It seemed way too tempting a target to pass up."

"Sounds like a trap," Anne muttered.

"Of course it's a trap," Skyler agreed. "Which just makes the whole thing that much more intriguing. At any rate, Lathe took a team there to see if we can turn it to our advantage."

"Enough of an advantage for a final victory?" Anne countered. "That *is* what you meant about this being the last hornets' nest we'd ever need, isn't it?"

"What do you mean, victory?" Reger echoed, frowning. "As in throwing the Ryqril out of the TDE?"

Skyler shrugged. "Basically."

Reger shook his head. "That's impossible."

"Lathe doesn't think so," Skyler said. "Between us and the Chryselli, we've got the Ryqril in a pretty tight place right now. A big enough push in the right direction might just do the trick."

"The right direction being this Ryqril tac center, I presume," Reger said, his eyes settled into a sort of distant stare. "So why are you here?"

"Because chaos in one place is less impressive than simultaneous chaos in two widely separated places," Skyler told him. "The idea is—was—for us to help you and Phoenix and your loyalty-conditioned moles turn this city upside down."

Anne shook her head. "It's not going to happen," she said. "The system here is just too set and stable. Nobody wants to rock the boat."

Skyler rubbed his chin, gazing at Poirot's sleeping face as he tried to think. Lathe was the tactical genius of the group, and the plan he'd worked out for the Earth part of the operation was a typically solid piece of work.

Unfortunately, it had assumed a thriving Phoenix and a large number of Whiplash-treated moles. Without that, it wasn't going to work.

Which meant they needed a Plan B. Only at this point, Skyler didn't have one. And he wasn't at all sure he could come up with one.

"For myself, I'm not convinced the moles are as resistant to the idea of rebellion as Anne believes," Kanai put in. "Perhaps each one merely thinks there's nothing he or she personally can do."

"Maybe if they knew they weren't alone but that they had allies," Reger agreed. "Possibly even allies in high places." He gestured at Poirot.

Skyler pursed his lips. That *was* why he'd brought the general here, after all.

But if Poirot also wasn't willing to cooperate, the secret of Whiplash's existence would be broken the minute he stepped foot inside the Athena government center. Was that a risk they wanted to take right now?

Anne was obviously thinking along the same lines. "I don't think any of you has the slightest idea what Security can do when they're genuinely panicked," she warned. "If they find out about Whiplash, they'll turn this entire district inside out."

Abruptly, Skyler made his decision. "It's a risk," he agreed. "But this is war. Risks are part of the job."

"Then let's quit wasting time," Reger said firmly. "Get the Whiplash out, and let's do it."

With a start, Caine snapped awake.

He held still in his bunk, maintaining the slow, steady breathing of a sleeping man. The cell was still dark, he could tell through his closed eyelids, and the faint background hum of the base's generator filled the room, its murmur effectively blanketing any sounds there might have been of stealthy footsteps or stealthier breathing.

But Caine had gone through all of Lathe's wearying and sometimes—he'd thought at the time—stupid blindfolded training exercises. As a result, he had sensory resources that had probably never even occurred to his captors. Effectively both blind and deaf, he focused instead on the patterns of moving air brushing across his face and neck and hands.

There was someone standing at the end of his bunk.

Carefully, he opened his eyes to slits. A big man was standing there, little more than a black shadow set against the faint light coming in through the open cell door. For a moment the man just stood there, doing something with the bunk supports. Once, he turned his head slightly, and Caine caught a profile of his face and the misshapen silhouette that showed he was wearing either infrared or light-enhancement goggles.

The man finished whatever he was doing and headed toward the other side of the room. As he moved away from the bunk, unblocking the view of the door, Caine saw that there was a second man standing framed in the doorway. From the lack of visible arms in his silhouette, he was probably holding a paral-dart pistol in a two-handed grip, pointed in Caine's direction.

And though the light out there was too faint for any genuine shadows, there was enough subtle movement against the background light to show there was at least one other backup man somewhere out of sight. Sleeping or not, they weren't taking any chances with their prisoner.

The intruder reached the bathroom area and stopped at the shower enclosure, and Caine suppressed a smile as he finally understood what was going on. The watchers in the monitor room had apparently been annoyed at Caine's earlier blockage of two of their three cameras, and had decided to take advantage of the nighttime hours to remedy the situation.

Perfect.

Because Caine could easily fix things back again in the morning. The only trick would be to wait just the right amount of time before "discovering" the reactivated cameras so that they wouldn't suspect he'd been awake tonight.

And if they thought they'd sneaked in once without waking him, they might be willing to try it again.

Yes, he decided. This had definite possibilities.

The Security man finished his work and left, closing the door soundlessly behind him.

Caine was still considering his options when he again drifted off to sleep.

CHAPTER 6

The air intake that Torch had used to create their back door into Aegis Mountain lay several kilometers to the northwest of their landing position. Jensen was pretty sure he could find it, but he knew better than to head directly there. If Security or the Ryqril succeeded in catching them, he didn't want their travel vector pointing directly toward their goal. Instead, he led Flynn due west, keeping a couple of ridges north of the highway that ran past the Ryqril base, watching for a good spot to start veering north.

They were perhaps two hours away from first light when he finally found it.

"Well, this is fun," Flynn groused as they waded ankle-deep through the icy rushing water of the creek. "You wilderness instructors are always talking about the marvels of running water as a way to hide your trail. You never mention how slippery these creek beds are. How far upstream are we planning to go?"

"Not too far," Jensen said, peering off to their right.

Halfway to the eastern horizon, he could see the faint blue-violet grav light of several aircraft crisscrossing the sky, clearly searching the likely landing area from the evening's drop. He hoped it was just standard surveillance, and not an indication that Skyler or one of the others had been caught.

He hoped, too, that they didn't take it into their minds to extend their search farther west.

"How far is not too far?" Flynn persisted. "The reason I'm asking is because if I remember the maps right, this stream will take us too far to the east of our target."

"You're right, it will," Jensen agreed. "The trick is going to be with the timing and placement of our departure. You see, the problem with the running water trick is that everybody knows it. That means that if, say, a pursuing Ryqril chase squad tracks us to this creek, they'll know we've gone one of two directions. All they have to do is split up and try to find the spot where we left the water."

"So we look for a rocky area where our tracks won't show?"

"No, because they know *that* one, too," Jensen said. "They'll stop at every such likely spot and search the area where the rocks quit, looking for the spot where we would have had to take to softer ground."

Flynn pondered that a moment. "So, what, the goal is just to keep them busy running down blind alleys until we've built up a decent lead?"

Jensen smiled. "Actually, I had something a little classier in mind. I'll let you know when I find it."

Fifteen minutes later, he did.

"Here we go," he said, the water swirling around his boots as he pointed to their left.

"Here we go where?" Flynn asked, clearly bewildered as he looked at the wide patch of open mud that stretched eight meters from the edge of the creek to the trees beyond. A few patches of grass poked out of the mud, and a few leaves and bits of bark and rotted wood were scattered around, but aside from that the mudflat was pretty much empty. "We cross that and we'll leave tracks a toddler could find."

"O ye of little faith," Jensen said reprovingly, slipping his pack off his shoulders and pulling out his grapple and a length of slender line. "Watch and learn."

He fastened the grapple to one end of the line and draped the rest in a loose coil across his left forearm. Holding the line half a meter below the grapple, he swung the hook in a slow vertical circle, studying the row of trees bordering the far side of the mud flat. What he needed was a sturdy branch at least three meters from the ground, and he had exactly one chance to nail it. If the grapple didn't catch and he had to drag it back to himself through the mud, they would have to go on and try a different spot. Picking a likely looking branch, he aimed at its intersection with the trunk and sent the grapple on its way.

Years of practice paid off. The grapple arced almost lazily through the air and dropped neatly into the notch between branch and bole. Pulling back carefully on the line, he felt the hooks dig themselves solidly into the wood.

"Very nice," Flynn complimented him. "I hope you're not expecting us to do a group Tarzan swing."

"Not to worry," Jensen assured him, handing him the rope. "Here—keep some tension on it."

Flynn took the line, draping it over his arm as Jensen had and holding the grapple end firmly. Jensen backtracked a few steps down the creek, studying the vegetation and terrain on their right. Across from the mud flat the ground rose sharply from the creek bed, cresting into one of the many ridges that wrinkled this part of the world. Fortunately, despite the angled ground, there were several trees situated only a meter or two back from the edge of the water. Picking the one directly across from where he'd hooked the grapple, he pulled out a *shuriken* and hurled it into the trunk three meters off the ground, burying it vertically nearly to its center.

Flynn was gazing thoughtfully at the throwing star as Jensen rejoined him. "Okay," the boy said. "But how do we anchor it?"

"*We* don't," Jensen said. "*I* do. Give me the rest of that line, but keep tension on the grapple end."

Flynn handed back the coil. Stepping to the edge of the stream, Jensen tossed a loop of the line over the embedded *shuriken*, dropping it between the sharpened points where it could lie against the nonsharp center. "Ah," Flynn said, nodding, as Jensen pulled on his end of the rope and took in the slack. "But wouldn't a branch work better? This way we're going to have to leave the *shuriken* behind."

"True, but if we used a branch we'd probably leave some rope burn behind that would indicate the direction we'd gone," Jensen explained as he pulled the rope tight around the *shuriken*. "This way, there's no burn, and they're just as likely to conclude we used the *shuriken* to haul ourselves up into the trees and over the ridge and are doubling back east toward civilization. That's if they even lift their eyes high enough from the creek to spot the star at all, which I'm guessing they won't." Wrapping the rest of the line around his waist, rappel-style, he braced himself and nodded. "Go."

Flynn leaped upward and caught the taut rope now stretching between the *shuriken* and the grapple. For a moment the line sagged as the sudden weight tried to pull Jensen off his feet. The blackcollar got his balance back and leaned hard against the strain, and the rope once again tightened. Flynn was already on the move, rapidly walking hand over hand over the mudflat. He reached the other side and pulled himself into the tree. "Clear," he called softly.

Unwrapping the rope from his waist, Jensen tied a loose, multiple knot in the end, making sure he had enough line left over to make it all the way across the mud. Then, again swinging it over his head, he threw it to Flynn.

The other caught it and wrapped it a couple of times around another thick branch, this one on the far side of the tree, and braced himself. "Go," he called.

Leaping upward, Jensen caught the rope. Thirty seconds later, he was across the mud and crouched in the branches beside Flynn. Taking the loose end from the boy, he gave the line a little slack, then flicked his wrist to send a ripple wave through it toward its *shuriken* anchor. The wave hit the *shuriken* and popped the line free; yanking his end hard, Jensen whipped the whole line over the mud to catch in the branches of their tree.

"See?" he murmured as they gathered in the rope and freed the grapple. "Piece of cake."

"Cake wasn't exactly the word that came to mind," Flynn countered dryly. "But it *did* work."

"Which is really all that matters," Jensen pointed out. "Besides, considering the crazy moves Mordecai's been teaching you, you're hardly in a position to point any fingers. I'll finish with the rope; you get going down the far side of the tree and see how we get out of here. And watch where you step."

The first hundred meters of terrain turned out to be considerably rougher than they'd had to cross thus far, and more than once Jensen wondered if they should backtrack to the creek and look for a clearer route. But by the time the stars in the east began to fade into the approaching dawn, they had made it through and into a much clearer area.

"How much farther are we going?" Flynn asked as they crossed another, narrower stream and started up yet another slope.

"Let's get over the top here and see what's on the other side," Jensen said, pointing upward. "Must have had some bad storms come through this past winter—see how many trees have had their lower branches bent over nearly to the ground. We'll find one big enough to hide both of us and wait out the daylight."

"Sounds good," Flynn said. "Too bad we don't have any entrenching tools."

"Well, we weren't exactly planning an excursion outside the bounds of civilization this way," Jensen reminded him.

"Weren't we?" Flynn asked, a slight edge to his voice.

Jensen gave him a long, cool look. "Are you implying something, Trainee Flynn?"

And because he was looking at Flynn and not where he was going, he stepped around a scraggly pine and got a full three steps into the small clearing beyond before he spotted the bear.

"Freeze!" he hissed, braking to a sudden halt.

But it was too late. With a roar, the bear reared up on its hind legs, its paws stretching threateningly toward the sky. Jensen had just enough time to notice a small cub bolting away across the clearing; and then, with a thud he could feel ten meters away through the ground, the bear dropped back to all fours and charged.

"Get out of here," Jensen snapped to Flynn, reflexively snatching out a *shuriken* and hurling it at the bear's head. But a weapon tailored to penetrate rubbery Ryqril skin was no match for fur and thick bone. Instead of collapsing, the bear merely roared in pain as the throwing star buried itself in its forehead and paused to bat at the irritant with a paw. The *shuriken* popped free and spun off into the matted leaves covering the ground, and the bear resumed its attack.

There was, Jensen knew, no way he could outrun the creature, particularly not on uneven ground. Without any other real options, he waited until the bear was too close to change direction, then threw himself in a flat leap to the right.

The bear was faster than he expected, slashing out its paw and catching the edge of his coat with a multiple tearing sound as the claws sliced through coat and shirt and scraped across the flexarmor beneath. Even the relatively slight impact was enough to throw Jensen off balance and send him into a fall that could have left him flat and helpless on the ground.

Fortunately, he was fast, too. As he hit the ground he let his leading leg collapse beneath him, turning the fall into a roll that brought him back to his feet with *nunchaku* ready in his hand. The bear braked to a halt and turned back toward him, growling angrily as it lumbered again to the attack. Jensen braced himself; and as the bear got within range, he leaped aside again, this time bringing the *nunchaku* blurring through the air to slam into the side of the bear's head.

But again, the furry animal was tougher than any Ryq Jensen had ever faced. For a moment it seemed to stagger, but then it shook itself and turned again to its prey.

There was a faint whistling sound from the side and something shot nearly invisibly across the clearing to ricochet off the side of the bear's head. Jensen glanced over in time to see Flynn hurriedly loading a second pellet into his slingshot. But the bear paid even less attention to the pellet's impact than it had to the *nunchaku*. Bracing himself for another slash-and-leap maneuver, Jensen waited for the bear to reach the right spot.

But as he started to push off the ground, something unseen beneath the matting of dead leaves shifted beneath his feet. His leap faltered, and for a crucial fraction of a second he was caught flat-footed.

And before he could recover, the bear's swinging paw caught him squarely across his left side.

He gasped as a multiple spike of agony stabbed through his rib cage. The force of the blow spun him around in midair, sending him crashing bodily into a squat bush. Clenching his teeth against the pain in his side, he tried to bring his *nunchaku* back into fighting position. But the weapon had gotten itself ensnared in the bush's branches. Letting go, he instead dug a knife from its forearm sheath and twisted it up to point at the bear loping toward him. He would have only one chance at this, he knew; one chance to catch the animal in the eye and hopefully kill it quickly enough that it didn't have time to deliver a killing blow of its own. The bear closed to within two meters, its jaws opening wide to show huge white teeth—

And like a black-clad cannonball, Flynn shot into view, his body sideways and flat to the ground, his knees curled tightly to his chest, arcing straight at the bear's side. His legs straightened out in a convulsive double kick, the heels of his boots catching the bear with devastating force in the side of its neck and sending the animal toppling over onto the ground.

Flynn hit the ground and scrambled to his feet, *nunchaku* in hand. But the bear had finally had enough. Hauling itself upright, it bared its teeth once more at its attackers and then turned and lumbered off in the direction the cub had taken. A few seconds later, it was out of sight.

"That has got to be the single craziest move I've ever seen," Jensen said, breathing as shallowly as he could. His whole left side felt like it was on fire, with someone jabbing a poker in the blaze with each breath. "Must be one of Mordecai's."

"It's called a door-clearer," Flynn said, shoving his

nunchaku back into its sheath and dropping to his knees beside Jensen. "You all right?"

"Hardly," Jensen admitted, probing gently at his side. "I'm guessing I have a broken rib. Possibly more than one."

"Damn and a half," Flynn muttered, carefully peeling back what was left of Jensen's coat and shirt. "At least the claws couldn't get through the flexarmor."

"No, this way I get to bleed to death internally," Jensen agreed. "Much tidier that way. I'm kidding, I'm kidding," he hastened to add as Jensen's eyes went wide. Sometimes he forgot that these trainees were only kids, without the history of dark wartime humor he and the other blackcollars shared. "Actually, I don't think I'm bleeding at all, at least not very much. Besides, any fight you can walk away from counts as a win. Speaking of which, help me get up."

"Shouldn't you stay put until we get you checked out?" Flynn asked, grabbing Jensen's arm as he started to push his way out of the bush.

"Good idea," Jensen said, biting down hard as the pain level jumped into the red-haze zone. "Nearest medical facilities are back at the Ryqril camp. I'll wait here."

"I just meant—"

"I know what you meant," Jensen assured him. "And it's something we'll definitely want to look into. But it's getting light, and we need to find some cover."

Flynn grimaced, but nodded. "You're the boss. Nice and easy, now."

With Flynn taking most of his weight, they managed to get him up out of the bush and back to vertical again. "How's that?" Flynn asked as he freed Jensen's *nunchaku* from the bush and slid it into the blackcollar's thigh sheath.

"Not too bad," Jensen said. His side was throbbing even harder in this position than it had been when he was lying down. But at least he didn't feel like he was going to black out. "Okay, let's go. Westward, ho."

"Northwestward," Flynn corrected as he got under Jensen's arm and wrapped his own arm carefully around the blackcollar's waist.

"Whatever."

It wasn't a pleasant journey. With every step he took a white-hot pain jabbed through his side, and even with Flynn taking a good fraction of his weight, his legs were shaking with fatigue by the time they reached the crest of the ridge.

Fortunately, the downward slope on the other side was fairly gentle, and there was one of the bowed-branch trees he was looking for a half dozen steps away. Flynn got them to its base and pulled up the drooping branches on one side while Jensen crawled beneath. The younger man followed, adjusting the branches again to hide them and then helping Jensen settle himself into a seated position against the trunk.

"How's that feel?" Flynn asked as he eased Jensen's pack behind the small of the other's back. "I think there's enough room to lie down if you want."

"Maybe later," Jensen said, pulling out his medkit. Now that they'd reached cover and the danger of masking his injuries with painkillers was over, it was definitely time for a shot.

"I'll leave you all the food and water," Flynn went on,

sliding off his own pack and setting it beside Jensen. "I'll signal via tingler before I come close so you won't have to worry that—"

"You going somewhere?" Jensen interrupted.

"I'm going to look for civilization," Flynn said. "Your report from the last trip said there were some small towns and villages scattered through these mountains."

"You think any of them will have a qualified doctor?"

"They should at least know where to find one," Flynn said doggedly. "Unless you'd rather sit here until you heal on your own."

"No, a doctor would be nice to have," Jensen conceded. "But neither of us is going to go walking around out there in broad daylight."

"The residents will be easier to find during the day," Flynn reminded him.

"So will you," Jensen said flatly. "We stay put until dark."

For a long moment Flynn just looked at him. Then, with a sigh, he turned around and settled himself cross-legged beside Jensen with his back to the tree trunk. "Fine," he said. "While we wait, how about telling me a story?"

"What kind of story?"

"You know what kind," Flynn said bluntly. "You didn't take us down to look at Aegis Mountain on the spur of the moment. You were planning it all along, or at least considering it. Given the present circumstances, I think I should know why."

Jensen grimaced. But he was right. "You already know most of it," he said. "A year ago one of the local blackcollars, Bernhard, took us to the back door the old Torch resistance group had opened up into Aegis Mountain and we all went inside."

"And found the Whiplash they'd created before they died."

"Right," Jensen said. "What you don't know—and Skyler may not know it, either—is that the day we went into the mountain, someone was watching us."

He sensed Flynn stiffen. "How do you know?"

"I saw a glint off the binoculars or telescope he was using," Jensen said. "It was halfway up a slope about a klick west of us."

"And you didn't tell the others?"

Jensen started to shrug, quickly changed his mind. "I told Mordecai, who was staying topside on rearguard duty. I didn't see much point in mentioning it to anyone else. It wasn't like we had extra personnel or reinforcements we could call on."

"I presume no one was waiting for you when you came out again?"

"Only Mordecai," Jensen said. "And we know that Bernhard, who left before us, didn't run into any opposition either."

"Maybe it was someone out hiking," Flynn suggested. "There's a good chance he was just admiring the mountains and never even saw you."

"That's one possibility," Jensen agreed. "The other is that it was some kind of observation post someone had set up."

"Someone like Security?"

"If it was, the Ryqril at the main Aegis entrance would have had a conveyer belt already set up to cart stuff out,"

Jensen pointed out. "That's why I wanted to go check that out right away."

"I see," Flynn said, his voice suddenly thoughtful. "But if it wasn't Security, and it wasn't a random hiker, the only possibility left is that it was Torch."

"Bingo," Jensen said, nodding. "And of course, a Torch observer wouldn't have interfered with us because we had Bernhard and Anne along, both of whom he would have recognized."

"Okay," Flynn said. "The question then is whether he's still there. That's the first question, I mean."

"And the second question?" Jensen asked, frowning.

"Whether he's going to like what you're planning to do."

Jensen grimaced. Had Flynn figured it out? "All I said was that I was going to make sure the Ryqril didn't get into the mountain," he reminded the other.

"And there aren't a lot of ways for a couple of men to do that," Flynn countered. "Even if one of them *is* a blackcollar."

"There's no *couple of men* involved," Jensen said firmly. "I'm going in alone. *You're* going to Denver to hook back up with Skyler."

"Jensen—"

"No arguments," Jensen cut him off. "This is *my* job, not yours."

For a minute neither of them spoke. "Well, at the moment it's all rather academic," Flynn said at last.

"I'm not dead yet," Jensen reminded him. "Give me the rest of the day. I'll be ready to travel by nightfall."

"Yeah," Flynn said. "We'll see."

✳　　✳　　✳

The corridor outside the interrogation rooms was silent and mostly deserted, the bright overhead lights belying Bailey's own dark mood. He'd been pacing back and forth for nearly five hours now, stopping at each room in turn to eavesdrop for a few minutes on the intercom, then moving on to the next, eventually restarting the whole cycle. The interrogators had been at it for those same five hours, through the night and to the dawn that was breaking across the prairie land to Athena's east.

Six interrogation rooms. Six prisoners. Hardly the twelve suspects he'd hoped to bring in when he'd set the operation in motion.

Still, he should probably consider himself lucky they'd gotten even that many. Only two of the rebels had actually escaped the nets, and one of those—Silcox—had had a good deal of help. Of the remaining four, three had been killed as they tried to escape, and the fourth was in the hospital undergoing emergency surgery for the gunshot wounds he'd received after being clever enough to avoid the paral-darts.

At the end of the hallway the elevator opened, and Bailey turned to see Lieutenant Ramirez step out, nodding as he passed the duty guard at his station. "Any news?" Bailey asked as the other came up to him.

"Nothing from the hospital," Ramirez said. "And Major O'Dae says he's drawn a blank on the interrogations of Reger's men. They're all apparently standard homegrown thugs, with no idea what his involvement with Phoenix might be."

Bailey nodded. "I suppose I shouldn't have expected the blackcollars to be caught that easily."

"No, sir," Ramirez said. "Speaking of whom, we've found the remains of the drop pod they arrived in. You said there were *four* blackcollars at Reger's place?"

"That's what I saw," Bailey said. "That local trouble-maker—Kanai—plus Skyler, Hawking, and one other I didn't recognize. Why?"

"Because the men who found the pod said it was bigger than the four-man ones Lathe and Caine used to bring in their teams last year," Ramirez said. "This appears to have been a *six*-man version."

Something cold ran up Bailey's back. "Are you suggesting there could be three *more* blackcollars running around loose out there?"

"Yes, sir," Ramirez said grimly. "I'd like permission to expand our search to the entire area around where the drop pod came down."

"Granted," Bailey said grimly. The local blackcollar activity that had rumbled through Denver over the years had ceased last summer after Lathe and his team left Earth. But it wasn't until a tip a few months ago had led them to a mass grave with six flexarmor-clad bodies that he'd dared to hope the problem had gone away for good. Now, it seemed, the Plinry blackcollars had decided to bring their insane war back for another round. "Get hold of Major McKarren—he should be in the main communications room—and have him put together some more search parties. You and he can coordinate which areas your respective offices will handle."

"Yes, sir," Ramirez said, not moving. "There is one other possibility we should consider."

"You mean the chance that the larger pod is a diversion

designed to pull our men out of the city and waste their time in a wild-goose chase?" Bailey suggested.

Ramirez's face flushed slightly. "Yes, sir," he said, sounding embarrassed. "I'm sorry—I should have realized you'd already have thought of that."

"No apology necessary," Bailey assured him. "Actually, I tend to agree with you. The blackcollars were trained to be city guerrilla fighters, not alpine troops. Unless there was an accident or malfunction, I can't see them voluntarily tramping up and down the mountains."

"Though they did plenty of that last time they were here," Ramirez pointed out.

Bailey grimaced. Yes; Trendor's strange and still unexplained assassination. "That operation was still based out of the city," he said. "Still, it wouldn't hurt to see if there are any other likely targets out there they might be gunning for."

"Shall I get started on a name search?"

"O'Dae can put someone on that," Bailey said. "You concentrate on getting every spotter we've got into the—"

From down the corridor came the sound of a door opening, and Bailey turned to see one of the interrogators step out into the corridor. He spotted Bailey and Ramirez and gestured urgently.

Bailey hurried over, Ramirez right behind him. "What is it?" he asked as he reached the door.

"You'll want to hear this, Colonel," the interrogator said, gesturing them into the room. Inside, Bailey found a dark-haired young woman slumped in her chair in a verifin-induced daze. "Go ahead, Bryna," the interrogator said encouragingly. "Tell me again about Whiplash."

"Wonderful stuff," the woman said, her words slurred

and dreamy-sounding. "It makes you . . ." Her voice trailed off.

"Bryna?" the interrogator prompted. "Tell me what Whiplash does."

"It makes you . . . you don't have to like the hose-snouts anymore."

"Hose-snouts?" Ramirez murmured.

"South Denver street slang for Ryqril," Bailey told him, frowning. *Don't have to like the hose-snouts anymore?* What the hell did that mean?

And then, steel bands seemed to close around his chest. "My God," he said softly. "Does she mean—?"

"I think so, sir," the interrogator said tightly. "She's said it at least three times now, and in different ways. I don't think it's an artifact of the verifin."

"I don't get it," Ramirez said, sounding confused. "What's she trying to say?"

"She's saying," Bailey said quietly, "that Phoenix has found a way to break Ryqril loyalty-conditioning."

Ramirez stared at Bailey, then back at the girl. "I think I'd better get those spotters in the air."

"Yes," Bailey said mechanically. "Wilsonn, keep at her. See if you can find out how much of this Whiplash stuff they have, where they got it from, and where they keep their supplies."

"Yes, sir," the interrogator said, and turned back to the girl.

Bailey gestured to Ramirez, and together they left the room. "You see to the spotters," he said. "I'm going to give the Ryqril a call. They're sure as hell going to want to know about this."

* * *

With a grunt, Foxleigh drove the last nail into the rough board and stepped back to inspect his work. It wasn't pretty, that was for sure. But once the south and west walls had been completely redone the cabin should be a lot cozier when the winter winds started blowing.

Or at least it would until new gaps opened up between the boards. A fact of life here in the mountains.

Rubbing the sweat off his forehead with his sleeve, he looked away from the new siding to the sunlight glistening off the mountains to the west. There were still times when he missed the level of human companionship he'd enjoyed before the war, but he had to admit there were compensations to living out here. He let his gaze sweep across the sky, drinking in the magnificent panorama as he shifted his eyes from west to south to east. . . .

He paused, frowning. There were a lot of Security spotters drifting around over there today. A *lot* of them.

For a minute he watched the spotters, an old sensation tingling the back of his neck. Then, setting down his hammer, he limped around to the front of the cabin and went inside. Crossing to the south-facing window, the one that looked down on the handful of houses below, he selected the red shade and pulled it all the way down. Toby's old signal to let his semiestranged family know that he urgently needed help.

Foxleigh could only hope someone down there would notice it soon. He hoped even more strongly that Adamson or his son would be willing to make the trek up here.

Because something was brewing out there to the east. Something big, judging from Security's reaction to it.

Maybe the blackcollars had returned.

He hoped so. He desperately hoped so. A year ago, when they'd sneaked into Aegis Mountain, he'd hesitated too long and missed his opportunity.

But not this time. This time he would be ready for them.

Throwing another look at the spotters drifting through the sky, he headed back outside and returned to his work.

"General Poirot?"

With an effort, Poirot pried open his eyes. Two men stood over him, their faces silhouetted against soft lights. "How do you feel, General?" one of the men asked.

Poirot frowned. That was a good question, actually. His head hurt fiercely, and his mouth had that peculiar dryness that usually meant a long night's sleep. His body seemed heavy, too, as if he'd slept either too much or too little. Memories were starting to tiptoe back now: the fiasco at Reger's estate, the blackcollar Skyler knocking the world out from under him. Skyler would pay for that, he promised himself distantly.

But there was something else, too, mixed in with the subdued embarrassment and irritation. A brand-new sensation he couldn't quite put his finger on.

"How do you feel about the Ryqril, for instance?" the second man suggested.

The Ryqril? Poirot frowned, the open-snouted faces of humanity's enslavers floating up in front of his mind's eye.

He stiffened. No—it was impossible. He'd been loyalty-conditioned. *Loyalty-conditioned*. The images and thoughts and feelings trickling through him simply could not exist.

But they did.

"That's right, General," the first man said quietly. "Welcome to your new world."

CHAPTER 7

Lathe had had everyone spend a couple of hours looking over the maps and other data Shaw had given them, and then had ordered them all to get some sleep.

It was late afternoon by the time Judas woke up. "Morning, Caine," Spadafora greeted him as he passed Judas's couch, a heavy-looking box in his hands. "Afternoon, rather. Better get dressed—Shaw's coming by in half an hour for a drive up into the Deerline Mountains."

Judas felt his stomach tighten. The real Caine was hidden away somewhere in those mountains. "What are we going there for?" he asked cautiously.

"He says there are some places where we can get a good look at the Khorstron center," Spadafora called over his shoulder as he disappeared into one of the house's bedrooms. "Move it or get left behind."

The safe house had come equipped with a fully stocked pantry. Judas fixed himself a quick breakfast and then hit the shower. By the time Shaw arrived, he was dressed and ready to go.

"Come on, come on—it's not getting any earlier out there," the tactor said briskly as he looked around. "Where's Spadafora?"

"He's not going," Lathe said, gesturing to Mordecai and Judas. "It'll just be the three of us."

Shaw made a face. "I wish you'd said something—I could have brought a car instead of a van," he growled. "Cheaper to run. Never mind; let's just do it."

The foothills of the Deerline Mountains ran right up to the southern edge of Inkosi City, with a couple of the pricier suburban areas scattered around its lower slopes. The Ryqril had refused to let Judas inside the tac center even after he'd been loyalty-conditioned, but Galway had brought him up into the mountains once during his training to give him a view of the place. As the rectangular city street grid gave way to winding mountain roads, he wondered if Shaw would end up taking the blackcollars to the same spot Galway had chosen.

Oddly enough, though their route was very different, they ended up not more than a hundred meters from the spot where Judas had been the last time. Perhaps Galway really *did* understand how these blackcollars thought.

"I really don't know what Lepkowski was thinking," Shaw said as they stood among the trees at the edge of the cliff. "If he thought your team was just going to walk in there, he was badly mistaken."

"I'm sure he wasn't expecting it to be that easy," Lathe said, peering through a set of binoculars at the squat, two-story octagon rising from the lightly forested plain east of the city.

"That's for sure," Judas murmured, shading his eyes

against the glare of the sunlight as it sent evening shadows across the ground. The place had looked pretty impenetrable when Galway had showed it to him a few months ago, and at that time the Ryqril had still been working on it. Now, with everything up and running, it looked even worse.

The building had no windows and only four doors, one each facing east, west, north, and south. A pair of bunkers flanked each of the doors, with firing slits that would allow targeting in a nearly hundred-eighty-degree horizontal arc. The building's ventilation exhaust vents were on the roof, encased in armored boxes with heavy grates over the vents. There were no visible intake valves, and Judas had no idea where they actually were. Also atop the building, set back a few meters from each of the eight corners, were antiaircraft laser batteries, their muzzles pointed vigilantly skyward. The trees and shrubbery for fifty meters around the center had been cleared away, and a two-meter-tall mesh fence marked the outer perimeter. Like the building itself, the fence had just four entrances, each flanked by another pair of guard bunkers.

"It's going to be a challenge, all right," Lathe agreed. "But one of the truisms of war is that there's a way into anything."

"Good luck," Shaw muttered.

"For instance," Lathe continued, "that fence isn't nearly high enough to keep out determined trespassers."

"It doesn't have to be," Shaw said acidly. "Notice how thick the fence posts are? Not only are there a full range of sensors in there, but there's also a sonic net anchored above the fence. Even if you managed to sneak up to the fence without them spotting you, jumping or climbing over it would scramble your balance and dump you on your face."

"Allowing the Ryqril to stroll out of the bunkers and beat the sand out of you?" Judas suggested.

"They can't get out of the bunkers, at least not directly," Shaw said. "But then, they really wouldn't have to. The whole area inside the fence, for about three meters back, is booby-trapped with scud grenades and hedge mines." He lifted his eyebrows at Judas. "If you managed not to trigger one of them, and the Ryqril shooting at you from the building bunkers somehow kept missing, *then* they'd send the warriors outside to beat the sand out of you."

"Must do things in their proper order, Caine," Lathe agreed mildly. "However, I wasn't implying we'd actually be going in over the fence. My point was simply that the fence's height is an enticement, and the fact that the Ryqril seem interested in luring in sightseers implies a level of overconfidence that can be exploited."

"Of course that's what you meant," Shaw said, an edge of sarcasm in his tone. "Again, good luck."

"Oh, we'll get in," Lathe assured him. "Actually, we have no choice. Lepkowski's already gone off to rendezvous with the Chryselli to tell them what we're up to. Pride alone dictates that we succeed."

"Unless the whole thing is a trap," Mordecai spoke up.

"What do you mean?" Shaw asked, his tone suddenly ominous. "If you're even *suggesting* I'm cooperating with the Ryqril—"

"He's not," Lathe cut him off. But there was a sudden new edge to his voice. "Go on, Mordecai."

"I was just wondering if this whole thing could be a Ryqril plan to turn the tables on the Chryselli," the other blackcollar said. "If the tactical data is going to be of any use, the Chryselli have to be here to collect it pretty much as soon as we dig it out. The Ryqril could have leaked word of this place in hopes of luring them into an ambush."

The lump that had been forming in Judas's throat relaxed. Mordecai had come close to the truth, but not close enough. Galway's plan was still safe. "Sounds kind of iffy to me," he said. "The Chryselli wouldn't be foolish enough to send anything too valuable into a Ryqril-held system, would they?"

"Of course not," Shaw said scornfully. "Besides, in order to set up that kind of ambush, the Ryqril would have to pull some major ships of their own off the battlefront, which they can't afford to do."

"I suppose," Mordecai said. "I just thought that—"

"And we appreciate the effort," Shaw cut him off. "But next time do us all a favor and leave the tactical thinking to the experts, all right?" Deliberately, he turned his back on the other and looked at Lathe. "Is there anything else you wanted to see up here?"

"No, I think we've seen enough," Lathe said. If he was upset at the tactor's verbal abuse of one of his men, he wasn't showing it. "You said you had some schematics of the place?"

"We have some fairly good guesses, based on long-range photos we took while they were building it," Shaw said. "But they're hardly comprehensive."

"They'll do for starters," Lathe said, returning his

binoculars to their pouch. "Let's get back to town and take a look."

The sun had disappeared completely below the horizon by the time they retraced their steps to the off-road clearing where they'd parked the van. With Shaw again at the wheel, they headed to the main road that would take them back down the mountain.

They were out of the foothills and once again into the more orderly city streets when Judas first realized they were being followed. "Lathe?" he spoke up hesitantly, tapping the blackcollar on the shoulder.

"Yes, I see them," Lathe said.

"We all see them," Shaw growled, his profile tight in the shifting streetlight. Taking his left hand off the wheel, he reached under his right sleeve, and Judas felt his wrist tingle with blackcollar code. *All blackcollars in range respond for assist.*

There was no answer. "Been on our tail for the past eight blocks," Shaw went on, tapping out the message again. "Prefect Haberdae is nothing if not unsubtle. Looks like we're on our own, too."

"What are we going to do?" Judas asked, an unpleasant sensation crawling up his back. This wasn't part of the plan, at least not any plan he'd been told about. Once he'd been swapped in for Caine, Security was supposed to back off and leave the blackcollars alone.

"Well, we're sure not going to lose them in this beast," Shaw commented. "We'll have to ditch it."

"Where?" Lathe asked.

"There's a viaduct eight blocks ahead to the left," Shaw said. "Where Oak passes under Eleventh."

"That the one with a shopping mall on one side of the overpass and a casino on the other?"

"Very good—you've been doing your homework," Shaw said, a hint of reluctant approval seeping into his voice. "Yes, that's the one. What the current maps *don't* show is that one of the entrances to the old subway system used to be at that intersection."

"Subways are always promising," Lathe said.

"Very," Shaw agreed. "Which is why the Ryqril went around plugging all the entrances when they took over. The maps also don't show that Inkosi City's less reputable citizenry have sunk a few new entrance shafts to the system, using them to move contraband and for private meetings. One of the rabbit holes just happens to be in the casino restaurant's back room."

"Handy place to disappear to," Mordecai murmured. He already had his flexarmor gloves on, Judas noted. Reaching beneath his coat, he got out his own gloves and started pulling them on.

"Provided we can get out once we're in," Lathe said. "How well do you know the system?"

"Well enough," Shaw said. "I can certainly get us in and back out again."

"And how well does Security know the system?" Mordecai asked.

"No idea," Shaw conceded. "I'm sure they've located at least some of the rabbit holes, but I doubt they've explored the whole thing. Security snogs who go down there don't always come out again."

"We'll just have to chance it," Lathe decided. "What's the shopping mall like?"

"All sorts of back entrances, hallways, nooks, and crannies," Shaw said, throwing him a frown. "But the subway shaft's from the casino, not the mall."

"I was thinking we might want to split up," Lathe told him. "Make them chase two targets instead of one."

"Bad idea," Shaw warned. "Especially since I'm the only one here who knows the tunnel system."

"Which just means the other pair stays above ground," Lathe countered. "Plenty of crowds and buildings out there to disappear into."

"Still not a good idea," Shaw said sourly. "But I take it your mind's already made up. Fine. I'll take Caine underground; you two can play dodgeball with Security. Get ready; we're coming up on our turn."

"Caine, stay with him and do exactly as he says," Lathe said, glancing over the seat at Judas. "What's our drop strategy?"

"There are stairs leading up both sides of the viaduct to the overpass above," Shaw said. "As soon as I reach them, I'll do a fishtail stop and try to block traffic in both directions. That ought to snarl the pursuit long enough for us to at least get up the stairs."

"All right," Lathe said. "Caine, keep your battle-hood ready, but don't put it on until Tactor Shaw tells you to. We'll try first to melt into the crowds."

"Got it," Judas said, trying to calm his racing heart. What the *hell* was Galway up to?

"They're moving into the left lane," the tech at the command van's status board announced, pressing his headset tightly to his ear. "Looks like they're planning to turn on Oak or Elsbeth."

"Stay with them," Haberdae ordered, a grim half smile on his face as he gazed at the board. "Guess they're not heading for the Queel District, after all."

Galway didn't reply, his eyes also on the board, a sense of imminent doom tugging at him. The spotters were in place over the city, the trackers were on Shaw's tail, and the intercept units were constantly updating their positions to be ready whenever Haberdae decided to make his move. The numbers were there; the ground and air support were there; and the landscape definitely favored the hunters. On paper, this should be a textbook-simple operation.

But no operation was ever textbook-simple. They were always riddled with variables and unknowns, uncertainties that blackcollars were experts at exploiting.

And even if it *did* work the way Haberdae expected— even if all the variables fell to the hunters—the evening might still end with the entire operation dead and buried in the dust.

Certainly, Shaw couldn't be permitted to snatch the Khorstron planning job away from Lathe. No one was arguing otherwise, least of all Galway. But Lathe himself hadn't even exhausted his options yet, let alone the various schemes Galway might be able to implement through Judas. And even if all other options *were* gone—even if Shaw was irrevocably hell-bent on running the show—trying to pull off this kind of surgical strike against the tactor while leaving Lathe and the others free and unscathed would take a finesse that Galway wasn't at all sure Haberdae and his men possessed.

But there was nothing he could do about it. He'd argued and warned and pleaded; but in the end Taakh had chosen to go with Haberdae's raid.

Perhaps that shouldn't have surprised him, Galway thought with a touch of bitterness. *Khassq*-class warriors were trained for direct action, not the kind of subtlety that was required here. Perhaps he, like Haberdae, was hungering for combat, even combat where all the Ryq and prefect themselves would do was watch.

"They've turned left on Oak," the tech reported.

"Means they're probably not heading for the Ring Village quarter, either," Haberdae muttered. "Too bad. I'd have liked a good excuse to go in and clear out that snake pit. All right, pull one of the units out of Ring Village area and shift it to—let's see—"

"Sir—accident in the Eleventh Street viaduct!" the tech said suddenly. "The van's gone into a fishtail."

"Were they hit?" Haberdae demanded, grabbing the headset he'd taken off earlier and jamming it back onto his head. "Tracker One, what the hell's happening?"

"Get one of the spotters down there right away," Galway ordered, his heart thudding suddenly in his chest as his eyes swept the board. If they got the nearest intercept teams moving immediately—

"Cancel that," Haberdae snapped, throwing a glare at Galway. "Someone's clipped them, that's all. The last thing we want to do is panic—what?" he interrupted himself, pressing hard on his earphone.

"What is it?" Galway demanded.

"They've left the van, all four of them," the tech said tightly. "They're on the stairs heading up to Eleventh."

"Scramble all units," Galway ordered. "*Now*. And get that spotter down."

"Do it," Haberdae confirmed. He glared at Galway again, but there was a sudden tightness now to his throat muscles. "How in hell's name did they spot the trackers?"

"They're blackcollars, that's how," Galway told him grimly. "Where are they going?"

"They've split up," Haberdae told him, pointing at the board. "Looks like Shaw and Judas are headed south toward the casino, with Lathe and Mordecai heading north toward the mall." He snorted gently. "Well, *that's* convenient. We can grab Shaw without having to worry about the wrong story getting back."

"Maybe *too* convenient," Galway cautioned. Sending a superior officer *and* the least capable fighter of their group to go running off on their own? That didn't sound like Lathe.

"I'll take what I can get at this point," Haberdae said. "Units Five through Eight: converge on the Spinning Wheel Casino—capture formation. Units One through Four: hold containment around Eleventh Street Mall. Stand ready to assist Spinning Wheel units."

"You should send at least a couple of units after Lathe and Mordecai," Galway said. "They're going to think it suspicious if we ignore them completely."

Haberdae made a face. "Fine. Unit One: move on the mall." He looked back at Galway. "They'd just better not actually interfere with them," he added ominously.

Galway looked back at the board. "Somehow, I don't think that's something you need to worry about."

✳   ✳   ✳

Judas and Shaw were nearly to the casino's front entrance when Security cars suddenly appeared, screeching around various corners as they sped into the parking lot, their red and blue lights flashing. "Like I said, Haberdae's nothing if not unsubtle," Shaw said, picking up his pace and digging beneath his coat. "Button up."

"That'll make us awfully conspicuous," Judas objected, searching desperately for a good reason why they should leave their battle-hoods off. He had a fair guess now as to what was going on, and with Lathe and Mordecai out of sight a straightforward paral-dart attack would be the easiest way to get Shaw out of the picture.

Unfortunately, Shaw knew that, too. "You want a face full of paral-darts?" the tactor countered as he pulled on his battle-hood and snugged it down over his flexarmor turtleneck. "Get it *on*."

Grimacing, Judas pulled out his own hood. So that was that. With Security's best weaponry now useless, he would just have to look for an opening to take Shaw down himself.

He had the hood on and was adjusting the goggles over his eyes when a spray of paral-darts from the approaching cars washed over him, jabbing tiny needles into his outer clothing and ricocheting off his battle-hood. A pair of passersby, caught by the edge of the spread, collapsed silently onto the sidewalk. "Watch your mouth," Shaw warned, holding a gloved hand up to protect his own exposed skin as a second burst swept over them. Running past the casino's startled doorman, the tactor straight-armed one of the two side doors flanking the elaborate central revolving door and headed inside.

Judas was two steps behind him, slipping neatly through the opening as the door swung closed again. "Where to?" he asked, breathing hard.

"A moment," Shaw said. He spun around to face Judas—

And to his horror, Judas saw the other had a *shuriken* in his hand. He had barely enough time to flinch back before Shaw cocked his arm and let the star fly.

But it didn't slash through Judas's cheek and teeth, as in that frozen second he'd fully expected it to. Instead, the *shuriken* whistled harmlessly past his ear; and as he turned to follow its path he saw it bury itself in the edge of the door they'd just come through, cutting through the panel and into its frame, effectively jamming it shut. Two more stars followed the first, sealing the revolving door and the other side door as well.

"Can't make it too easy for them," Shaw said casually. "This way."

Pulling out another *shuriken*, he headed off in the direction of a gaudy restaurant sign set into the high ceiling to their right. Judas followed, a creepy numbness settling into his gut. Barely thirty seconds earlier, a distant part of his mind reminded him, he'd actually been considering trying to personally take this man down.

Like the doorman, the restaurant's hostess merely gaped in surprise as the two men charged past her. Some of the patrons did the same, while others simply ignored the sight, as if a pair of masked men in a hurry were nothing particularly out of the ordinary. No one tried to stop them as Shaw led the way across the main dining area and through a service doorway. "Hood off," he muttered to Judas, pulling off his own battle-hood and goggles as he led the way down a wide service corridor.

Frowning, wondering what the other was up to now, Judas complied. They reached a T-junction and Shaw turned into the cross corridor, and Judas saw an unmarked door five meters ahead.

A door flanked by two of the biggest and ugliest men he'd ever seen.

And with that, Shaw's plan became clear. Neither guard had a gun in his hand, but that would have quickly changed if they'd seen a pair of blackcollars in full battle gear charging down on them. Their weapons wouldn't have been much use against flexarmor, of course, but the sound of shots would have shown Security which way they'd gone.

But with their hoods off and the rest of their flexarmor concealed, he and Shaw were just a couple of guys who might have taken a wrong turn. The sort of intruders toward whom even professional bodyguards might be inclined to show a little initial restraint.

Sure enough, one of the guards took a step forward, holding up a hand palm outwards. "This here's a private party," he said as Shaw continued striding toward him. "The main room's back that—"

The last syllable came out in a grunt as Shaw leaped across the last two meters, pivoting on his left foot and snapping his right up in a side kick to the man's stomach.

The second guard threw himself back against the door, his hand diving beneath his jacket. Without bothering to put his right foot down, Shaw cocked it back and did a little chicken hop past the crumpled body of the first guard. As the second man's hand emerged gripping a flat handgun, Shaw kicked the weapon hard into the man's chest.

His breath went out in an explosive gasp, and Shaw again cocked his leg back and threw one final sweeping kick across the side of his head. Toppling to the floor beside his partner, he lay still.

"Whoa," Judas muttered as he stepped gingerly over the crumpled bodies. "I thought you tactors were just the planning end of the organization."

"We're also blackcollars," Shaw reminded him tartly. "Quickly, now."

To Judas's mild surprise, the back room itself was empty. But as Shaw headed toward a shallow coat closet he saw that the back of the closet was open a crack, with a wide circular stairway visible beyond it. With Shaw in the lead, they headed down.

The subways of central Europe had similarly been sealed down when the Ryqril had taken control of the TDE three decades earlier. But Judas had seen old photos of some of them, and Inkosi City's system seemed fairly typical. A wide, dome-topped tunnel stretched out, heading east and west, with a pair of monorail tracks set into straight-walled trenches in the center. From the size of the area, he guessed they'd come down in one of the original stations, with wide platforms and empty booths where venders would have sold food or reading material or trinkets. The ceramic wall and floor tiles were done up in flowing patterns of yellow and green and brown, though with the low-power overhead lighting creating only isolated pools of light the décor was difficult to properly appreciate.

Rather to Judas's disappointment, there were no actual subway cars in sight.

What *was* there, centered in one of the light pools, was a circular graystone table that looked glaringly out of place. Seated around it were a half-dozen hard-faced men.

All of them looking up at the intruders.

The two men standing guard at the bottom of the stairway, unlike those Shaw had dealt with above, had their guns out and aimed by the time Shaw and Judas reached the bottom. "My apologies for the intrusion, gentlemen," the tactor said, coming to a halt a couple of meters from the gunmen and motioning Judas to do the same. "I'm afraid the rest of your meeting will have to be postponed. Security's on the hunt upstairs."

"Hunting you, I presume?" one of the men suggested.

"As it happens," Shaw said.

"Is there some reason we shouldn't just give you to them?" someone else put in sarcastically.

Shaw inclined his head slightly. "You could try."

There was a short silence. Judas found himself staring at the guns pointed at him, hoping fervently the guards wouldn't try anything rash. Not for his and Shaw's sake, but for theirs.

The first man stirred and got to his feet. "Don't think it's really worth it," he said calmly, gesturing to the others. "Besides, whoever they're after, they'd be happy enough to bag one of us. Anchor, Veeling—go secure the exit."

Silently, the two guards lowered their guns and brushed past Shaw and Judas to the staircase. "Good luck to you," the first man said, nodding to the blackcollars as he headed up, the others trailing behind him. "If they catch you, try not to mention us."

"No problem," Shaw promised.

A minute later, they were gone. "Come on," Shaw said, heading west down the tunnel at a quick jog. Fifty meters away, Judas saw, the station ended and the tunnel narrowed down into permanent darkness. "As quietly as possible."

Grimacing, Judas ran after him. So not only was Shaw a tactor with other blackcollars to call on, but he was also apparently on speaking terms with the city's criminal underground, with its potential for additional manpower. More than ever, it was becoming clear that Shaw needed to be taken out of the equation.

Judas only hoped Galway was up to the task.

Lathe and Mordecai had made it nearly to the mall's south entrance when a lone Security car appeared at the western end of the parking lot and headed their direction. "About time," Mordecai commented. "I was starting to think they'd forgotten about us."

"They *do* seem more interested in the others, don't they?" Lathe agreed, turning to look back at the casino parking lot. There were at least three Security cars already there, their flashing lights strobing eerily off the buildings and cars. At the casino's western end, a fourth car was heading in to join the party. "I suppose we should do something about that."

"We can't just let Security have them?"

Lathe smiled. "He *does* have a gift for rubbing people the wrong way, doesn't he? Still, it would be unprofessional to throw him to the wolves."

"I suppose," Mordecai conceded. "What's the plan?"

"Let's first see how much they really want us," Lathe said, eyeing the approaching Security car and picking up his pace. "We'll beat them to the mall, do a flip and drop, and see what happens. Ready . . . . go."

Abruptly, he and Mordecai abandoned their unconcerned walk and broke into a dead run toward the mall entrance. The Security car surged forward as the driver saw their quarry rabbiting, but he was too far back and the two blackcollars had too much of a lead. The car was still fifty meters away as Lathe shoved open one of the tall glass doors and slipped inside.

Beyond the outer doors was a wide vestibule with another line of glass doors four meters back. Slowing to a fast walk, he headed toward the inner doors, peeling off his flexarmor gloves as he did so and giving the area beyond the vestibule a quick scan. Off to the left was a small, open-air coffee-and-pastry shop with a dozen small tables scattered around at the edge of the main corridor. Stuffing his gloves into his coat pockets, he shifted direction to angle across the vestibule toward the shop. He reached the inner doors, pushing open the nearest with one hand as he unzipped his coat with the other, and stepped through into the warm air and soft background music of the mall. As he walked toward the coffee shop he pulled off his coat, grabbing the sleeves with his hands as he did so, and turned the garment inside out, replacing the plain navy blue he'd been wearing with a black-and-burgundy herringbone pattern. By the time he reached the first group of tables he had it back on and zipped up.

One of the tables had recently been vacated, the previous

patrons' discarded cups, plates, and napkins still there. He sat down in one of the chairs facing the mall entrance as Mordecai, his own appearance also transformed, took the seat across from him.

They were barely settled when the vestibule doors burst open and four armed Security men charged in.

Lathe had already lowered his head, looking down at his chest as he daubed vigorously with a napkin at an imaginary coffee spill on his coat. Mordecai picked up one of the empty cups with one hand as he rested his chin in the other, his fingers partially covering the side of his face as he pretended to watch Lathe's cleanup operation. Out of the corner of his eye Lathe saw the Security men pause for a moment and look around, then continue down the hallway, spreading out into a loose sweeping formation as they searched for their quarry.

"Clear?" Mordecai murmured.

"Clear," Lathe confirmed, giving his coat one last swipe. The Security men were still moving down the hallway, peering into each shop door as they passed. "They'll give anyone a uniform these days."

"Or else they had orders to leave us alone."

"No, they didn't spot us at all," Lathe told him. "I'd have caught the body language if they had. As an overall command decision, though, I think you're probably right."

"So what's our next move?"

Lathe nodded his head toward the door. "Car's right out front. Let's go see if the others want a ride."

The Security car had been pulled quickly and rather sloppily to the curb, its engine off but its lights still flashing. The driver had remembered to take the key with him, but that was only a minor inconvenience. Thirty seconds later, Lathe pulled away from the curb, made a tight U-turn, and headed back westward across the parking lot.

"Any idea where they'll be coming out?" Mordecai asked as he shut off the flashing lights.

"There's another of these private subway entrances half a klick west of the casino," Lathe told him, pointing ahead. "I'm guessing that's where the rest of the Security force will be congregating, either to go in after them in a pincer or else just wait topside for them to pop out."

"A pincer would be risky," Mordecai pointed out. "Still, against an aging tactor and a nonblackcollar they might be stupid enough to try it." He slipped his fingers under his sleeve. "I wonder how well these things transmit underground."

On his own wrist, Lathe's tingler tapped out Mordecai's message: *Shaw—Caine—respond.*

There was no answer. "Not very well, I guess," Mordecai concluded. "Maybe when we're closer—"

"Unit One, report," a voice called suddenly from the car's radio. "You're out of position."

"At least they've got competent people in their spotters," Mordecai commented, rolling down his window and peering skyward. "That could be trouble."

"We'll just have to do something about it," Lathe agreed as he pulled the microphone from its clip and thumbed it on. "Unit One," he reported, dropping into the characteristic Security style of clipped speech. "Suspects inside mall, heading west. We've split forces and are attempting to cut off their escape."

"Cancel that," a different voice growled. An officer's

voice, Lathe decided from the medium-high arrogance level in his tone. "We're concentrating on the others now. Pick up the rest of your team and proceed immediately to the casino."

"Yes, sir," Lathe said. "I'll park and wait for the others to catch up."

The radio clicked off, and Lathe shut off the mike and returned it to its clip. "You see him?" he asked.

"Yeah, he's right up there," Mordecai said, nodding upward. "Looks like he's directly over the other subway entrance you mentioned." He pulled his head inside again. "They aren't *really* going to send this unit over to the casino, are they?"

"I doubt it very much," Lathe assured him. "I'm pretty sure that was wholly for our benefit."

"That's what I thought," Mordecai agreed. "So you feel like an evening's stroll by the light of a spotter's searchlights?"

Lathe smiled tightly. "Don't worry," he said. "We'll figure something out."

Haberdae clicked off the comm and turned to face Galway. "Clever little things, aren't they?" he said sardonically as he draped his headset around his neck. "Obviously think we're as stupid as they are smart." He gestured to the tech at the board. "You still in contact with Unit One Leader?"

"Yes, sir," the other said. "He requests orders."

"Tell him they'll be leaving his car near the west mall entrance," Haberdae instructed. "He's to double-time it there, then get over to Intercept Two and join the net

Units Two, Three, and Four have set up. Then tell Spotter Two to watch the area west of the Unit One car and make sure Lathe and Mordecai don't go that direction. I know he won't be able to keep track of them long with all the pedestrian traffic out there, but he's to make damn sure they don't head for Intercept Two."

"Yes, sir." The tech turned to his mike and began issuing the orders.

"This all assumes, of course, that Shaw and Judas will come up that particular stairway," Galway warned. "What if Shaw decides to keep going to the next exit instead?"

"He won't," Haberdae said. "Next exit's over two kilometers away, and it's one he should know we've already found. No, he's got to be figuring the Thirteenth Street slot is still secret. Besides, with two units on their way down behind him from the casino he can't afford to spend any more time down there than he has to."

"Sir, Spotter Two reports Unit One's car has parked near the west mall entrance," the tech announced. "Two men getting out—"

Distantly, through the headset around Haberdae's neck, Galway heard a yelp. "What is it?" he snapped.

"Nothing," the tech assured him as Haberdae hastily put his headphone back on. "They turned the car's search-light on Spotter Two, that's all. Dazzled them for a moment until they could get out of the beam."

"So where are they now?" Haberdae demanded into his mike. He listened a moment, his lip twisting. "They were dazzled just long enough for Lathe and Mordecai to slip away," he said sourly, looking at Galway. "No idea which way they went."

Galway looked at the board, his stomach tightening. "They're heading west," he said.

"No." Haberdae was positive. "There's no one heading west. Both spotters agree on that."

"Then they're going the long way around," Galway insisted. "Or maybe they're going to grab one of the civilian cars in the lot and drive there."

"Galway, will you calm down?" Haberdae said in a tone of strained patience. "We have spotters in the air, we have men and cars on the ground, and every one of them knows Lathe and Mordecai by sight. They're not going to get within a hundred meters."

"A hundred meters might be close enough."

"Fine—they won't get within *two* hundred meters," Haberdae growled. "You want me to make it *three* hundred?"

"Prefect, Lathe isn't going to abandon the others," Galway said, forcing his voice to remain calm and reasonable. "That's not the way he does things. Unless you get to them first, he *is* going to rescue them."

"And what exactly do you suggest?"

Galway looked up at the board. "Send your men down the Thirteenth Street entrance now," he said. "Catch Shaw between them and the casino units and make the capture underground where Lathe can't interfere. Once you've got him, flip a coin as to which exit you use to bring him out. Even Lathe can't be two places at once."

"You want me to send my men down a dark subway tunnel where the quarry has all the advantages?" Haberdae countered. "Don't be ridiculous."

"You'll have them in a pincer—"

"I'll have my men in a crossfire situation, that's what I'll have," Haberdae cut him off. "Look, Galway, Lathe is a blackcollar, not a magician. He can't fly, he can't demate-rialize, he can't cloud men's minds. And flexarmor or not, he can't just charge through a line of men armed with lasers. Not without getting himself killed."

"Prefect—"

"We're going to do this according to plan," Haberdae cut him off. "We're going to push Shaw to the rat hole and nail him as he comes out. If you're that worried about Lathe, I'll call a car and you can go over there and help watch for him."

"You know I can't do that," Galway bit out. "If he finds out I'm on Khala, it could wreck the whole operation."

"Exactly," Haberdae said with satisfaction. "And if you're not really here, you can't tell me how to do my job, can you?"

Galway sighed silently to himself. Haberdae simply refused to understand. "Fine," he murmured. "It's your show."

"Damn right it is." Haberdae turned back to the board. "What's happening with Unit One?"

"They've reclaimed their car and are heading over to Intercept Two," the tech reported.

"Good." Haberdae looked back over at Galway. "Tell them to keep an eye out for Lathe and Mordecai along the way," he added, almost reluctantly.

"They're already doing that, sir," the tech said. "So far, no sign of them."

"Fine," Haberdae said. "Alert all units to stand ready. Let's get this done."

CHAPTER 8

The short ride from the mall parking lot had been a rough one, Lathe thought as he braced himself against the inside of Unit One's trunk. Still, he had little cause to complain. Mordecai, hanging to the underside of the vehicle, had it considerably harder. He just hoped the other hadn't fallen off somewhere along the way.

The car made one final turn and braked to a halt. Four doors opened and closed as the Security men made their exit, and then all was silence.

Lathe gave it a fifteen count, then dug to his tingler. *Mordecai—report.*

Inside Security perimeter, the reply came promptly. Clearly, the other had made it through okay. *Estimate fifteen to twenty in ambush formation—eight more in backstop position.*

Lathe nodded to himself. So he'd been right. Security expected the others to pop out of the subway at the allegedly secret Thirteenth Street exit and were hoping to nab them as they did so. *Clear to exit?* he signaled.

Clear.

Lathe found the trunk release and popped the lid. Easing it open a crack, he looked outside.

He was facing away from the main ambush ring, looking back toward the mall half a kilometer away. The eight-man rear guard was positioned a dozen meters behind him, a thirty-degree arc of protection standing silent vigil behind the row of parked Security cars, waiting alertly for the missing blackcollars to appear.

Only they were facing the wrong way.

He opened the trunk a few centimeters more and looked up at the sky. The spotters hovering overhead wouldn't be making that same mistake, of course, at least not to the same degree. Still, he would bet heavily that their attention was currently split between the subway exit and the area west of the mall where he and Mordecai had disappeared. Theoretically, parked Security cars should be of little interest to anyone at the moment.

Time to find out whether or not that was true. Giving the rear sentry line one last look, he opened the trunk just far enough to roll out, pulling the lid mostly shut again as he landed on hands and knees on the pavement. Dropping to his belly, he crawled quickly out of sight beneath the car.

"Pleasant ride?" Mordecai murmured as Lathe joined him. The smaller man was working industriously at one of the throwing knives he'd wedged into the car frame earlier to serve as a handhold.

"A little bumpy," Lathe told him. "You?"

With a final tug, the knife came free. "I've had worse," Mordecai said, slipping the weapon back into its thigh sheath. "How do you want to work this?"

Lathe crawled to the side of the car where he could get a better look at the Security cordon. It was a fairly standard containment formation: four men in each of four clusters, the nearest of them about twenty meters away, crouching behind small bushes and parked vehicles at the edge of a narrow and mostly empty parking area. The focus of their semicircle was a large storage shed fastened against the rear of what seemed to be a hardware store on the other side of the lot.

The hunters' equipment was something of a hardware store in its own right. Two of the men in each foursome sported paral-dart rifles, the third carried a flechette rifle, and the fourth had one of the snub-nose laser rifles that had once been Security standard issue. Each man also had a couple of grenades in a sling carrier at his belt. Everyone wore visored helmets and protective vests.

Mordecai crawled up beside him. "Is that the exit?" he asked.

"Up through the ground and out the shed," Lathe confirmed. "You don't see Galway anywhere, do you?"

"Not in this group," Mordecai said. "Were you expecting him to show up personally for the capture?"

Lathe shrugged. "I thought he might."

"Galway's not that stupid," Mordecai said. "Did you notice the grenades?"

Lathe nodded. "Concussion, most likely. No one's wearing enough armor for them to risk frags."

"Still shows they're pretty serious," Mordecai said. "I presume we'll be doing a standard cannonball with the two nearest groups?"

"Cannonball with those, steamroller with the others," Lathe confirmed.

"Taking out the flanking laser gunners first?"

"Yes," Lathe agreed reluctantly. Ideally, he would have preferred to neutralize the entire bunch with hands and feet and *nunchaku*, minimizing the risk of killing any of them. With Whiplash, enemies like these were also possible future allies.

But two shots with those lasers could punch through their flexarmor, and they couldn't afford to let anyone get that second shot. "Of course, once we're finished we'll still have that sentry line behind us to deal with," he reminded Mordecai.

"Plus the spotters overhead," Mordecai said.

"True." Lathe rubbed his cheek. "Maybe Shaw will have some ideas."

Right on cue, his wrist tingled. *At exit. Situation?*

Lathe slid two fingers beneath his sleeve. *Sixteen-man Security trap cordon—eight-man rear guard—one or more spotters in air.*

Weaponry?

Paral-darts, flechette rifles, lasers, grenades.

There was a short pause. *Take out cordon—get laser to me.*

Lathe cocked an eyebrow at Mordecai. "He *is* a tactor," Mordecai pointed out. "I assume he knows what he's doing."

"We can hope," Lathe agreed. *Acknowledged*, he sent. *Attack in ten.*

Acknowledged. Laser to me in thirty.

Giving him and Mordecai a whole twenty seconds to

deal with the rest of the cordon, Lathe noted wryly. The man was too generous. "Ready?" he murmured.

Mordecai had already shuffled across to the other side of the car. "Ready," he murmured back.

Pulling out two *shuriken* and his *nunchaku*, Lathe counted down the rest of the seconds; and as his mental clock reached zero, he rolled out from under the car, got to his feet, and headed silently toward the nearest group.

With their attention the other direction, the Security men never saw him coming. But someone in one of the spotters obviously did. He'd covered only half the twenty-meter gap when suddenly everyone gave a sort of simultaneous group twitch and spun around.

Lathe's first *shuriken* took out the closer of the two laser gunners, catching him in the narrow gap between helmet visor and the top of his chest armor. The second, more distant target fell with the other throwing star buried in the same place. A cluster of paral-darts bounced off Lathe's shoulder, while another cluster and a high-velocity flechette whistled past without even touching him. The rest of the gunners, taken by surprise and clearly rattled, were firing wildly.

Given time, they would undoubtedly correct their aim. Lathe had no intention of giving them that time. A second volley of paral-darts caught him in the stomach; and then he was in the middle of his target group.

He took out the first of the remaining three men with a side kick to the other's chest, the power of the blow against his armor sending him crashing hard onto the pavement. The second man swung his gun sideways toward Lathe's head; dropping into a one-legged crouch,

Lathe slammed his fist into the man's thigh in a punch that paralyzed the muscle and likewise dropped him to the ground. The last man sent a final burst of paral-darts uselessly at Lathe's back before the blackcollar's *nunchaku* swung around and slammed into his helmet.

One group down; one to go. Lathe snatched up the laser rifle still gripped in the dead gunner's hands, using the momentary pause in the action to check out Mordecai's progress. The other blackcollar had likewise taken out his first batch and was sprinting toward his next set of targets. With the borrowed laser rifle in his left hand and his *nunchaku* in his right, Lathe turned and headed toward his own second group.

They were holding their ground, he noted with a touch of professional admiration. Two of the men had dropped to one knee, the third standing behind them in a standard volley formation. As Lathe started toward them, they opened fire.

The flechette gunner was good, his first shot catching Lathe squarely in the chest. The impact staggered him, slowing his charge and throwing off his balance as the flexarmor went rigid to absorb the blow. The gunner's second shot was nearly as well centered, this one bouncing off his abdomen and impeding his charge even more. Then, as his third shot also connected, the gunner shouted something to his companions.

And one of the kneeling paral-dart gunners dropped his weapon and dived for the laser rifle lying on the ground beside the dead gunner.

Lathe swore under his breath, dropping the laser rifle he was carrying and trying to get to his *shuriken*. But the flexarmor rigidity that had protected him from the high-velocity flechettes was now unexpectedly working against him. He was still trying to force his stiffened arm down to one of his weapons pouches when the Security man reached the laser rifle and scooped it up, swiveling back around as he brought it to his shoulder.

And then, as Lathe's fingers finally closed on one of his throwing stars, a flash of light sizzled past his face from the right.

The rear sentry line had joined the battle.

Clenching his teeth, Lathe dropped to one knee, the agonizingly slow movement slowed even further as a fourth flechette hammered into his abdomen. The laser gunner in front of him was nearly into position now, the barrel of his rifle swinging around to point directly at him. Lathe finally got his *shuriken* free and struggled to raise his arm to throw, knowing he wouldn't be in time.

But as he braced himself for the blast, the gunner jerked suddenly to the side, his laser swinging wildly away as both man and weapon sprawled onto the ground.

Lathe had forgotten about Shaw. Apparently, so had everyone else.

He looked to his left. The tactor was framed in the open shed door, his arm windmilling as he sent a second *shuriken* on its way, this one taking out the flechette-gunner marksman. Reaching down, Lathe picked up the laser rifle he'd dropped and tossed it toward Shaw, then half turned to send his own *shuriken* in the direction of the rear picket line. There was a burst of laser light from behind him—

And from the center of the picket line came a brilliant

flash and a thunderclap that slammed Lathe flat onto his back.

Trained reflexes took over, bringing his arm down to slap out the impact and then rolling himself back up into a crouch. His ears were still ringing; fortunately, the battle-hood had protected him from most of the concussion from the grenade Shaw had set off with his laser shot.

The men in the rear picket line, though, were definitely down for the count. The man who'd been wearing the particular grenade Shaw had hit was probably down permanently.

The final gunner in the group Lathe had been heading for had also been thrown to the ground by the concussion, and Lathe could see him visibly twitching with the after-effects of the blast. For a second he considered making sure the man stayed put, decided it wouldn't be necessary, and turned again to Shaw.

The tactor was still standing in the shed doorway, his eyes and laser now pointed upward. "Need any help?" Lathe called.

"Get us some transport," Shaw called back, firing a pair of shots into the sky. "Caine? Let's go."

All of the Security cars, as Lathe had noted earlier, were parked in a loose group between the two lines of Security men. He ran to the closest, found the key still in it, and climbed behind the wheel. *Ready*, he signaled with his tingler.

No one tried to stop the others as they piled into the car. Twenty seconds later, they were back on the street.

"Everyone all right?" Lathe asked as he pulled onto one of the major thoroughfares, throwing a quick look at the two men in the rear seat.

"Quite all right," Shaw assured him, his head halfway out the window beside him as he stared up at the sky. "I don't suppose you happened to get a count of how many spotters they had deployed."

"Sorry," Lathe said. "We must have missed the sign marking the command van."

Shaw grunted. "Well, as long as they stay out of my range, they also won't be close enough to track us when we dump the car. Take a left at that next light."

"Where are we going?" Mordecai asked.

"Ring Village quarter," Shaw told him. "Largely controlled by a fairly unsavory crime boss named Bilnius. One more stolen car won't even be noticed there."

"Not to mention the one we plan to steal on our way out?" Lathe suggested.

"Borrow, not steal," Shaw corrected him. "Speaking of plans, I seem to remember you having a plan for getting into Khorstron."

"I have the start of one, yes," Lathe said. "It still needs some fleshing out."

"And some extra personnel, too, I expect," Shaw said. "Fine. I'll start pulling my people together tonight." He pulled his head back inside the window and looked meaningfully at Lathe's profile. "But *I'll* be the one in charge of them."

Lathe cocked his head. "As you wish."

"Good," Shaw said, poking his head out the window again. "As long as that's clear. Tomorrow, after we've had a chance to rest, we'll see about fleshing out this plan of yours."

The bodies had been removed, the injured had been sent for treatment, and the wreckage and weaponry had been collected and carted away. From all appearances, the parking area behind Sheffer's Hardware was once again back to normal.

But it wasn't, Galway knew as he stood gazing across the bloodstained pavement. It would never be normal again. Men had fallen here, and with their deaths this place was subtly but forever changed.

He'd seen the same thing back on Plinry. Far too many times.

He heard a footstep, and turned to see Haberdae come up behind him. "They gave the spotters the slip," he said, his voice dark and cold. "Dumped the car and slipped away while it was dodging one of Shaw's laser barrages."

Galway nodded. He'd known that would happen, of course. He'd predicted as much in the command van as soon as the blackcollars had commandeered the vehicle and roared their way out of Haberdae's trap.

But there was nothing to be gained by bringing that up now. For the first time in the six months since Galway and Judas had first arrived on Khala, Haberdae had completely lost his condescending smugness. Now, finally, he truly understood what it was the blackcollars represented.

And he was angry. Deeply and bitterly angry.

"At least they don't have the car anymore," Galway

commented, searching for some bright spot in all this. "With those onboard transponders that let the cars into the government center—"

"Into the inner garage areas," Haberdae cut him off tartly. "And you know perfectly well they're as secure as the wall itself."

"Of course," Galway said quickly, not believing it for a minute. Unlike the Security men on the wall and outer gates, the guards in the garages wouldn't be expecting anyone but high government officials to be driving into their areas. It was exactly the sort of mental blind spot that blackcollars loved to play with.

"Never mind the car anyway," Haberdae went on grimly. "You know Taakh better than I do. When's he going to pick out a few of my men to kill over this?"

"Actually, I don't think he will," Galway said. "Don't forget, he personally signed off on—" *your plan* "—on tonight's plan. He can't start passing out responsibility for the defeat without taking some of it for himself, and he has way too much pride for that. I'm guessing he'll stay as quiet as possible and wait for it to go away."

Haberdae let his gaze sweep slowly over the area. "You're the one who brought these men here, Galway," he said. His voice was controlled, almost calm, but there was the odor of death beneath it. "You're the one who turned them loose on my city and my world."

"They're not *loose*, Prefect," Galway said, an icy shiver running through him. Haberdae was looking for someone to kill . . . and Galway was the closest likely target. "Judas is with them. They *are* under control."

"Eight of my men just died," Haberdae reminded him,

the death-odor growing stronger. "You call that being under control?"

"We pushed them too hard, and we paid the price," Galway said, again fighting against the urge to remind Haberdae that it was his rashness that had brought this disaster down on them. "There's nothing we can do about it now except make sure those deaths ultimately serve some purpose."

Haberdae snorted. "Like proving to the blackcollars how infallible they are?"

"Like making this work," Galway countered, some anger of his own starting to stir inside him. He'd had just about enough of Haberdae's attitude. *All* of his attitudes. "We've made an attempt to capture them, which Lathe probably would have expected somewhere along the line anyway. So now we pull back as if we're licking our wounds and let him have a free hand to plan the Khorstron attack."

"Unless Shaw still insists on running the show," Haberdae pointed out. "In which case we're right back where we started."

"We'll find out soon enough," Galway said. "But even if Shaw still wants overall command authority, he has to be smart enough to realize now that he's in a real war. And war is no place for petty rivalries."

Haberdae looked sideways at him. "Like ours?"

Galway grimaced. "That's not what I meant."

"No, of course not." Haberdae looked back at the parking lot. "You can call it petty if you want, Galway. But *I'm* the one responsible for what happens on Khala. Not the Ryqril; certainly not you. It was *my* men who died here tonight . . . and someone's going to pay for that."

Galway shivered. "You're welcome to hold that thought," he said. "Just be careful to keep it within the guidelines of the plan."

"Oh, don't worry," Haberdae said tartly. "I would never do anything to upset *the plan*. Are you finished here?"

"Yes," Galway said. In fact, he'd been finished several minutes ago. "We should get to the hospital and start debriefing any of the injured who are ready to talk."

"You go ahead," Haberdae said. "I've got some other business to attend to first." Turning, he strode off toward the handful of vehicles parked behind them.

"Fine," Galway murmured softly to himself as he watched the other go. "I guess I'll see you later."

Caine's breakfast delivery had come early, despite his late-night arrival at his new quarters. Unlike the silent midnight raid, though, this one had come with all the casual noise and bustle that one would expect from a normal operating prison.

It was only after he'd finished the meal bars and tea and was able to surreptitiously check the cameras that he realized he'd underestimated the opposition. Instead of simply and obviously removing the moistened bits of paper Caine had used to blind them, they'd replaced the paper with something that looked almost exactly the same but was presumably treated to actually be transparent.

He'd spent the day again listening at the door while pretending to fiddle with the lock, all the while trying to decide how he should respond to their little reverse sabotage gambit. Now, as evening began to fade toward night, he still didn't have an answer.

But there were other answers he did have, at least preliminary ones. The building's power generator appeared to be on this level, somewhere at the far end of the corridor from the elevator they'd brought him in on. There were always two guards on duty outside his cell, that number doubling whenever his door was going to be opened for meal delivery. There were also at least six other guards quartered in other rooms on this level, with duty shifts changing three times a day. His watch, like his clothes, had gone with Galway's imported replacement, but Caine had a good time sense and was pretty sure the shift changes were at more or less the standard eight/four/midnight hours.

Occasionally, the pitch of the generator hum would change, and shortly thereafter he would hear one or two men arrive and head down the corridor at a more casual civilian gait than the crisper step of the guards. Either the generator required periodic care and feeding, or else it was old and cranky enough that it had to be occasionally persuaded to keep working.

Those, at least, were the basics of what he had to work with, though he would need another day or two of observation before he would feel confident enough of the prison's routine to make any sort of overt move. Hopefully, he would have that time.

In the distance, he heard the elevator doors open, and the footsteps of three Security men heading his way.

Quickly, he slid his paper probe out of sight inside the collar of his jumpsuit and hopped up from the comfort chair. Grabbing the arms, he lugged it back across the floor to where it usually sat near the center of the room and picked up the top few sheets of paper from his reading stack on the floor.

He was settled again in the chair, pretending to be engrossed in the book, when the lock clicked and the door swung open.

But it wasn't the evening meal he'd been expecting. Instead, a big man he'd never seen before strode into the room, his eyes hard as he gazed at Caine. "So you're Caine," he said without preamble.

"Unless Galway got the two of us mixed up," Caine said. "You my new roommate?"

The other's eyes hardened even more. "You think you're cute, don't you?" he said softly. "You think you're like all those other blackcollars, ready to take on the world and beat it to a pulp."

"Actually, people in orange jumpsuits usually aren't the ones doing the beating," Caine reminded him. "Mr.—ah . . .?"

"Prefect," the other corrected him darkly. "Prefect Daov Haberdae, commanding all Security forces on Khala."

"Ah," Caine said, nodding. "Except for the ones Prefect Galway's commandeered, I assume."

Haberdae hissed out a breath. "I don't know what it is with you backwater Plinry rats," he ground out, taking a step forward. As he did so, a pair of guards stepped hastily into the room behind him, their paral-dart guns leveled warningly at Caine's chest. "What is it that makes you think you're better than the rest of us?"

"You got me," Caine said, wondering if he should mention that, strictly speaking, he was actually from

Earth, not Plinry. "What's the matter? Isn't Galway saluting or sirring you properly?"

Without warning, the big man charged.

He was at the chair in three quick steps, slapping the pages out of Caine's hand and hauling Caine bodily to his feet by the front of his orange jumpsuit. "I lost eight men today, you son of a snake," he snarled, his nose bare centimeters from Caine's. "*Eight men.*"

With an effort, Caine forced himself to remain impassive. He could drop the man in an instant, he knew. A single properly placed blow could stun him, knock him cold, or permanently cripple him—Caine's choice.

But this wasn't the time. The cell door was open, but the guards were deployed and alert, their guns out and ready. All an attack on Haberdae would buy him would be another period of paralysis.

Besides, if he was very, *very* clever . . .

"Eight men, huh?" he commented, looking Haberdae straight in the eye. "Lathe must have been feeling generous."

And an instant later Caine was flying across the room as Haberdae hurled him sideways toward the wall.

Reflexively, Caine twisted his legs and arms around, trying to get his feet back under him. He made it in time and hit the floor a meter from the end of the bunk bed.

He could have stuck the landing like a professional gymnast, a feat which would no doubt have impressed the watching guards. Instead, he continued to stagger in the direction he'd been thrown, his arms flailing as if he was fighting to get his balance back, watching out of the corner of his eye as he aimed for just the right spot. With an impressively loud clatter, he slammed into the end of the bunk bed, the impact turning him halfway around as his hands again waved around as if for balance.

And under cover of the movement, his fingertips deftly flicked off the gimmicked paper his midnight visitors had put over the hidden camera lens.

He turned back around to find that Haberdae had followed him across the room. Again the big man grabbed a fistful of his jumpsuit, hauling him completely upright. "You're going to die, Caine," Haberdae said, his voice too low for anyone but Caine to hear. "You hear me? Whatever Galway said or promised, you *are* going to die before this is over. And Lathe and your other friends are going to die, too."

"You'll have no trouble killing me," Caine assured him. "Best of luck with the others."

"Oh, there won't be any luck involved," Haberdae assured him. "I already know how I'm going to do it. The Khorstron Tactical Center, the one Galway thinks Lathe can break into? Right outside the central core area are a set of autotarget defense lasers strong enough to punch straight through your fancy flexarmor. Galway plans to have them shut off, to make sure the blackcollars can get all the way to the very center."

He tightened his grip. "Only they won't be," he said. "I'm going to be right there when they attack . . . and I'm going to make sure they're live and tracking. I only wish there was a way to let them know who it was who beat them."

Letting go of the jumpsuit, he gave Caine a sharp shove backward into the end of the bunk bed. "Enjoy your night," he said. "It's one of the last you'll ever have."

Turning, he strode out of the room. The two guards waited until he was in the corridor, then backed out behind him. "Don't forget your people still owe me dinner," Caine called after him as the door swung shut.

He stayed where he was for another minute, half expecting Haberdae to decide he had a little more anger to get out of his system. But the door remained closed, and eventually Caine headed across the room and began collecting the papers the prefect had knocked out of his hand. By and by, as he went about his limited range of options for his evening activities, he would pretend to notice that the camera by the bed had been unblocked and use another bit of soapy paper to block it again. Then, just to make sure, he would naturally replace the paper on the other camera.

And then he would see whether they would be brave enough to make another quiet excursion into his room tonight to again undo his sabotage.

He hoped they would. He hoped it very much.

The last of the debriefings had been completed, and Galway had returned to his quarters and was preparing for bed when Judas's message came. While insisting he maintain overall command of the Khorstron Center operation, Shaw had nevertheless agreed to turn over planning to Lathe.

It was a victory of sorts, Galway knew. Moreover, it was exactly as he'd predicted. Maybe it would finally convince Haberdae that he did indeed know what he was doing, and persuade the other to give him at least a little genuine cooperation.

But ultimately, it didn't matter whether Haberdae came around or not. Lathe would succeed in penetrating the Khorstron center; and when he did even the most skeptical Ryq would have no choice but to recognize the valuable resource they had in the blackcollars.

After that, there would be nowhere to go but up. Galway would guide, and Lathe would serve, and Plinry's safety would be assured. After years of bare subsistence, the Ryqril would finally be forced to do right by his people.

He was still smiling at that thought when he drifted off to sleep.

CHAPTER 9

The meal they'd set out in front of Poirot reminded him of the Sunday brunches his parents had sometimes taken him and his sisters to before the war: a strange combination of breakfast and dinner foods, all served together. Apparently, at four o'clock in the afternoon following a fifteen-hour sleep, no one had been quite sure exactly which meal it was.

Poirot didn't care. He was ravenously hungry, and devoured the eggs and sausage and roast pork and garlic bread without worrying about whether they really went together or not.

When he was finished, the entire crowd went back to the conversation room and Skyler told him the whole story.

"I'll be damned," Poirot murmured when he'd finished, eyeing Anne Silcox with new appreciation. "And your people came up with this stuff all by themselves?"

"Basically," she said, her eyes staring unblinkingly at him. Clearly, she wasn't nearly as comfortable in the presence of Denver's Security chief as Skyler was.

Which, as far as he was concerned, made her considerably smarter than the big blackcollar. "It's amazing," he commented, looking back at Skyler. "So what exactly is the plan?"

"The plan *was* to use Phoenix and their Whiplashed people to create a level of chaos the Ryqril have never experienced on any of their conquered worlds," Skyler said. "Unfortunately, you now have most of Phoenix's leaders, and it further appears that none of our potential moles are willing to play ball. The plan therefore is going to require some drastic revision." His lip twitched. "We were thinking you might be able to help us out with that."

Silcox shifted in her chair, but remained silent. "I'm flattered that you think I could be of assistance," Poirot said, choosing his words carefully. "But I have to admit this has thrown me for a double spin. It's going to take a while to get used to it."

"You've got three hours," Skyler said bluntly. "We're sending you back into Athena tonight."

Poirot shook his head. "Impossible."

"*Make* it possible," Silcox retorted. "Those are my people in there."

"I didn't mean it was impossible to go back," Poirot said hastily, lifting his hands. "I meant it's going to take a while for me to come to grips with my new brain and figure out how to best be of service."

"I want my people," Silcox insisted.

"We'll get them," Skyler assured her, his eyes steady on Poirot. "You can at least get them moved out of Athena, can't you?"

Poirot felt his forehead creasing. "Are you thinking about grabbing them en route to somewhere else?"

"Why not?" Skyler asked. "We've got Anne and Phoenix's cache of weapons, plus Reger and whatever manpower he can pull together. And now we've got you and your intimate knowledge of how Security does things." He gestured to the three black-clad men standing a silent half circle behind him. "And we have four black-collars. What more do we need?"

Poirot looked around the room, his skin prickling. An actual blackcollar strategy session . . . and here he was, right in the middle of it.

The question now was how to take full advantage of the opportunity. "Offhand, a few more blackcollars comes to mind," he commented, keeping his voice light and casual. "I don't suppose you have any more stashed away any-where."

Skyler grimaced. "We should have one more, but his hang glider went down early and we haven't been able to make contact. Reger sent out some searchers, but the whole area is crawling with your people and they had to pull back."

"Any idea where he might be?"

"Probably gone to ground waiting for everyone to clear out," Skyler said. "I'm not particularly worried, but it does look like we're going to be short handed the next couple of days. Still, as near as we can figure, you only have six of Anne's people. Four of us should be plenty."

"They've also got fifteen of *my* men," Reger spoke up tartly. "You *were* planning to get them out, too, weren't you?"

"They won't be a problem," Skyler assured him. "As soon as Security confirms they don't know anything about Phoenix, they'll probably let them go."

"Not necessarily," Poirot warned. Actually, Skyler was right, but the more he could confuse and muddy this whole thing, the better. "Given what we suspect about Reger's connection to Phoenix, Colonel Bailey might decide to keep his men on general principles."

"Fine," Reger said, a subtle menace in his tone. "But once you're back in Athena, *you* could let them go. Right?"

Poirot suppressed a grimace. This was no time to get backed into a corner. "Provided I can come up with a good reason to do so, yes," he said. "But with me having been in your hands this long, Bailey may have some suspicions."

"What suspicions?" Reger scoffed. "What could we possibly have done to you?"

Poirot felt a flicker of contempt. Was he going to have to do *all* their thinking for them? "Well, you *did* mention Whiplash in his presence," he reminded them. "He'll certainly be trying to chase down that reference."

"Which just means we'll need a good excuse to let them go," Skyler said. "These are the pieces we have. Let's start putting them together."

Flynn was munching quietly on a ration bar, wondering how much more daylight was left, when he heard the sound of a large animal coming through the underbrush.

He looked over at Jensen. The blackcollar was asleep, his head pillowed on his pack, his breathing shallow but steady. Setting his ration bar on the ground, Flynn slid his *nunchaku* from its sheath. The sound came again, this time loud enough for Flynn to tag its direction as coming from due north. Getting up into a crouch, careful not to brush the low branches sagging down above him, he worked his way around to the south side of the tree and eased his way out from beneath the branches.

The sky had clouded over since they'd gone to ground that morning, with furrows of gray now forming a backdrop to the mountain peaks. *Nunchaku* in hand, he moved toward a stubby bush a few meters away, wincing at the soft crunching sounds he made in the leaves as he walked. So far the approaching animal hadn't appeared, but from the increasingly loud swishing sounds it could be anytime now. Flynn made it to his target bush and crouched down, gripping his *nunchaku* tightly, hoping like hell it wasn't the bear back for a rematch. Through the branches of his cover he caught a glimpse of a large, dark shape approaching—

And to his amazement, the biggest brown Labrador retriever he'd ever seen ambled into view.

He exhaled silently, his first instinctive relief that it wasn't the bear quickly giving way to the more sobering reality that this might actually be worse. The dog, he could see now, was wearing a collar of some sort; and dog plus collar equaled owner. Here, a few klicks from a Ryqril base, dog plus owner might very well equal Security tracker.

The Lab was wandering toward the tree where Jensen lay hidden, his tail wagging back and forth as he snuffled at bushes and exposed tree roots. Behind him, Flynn could hear a couple of sets of footsteps approaching.

Shifting his *nunchaku* to his left hand, he pulled out a throwing knife and settled his mind into combat stance. Jensen, it was whispered among the trainees, had once undergone a full-blown Security interrogation. He wasn't going to have to go through that again, not if Flynn could help it.

Once again, the expectation proved worse than the reality. The two men who strode into view were tall and bearded, wearing haphazard and threadbare outfits that a proper Security man wouldn't be caught dead in. The younger of the two was probably no more than a year or two older than Flynn's own twenty-three, while the older was well into his fifties, with the leathery skin that came of a lifetime outdoors. There was also a distinct family resemblance, he noticed, particularly around the mouth and eyes.

The resemblance between the long-barreled flechette rifles they carried propped over their shoulders was even more pronounced.

Flynn sank a little lower behind his bush, indecision twisting through him. On the one hand, these could be precisely the sort of people he'd planned to go looking for, locals who could point him to the doctor Jensen needed so badly. But on the other hand, through his long hours of forced idleness he'd reluctantly concluded that Jensen's analysis of the possibilities had probably been more accurate than his own. Finding a competent doctor out here in the wilderness might be well-nigh impossible.

And even if they did find one, there would be no way of knowing where his loyalties lay. Not until it was too late.

No, he decided suddenly. Best to just let the two rabbit

hunters pass by and hope Jensen's injuries weren't as bad as they'd seemed this morning.

And then, to his dismay, the Lab stopped in his tracks, turned his massive head, and bounded straight toward the tree where Jensen was hidden.

There was no time for Flynn to think it through. An instant later he was on his feet, his right arm cocked over his shoulder with the knife poised to throw. "Hold it," he snapped.

The younger man jerked in surprise at Flynn's sudden appearance, his rifle bouncing off his shoulder as he swung the weapon down toward firing position. But the older man was quicker. His left hand snaked out to catch the barrel as it fell, his own rifle staying firmly against his shoulder. "Easy, son," he called calmly toward Flynn. "We ain't gonna hurt you."

"That's good to know," Flynn said, trying to watch the younger man and the dog at the same time. The animal had turned at Flynn's warning and now seemed to be torn between the idea of checking out the newcomer or continuing on to the tree.

The older man apparently misinterpreted Flynn's split attention. "You ain't worried about Joe Pup, here, are ya?" he asked, gesturing toward the dog. "He ain't gonna hurt you none, neither." He gave a short whistle. "C'mere, Joe Pup. Heel."

Obediently, the Lab loped over and came to a halt at his side, panting cheerfully. "So who are you, anyway?" the older man went on. "Don't hardly think I seen you around here afore."

"No, I'm just passing through," Flynn said.

"Goin' anyplace special?"

Flynn braced himself. This was going to be uncomfortably risky, he knew. But as Lathe had often said, when data was inadequate instincts were all anyone had, and his instincts told him these men were no friends of the Ryqril or their loyalty-conditioned collaborators. "I was hoping to find a doctor, actually," he said, watching them closely.

"Yeah?" the younger man said suspiciously. "You look pert' healthy t' me. Got some disease that don't show?"

"I've got a sick friend," Flynn said. "But you were obviously on your way somewhere. If you can point me in the direction of a doctor, I'd appreciate it. If not, I'll let you be on your way."

"Right decent of you," the older man said dryly. "But this here's *our* home, not yours. *You're* the one who gets to move on if someone's gotta get goin'."

Abruptly, his eyes hardened. "Unless you want to come clean and tell us who you really are," he warned. "And I mean right now." And on the last word, he let go his grip on the younger man's rifle.

And before Flynn could react, the barrel finished its downward swing to land with a slap in the younger man's left hand.

Pointed directly at Flynn's face.

Flynn dropped into a crouch, twisting at his knees and waist as he fell, using the momentum of his corkscrew spin for extra power as he whipped the knife around and threw it at the gunman. At the last instant he gave the weapon just enough extra torque for an additional half turn, and as he completed his spin he saw it slam hilt first against the younger man's forehead. The other's gun swung wildly off target as he staggered a couple of steps back, and Flynn shifted his attention to the other man.

He was still standing motionless, apparently frozen in place by Flynn's unexpected counterattack, his own gun still propped against his shoulder. Leaping back to his feet, Flynn shifted his *nunchaku* to his right hand and charged, hoping he could cover the distance before either man recovered enough for another attack.

But he was too late. The younger man was tougher than he looked; and even as the Lab gave out a startled yip and laid his ears back he got his gun back under control. Once again the weapon swung to point at Flynn.

And with the flat *crack* of stone on metal, the gun leapt sideways out of his hands.

"That'll do, gentlemen," a croaking voice came seemingly from nowhere. Even knowing who it was, it still took Flynn a second to recognize the voice as Jensen's. There was a swish of branches, and Jensen appeared from beneath the tree, his slingshot cocked and ready. "Put the gun on the ground," he continued, pointing the weapon at the older man, whose rifle was still propped against his shoulder. "Then both of you get going."

"That won't be necessary," the older man said calmly, lowering his gun to the ground. "My apologies for the test, but we had to be sure."

"Sure about what?" Flynn demanded. "That we weren't easy targets?"

The older man inclined his head toward Jensen. "That you were blackcollars."

"Toby was right," the younger man said, massaging his forehead where Flynn's knife had caught him. "You must have come in on last night's shuttle glide path. Security's spotters have been buzzing over that area all day."

Flynn glanced over his shoulder, but the trees blocked his view of that part of the sky. "Toby keeps track of such things, does he?"

"He's got a fair amount of time on his hands," the older man said dryly. "He's also got a cabin a couple hundred meters upslope of our town where he gets a good view of pretty much everything that goes on."

"And whose side is Toby on?" Jensen asked.

The older man shrugged. "All he needed to do was call Security and suggest they might be looking too far east," he pointed out. "But he asked us to come look for you instead." He lifted his eyebrows. "And you, my friend, are in considerable pain. What can we do to help?"

"I don't know," Jensen said. "What *can* you do to help?"

"Anything I can." To Flynn's surprise, the older man straightened up into military attention. "John Adamson, former sergeant-medic with the TDE Army of Western America."

For a moment, Jensen didn't speak. Then, slowly, he released the tension on his slingshot pouch and lowered the weapon. "I may have a cracked rib or two," he said.

"And you made it this far?" Adamson asked as he crossed over to Jensen and carefully opened his coat and shirt.

"Actually, it only happened on the far side of that ridge," Jensen said. "We ran into a bear."

"You fought a *bear*?" the younger man said, his eyes widening.

"Only a little one," Jensen said, wincing as Adamson's fingers probed gently at his side.

"Yeah, right," the younger man said. "Five to one it was Bessie."

"You name the animals around here?" Flynn asked.

"Just certain ones," Adamson said. "Bessie's sort of a fixture in these parts. By the way, this is my son, Vernon."

"Call me Trapper," the younger Adamson said. "Okay if I get the rifles?"

"Go ahead," Jensen told him. "How bad is it?"

"Bad enough," Adamson said. "I'll need to get you to my house and get this—what's it called? flexarmor?—get this flexarmor off you before I'll know for sure."

"We going to want a stretcher, Dad?" Trapper asked as he retrieved the two rifles.

"Probably," Adamson said, looking at Flynn. "You've got the longest coat. Mind if we borrow it?"

"Sure," Flynn said, unfastening his coat as he walked toward them.

"His name's Flynn, by the way," Jensen said. "How far are we going?"

"A kilometer or so," Adamson said. "Not too far." His lips compressed briefly as he took Flynn's coat and started fastening it closed again. "The trick's going to be sneaking you in past the rest of the townspeople."

"And the sensor pylon," Trapper added.

"The *what*?" Flynn demanded, his hand involuntarily squeezing his *nunchaku*.

"Relax—it's mainly an aircraft spotter," Adamson assured him. "Fully automated, put there to make sure nothing sneaks up on their homestead out at Idaho Springs. Should be easy enough to keep you out of its view."

"Our job as a town is to keep it maintained," Trapper explained. "That was the price thirty years ago for Security to let us stay out here instead of herding us back to Denver like they did with the people in a lot of the other small towns."

"With all of you being properly loyalty-conditioned, of course?" Flynn asked.

"Oddly enough, no," Adamson said, kneeling down and spreading Flynn's coat flat on the ground, flipping over the sleeves to point above the collar. "You have to remember that this was right after the Ryqril occupation began, when they were scrambling to loyalty-condition every possible threat. Someone apparently decided a hundred or so people out in the middle of nowhere weren't worth the effort."

"Especially since the pylon was mostly automated anyway," Trapper added, handing his father one of the rifles.

"Doesn't mean we're all rabidly anti-Ryqril, of course," Adamson said, sliding the rifle up the hem of the coat and pulling the barrel up into the right-hand sleeve. "Actually, most people are in a kind of live/let live mode these days." He slid the other rifle up the other side, poking it through the left-hand sleeve. "But there are still some of us left who haven't forgotten," he added, straightening up and looking at Jensen. "Your carriage awaits you, Commando. You need a hand getting down?"

"I can make it," Jensen said. "Shouldn't we wait until nightfall, though?"

"It'll be tricky enough when we can see where we're going," Adamson said. "Don't worry, we'll hear anything that's coming long before it can see or hear us."

Jensen gave him a rather wan smile. "Because this here's your home, and you know pert' much what you're all doin'?"

"Something like that," Adamson said, smiling back. "Don't worry, no one in Shelter Valley actually talks that way. We just bring it out for the tourists."

"I'm sure you get so many," Jensen said. "Flynn, go get the packs, will you?"

By the time Flynn emerged Jensen had made it to the ground and was lying on his back on the coat. "Afraid I don't have as much strength and stamina as I used to," Adamson confessed, gesturing Flynn toward the rifle stocks sticking out of the coat by Jensen's feet. "But I can carry the packs."

"We've got them," Trapper said, taking one of the packs from Flynn and putting it on as he moved to the front of the makeshift stretcher. "Dad, can you help Jensen with his legs?"

"Sure," Adamson said, stepping over and getting a grip on Jensen's ankles.

"Shouldn't we unload the guns?" Flynn asked as that thought suddenly struck him.

"They aren't loaded," Adamson assured him. "We didn't want a misfire or accident hurting anyone."

"We've got a few rounds in our pockets if we need them," Trapper said, squatting down and getting a grip on the coat sleeves and the rifle barrels inside them. "Say when."

A moment later he and Flynn had the makeshift stretcher up, with Jensen's back and head lying on the coat and his legs angled up to rest on Trapper's shoulders. "I know this is going to sound ridiculous," Adamson said, stepping in front of his son, "but try not to bounce him more than necessary."

"Don't worry," Flynn said, cocking an eyebrow down at Jensen. "It'll be as smooth as a drop pod entry."

"Terrific," Jensen said, closing his eyes melodramatically. "I'm dead."

"Not on my watch, you aren't," Adamson said firmly. He gave a short whistle, and the big Lab bounded back into view from behind a stand of trees, clearly eager to get moving. "Let's go."

CHAPTER 10

They dropped Poirot off in a quiet part of town five blocks from the main Athena entrance, and by the time he got the blindfold off their car had disappeared around a corner.

They'd left him his hailer, and for a minute he considered calling an autocab to take him the rest of the way. But it was a nice night, and he had a lot to think about. Squaring his shoulders, he got his bearings and headed off at a brisk walk.

He quickly regretted the decision. Quiet though the area might have been, there were still plenty of people around, none of whom had apparently ever seen a Security general before. Everyone seemed to find it necessary to stop and stare, many of them turning around and continuing their examination even after he'd passed. Some of those stares, he noted uncomfortably, had a degree of hostility to them.

But no one tried to stop him, or even talk to him, and fifteen minutes after leaving the car he turned at last into the wide, well-lit thoroughfare that led to the high fence and heavy gate of the Athena government center.

The guards at the gatehouse saw him coming, of course, and they certainly recognized him. But to his irritation, none of them made any move to leave their bunker to come out and meet him. By the time he came to a halt in front of the gatehouse's thick-glassed window, he was ready to break all four of them back to private.

"General Poirot," he identified himself tartly, as if there could be any doubt. "Open up."

No one made a move toward the gate control. "Welcome back, General," the duty lieutenant said, his voice strangely flat as it came through the speaker grill below the window. "Colonel Bailey's been extremely concerned about you."

"Then Colonel Bailey will want to see me, won't he?" Poirot growled.

"Yes, sir," the lieutenant said, still not moving. "Your escort's on its way."

His *escort*? "I don't need an escort, Lieutenant," he said, letting his tone drop into official warning territory. "Just open the damn gate."

The other looked down at the bank of monitors beneath the window and nodded. "As you wish, sir," he said. Reaching down, he twisted the release and the gate swung open. Giving him one final glare, Poirot left the window and strode through the gateway.

And stopped short. Lined up facing him were three cars and a group of eight Security men, some still in the process of getting out of the vehicles. "What's all this?" he demanded.

"We have orders to take you to headquarters, General," the sergeant in charge said, his voice as stiff as the duty lieutenant's had been. "If you'll come this way, please?"

"Absolutely," Poirot said between clenched teeth. Bailey, he promised himself darkly, was going to hurt for this.

He stomped over and got into the nearest vehicle's rear seat. A moment later he had to move quickly to the center as two of the others climbed in with him, one on either side. Two more got into the front, the rest sorting themselves out between the remaining two cars, and a minute later all three vehicles were headed inward through Athena's streets. The other two cars, Poirot noted, had taken up positions in front of and behind him, standard configuration for transporting VIPs. At least Bailey—or the sergeant—had gotten that part right.

A few minutes later they reached the Security building. To Poirot's continued annoyance, though, they bypassed the main entrance and took him instead in through the tunnel. There, his protests ignored, he was put through the full battery of scans as the techs checked him for weapons, explosives, and poisons.

He half expected them to go all the way and do a strip search. Fortunately for Bailey, even the colonel apparently didn't have quite enough nerve to try that one.

Bailey was waiting for him in the middle of the situation room, a young lieutenant Poirot didn't recognize at his side. "Welcome back, General," Bailey said, nodding as Poirot strode up to them. His words were polite enough, but there was an odd sort of distance to his tone and expression. "I'm pleased to find you alive and well."

"I'm rather pleased about that myself," Poirot growled.

"You'd better have a damn good reason for what you just put me through." He shifted his glare to the lieutenant. "Who are you?"

"Lieutenant Ramirez, Boulder Security office," the other identified himself. "I've been assisting Colonel Bailey with his efforts to find you."

"Well, I'm found," Poirot said. "Thank you for your assistance. Now go home."

"I'd like the lieutenant to stay a little longer, if you don't mind," Bailey put in. "There are a few matters we all need to discuss." He gestured to the row of office and conference room doors at the rear of the situation room. "If you'll come this way, please?"

"No, we're going to do this right here, Colonel," Poirot ground out, not moving a millimeter. There were a dozen other Security men working the various status and command boards, and it wouldn't do them any harm to hear what happened to a subordinate who forgot how to properly treat a superior officer. "Let's start with why I was put through a weapons scan before even being offered medical treatment."

"Do you *need* medical treatment, sir?"

"Answer the question, Colonel."

Bailey's lip twitched. "You've been in enemy hands for nearly a day, sir," he said reluctantly. "We had to make sure you weren't bringing in anything dangerous."

"And you don't think I'd have noticed if something like that had been planted on me?"

Bailey glanced at the other men at the boards. "Sir, I really think we'd be more comfortable in the conference room—"

"Answer the *question*, damn it."

Bailey seemed to brace himself. "If you insist, sir. No, not necessarily."

"Not *necessarily*?" Poirot echoed, hardly believing his ears. "You think they could have planted a bomb or loaded my pockets with cyanide ampoules without—?"

"Have you ever heard of Whiplash, General?" Ramirez asked.

Poirot glared at him. How *dare* he interrupt—?

And then, abruptly, it hit him . . . and in that single heartbeat his simmering anger vanished into a chill like an arctic breeze. "What exactly are you implying, Colonel?" he asked between stiff lips.

"I think you know, sir," Bailey said. "You've been in blackcollar hands, and the blackcollars apparently have a drug that removes loyalty-conditioning. What would *you* be thinking in my place?"

For a long moment Poirot couldn't find his voice. This couldn't be happening. "All right," he said at last, forcing a calmness he most certainly didn't feel. "Yes, they injected me with the stuff. And yes, they think I'm on their side now. But I'm not."

Bailey's expression didn't even twitch. "No?"

"Of course not," Poirot insisted. "If we move fast, we have a chance to nail them once and for all."

"I suppose they sat down and discussed their plans with you, too?" Bailey suggested.

Poirot curled his hand into a frustrated fist. "They think I'm on their side," he repeated. "They think that once someone's loyalty-conditioning is gone he's automatically filled with revolutionary fervor."

"And that's not true?" Ramirez asked.

"Don't be ridiculous," Poirot snapped. "These people have no idea how much destruction the Ryqril could rain on Denver if they got it into their heads to do so. But I do. The only reason they don't—the *only* reason—is that they're secure in the knowledge that we have the district under control. Do you think I'd be stupid enough to deliberately wreck that status quo?"

For a minute Bailey gazed at him in silence. Poirot stared back, feeling sweat trickling down his back. "All right," the colonel said at last. The words were conciliatory, but Poirot could tell from his tone that he still wasn't convinced. "Let's go sit down and you can tell us all about it."

Poirot looked around the room. All the other Security men were busy at their posts, none of them giving any indication that they might have overheard the conversation.

But he knew they had. All of them. "Of course," he said. "Lead the way."

Silently, they all headed back to the conference room. Bailey opened the door and gestured, and Poirot stepped inside.

And came to an abrupt halt. Seated at the far end of the table were a pair of Ryqril. "Please sit down, sir," Bailey said, squeezing through the doorway past Poirot and pointing to the chair at the near end.

Silently, Poirot started forward again and sat down in the indicated chair, his brain mechanically registering the patterns on the aliens' baldrics. One of them was a battle architect, a senior tactical officer and the highest non-command rank in the Ryqril military.

The other was a *khassq*-class warrior.

"General Poirot, let me introduce Battle Architect Daasaa and *Khassq* Warrior Halaak," Bailey said as he and Ramirez sat down on either side of Poirot. "They'll be supervising us during this crisis."

Poirot felt his stomach tighten. So it was a crisis now? "With all due and proper deference," he said, "I don't see it being quite that serious yet. As I told Colonel Bailey, my loyalty remains firmly with the government and the Ryqril."

"Yet the re'els think otherrise?" Daasaa asked.

"Yes, they do," Poirot said. "And in that error lies the key to their defeat, because I know what they intend to do."

Daasaa's dark eyes bored into Poirot's face. "Tell us."

Poirot took a careful breath. This was it. Somehow, he had to convince them that he was still on their side. "First of all, they want to rescue the members of Phoenix that Colonel Bailey arrested yesterday." He looked at Bailey. "I take it they're undergoing interrogation?"

"That's how we found out about Whiplash," Bailey said.

"Ah," Poirot said, feeling a flush of embarrassment. Of course that was how they would have learned about it. "At any rate, they want me to order the prisoners transferred someplace else—Silcox suggested the Colorado Springs interrogation center—so they can ambush the convoy along the way."

"They dae not intend tae in'ade Athena to rescae they?" Daasaa asked.

"They invaded Athena once before," Poirot reminded him, wincing at the memory. "I don't think they'd want to try that again."

"I disagree," Daasaa countered. "They ha' done that runce. They there'ore know they can dae it again."

"I understand, Your Eminence," Poirot said. "But I don't get the sense that that's how blackcollars do things."

"It is 'asic tactics," Daasaa insisted. "A rarrior uses the skills he has."

"In general, that's certainly true," Poirot agreed carefully. "But if the warrior's opponent has already seen a particular tactic in action, it might make sense to switch to something—"

"The re'els are o' no use tae they," Halaak cut him off firmly. "They rish yae tae send out a con'oy tae draw yaer nen aray fron Athena."

Poirot looked at Bailey in silent appeal. But the colonel's face was expressionless. "All right, perhaps they are planning an attack on Athena," he said, conceding defeat. "There's no reason we can't prepare for both possibilities."

"Tae in'ade Athena, they rill need an aircra't," Daasaa went on. "Re nust guard against that."

Poirot squeezed the arm of his chair tightly. Was Ryqril thinking really so limited that they could only look back at what had already been done? Was that why they needed to loyalty-condition their conquered peoples, so those peoples could be trusted to do their thinking for them? "This time they won't have access to any aircraft, Your Eminence," he promised. "We won't be sending out any ambulances they can commandeer, or patrol boats, or—"

"The spotters," Ramirez said suddenly.

All eyes turned to him. "What?" Poirot asked.

"We have spotters flying all over the mountains west of Boulder," Ramirez said, a note of urgency in his voice. "We think one to three more blackcollars might have come in with Skyler's team."

"Skyler said they'd only lost one on the way in," Poirot said. "You haven't found him yet?"

"There's a lot of forest out there," Bailey reminded him. "Not to mention a lot of animals to mess up IR readings. You saying Skyler just volunteered this information?"

"Yes," Poirot murmured, gripping the chair arm a little tighter as a sudden uncertainty dug at him. Now that he thought about it Skyler *had* been pretty loose with that comment. Could the blackcollar have been deliberately feeding him misinformation, expecting that he wouldn't betray his job and his people? "He said the man was probably waiting for the searchers to go away."

"How convenient," Ramirez murmured. "So while we waste time and manpower—"

"It is not rasted," Halaak cut him off sharply. "There *is* another 'lackcollar." His dark eyes seemed to go even darker. "He has killed a Ryq rarrior."

Poirot felt his breath freeze in his throat. "Where?"

"In the hills a'ove our Aegis 'ase," Daasaa said, his eyes going back and forth between the three humans, clearly looking for some kind of reaction. "He ras killed rith a star rea'on in his throat."

Poirot winced. A human killing a Ryq was about as bad as it got. Dimly, he wondered if Skyler had any idea of the crate of snakes his wayward commando had just opened up. "He must have gotten lost," he said. "Probably saw the warrior and panicked."

"Or else was deliberately heading for the base," Ramirez murmured thoughtfully.

"Re *rill* ca'ture he," Halaak said, and Poirot shivered at the menace beneath the words. "Yae rill continue yaer search."

"Yes, Your Eminence," Bailey said, his voice suddenly hesitant. "Are we sure there was just one of them?"

"Re 'ound his glider," Daasaa said. "It had a second glider 'astened 'eneath it."

"One man pretending to be two," Poirot said, nodding. "Splits up the search parties."

"Or intensifies the search," Bailey said. "More to the point, that still leaves one slot unaccounted for in this six-man pod of theirs. What we may have is one blackcollar stirring up trouble while his partner waits quietly for one of the search teams to land an aircar in a convenient location."

"And then uses the s'otter tae in'ade Athena," Daasaa concluded, a note of vindication in his voice. "It is as I said."

"Or they might even be planning to attack the Aegis Mountain base," Ramirez said. "Maybe the first blackcollar wasn't just stirring up trouble, but was scouting it out."

Halaak made a rumbling sound in his chest. "That cannot 'e allored," he ground out. "The 'ase nust 'e 'rotected."

Daasaa motioned to him, and for a minute the two Ryqril held their heads close together as they conversed quietly in Ryqrili. Then, Daasaa straightened up again. "Yae rill rithdraw the s'otters at runce," he ordered. "The ground search rill continue."

A muscle in Bailey's cheek tightened momentarily. "As

you command, Your Eminence," he said. "But I must warn you that without the spotters—"

"Dae yae kestion ne?"

The same cheek muscle twitched again. "No, of course not, Your Eminence," he said hastily. "The spotters will be withdrawn immediately." He looked at Ramirez. "See to it, Lieutenant."

"Yes, sir," Ramirez said, looking quietly relieved to be getting out of this particular frying pan. Standing up, he hurried from the room.

"General 'Oirot?" Halaak asked.

Poirot started. "Yes, Your Eminence?"

"A'ter the 'risoners rere taken, rhat ras their 'lan?"

"Basically, just to cause as much trouble as they could," Poirot said. "Skyler didn't go into details, but I got the feeling they planned to launch attacks on any Security men they could find outside Athena. He also mentioned a cache of weapons Phoenix had hidden somewhere."

"Rhat sort o' rea'ons?" Halaak asked.

"I don't know," Poirot said. "Again, he didn't give any details."

"None of the prisoners has said anything about a weapons cache," Bailey put in.

"Yae rill ask they," Daasaa ordered.

"As you command, Your Eminence," Bailey said. "I'll speak with the interrogators as soon as we're finished here."

"Re are 'inished," Daasaa said. "Go."

Poirot braced himself. "Your Eminence?" he said carefully. "May I ask what you plan to do with the prisoners? If we don't transfer them to Colorado Springs, or at least make some preparations that direction, Skyler will suspect I'm still loyal."

"And?" Daasaa asked.

"And if he suspects that, I won't be able to get any further information from him."

"Re rill *not* gi' u' our 'risoners," Halaak insisted.

"I wasn't suggesting we let the blackcollars actually take them," Poirot assured him. "I'm sure we can keep any rescue attempt from succeeding."

"The general does have a point," Bailey said. "It might prove useful to keep him in their good graces as long as possible. Besides, if we can delay the transfer another day or so, we'll have learned pretty much everything they can tell us anyway. It might be worth the risk to use them as bait."

Again, the two Ryqril huddled into a private conversation. "'Ery rell," Daasaa said. "Yae rill nake 'lans tae trans'er the re'els. They rill lea' Athena the night akhter taenorror."

"As you command, Your Eminence," Poirot said. Finally, they were listening to reason. "I'll have the orders cut—"

"Not yae," Halaak said. "Colonel 'Ailey rill connand."

Even though he'd been half expecting it, it was still a shock. "As you command, Your Eminence," Poirot said again, his throat tight.

Daasaa inclined his head fractionally. "Go."

Neither Poirot nor Bailey spoke until they were back in the situation room, with the door to the conference room firmly shut behind them. "I'm sorry about this, General," Bailey apologized.

"No, you're not," Poirot said sourly. "But I can't really blame you. *Or* them. I just wish there was some way I could prove to you that I'm still loyal."

"I wish there were, too," Bailey said. "But until we come up with something. . . Look, why don't you head down to the infirmary and have yourself checked out? You were right; I really *should* have done that before bringing you up here."

"I'd rather get started on the plans for the prisoner transfer." He eyed Bailey. "You *will* accept my assistance on that, won't you?"

"Of course, sir," Bailey said. "But there'll be time for that after the doctors have checked you over."

Poirot grimaced. But it was clear that the other wasn't going to budge on this one. "As you command," he said, trying not to sound too sarcastic. "I'll be back soon."

He was halfway across the situation room when a pair of Security men detached themselves from the wall and fell quietly into step behind him.

But again, there was nothing he could do about it. With loyalty-conditioning, he reflected grimly, a man always knew who he could trust. Without it, how could anyone know anything?

But there was one thing he *did* know. Skyler would pay for this. He would pay dearly.

Ramirez was waiting by the spotter command console. "Well?" Bailey asked as he walked up.

"They're on their way back," Ramirez confirmed. "We've been in contact with each of the pilots, and they all appear to be our people. Interesting footnote: one of the search teams reports they found a section of drop pod that hadn't deployed."

Bailey frowned. "Someone was killed?"

"No, it hadn't deployed because there was apparently no one using that section," Ramirez explained. "With one slot empty, one man doubling as two, and three of them now in Denver—"

"We have a match on our numbers," Bailey said. "So there *is* just one blackcollar loose in the mountains."

"Which fits with what General Poirot said," Ramirez reminded him. "You think he could be telling the truth about still being loyal?"

"I don't know," Bailey said with a helpless shrug. "Maybe he just gave us the number knowing it's something we'd have been able to chase down on our own anyway."

"Though they certainly went to some trouble making the one man look like two," Ramirez said.

"Unless that was just a giveaway," Bailey said, scowling at the back of the spotter controller's head. This was getting way too complicated for his liking.

"The searchers will keep at it," Ramirez promised. "Speaking of which, I was thinking it might be a good idea to rotate everyone through the Boulder office, even people from Athena. Make sure there aren't any imposters mixed in before we send them trooping back through your gate."

"Good idea," Bailey agreed. "Go ahead and give the orders."

"I already have, sir."

"I see," Bailey said, an odd sensation creeping up his back. "Well. Good."

"We should know about everyone by midnight at the latest," Ramirez went on. "Was anything else decided in there after I left?"

"We're going to pretend General Poirot's genuinely a traitor," Bailey said, studying the other's face. "He and I are going to work out a plan to transfer the Phoenix prisoners to Colorado Springs forty-eight hours from now and see if we can lure the blackcollars out from under their rock."

"All right," Ramirez said slowly. "If you do capture them, you'll be bringing them back here?"

"Yes, we will," Bailey growled, wincing at the memories. "And you can rest assured it will *not* end up like the last time."

"I hope not, sir," Ramirez said evenly. "What would you like me to do next?"

"What do you *want* to do next?" Bailey countered.

A hint of a frown crossed Ramirez's forehead. "Whatever you need, Colonel," he said, sounding a little puzzled. "I'm just here to help out."

"Of course," Bailey murmured. "In that case, why don't you head up to Interrogation and see if they've been able to dig out anything new."

"Yes, sir." Turning, Ramirez headed across the room at a brisk walk.

Bailey watched until he'd disappeared out the door, then crossed over to the tech at the comm station. "I want you to contact the Boulder Security office," he told the other quietly. "Get me the names and files of everyone on duty there tonight."

"Yes, sir," the tech said, frowning briefly up at him. "Anything in particular you're looking for?"

"Not really," Bailey said, trying to sound casual. "I just want to know who's up there. In case something goes wrong."

The tech's lip twitched as he turned back to his board. "Yes, sir."

"And after you do that," Bailey went on, "have someone pull Lieutenant Ramirez's file and send it down to Analysis. I want to know if there've been any reports of peculiar behavior over the past year."

He looked over at the door. "In particular, whether or not he's had any long, unexplained absences."

The woods were dark by the time the lights of Shelter Valley began to wink at them through the trees. "Where exactly is this sensor pylon?" Flynn whispered.

"About ten meters that way," Adamson murmured back, pointing ahead and to the left. "Don't worry—there's no audio pickup."

"What about the rest of the townspeople?" Jensen asked, his voice sounding strained. "Will they all be indoors?"

"I'll keep an eye out," Adamson said. "I'm thinking that maybe you should go straight to Toby's place instead of stopping at the house—it's a lot more private. I can collect my gear and treat you up there."

Flynn looked down at Jensen. He hadn't complained during the trip, but Flynn could tell that the swaying and bouncing were taking their toll. Now Adamson wanted them to extend the trip another half hour or more? "What do you think?" he asked.

"Sounds good to me," Jensen said, clearly working hard to filter the pain out of his voice. "Assuming your arms can hold out that long."

"Our arms are fine," Flynn assured him. "Lead on, Trapper."

Even by Plinry standards the twenty or so haphazardly scattered houses that made up Shelter Valley hardly qualified as a town. Fortunately, as Adamson had predicted, everyone was already indoors. They passed between the houses like shadows, and twenty meters past the last house they reached another path. There Adamson doubled back, and Trapper and Flynn headed up.

It was the steepest patch of ground they'd hit yet, and by the time the slope began to level out Flynn's legs were trembling with fatigue. Fortunately, that was the worst of it, and he made it the rest of the way without the embarrassment of having to call for a break.

The occupant must have been watching for them, because they were still a few steps from the cabin when the door swung open. A short, slender man stood there, framed against the glow of a wood stove behind him. "So I was right," he muttered, stepping back out of their way. "Or maybe not," he corrected himself, turning his head around to peer down at Jensen. "What happened, Trapper? You shoot him?"

"They ran into Bessie," Trapper said, glancing around the cabin and turning toward a section of open floor near the stove.

"No, no—on the bed," the other man said, pointing toward the narrow cot pushed against the rear wall. In contrast to the ramshackle appearance of the rest of the cabin, the bed was neatly made. "Bessie, huh? You have to kill her?"

"Never even saw her," Trapper told him as he and Flynn set Jensen and his makeshift stretcher onto the bed. "They chased her away themselves. Toby, this is

Blackcollar Commando Jensen and Trainee Flynn. Gentlemen, meet Toby, Shelter Valley's very own professional hermit."

"So I was right," Toby murmured, a strange expression on his face. "Blackcollars."

"Just the one," Flynn said, studying what he could see of Toby's face through the full beard. The man was roughly Jensen's age, with a hint of bitterness at the corners of his mouth. "As Trapper said, I'm just a trainee."

"You dress like one, though," Toby said. "So what'd Bessie do to you?"

"Little love tap on the ribs," Jensen told him.

"Lucky you didn't *really* rile her," Toby said grimly. "You want something to eat or drink?"

"Some water would be nice," Jensen said. "Flynn can get it, if you want to point him to the well or stream or whatever."

"No need," Toby said. Picking up a glass from a small table set by the window, he crossed to the opposite corner and a hand-carved wooden sink set into the wall with a faucet above it. He turned the spigot; and to Flynn's mild surprise water gushed out. "You have a cistern on the roof?" he asked as Toby filled the glass.

"Just a little one," Toby said, shutting off the flow and taking the glass to Jensen. "Actually, the water's piped in from a stream that runs down the side of the hill back there. A man can live without a lot of things, but running water isn't something I'd ever want to be without."

"Especially when you've got a bad leg?" Jensen said as he eased himself up on one elbow and accepted the glass.

"You got sharp eyes," Toby commented. "I'm not even limping that much today."

"The benefits of training," Jensen said. "Speaking of sharp eyes, I understand you're the one who sent Adamson and Trapper out looking for us."

Toby shrugged. "Saw all the Security spotters buzzing around. Figured there was some trouble that oughta be looked into."

"Trouble like this happen very often?" Jensen asked.

"Happened last year," Toby said significantly. "About the same time Athena Security went a little berserk, in fact."

"You heard about that?" Flynn asked.

"We're not *that* close to the edge of the universe," Trapper said. "We get a couple of the local radio news stations just fine. We've also got two cars and some old logging roads that'll get us to one-nineteen and from there into Denver."

Flynn nodded understanding. "I was wondering how you all survived out here."

"Mostly, we live off the land," Trapper said. "We hunt and fish and trap, and there's a couple of decent-sized crop areas over the ridge behind town where we grow wheat and vegetables. But there's also a market for our furs in Denver, and some of us also do carvings and pottery that seems to appeal to big-city people. We get by."

"They probably think of you as adorably quaint," Jensen said dryly.

"Let them," Trapper said, a hint of contempt in his voice. "We prefer to think of ourselves as having given up a little civilization for a hell of a lot more freedom."

"As much as you can get on a Ryqril-run world, anyway," Toby growled as he took Jensen's empty glass from his hand. "More?"

"Not right now, thanks," Jensen said, easing himself back flat again.

"Well, there's plenty when you want it," Toby said. He stood gazing down at Jensen for a moment, then turned away and took the glass back to the table. "The other plumbing's even simpler," he said, pointing to a toilet seat fastened to the top of a meter-cube box in the corner by the sink. "That commode over there just opens up over a ravine. Sort of a natural latrine."

Flynn had wondered about the lack of any obvious plumbing on the fixture. "Beats the hell out of digging one yourself every few years," he commented.

"Sure does," Toby agreed. "Smells a lot better, too."

Behind Flynn, the door opened. Instinctively, he snatched out a *shuriken* and snapped his arm into throwing position.

But it was only Adamson. "Friend," he said hastily, lifting his free hand palm outward as he swung a large case in through the door with the other.

"You didn't bring enough stuff, did you?" Toby asked, eyeing the case as Adamson closed the door behind him.

"Cracked ribs require a little more than just seal-strips and painkillers," Adamson told him. "Okay, Jensen, let's get that flexarmor off and see what we're dealing with."

Properly fitted flexarmor never came off easily even at the best of times, but with persistence and a fair amount of wincing on Jensen's part they were able to remove his shirt. Adamson's equipment was hardly top-line, Flynn noted, but it was adequate for the job and had obviously been well cared for. Adamson, too, seemed to know what he was doing.

"We've got the traditional good news and bad news," Adamson said when he'd finished. "Good news is that you have two cracked ribs, but they're only *slightly* cracked. Even better news is that I still have some Calcron that will help stimulate the healing process. A thincast, a few days of complete rest plus a few more of limited activity, and you should heal just fine."

"Sounds great," Jensen said. "What's the bad news?"

Adamson sighed. "That I doubt you're going to follow a single instruction I give you," he said soberly. "Whatever you came to Denver for, I don't think it was to take time off to stare at the clouds."

"Maybe we can compromise," Jensen suggested. "Trapper implied the townspeople make occasional runs to Denver. Are there any Security checkpoints along the way?"

"Not normally," Adamson said. "Though with you here, they might have set some up. You're looking for a ride to town, then?"

"Flynn is," Jensen said, looking over at Flynn. "I need him to find the rest of the team and let them know where we are."

"Wait a minute," Flynn said, trying to keep his tone under control. The last thing he was going to do was leave Jensen here alone. Not after that veiled comment about making sure the Ryqril didn't get into Aegis. "You're going to need me here."

"I'm fine," Jensen said, warning him with his eyes. "I need you to go contact Skyler."

"But—"

"I have a message only you can deliver," Jensen said, his tone leaving no room for argument.

Flynn sighed silently. Whatever Jensen was planning, it was clear he intended to do it alone. "Understood," he murmured.

"I hope the message isn't too urgent," Trapper warned. "Denver's a big place. It may take a while to find them."

"Don't worry, we know some shortcuts," Jensen said. "He'll find them."

"Still cost at least a day." Trapper looked at his father. "And you'd be missed faster than I would."

"Probably," Adamson agreed reluctantly. "I take it you're volunteering?"

"Yes," Trapper said. "Though we can't leave until day after tomorrow."

"Why not?" Adamson frowned. "Oh, that's right. Martin won't be coming back with the sedan until tomorrow night."

"And Alex and Jane are taking in a load of spices with the pickup tomorrow," Trapper said, nodding.

"Couldn't we hitch a ride with them?" Flynn asked.

"No," Adamson said firmly. "They're probably trustworthy, but I don't want any more people than necessary in on this. If Security comes calling, I want their interrogations to show that no one but us had any idea what was going on."

Flynn grimaced. Lathe had warned them during their training that their very presence would put innocent people at risk, but this was the first time that fact had taken on any flesh-and-blood meaning. It was a sobering thought. "Maybe we could leave as soon as Martin gets back tomorrow," he suggested. "The sooner we're out of your way, the better."

"Agreed," Adamson said. "But Martin will be back too late for us to take off. There are a couple of places along the road you definitely don't want to tackle in the dark."

"Then I guess it's first light the day after tomorrow," Flynn concluded. He looked questioningly at Jensen. "That all right?"

Jensen didn't look particularly happy about it, but he nodded. "I guess it'll have to be," he said. "I just hope Skyler doesn't start the party without us."

"First light it is, then," Adamson said. "Even that early we can't have you showing up in town, though, so I'll come up and take you to a rendezvous spot."

"Make it Goldfinch Hook," Trapper suggested. "I can wait there out of sight as long as I need to."

"Fine." Adamson looked at Jensen, a small smile touching his lips. "Well, it looks like you'll have at least one of those bed-rest days I asked for."

"Looks like it," Jensen agreed. "Speaking of days, mine has been long and fairly uncomfortable," he added, easing himself up off the bed again. "I'd like to find myself a corner and settle down for the night."

"You stay right where you are," Toby said firmly. "I've got a couple of old bedrolls the kid and I can use."

"He's right," Adamson seconded. "Let me get a thincast on you, then mix you up some of that Calcron."

Adamson got the blackcollar fixed up, and he and his son headed back to town.

Leaving Foxleigh and his new houseguests alone.

Despite the long day Jensen had mentioned, he and Flynn didn't go immediately to sleep. Instead, they whispered together for nearly half an hour, Jensen on the bed, Flynn on his borrowed bedroll on the floor beside him.

They kept their voices too low for Foxleigh to hear what they were saying. But that didn't matter. Three things were already certain, and they were all he needed. One: in a little over a day Flynn would be going to Denver, leaving Jensen behind. Two: Jensen was definitely one of the blackcollars he'd seen slipping into Aegis Mountain a year ago. And three: with Adamson's thincast wrapped around his torso, Jensen wasn't going to be fitting into his fancy flexarmor shirt anytime soon.

Which meant the time had finally come.

Rolling over on his bedroll, wincing at the unaccustomed hardness of the floor beneath him, Foxleigh drifted off to sleep.

CHAPTER 11

"As I said before, there's a lot of guesswork here," Shaw warned as he dropped the stack of rolled papers on one end of the kitchen table and selected one from the pile. "But it's all we've got."

"Understood," Lathe said. "Let's take a look."

Standing beside Mordecai at the side of the table, Judas craned his neck as Shaw unrolled the sheet and spread it out. To his surprise, it looked nearly as detailed as an actual blueprint would have been. If this was guesswork, he thought with a shiver, he would hate to see what blackcollars came up with when they actually had something to work with.

"This is the main floor," Shaw identified it. He tapped at the four sides in turn. "Here are the four entrances we saw yesterday; the eight entrance bunkers, two per door; and the reinforced bases at each of the eight corners for the antiaircraft lasers."

"Where's Spadafora?" Judas asked, looking around as he suddenly realized the third Plinry blackcollar wasn't there. In fact, now that he thought about it, he realized he hadn't seen the other since leaving for their look at Khorstron the previous afternoon.

"He's out on another job," Lathe said.

"Comsquare Lathe has him dealing with the sensors in the fence," Shaw added.

"The sensors?" Judas asked, his stomach tightening. Surely they weren't attacking *today*, were they? "You mean we're—*today*?"

"No, no," Shaw soothed, looking rather amused. "Certain things take time, Trainee Caine. Aged whiskey and out-link sensor systems are two of them."

Judas swallowed. "Oh," he said, feeling his face warming. "Sorry."

"Looks like there are mantrap foyers inside each entrance," Lathe said, tapping the large oval rooms behind the east entrance.

"Probably," Shaw agreed. "We don't know how they're furnished, of course, but from the thickness of the walls and these support points we assume each will have a couple of autotarget lasers flanking the inner door and a pair of guard holes a meter or two around the curve from them."

Judas winced. "That doesn't sound good."

"Depends on how they're set up," Lathe said. "Autotargeters can sometimes be disabled with a *shuriken* or two."

"Though you *do* tend to get only one shot at a given laser," Shaw said.

"There's that," Lathe agreed. "Tell me more about these entrance guard bunkers. You implied earlier that they didn't have any outer doors?"

"Right—they open directly through the wall into the base."

"So you could get inside through the bunkers?"

"Yes, but I wouldn't count on that being very useful," Shaw said. "The bunker walls themselves are relatively thin, but the entry doors behind them are every bit as tough as the main door they're protecting. And of course, with no external door on the bunker you'd have to blow the front off the thing to even gain access."

"Still, it would avoid the mantrap problem," Lathe pointed out. "What about the outer bunkers, the ones at the gate entrances?"

"Same deal, only the guards get in from the base via underground tunnels," Shaw said. "Here, here, here, and here. And, of course, once you were through the tunnels you'd have the same serious door to get through at the base end."

"Plus whatever additional goodies the Ryqril put in the tunnels themselves to discourage trespassers," Lathe said.

Shaw nodded. "Plus that."

"Why four entrances?" Mordecai asked suddenly.

"What?" Shaw asked, frowning at him.

"Four entrances, but the only thing nearby is Inkosi City to the west," Mordecai said. "There aren't any towns shown anywhere else, or even any real roads leading to the area. So why bother with the north, south, and east gates?"

Shaw shrugged. "Maybe they're just there for emergencies. Maybe they're planning to build barracks or auxiliary facilities on those sides. Or maybe they just got a good deal on reinforced doors. The point is that we have four possible ways of getting in and not just one."

"Yes," Lathe murmured. "Convenient."

"You want to look at this or don't you?" Shaw growled. "You do? Fine." He leaned over the table and tapped a circular opening in the center. "Here's the heart of the place, dead center on the first floor. No big surprise there—it's the most protected spot in the building."

"What's in there?" Judas asked.

"The gold at rainbow's end," Shaw said. "Or at least, all the gold we care about. The core's where all the data comes in, which is then parceled out to the various collation and analysis stations in other parts of the building. Once everything's been sifted, the analyses and conclusions are sent back to the core, where the permanently stationed half circle of Ryqril command officers make decisions and send out orders. There are things we could glean from offices all over the building, but the core's the only place to get everything at once."

"And they obviously know it," Lathe said. "I see they've got a complete double wall around it."

"With plenty of room between the layers for pressurized gas traps, antipersonnel explosives, or even a few roaming *khassq* if they feel so inclined," Shaw said grimly. "You can also bet they've got more autotarget lasers set up outside the doors, ready to turn the last five or ten meters of corridor into a killing zone."

"Only three doors into the place, too," Judas commented. "What about these three narrow rooms wrapped around the big central one?"

"One of them will be the base's main security monitor room," Shaw said. "This one, probably, from the number of secure display conduits we saw them putting in the walls. The other two are probably a guard room and a lounge for the command officers."

"Seems horribly inefficient," Judas said, studying the three wide corridors that led from the perimeter corridor to the central circle and its wraparound rooms and the five sets of cross corridors cutting across them. "With an octagonal shape, wouldn't it make more sense to parallel that design on the inside? Or at the very least to go with a four-sided corridor/room pattern instead of a triangular one?"

"They probably borrowed it from one of their victims," Lathe said. "They borrow everyone else's technology. Why not their architecture, too?"

"Anyway, that's the overview," Shaw said. "We've also got a little more detail on some of the areas—"

"Why the first floor?" Mordecai interrupted, gazing at the diagram.

"Excuse me?" Shaw asked.

"Probably because the second floor's more exposed to air attacks," Judas explained, frowning. Even to him that one seemed obvious.

"I meant why on the surface at all?" Mordecai said. "Why not put it underground? We know the ground can be dug into—they've got tunnels leading to the fence bunkers."

"He's got a point," Lathe agreed, stroking his beard thoughtfully. "For that matter, why not put the whole base underground?"

"For starters, underground facilities take a lot longer to build," Shaw pointed out. But he, too, was frowning down at the paper.

"Or the place may not be as valuable as they want us to believe," Mordecai said.

There was another silence, a longer one this time. Surreptitiously, Judas looked at each of the others in turn, his heart pounding uncomfortably. If they gave up now, this whole thing would have been for nothing.

And if that happened, there was no telling what might happen to his family back in Interlaken. Galway had promised them safety and security, but the unspoken condition was that Galway would continue to be in a position where he could make good on that guarantee. If the mission failed, the Plinry prefect wasn't likely to remain in the Ryqril's good graces for long.

To his relief, Lathe shook his head. "No," he said. "Haberdae must have deduced by now that Khorstron is the reason we're here. If they didn't care whether or not we got in, they wouldn't have tried to take us out of the game last night."

Judas breathed a quiet sigh of relief. "Besides, as you said earlier, Lepkowski's already gone to tell the Chryselli about it," he added. "We have to get inside."

"Right," Lathe agreed. "So let's quit worrying about why Ryqril do things the way they do and concentrate on how we're going to get in there. Tactor?"

"Okay," Shaw said, selecting another roll of paper. "This one's a closer look at the west door area. . . ."

Neatly framed in the center of the display was a wide rectangular post, a meshwork pattern extending out from it on both sides. "It's one of the Khorstron fence posts," Haberdae identified it. "So?"

"Just keep watching," Galway told him. "Especially the upper third."

"Galway, I don't have time for gam—"

He broke off in midword as a gray projectile suddenly shot in from the edge of the display and slapped into the upper part of the fence post, the impact flattening it into a misshapen blob. "What the *hell*?" Haberdae muttered.

"You were wondering earlier where Spadafora had disappeared to?" Galway gestured to the display. "There you go."

"There I go where?" Haberdae growled. "What the hell *is* that?"

"A small piece of plutonium embedded in a putty-like substance, delivered via slingshot by a blackcollar sharpshooter," Galway told him. "That was the fifteenth he's landed on the post since dawn. The fifteenth we've noticed, anyway—he might have sent in more of them before we caught on. You can see how well the putty matches the color of the post."

"And this is in aid of what?" Haberdae asked. "I trust you're not going to suggest there's enough radiation in there to decrystalize the metal of the post and bring it down."

"No, of course, not," Galway said. "But if you place the pellets over critical sensor or sonic net electronics—and all fifteen of them *are* over such places—there's more than enough radiation to begin slowly degrading them. Fairly unnoticeable, too, since the diagnostic sensors are being scrambled at the same time."

Haberdae looked sharply at Galway, then back at the

display, then a little less truculently at Galway. "How slow are we talking about?"

"I don't know yet," Galway said. "Hours, or a low number of days. The techs are researching that now. The point is that they've actively started their plan."

"I guess so," Haberdae said, scratching his chin. "So where is he?"

"We're not sure about that, either." Galway gestured to the tech, who tapped his control board. With dizzying speed, the view on the display pulled back from the fence post and settled down into an overall view of the southwest quadrant of the Khorstron area. "Here's the affected post," he said, touching a spot on the southwest part of the fence. "We're guessing he's in a camouflage setup in or near one of the trees over here to the south of the base." He ran a hand over a thirty-degree arc through the forested area outside the fence. "There's also this abandoned shack over here, along with this shed, either of which he could also be using."

"He'd have to shoot a hundred meters from either of those buildings," Haberdae objected. "*And* through that whole patch of forest on top of it."

"As I said, he's a sharpshooter," Galway reminded him. "Which is why he's here instead of one of the others. Neither Lathe nor Mordecai has anywhere near the necessary skill with a slingshot."

"But a hundred *meters*?"

"Actually, I don't think he's that far away," Galway said. "I'm guessing he's somewhere in the woods. Unfortunately, no one saw him get in there and set up shop, and the pellets themselves are too small to get a

decent trajectory vector from. And we certainly don't want
to send in a team that might spook him."

"No, of course not," Haberdae said darkly. "We want
them to feel nice and safe for their little raid."

"Actually, yes, we do."

"That's what I said," Haberdae insisted. "Did you think
I was being sarcastic?"

Actually, Galway wasn't sure what kind of tone that had
been. But there'd been something there, something nasty
lurking beneath the surface. "No, of course not."

"Good." Haberdae nodded toward the display. "Let me
know as soon as you have an idea how long it'll take for
them to wreck the sensor system. I want to know when
they'll be ready to move."

The public phone Skyler had specified was on a busy
corner squarely in the middle of downtown lunchtime
traffic. Poirot arrived two minutes early and stood to the
side, watching the passing pedestrians and cars and feeling
decidedly uncomfortable in his civilian clothing.

The phone rang, and Poirot scooped up the handset.
"Yes?"

"You alone?" Skyler's voice came back.

With an effort, Poirot forced himself not to look at
the van parked half a block away where Bailey and his
tech team were monitoring the call. "I'm on a street
corner in Denver," he countered instead. "How alone
can I be?"

There was a soft chuckle. "Point taken," Skyler said.
"What have you got for me?"

Poirot took a deep breath. This was it. "I've persuaded

them to let me move the prisoners tomorrow night," he said. "They'll be—"

"Who's this *them* you had to persuade?" Skyler interrupted. "I thought *you* were the head of Security here."

"I am," Poirot said, and it took no acting at all to add a bitter edge to his voice. "The Ryqril are taking a personal interest in this. It seems your missing blackcollar killed one of their sentries last night."

There was a long moment of silence. "Really," Skyler said at last, his voice giving no hint as to what he was thinking.

"Yes, *really*," Poirot said. "I hope to hell whatever he's doing is worth the trouble he's stirred up."

"I hope so, too," Skyler said evenly. "Tomorrow night, you said?"

"Yes," Poirot confirmed. "They'll be loaded aboard a group of vans which will leave Athena at seven o'clock and head for Colorado Springs."

"That's when city traffic will be at its minimum, I presume?"

"Correct," Poirot said. "It's lightest between six-thirty and seven-thirty. That'll make it easier to spot any tails. They'll also have five or six spotters at high cover, and probably an armed patrol boat or two ready in case they need extra firepower."

"That last part could be unpleasant," Skyler said. "Any chance of getting it cancelled?"

"I doubt it," Poirot said. "It was the Ryqril's idea."

"Well, if we can't ground them, we'll just have to work around them. How many vans will you be using?"

"The current plan is to have six," Poirot said. "One prisoner per van, with a driver and a couple of guards along. Of course, bear in mind that the Ryqril could come in at any time and change any or all of that."

"I understand," Skyler said. "What about Reger's people, the ones you picked up after we crashed your party at his estate?"

"Crashed rather literally," Poirot growled, rubbing the side of his neck in memory. "Don't worry about them. We've established that none of them know anything about Reger's connection with Phoenix, and we've got more urgent things to do right now than bother with minor flight and resisting-arrest violations. They're all being released, probably this afternoon."

"That should make Reger happy," Skyler said. "Then I guess we're set."

"I hope so," Poirot said, and meant it. If this worked, and if they were able to capture even one of the blackcollars, it would go a long way toward convincing Bailey and the Ryqril that he was still loyal. "Anything else you need?"

"I don't think so," Skyler said. "Oh, wait—there was one other thing. What's the threshold size for Athena's defense lasers?"

Poirot blinked. "The *what*?"

"The size something has to be to trigger those big Green Mountain autotarget lasers that guard Athena's outer fence," Skyler said. "Is it basketball size, baseball size—what?"

A cold chill ran up Poirot's back. Could Daasaa have been right about Skyler planning to attack Athena? "I don't have that number off the top of my head," he said through stiff lips. "I'll have to look it up."

"Do that," Skyler said. "Let me know tomorrow when you call to confirm the final details for the transfer."

"Look, I can't keep leaving my post at odd times and coming out here this way," Poirot insisted. "Someone's bound to get suspicious."

"Since when is lunch an odd time to be coming and going?" Skyler countered.

"Since most government workers eat in Athena, not out in the city," Poirot said with strained patience.

"Okay, fine," Skyler said reasonably. "Give me a time that *wouldn't* be odd. You must come out to make your rounds or pick up your laundry or *something*."

Poirot grimaced. He didn't want to come out here again—every contact with Skyler just increased the chances that he'd make some sort of slip. Unfortunately, he couldn't think of a plausible reason to decline. "Let's make it midmorning," he said reluctantly. "I can tell them I'm checking with one of my informers. Say, ten-thirty?"

"Ten-thirty it is," Skyler confirmed. "Here's your new rendezvous." He read off a street corner halfway across town. "Talk to you then."

The phone went dead. With a curse, Poirot hung up and headed back to his car. The van would be making its own return to Athena along an entirely different route and timetable, but in an hour or so he and Bailey should be able to sit down and discuss this new twist.

If, that is, Bailey wanted to discuss it with him. *If* Bailey was interested in helping Poirot clear himself, rather than just trying to keep his own nose clean as far as the Ryqril were concerned.

If Bailey wasn't actually after Poirot's job.

He shook his head in annoyance at the absurdity of that thought. Bailey was ambitious, but not enough to stab his superior in the back. Not even with this damned Whiplash thing giving him the perfect excuse to do so.

At least, he hoped not.

He shook his head tiredly. With loyalty-conditioning, the thought once again flicked through his mind, a man always knew who he could trust.

Without it, how could anyone know anything?

Skyler hung up the phone and glanced around at the pedestrians and cars moving along the streets and walkways around him, wondering if Security could have traced the call and gotten a team here this quickly. Unlikely, he decided. Taking a quick look at the cloudy sky above him, he headed down the street to where Anne and the car were waiting.

He'd gone five steps when his tingler came on. *Tracker confirmed*, O'Hara reported. *White van with surveillance equipment*.

Skyler slid his fingers to his own tingler. *Subject aware of tracker?*

There was a pause as O'Hara mulled at the question, running his observations through the filter of his blackcollar instincts. *Probably*.

Skyler grimaced. But it was hardly an unexpected development. If the lower-level government workers Phoenix had freed from their loyalty-conditioning weren't interested in risking their comfortable jobs, there had always been little hope that the head of Security himself would be willing to do so.

But Skyler had a secret streak of optimism, and he'd quietly nurtured that hope. Still, now they knew for sure. *Return home*, he told O'Hara. *Watch your backtrack.*

Acknowledged.

So they would have to do this the hard way. Moreover, they would have to do it shorthanded.

He scowled. *Blast you anyway, Jensen*, he growled silently toward the distant mountain peaks. He'd wondered if the other had had some private agenda when he'd volunteered so quickly to stay with Flynn and his damaged hang glider. Possibly an agenda involving that observer he claimed to have seen when they'd entered Aegis Mountain on their last trip to the area. Skyler hadn't known about that at the time, but Mordecai had clued in him and Lathe afterward.

And now, if Poirot was to be believed, he was out there killing Ryqril.

Lathe had warned him not to bring Jensen along. Skyler, of course, had known better. Now look where it had gotten him.

Above the sound of the traffic came the faint but distinctive whine of a spotter. Instinctively, Skyler lowered his head to make his face harder to see, while simultaneously craning an eye upward toward the incoming vehicle.

It turned out not to be a single spotter but a pair of them, flying low and slow a dozen meters apart with a wide, flat sensor disk strung on cables between them. Not a visual scanner, as Skyler might have expected, but rather the kind of microradar and materials echo-sensors designed to look for particular metals and compounds, plus power sources and other forms of radiation.

The blackcollars' own equipment, of course, didn't have enough metal to lift them out of the background clutter, and aside from tinglers and short-range radios they used no power sources at all. That was the whole reason they'd adopted such low-tech weapons in the first place.

Which meant those spotters weren't hunting for Skyler's team. So what *were* they hunting?

And then it clicked, and he smiled tightly to himself. Of course: his throwaway comment to Poirot about Phoenix's secret cache of weapons. He'd dropped the line mainly to make the rebel forces look bigger and more powerful than they really were, trying to make them look more like the probable winning side. Apparently, the general had taken the line seriously.

Which was fine with Skyler. The more men and vehicles Security wasted on useless searches for huge organizations and nonexistent weapons dumps, the fewer they would have available for actually tracking down the real threat.

He reached the car and got in. "Well?" Anne asked.

"You were right," Skyler admitted. "He's still on their side."

"I told you," Anne said. "So what now?"

"We play them like they're trying to play us," Skyler said, trying to sound more confident than he felt. This tactics stuff really wasn't his strong point.

"Meaning we go ahead with the plan?"

"Unless you want to let them keep your people."

"The people who would be leading their normal lives right now if you hadn't shown up?"

"We'll get them back," Skyler assured her. "Let's head home."

Reaching down, Anne started the car. "I talked to my contact in Boulder this morning while you and O'Hara were reconnoitering the area," she said as she pulled out into the traffic flow. "She isn't happy about it, but she's agreed to get us the rolling scramble-freq radio system Security's spotters use and a couple of the general authorization codes. That's *all* she'll do, though."

"It'll be enough," Skyler said. "Don't worry—this is going to work."

Anne didn't answer.

"And you're *absolutely* sure you weren't followed?" Poirot asked as he and Bailey walked together across the situation room.

"I'm sure," Bailey said, trying hard to hold onto his temper. It had been a highly unproductive and frustrating morning, and having Poirot asking different versions of the same question over and over wasn't helping. "Trust me, General, we *do* know what we're doing."

Poirot made as if to speak again, seemed to think better of it, and fell silent.

The two Ryqril were waiting for them in the conference room, poring over maps and sifting through pages from a stack of reports. "Sit," Battle Architect Daasaa said without preamble, pointing the two humans to seats across from them. "*Khassq* Rarrior Halaak and I are not 'leased rith yaer re'ort."

"We do have more information now, though," Poirot offered. "The blackcollars—"

"I an not s'eaking tae yae," Daasaa cut him off. "Yae—Colonel 'Ailey—yaer sur'ey is not acce'ta'le."

"My apologies, Your Eminence," Bailey said, feeling his stomach tighten. His men had been working like demons to get their aerial survey of the city finished in the time Daasaa had allotted them, and for the most part they'd succeeded. But all they had to show for it was negative information. "We've begun a second sweep of the city proper, but I don't expect to find anything on this one, either. Still, there are many large tracts in the outlying rural areas that are still being searched."

"Searched for what?" Poirot asked in a low voice.

"The weapons cache you said Phoenix had buried away somewhere," Bailey told him.

"Are you fine-tuning for gunmetal?" Poirot asked. "Because if you're looking just for metal—"

"I know how to do a weapons search," Bailey cut him off, turning back to the Ryqril. "My apologies for the interruption, Your Eminences."

"Yae rill continyae the search," Daasaa said. "General 'Oirot. Tell us a'out yaer contact."

Bailey listened with half an ear as Poirot detailed the brief conversation with Skyler, most of his mind busy trying to extrapolate to what the blackcollars might be planning.

"The 'lackcollars rill attack Athena," Halaak said firmly when Poirot had finished.

"That does now seem more likely," Bailey said cautiously. "On the other hand, Skyler might have asked about the defense laser thresholds just to mislead us."

"Dae yae think they dae not trust General 'Oirot, then?"

"They *do* trust me," Poirot insisted. "They have no reason to think I'm working against them." He glared at Bailey. "Unless they spotted Colonel Bailey's van and figured out that he was tapping the conversation."

"No," Bailey said firmly. "We were very careful. There's no way they could have made us."

"Then the 'lackcollars rill attack Athena," Daasaa concluded. "Yae rill nake ready to sto' this attack."

Bailey grimaced. More of his men diverted from the task at hand, this latest batch earmarked to guard against an attack they all knew couldn't possibly succeed. But Daasaa's mind was clearly made up, and it would be dangerous to argue further. "As you command, Your Eminence," he said, suppressing a sigh. "What about the prisoner transfer? Do we still go ahead with that?"

"Yae rill trans'er they as 'lanned," Halaak said. "If re nust s'lit forces, then so nust they."

Which wasn't at all how it worked, Bailey knew. Skyler could just as easily choose to concentrate his forces against one of his possible targets and ignore the other completely. But again, it wasn't something he dared argue at this point. "As you command, Your Eminence," he said again. "In the meantime, Skyler will expect General Poirot to provide some numbers on the laser threshold tomorrow. What do you want us to tell him?"

"Re rill consider," Daasaa said. "Yae rill gi' the orders."

"As you command, Your Eminence," Bailey said, standing up and gesturing to Poirot.

But instead of getting out of his chair, the general was

frowning hard at the far side of the room. "A moment, please," he said slowly. "It just occurred to me that there's another possible location for this Phoenix weapons cache, a location I know you haven't searched."

"There are a lot of places we haven't yet—"

"I mean Aegis Mountain."

Bailey broke off, staring at the other. "That's impossible," he said. "Even the Ryqril haven't been able to find a way in."

For a moment Poirot didn't answer, his lips moving slightly as if he was talking to himself. Then, abruptly, his head snapped around. "My *God*," he breathed, his eyes suddenly blazing with passion. "It fits. It all *fits*."

"General—"

"No—listen to me," Poirot cut him off, his words tumbling over themselves in his excitement. "Last year when Lathe came, we thought they were here to assassinate former Prefect Ivas Trendor. But that never made any sense."

"They also got into Athena and ran games through the Security building," Bailey reminded him.

"Only because General Quinn pushed them into it," Poirot said, wincing visibly at the memory. "And then once Trendor was dead, they suddenly closed up shop and left." He tapped a finger on the tabletop. "But what if the assassination was just a blind? What if what they were *really* here for was to get into Aegis?"

Slowly, Bailey sat down again. "All right," he said, thinking hard. "But if they have all these weapons, why haven't they used them?"

"Because they first needed Silcox and Reger to build

them a proper rebel force," Poirot said. "And we know they did—we've got six of the leaders locked away upstairs."

"And now Skyler's come back to lead them into battle?"

"Why not?" Poirot countered. "They have the personnel, they apparently have the weapons, and with the blackcollars they have some top-notch military leadership." He looked at the Ryqril. "*And* one of them was obviously snooping around the main entrance into Aegis," he reminded them.

"And of course, with Whiplash they also have the spies?" Bailey suggested.

Poirot stared at him, the excitement draining from his face. "You don't believe me, do you?" he said, his voice subdued again. "You think this is something Skyler told me to feed you."

Bailey shrugged uncomfortably. He hated having to think the worst of his superior this way. "All I know is that none of the Phoenix prisoners has even mentioned Aegis."

"Maybe none of them know about it," Poirot said. "Maybe only Silcox and the blackcollars know. In fact, maybe that's why they worked so hard to get her away from us in the first place."

"Aegis Nountain is sealed," Daasaa said. "Re ha' 'een trying 'or two years tae 'enetrate it. It cannot 'e done."

"Can you afford to take that chance?" Poirot asked.

Halaak's eyes narrowed, his left hand dropping to the short sword belted at his left hip. "Dae yae s'eak thus tae a *khassq*?" he demanded.

Poirot's lips tightened. "I meant no disrespect, Your Eminence," he said. His voice was properly deferential, but Bailey could hear the clenched teeth behind it. "But I'm concerned that if the blackcollars *do* intend an attack on Athena, we may find ourselves facing more than catapulted bowling balls or whatever else they can improvise."

"Yae rish tae di'ert e'en nore o' yaer nen tae search the nountain?" Daasaa asked.

"Actually, that may not be necessary," Bailey put in. He still wasn't ready to buy Poirot's conveniently timed reasoning, not by a long shot. But at the same time, he had to admit it wasn't something they could afford to dismiss out of hand. "We know they can't get in or out of Aegis through the main entrance, not with your base there, and you've got the highway blocked as well. All the rest of the terrain in the area is pretty rugged, far too rugged for land vehicles."

"Reach yaer 'oint, Colonel," Halaak rumbled.

"The point is that we have a ring of sensor pylons around the Idaho Springs area that were specifically designed to watch for aircraft," Bailey said. "If there is a back door into Aegis, and if the blackcollars try to move anything substantial out through it, those sensors ought to spot them."

"Assuming the pylons haven't been tampered with," Poirot warned.

"Exactly," Bailey agreed. "I propose, therefore, that we send out a couple of teams to inspect all the pylons and make sure they're functioning properly. Unless they find a problem they should all be back well before nightfall. Even if Skyler does intend to attack Athena, he surely won't move until then."

For a moment the Ryqril conferred between themselves. Bailey kept his eyes on Poirot, who in turn seemed to be carefully ignoring him. "'Ery rell," Daasaa said at last. "Send yaer nen tae exanine the sensors." His eyes bored into Bailey's. "They *rill* 'e 'ack 'e'ore dark."

"Absolutely, Your Eminence," Bailey assured him.

"What are your orders for me?" Poirot asked.

Daasaa regarded him thoughtfully. "Yae rill continue tae assist 'lanning 'or the 'risoner con'oy," he said.

Poirot bowed his head slightly. "As you command, Your Eminence."

Bailey grimaced. The battle architect was offering Poirot all the rope he would need to ultimately hang himself . . . and the general, for his part, was grabbing every bit of that rope that he could.

"Yae rill go," Daasaa said. He looked at Bailey. "'Oth o' yae."

"As you command, Your Eminence," Bailey said. Standing up, he and Poirot left the room.

"So?" Poirot asked when the door was closed behind them.

"What do you mean, *so*?" Bailey said. "We carry out our orders."

"That wasn't what I meant," Poirot said, his voice curiously hesitant. "What do you think—really—about this?"

Bailey sighed. "You're right about the blackcollars' last incursion not making any sense," he conceded. "Assassination was never one of their usual jobs, at least not according to the histories."

"And this particular killing made no sense on top of it,"

Poirot said. "Trendor was retired, hardly a threat to them or anyone else."

"True." Bailey cocked an eyebrow at the other. "But on the other hand, the Ryqril are right, too. They've been trying to get into Aegis for two years and haven't made it yet."

"True," Poirot said. "But Ryqril are hardly the most innovative people around."

Bailey looked at him sharply. How could he *say* such a thing? A senior officer of TDE Security?

Because he wasn't loyalty-conditioned anymore, that was how. It was something Bailey could never let himself forget. "Whatever," he said, letting his tone go plain-tan neutral. "I'll also admit that blackcollars in possession of Aegis Mountain weaponry is a very unpleasant thought."

"Then let's make sure we nail it down right now," Poirot said firmly. "You get those teams out to the pylons, and I'll see if we can come up with a way to nab them when they try to spring their friends." With a brisk nod, he headed across the situation room.

Bailey gazed at his back as he strode away. "Right," he muttered under his breath. "Assuming you really *want* to nab them."

"Sir?"

Bailey turned to see Ramirez come up behind him. "I've got the latest batches of reports from the scanning teams," the lieutenant said, waving a sheaf of papers.

"That can wait," Bailey told him. "I need you to find me a couple of tech teams, a few Security men to guard them, and a pair of aircraft to ferry them."

Ramirez seemed taken aback. "That's going to be a little tricky, sir. All the available techs and spotters are out with the scanning teams. The rest are on city monitor duty or getting some sleep."

"What about your Boulder people?"

"They're doing weapons scans up there, too."

"Have them put that on hold," Bailey decided. "I need someone to go check all the Idaho Springs sensor pylons and make sure they haven't been tampered with."

Ramirez grimaced, but nodded. "I'll see who I can find." He started to turn away, then paused. "By the way, I understand you had a check made of all my people last night."

"Just a precaution," Bailey assured him. "You'd already suggested the blackcollars might try to slip someone in through the returning spotter teams. I wanted to make sure the people checking them in also hadn't been infiltrated."

"Very prudent of you." Ramirez's eyes hardened a little. "I understand you also did a check on *me*."

Bailey felt a flicker of anger. How the *hell* had Ramirez found out about that? "Yes, I did," he said. "You have a problem with that?"

"I have a problem with my competence being questioned behind my back," Ramirez countered. "If you had questions about my performance, you should have brought them to me directly."

"It wasn't your competence that was at issue, Lieutenant," Bailey told him evenly.

Ramirez seemed to draw back. "You aren't serious."

"Deadly serious," Bailey assured him coldly. "As serious as our enemies are."

Ramirez's lip twitched. "And?"

Bailey studied the other's face, as plain-tan neutral now

as Bailey's own. True, the check hadn't picked up any suspicious absences or obvious attitude changes. But from Poirot's experience they knew the Whiplash change could be affected in under twenty-four hours, possibly with as little as a single injection of the damned stuff. So what did even perfect work attendance prove? "You seem to be in the clear," he told Ramirez. "At least, as much as anyone else is."

"I see," Ramirez said stiffly. "Thank you, sir. I'll see about getting you those tech teams." Spinning around in a military about-face that was just a shade crisper than it needed to be, he headed for the communications station.

For a moment Bailey watched him go. Then, turning the opposite direction, he headed for the door Poirot had disappeared through a few minutes earlier. Let Ramirez be annoyed if he wanted to be. Let him think he was under suspicion, too. In fact, it might be best if everyone in Athena started watching everyone else. Just let them get on with their work and their back-watching and leave him alone for a while.

Because it had suddenly occurred to him that there might be a way to prove once and for all who was telling the truth about this alleged Aegis Mountain weapons cache. True, none of the prisoners up in the interrogation rooms had mentioned anything about either the mountain or the weapons.

But then, not all of the prisoners were *in* the interrogation rooms.

He took the elevator up to the garage, where a handful of Security men and drivers were standing around talking quietly together beside the line of parked vehicles. "Yes, sir?" the duty sergeant said, breaking from the group and stepping over as Bailey came in.

"I need a car," Bailey said tersely, striding past him toward the nearest car.

"Yes, sir." The sergeant gestured, and one of the other men moved hastily to Bailey's target vehicle and opened the back door.

"I'll be driving myself," Bailey said, closing the door as he passed it and opening the driver's side.

"Yes, sir," the sergeant said, sounding a little uncertain. "Ah . . . your destination, Colonel?"

"I'll be back when I'm back," Bailey said, ignoring the question. "If there's an emergency, I'll have my comm on channel six."

The other might have said something else, but the slamming of the car door cut it off. Starting the engine, Bailey pulled away and out into the Athena traffic.

Smiling tightly to himself, he headed for the hospital.

CHAPTER 12

It was late afternoon, and Flynn was re-sorting his weapons pouches at Toby's rough-topped table, when through the open door he heard the sound of an approaching air vehicle.

Lying on the bed across the room, Jensen stirred. "Sounds like a patrol boat," he said, starting to get up.

"I'll check," Flynn told him, waving him back down. "You stay put."

He was two steps from the door when Toby appeared in the doorway, moving as fast as his limp would allow. "Security," he puffed. "Get up—get *up*."

"Where are they?" Jensen asked. He was already sitting on the edge of the bed, pulling on his boots.

"Looks like they're heading into town," Toby said, hobbling toward the corner that held the sink and toilet. "But I'm guessing they'll be up here soon enough."

"I don't suppose this mountain has a back door," Flynn said as he scooped up the rest of his weapons and refastened the various pouches to his belt.

"As a matter of fact, it does," Toby said. Getting a grip on the edges of the box the toilet seat was mounted on, he gave it a tug.

And to Flynn's surprise, the whole box swung forward on concealed hinges, revealing a large hole in the cabin floor.

He stepped over for a closer look. It was a large and very *deep* hole, he saw as he gazed down into the fissure that Toby had called his natural latrine. Narrow and steep-sided, it extended a good two hundred meters straight down. "Don't worry, I'm not expecting you to fly," Toby grunted, rummaging beneath the firewood in the bin built into the side wall. "Here—catch," he said, pulling out a coil of rope and tossing it to Flynn.

"Where'd you get this?" Flynn asked, frowning as he brushed bits of bark off the rope. It was old but in excellent shape, made of some unfamiliar synthetic. It was smooth enough to be easy to handle, but rough enough to hold secure knots.

"The tooth fairy," Toby said tartly. "Here's Jensen's."

Flynn caught the second coil. "Now what?" he asked, handing it to Jensen. "We tie knots in them and hang on?"

"Do it like this," Jensen said, shaking out the rope and finding one end. With deft movements, he wove the rope around his waist and thighs and chest in a deceptively simple pattern that left him securely trussed up. "Where does the other end go?" he asked Toby.

"There are a couple of pulleys under the floor on opposite sides of the hole," Toby told him, pointing toward the latrine as he resettled the wood in the bin. "Better make a knot in the end once it's through, just in case."

"Right." Carefully, Jensen lay down on his stomach by the hole and turned his head to look under the floor. "Got it," he said, reaching under the boards with his rope and fiddling with something out of Flynn's view. "Flynn?"

"Almost ready," Flynn said, tightening the last knot in his impromptu harness and giving it one last check as he stepped to Jensen's side. "These boards don't look all that sturdy," he warned as he handed over the end of his rope.

"No, but the beams the pulleys are actually attached to do," Jensen assured him as he put Flynn's rope through another unseen pulley.

"Come on, come on," Toby said urgently. "I think I see someone coming."

"Working on it," Jensen grunted, pulling industriously on his rope as he ran the slack through the pulley. He made it to the end and fed the knotted end through two of the ropes in his harness, again pulling the slack rapidly through and letting the end drop down through the hole. "Flynn?"

"As ready as I'm going to be," Flynn said, pulling his own rope taut and feeding the end through his harness the way Jensen had.

"Just do as I do," Jensen said. Gripping the rope, he slid his legs over the edge of the hole and disappeared through it.

Flynn leaned over. Jensen was dropping in a controlled fall down the ravine, playing out the rope as he lowered himself down. "This is nuts," he muttered under his breath as he sat down on the edge of the hole and prepared to follow.

"Wait a second," Toby said, hobbling toward him.

Flynn turned, flinching reflexively as he saw the small but nasty-looking slug pistol in Toby's hand. Before he could even reach for his *shuriken* pouch, though, the old man reversed the weapon, offering him the grip. "They might search the cabin," the other explained. "Don't drop it."

"I won't," Flynn said, his face warming in embarrassment as he took the weapon and stuck it into his belt.

"Now get moving," Toby ordered, leaning down and getting his fingers under the edge of the box. "I'll close up behind you."

Taking a deep breath, Flynn got a grip on the rope and pushed himself off into the abyss.

For a moment he hung there, fighting back a sudden flood of vertigo and a terrible sense of vulnerability. Hang gliders, even malfunctioning ones, were no big deal to him. But dangling at the end of a rope, with Security above and shattering death below, was a very discomfiting sensation.

Above him, the diffuse light abruptly shut off as Toby swung the box back into place. Grimacing, Flynn started down.

To his mild surprise, once he was actually in motion most of the discomfort evaporated. The harness design held him securely, and Jensen's method of threading the rope through it provided enough friction to take most of his weight. It wasn't really any worse than rappelling, he decided as he picked up his pace, with the extra bonus of not having to worry about twisting his ankle as he bounced his way down a building or cliff face.

Jensen was waiting for him as far down as he could go

without actually letting go of the rope. "Good," the black-collar said as Flynn brought himself to a halt. "Now hook the knotted end around these ropes here." He indicated the technique with his own rope and harness. "That should hold you, though you'll want to keep a hand on it just in case it starts to loosen."

"Right," Flynn said, copying the other's technique. "I wonder what Toby uses these pulleys for."

"Probably not much," Jensen said. "Been a while since they've been used."

"Oh?" Flynn asked, his vertigo threatening to return as he looked up at the floor of the cabin nearly a hundred meters above him. "How long a while?"

"Don't worry, they'll hold just fine," Jensen assured him. "Nice souvenir."

"What?"

"Your new toy," Jensen said, pointing at the gun in Flynn's belt. "Toby give you that?"

"Oh." Flynn looked down at the weapon. "Yes. He didn't want any visitors catching him with it."

"I don't blame him," Jensen said, his forehead wrinkling as he gazed at the gun. "Security doesn't like concealable weapons in civilian hands."

"Security barely tolerates hunting rifles in civilian hands," Flynn countered, studying the other's expression. "Anything wrong?"

"Not really," Jensen said. "I was just thinking that gun has a definite military look about it."

Flynn glanced up at the bottom of the cabin. "You think Toby was in the war?"

"It's possible," Jensen said. "I know that on Plinry, at

least, the Ryqril tried to tag all the vets when they took over, particularly the officers. Maybe Toby holed up out here hoping to evade the net."

Flynn thought about the old man living in a one-room cabin for the past thirty years. "Seems to me the hunt should be over by now."

Jensen snorted. "It was probably over three to five years after the occupation started," he said. "If he's hiding from the Ryqril, this is serious overkill."

"Maybe he likes it out here."

"Or maybe he got the gun some other way," Jensen said, his voice going dark. "Found it, or stole it."

A chill ran up Flynn's back. "Or killed for it?"

"Possibly," Jensen agreed grimly. "It might explain why he's still out at the back edge of nowhere."

"So what do we do?"

"For now, we stop talking," Jensen said, wincing as he rearranged his harness around his injured ribs. "Sound can carry strangely in the mountains."

"I just hope he's not planning to turn us in," Flynn murmured. "This would be a rotten position to fight from."

"We'd manage," Jensen assured him, peering upward. "*I* just hope his visitors don't ask to use the facilities."

Foxleigh was sitting at the table, whittling industriously at a random stick he'd grabbed from the wood bin, when the two Security men arrived.

Typically, they didn't bother to knock. "Boulder Security," the younger of the two said brusquely, as if their uniforms weren't enough of a clue. "Who are you?"

"Who wants to know?" Foxleigh countered, not looking up from his carving.

The man snorted and grabbed the end of Foxleigh's stick. "When I ask you a question—"

Foxleigh let go of the stick, shifted his grip to the man's wrist, and pulled it sharply downward toward the tabletop. The other stumbled forward, off balance; and as he did so, Foxleigh twisted the knife around to point toward him.

The man froze with shock and probably astonishment, the knife point no more than ten centimeters from his stomach. "Manners, sonny," Foxleigh said softly. "You'd be surprised how far they get you."

"Smith?" the kid demanded in a choked tone, his wide eyes staring at the knife.

"Easy, Griffs," the older man said soothingly. He had his paral-dart gun out, pointing it at Foxleigh. "You, too, friend. We're just here to talk."

"Tell *him* that," Foxleigh suggested.

"Everyone just relax," Smith said. "Griffs, apologize to the man."

"Me?" Griffs demanded. "Smith—"

"Apologize to the man," Smith said more firmly.

Griffs glared at Foxleigh, his throat working. "Sorry I grabbed your stick," he said through clenched teeth.

"There we go," Smith said encouragingly. "Now let him go, okay?"

"It's all about manners," Foxleigh said, releasing Griffs's wrist.

Breathing hard, the other took a step back from the table and yanked out his own paral-dart pistol. "Drop it," he snarled.

"It's dropped," Foxleigh said, laying the knife on the table and folding his arms across his chest. "Now ask your questions and get out."

"Let's start with your name," Smith said, lowering his gun to point at the floor.

"I'm called Toby," Foxleigh said.

"Toby what?" Griffs demanded. His gun, not surprisingly, was still pointed at Foxleigh's face.

"Just Toby."

"Look—"

He broke off at a gesture from Smith. "What do you do up here, Mr. Toby?" the older man asked in a more reasonable tone.

Foxleigh shrugged. "I live," he said. "Pretty much the same thing you do in the city."

"I meant, how do you survive?" Smith said. "Food and clothing and all?"

"There's plenty of game about," Foxleigh said. "I do some hunting and trapping, and I've got a small vegetable plot around the side of the cliff face over there."

"And the people in Shelter Valley help you out, too, I suppose?"

Foxleigh grimaced. "Sometimes," he admitted. "Some of them. Only when I can't do for myself."

"And that's not very often, I imagine," Smith said, glancing around the cabin. "You seem the self-sufficient sort. Tell me, how long have you been up here?"

Foxleigh shrugged as casually as he could. Here was where things were going to get dicey. "Don't remember exactly," he said vaguely.

"Since before the war?"

"Some, I guess," Foxleigh conceded.

"And you were, what, sixty or so when it began?" Smith persisted.

It would have been nice to be able to bring that number down to somewhere around thirty, Foxleigh knew. It would line up with his actual age and eliminate a lot of potentially unpleasant questions. Unfortunately, there were people in Shelter Valley who might remember the real Toby being in his upper fifties when he turned his back on humanity and moved out on them. "Closer to fifty," he said, fudging the number as far as he could.

"Which would make you about eighty years old," Smith concluded, peering closely at Foxleigh's face. "You're in mighty good shape for a man that age. Especially given the kind of life you lead."

"Life like this keeps a man healthy," Foxleigh countered. "You soft city folk ought to try it sometime." He lifted his eyebrows at Griffs. "Especially you."

Griffs bristled, but another gesture from Smith kept him quiet. "I'm sure it does," Smith said. "But it doesn't keep you *that* healthy." His eyes hardened. "You've been getting Idunine, haven't you?"

That was, of course, the obvious first assumption for them to make. Trouble was, it had the potential to get all of Shelter Valley into nearly as much trouble as the truth would. "What if I have?" Foxleigh growled. "Is that a crime?"

Smith shrugged. "Depends on how you've been getting it."

Foxleigh lowered his eyes. "Don't want to get anyone in trouble," he muttered.

"You won't," Smith assured him.

Foxleigh knew how much *that* promise was worth. But he had little choice in the matter. "It was the doc in town," he admitted. "Doc Adamson. He gave me a little once when my leg was acting up so badly I couldn't walk."

"When was that?"

"Ten years ago," Foxleigh said grudgingly. "Maybe twelve."

"Did it work?"

"Good enough," Foxleigh said, watching the other's face out of the corner of his down-turned eyes. So far he seemed to be buying it. "I still have some trouble, especially in the cold. But at least I can get by."

"So what other illegal drugs does Doc Adamson have?" Griffs asked.

"Who says Idunine is illegal?" Foxleigh demanded, glaring up at him. "Used to be you could get it all the time before the war."

"*Before* the war," Griffs repeated tersely. "This is *after* the war, and Idunine is strongly regulated. Somehow, I don't see a backwoods witch doctor having legal access to it."

"Maybe he had some left over from before," Foxleigh said, looking accusingly at Smith. "You said he wouldn't get in trouble."

"If he was just using up an old supply, he won't," Smith assured him. "But if he's black-marketing it . . . well, we'll see."

Foxleigh grimaced. That was, in fact, the story he and Adamson had worked out all those years ago in case someone started asking these very questions. He just hoped the doc hadn't forgotten the details. "So is that it?" he muttered.

"Just about," Smith said. "You said you did some hunting. That mean you have a gun?"

"No, I brain the deer with rocks," Foxleigh bit out sarcastically. "Of course I have a gun. It's over there beside the bed."

"Guns are regulated, too, of course," Smith pointed out as Griffs strode over for a look.

"Yeah, why am I not surprised?" Foxleigh said with a sniff, watching Griffs closely as he took the old scattergun off the rack. "Careful with it—*careful*."

"He is," Smith said soothingly. "Well?"

"It's within the limits," Griffs said, a note of disappointment in his voice. Clearly, he'd been hoping he could find an excuse to confiscate it. Setting it back into its rack, he pulled up the thin mattress and looked beneath it. "Any other weapons?"

"Just the knife, and it's mostly for eating with," Foxleigh said. "What are you doing?"

"I'm looking around," Griffs said, dropping the mattress and running his hands through the books and other odds and ends in the crate that served as a nightstand. "That all right with you?"

"Not really, no," Foxleigh said, looking back at Smith. "If he wrecks anything, it's coming out of his hide."

"He'll be careful," Smith said, his voice suddenly a little too casual. "You have any visitors up here recently?"

Foxleigh felt his stomach tighten. "Not unless the doc's visit way back when counts as *recently*," he said. "Why?"

"The thermal reading we took from the town a little

while ago seemed too high for one man," Smith said. "You have anything you'd like to tell us?"

"Aside from *go to hell*?" Foxleigh countered. "This is the cabin. You see anyone else here?"

"Don't get smart," Griffs warned as he sifted gingerly through the wood bin. "If you're covering for someone, you're going to be in serious trouble."

Foxleigh snorted. "I stopped covering for *anyone* forty years ago," he said. "You were probably just reading my stove—you can see for yourself it's still hot. That, or your equipment's no damn good."

"We'll have it checked out," Smith said. "Griffs?"

"Seems clean," Griffs said, standing in the middle of the room for one final look. His eyes lingered a moment on the sink and toilet area, and Foxleigh held his breath. But the young Security man turned away without comment and nodded to his partner. "Let's get out of this pig hole."

"Good-bye, Mr. Toby," Smith said, giving Foxleigh an almost friendly smile as they left.

Foxleigh watched through the window as the two men picked their way down the path back toward town, his stomach settling into a hard knot. Smith's smile had been almost friendly, all right. But Foxleigh wasn't fooled, any more than Smith had been fooled by his hot-stove story. A good IR sensor could tell the difference between a stove and a human body, and even if the analyzers on their Birren-7 patrol boat weren't good enough to sort that out the ones in Athena certainly were.

And if he'd been reading Smith's face right, running the track through those analyzers was the first thing he would do when he got back to base.

Half an hour later, he heard the Birren-7 lift back into the sky . . . and with that, the clock was now counting down. Still, he couldn't simply haul the two blackcollars back up. Not yet. Smith might have been suspicious enough to leave an observer or two behind.

Maybe there was a way to find out about that. Reaching to the top of the window, he pulled down the red shade. Then, crossing over to his larder, he started putting together a traveling pack.

Adamson must have been watching for the signal. Barely fifteen minutes later, the medic strode through the door. "What happened?" he asked.

"About what you'd expect," Foxleigh said, sinking down on the end of the bed and gesturing his visitor to the chair. "They came in, looked around, and made veiled threats against whoever'd given me my Idunine. I told them you'd used old stock."

"Yes, they asked me about that, too," Adamson said. "But they seemed satisfied with my answers. What did you say about the IR readings?"

"You knew about that?"

"I heard them discussing it," Adamson said. "That was just before they asked me who lived up here."

"I tried to blame the stove," Foxleigh said, grimacing. "But I don't think they bought it."

"I don't think so, either," Adamson agreed with a sigh. "Cracked ribs or not, Jensen and Flynn are both going with me tomorrow."

"They're going sometime in the next hour, you mean," Foxleigh said with a snort. "That's the round-trip time to Boulder."

"Relax," Adamson said, holding out a hand. "They already have their hands full checking on the other pylons."

Foxleigh frowned. "The pylons? *That's* all they were here for?"

"That's it," Adamson said. "And they're hurrying like crazy to get back to base before full night. Apparently, they're expecting trouble in Athena."

Foxleigh took a deep breath. So he had a little more time. Good. "Any idea what kind of trouble?"

Adamson shrugged. "They weren't talking about it, but my guess is blackcollar trouble." He lifted his eyebrows. "Now for the *big* question: What are *you* planning to do with all this?"

Foxleigh's first impulse was to lie. But Adamson deserved better. "I'm going into the base," he told the other. "Jensen knows the way—he was in once before."

"You think that's where he and Flynn were headed?"

"I don't know what else could possibly be out here he would want," Foxleigh said. "All I have to do is persuade him to take me in with him."

"How? With the truth?"

Foxleigh shrugged. "As much of it as he needs."

"As much as he needs, or as much as you want him to know?"

"Same difference," Foxleigh said. He smiled tightly. "Hell, doc, even *you* don't know *all* the truth."

"Yeah, I've always sort of figured that," Adamson said ruefully. "You *can* trust me, you know."

"I know," Foxleigh said with a sigh. "But there are certain truths that are better left hidden."

For a moment the two men sat in silence, each wrapped in his own thoughts. For Foxleigh, the thoughts were mingled with bitter memories. But they would soon be over. All of it would soon be over.

Eventually, Adamson stirred. "So what do you want me to do?"

"Take Flynn into Denver tomorrow as planned," Foxleigh said. "He needs to find the other blackcollars and let them know what's happening."

"You sure you and Jensen won't need him?" Adamson asked doubtfully. "That's not an easy hike, and you both qualify for walking-wounded status."

"We'll make it," Foxleigh said.

"If you don't, it's an equally long walk back," Adamson warned. "What then?"

"Then as far as I'm concerned, you're released," Foxleigh said. "Your life is completely your own again."

Adamson's eyes drifted toward the window and the mountain towering against the sky to the southeast. "You're not coming back, are you?" he said quietly.

Foxleigh shrugged, probably a little too casually. "That depends on what I can talk Jensen into. Hey, I may not even make it over the next ridge." He held out a hand. "But whatever happens, I want you to know how much I appreciate what you've done for me."

"I haven't done anything but my job," Adamson told him, gripping the other's hand tightly. "Good luck to you."

"And to you," Foxleigh said, letting go of his hand. "Now go home. Practice being shocked by the horrific revelations Security's going to bring when they come knocking on the door."

"Shocked I can do in my sleep," Adamson said with a wry smile. "Good-bye . . . Sam."

It was the first time in nearly three decades that he'd been called by his true name. The sound of it rang strangely in his ears. "Good-bye, Doc."

He waited until Adamson had disappeared around a turn in the path. Then, crossing the cabin, he pulled open the latrine box. "Clear," he called softly. "Come on up."

A few minutes later, the two blackcollars were back in the cabin. "What did they want?" Jensen asked as he disentangled himself from his rope.

"Adamson says they came to town to check on the sensor pylons," Foxleigh said, running a critical eye over the other. Jensen's voice was firm enough, but his face seemed a little pale and he was definitely favoring his side. Hanging down there for an hour wrapped in a rope harness couldn't have done his injuries any good. "They came up *here* because their IR sensors seemed to show more than one person present and accounted for."

"I was afraid of that," Jensen said, coiling the rope and setting it on top of the wood bin. "Is there someplace out there where Flynn can wait for Adamson's morning shuttle service?"

"Assuming they don't shut down the whole region," Flynn warned. "Anyway, I'm thinking maybe we should forget Denver and try the cross-country route."

"Relax—I don't think they'll be back tonight," Foxleigh said. "Doc says they have to check the rest of the pylons and then hotfoot it to Athena. Here, I'll take that," he added, holding out his hand as Flynn pulled his old pistol from his belt.

"What's happening in Athena?" Flynn asked, handing it over.

"No idea," Foxleigh said, putting the gun carefully in his own waistband. "But I get the feeing they're expecting a show from your friends tonight."

Jensen grimaced. "With us on the sidelines," he growled. "No way we can get out tonight, I suppose?"

"Cars aren't back yet," Foxleigh reminded him. "We may want to send Flynn down to Adamson's place overnight, though, just in case. The question is what we're going to do with *you*. You're not in any shape for a long, bumpy car ride."

"No, but I don't think we've got much choice," Jensen said. "If they come back with a full team, there's nowhere around here I can hide where they can't eventually chase me down."

"Unless you go—" Flynn broke off.

"Unless you go where?" Foxleigh asked.

"Unless I go somewhere outside this valley and go to ground," Jensen said, his eyes sending a warning look in Flynn's direction. "And I'd better get started while I've still got some light."

"You're not in any shape for a long walk, either," Foxleigh said firmly. "At least, not alone. I'm going with you."

"What, with your bad leg?" Jensen asked, gesturing toward it.

"I'll match my leg against your ribs any day," Foxleigh said. "Besides, the minute you're out of sight of the cabin and town you'll be completely lost."

"You might be surprised," Jensen said.

"Or *you* might be," Foxleigh countered. "There are

a lot of ways to get lost, sidetracked, or stuck out there."

"I could try to get you to cover tonight and then come back for my rendezvous with Adamson in the morning," Flynn suggested.

"You'd get just as lost together as either of you would get separately," Foxleigh said. "What are we still arguing about this for? The subject is closed. I'm helping Jensen to cover. Period."

Jensen and Flynn exchanged looks. "He kind of sounds like Lathe when he's in one of his moods, doesn't he?" Jensen commented.

"He does a little," Flynn agreed, clearly not at all happy with the situation.

"All right, Toby, you're on," Jensen said, looking back at Foxleigh. "When do we leave?"

"As soon as we've organized some provisions," Foxleigh said, a sense of relief rushing over him. Relief, and an odd sadness. "Give me a hand putting these travel packs together, will you?"

Twenty minutes later, the two men slipped through the door into the gathering dusk. Ten paces from the cabin, Foxleigh led them off the path that led to town and set off eastward through the wilderness.

As they headed down a small rise, he turned for one last look at the place that had been his home for so many years. Flynn was visible in the doorway, standing straight and tall and motionless, watching them leave.

He knew he would never see either the cabin or the boy again.

*   *   *

Three o'clock in the morning.

Bailey stood at the hospital room window, hands clasped behind his back, staring out at Athena's muted streetlights and quiet buildings. So the blackcollars hadn't attacked after all. True, there was no particular reason why they should have, especially given that they were still supposedly waiting for Poirot to deliver the data on the defense laser threshold. But somewhere in the back of his mind, he'd expected that question to have been a ruse, a ploy to lull him into a false sense of security while they hit the place a day earlier than expected.

But they hadn't. So where did that leave him?

"Colonel?"

Bailey turned. The interrogator he'd brought over earlier in the evening was leaning over the bandage-swathed figure in the bed, his ear close to the boy's mouth.

The boy. Mentally, Bailey shook his head, his mind flashing back to that fever dream Poirot had spun for them back in the conference room about Aegis Mountain and weapons caches and secret military forces. Whatever this Phoenix was that Reger and Silcox had created, it wasn't even close to being an army, and all the weapons and blackcollars in the world wouldn't change that. This kid, in particular, was barely even out of college—

"Colonel!"

"Yes, I'm listening," Bailey growled, feeling his face warm with embarrassment as he angrily shook the random thoughts away. Fatigue always made his mind drift that way. "What is it?"

"I think you'll want to hear this for yourself, sir," the

interrogator said, sitting upright and gesturing to the chair at the other side of the bed.

Frowning, Bailey sat down. The kid's eyes were closed, his breathing slow but steady. "Go ahead," he told the interrogator.

The other nodded. "Rob?" he called softly. "Rob? You need to tell our other friend here what you just told me."

For a moment the kid didn't move. Then, his head turned slightly, his eyes reluctantly opening to slits. "She knows," he murmured. "She knows the way inside."

Something with cold feet took a walk up Bailey's spine. "Who knows the way?" he asked, leaning close to the boy.

"Anne," Rob said. "Anne does."

"Anne Silcox?"

"Yes," the boy said. "They told her. You know. The blackcollars."

Bailey looked up at the interrogator. "Ask him the way into what," the other suggested quietly.

Bailey looked back at the injured prisoner. "What place does Anne know the way into?"

"You know," Rob said, his voice almost too soft to be heard. "Aegis Mountain."

Bailey's mouth was suddenly very dry. Could Poirot have been right after all? "Do *you* know the way in?" he asked.

"No," Rob said. "Just Anne. And the blackcollars."

Bailey locked eyes with the interrogator. "This had better be straight," he warned.

"It is," the interrogator assured him. "I never prompted him."

Bailey looked back down at the half-sleeping kid. So

there was a way in after all, a way the blackcollars had apparently found.

And at this very moment, across town, General Poirot was working with the tactical group who were trying to come up with a plan to capture one or more of those same blackcollars. Coincidence?

Abruptly, Bailey got to his feet. "Keep at him," he told the interrogator as he snagged his coat from the hook. "Find out everything he knows, and I mean *everything*. I'll send over a couple more men to assist."

"You don't need to do that, sir," the other assured him. "I can handle it."

Bailey gazed at him, an unpleasant tingle whispering through him. Whiplash . . . "I'll send a couple more men to assist," he repeated, his tone making it an order. "And you aren't to breathe a word of any of this to anyone but them and me. Clear?"

The interrogator's lips compressed. "Yes, sir."

Three minutes later Bailey was in his car, heading through the silent Athena streets toward the Security building. Yes, Poirot had been right about Phoenix and Aegis Mountain. The question now was, *how* had he managed to be so right?

More to the immediate point, did this wonderful revelation come with hidden strings attached?

He didn't know. But he was damn well going to find out.

CHAPTER 13

It was still dark when Jensen's mental alarm clock went off. Four o'clock in the morning, or near enough.

Time to go.

For a minute he lay still on the hard ground, listening to the night sounds around him playing counterpoint to Toby's slow, even breathing. The man was asleep, with the deep oblivion of a man who'd spent a couple of hours the evening before tromping through unbroken wilderness on a bad leg.

In a way, he hated to leave the old man out here alone. Unlike the Plinry blackcollars, it didn't look like Toby had been getting the periodic low-level Idunine doses that had kept their muscles and organs young while letting their outer appearances age normally. It had been a long, hard trek, and it would be an equally hard trek back to his cabin.

But where Jensen was going, he was going alone. Carefully, wincing as his ribs flared in protest, he rolled halfway over and started to get to his feet.

273

"Going somewhere?" Toby asked mildly.

Jensen frowned toward the dark lump a couple of meters away. He would have *sworn* the other was asleep. "Thought I'd see if I could find a place that was open for breakfast," he said.

"You've found it," Toby said, sitting up. "This bush right here's the best place in the Rockies. Here—special of the day."

He held something out; a ration bar, Jensen discovered as he took it. "You're a pretty light sleeper," he commented as he tore off the end of the wrapper.

"So are you," Toby said. "Luckily for me, you're also very predictable."

"In what way?"

"For starters, this little attempt to ditch me," Toby said. "That *was* what you were intending, wasn't it?"

Jensen grimaced. "I appreciate all your help, Toby," he said. "But where I'm going it isn't safe for you to go."

"Why not?" Toby countered. "Didn't you and the other blackcollars close down what was left of Aegis's defenses the last time you were in there?"

So there it was, out in the open at last. "Very good," he said. "Where did you hide your telescope? I never saw it in your cabin."

"I packed it away in a rotten log after I sent Adamson and Trapper out to look for you," Toby replied. "You're good, too. I didn't realize you'd spotted me."

"I caught a couple of glints from the lens," Jensen said. "So what do you want?"

"The same thing you do," Toby said. "I want into Aegis Mountain."

Jensen shook his head. "Sorry."

"If I don't go, neither do you," Toby warned.

"Is that a threat?" Jensen asked, wishing it was light enough for him to see whether or not the other was holding his pistol.

"It's a statement of fact," Toby said. "I'm guessing that whatever you want in there is going to involve at least a little bit of heavy lifting. There's no way you're going to do any of that, not with your ribs the way they are."

"And you're not going to make it with your leg the way it is," Jensen countered. "There's a lot of walking and climbing involved."

"I'll make it," Toby said firmly. "And not to push, but this *is* a limited-time deal. Eventually, Security's going to get around to analyzing the pylon team's IR data and come out here for another look. The only place we can go where they won't spot us is inside the base."

"Alternatively, that's exactly what they're hoping I'll think," Jensen countered. "Maybe the plan is for you to talk me into showing you the way in."

"And then what?" Toby scoffed. "I overpower you with my bare hands and call them in?"

"You have a gun," Jensen reminded him.

Toby snorted. "And I'm supposed to threaten a *black-collar* with a *gun*? That's hardly the way I want to die."

"How *do* you want to die?"

"Not that way," Toby said, a sudden oddness to his voice. "So are we going? Or would you rather be sitting here arguing about it when Security flies in to pick us up?"

Jensen grimaced as he gazed at the other's silhouette in the starlight. Toby was right, he had to admit—with his ribs in the shape they were he wasn't going to accomplish much alone. But there were still an awful lot of question marks swirling around the old hermit.

On the other hand, Toby was also right about Security coming out for a second look . . . and after personally sampling their torture methods on Argent, he knew he would eventually break down and show them the secret entrance.

And he was damned if he was going to lose by default. "All right," he said reluctantly. "But you're going to have to get me to the right area. I have no idea where we are."

"We're not too far," Toby assured him, using a tree branch to help himself to his feet. "I figured we might as well head that direction to start with."

"Yeah, I sort of figured that," Jensen said, pushing himself off the ground.

"Here." Toby offered a hand.

Jensen gripped it, and together they got him upright. "Thanks," he said, pausing while the stabbing pain in his side settled back down to a dull ache. "Did you want to eat something before we go?"

"I can eat along the way." Toby hesitated. "And if it would make you feel better about me, I can give you my gun."

"No, that's okay," Jensen said, waving away the offer. "Ribs or no ribs, if I can't take care of a single old codger with a gun, I probably deserve to get shot."

"You have no idea how comforting a thought that is, too," Toby said dryly.

"I try," Jensen said. Besides, if Toby was a Security plant, he would certainly have a backup weapon tucked away somewhere. "Which way?"

"Through there," Toby said, pointing toward a gap between two stands of trees. "Give me a hand, will you, until my leg unstiffens a little?"

"Colonel?"

Bailey started awake, rolling over on the cot he'd had set up in his office. Ramirez was standing in the doorway, a sheaf of papers in his hand. "Yes, what is it?" he asked, wincing as he stretched aching muscles.

"I have something here you should see," Ramirez said, coming in as Bailey sat up. "One of the pylon teams picked this up late yesterday afternoon."

Frowning, Bailey took the papers. On top was a print of an infrared-sensor photo with a small shack in the center. The legend at the bottom of the print gave the coordinates, plus the fact that it had gone through a three-stage computer scrubbing. "What am I supposed to see?" he asked.

"There appear to be two human images present," Ramirez said, pointing to two blurs in the shack. "One sitting near the window, the other lying down further back. Problem is, the cabin's owned by a hermit who allegedly lives alone."

The hairs on the back of Bailey's neck began to tingle as he peeled off the top sheet and looked at the next page down, a topo map of the region with the cabin marked with a circle. It was just above a place called Shelter Valley, a few klicks northwest of Aegis Mountain. "Didn't anyone have the brains to wonder about this?"

"Actually, sir, two of the Security men accompanying the techs did go up to take a look," Ramirez said stiffly, and Bailey belatedly remembered that those tech teams had come from Ramirez's office. "When they got there, the hermit was alone."

"Did they get any other readings?" Bailey asked, shuffling through the papers. There didn't seem to be any more prints. "Anyone have any idea where the other one might have gone?"

"Unfortunately, no," Ramirez said sourly. "The sensor data wasn't nearly clear enough for them to take any action or even send up any red flags. You can see yourself that it took three scrubbings to get it even this clear."

Bailey looked back at the first page, frowning as he spotted the time stamp. "This came through at *midnight*?" he snarled, jabbing a finger at the number. "Why the hell are we talking about it *now*?"

"I tried to talk to Battle Architect Daasaa as soon as it came through," Ramirez said, his voice under tight control. "But he wouldn't authorize me to release any of the spotters or men assigned to Athena guard duty."

"Then why didn't you bring it to *me*?" Bailey snarled. "Maybe *I* could have done something."

"Yes, sir, I thought you might," Ramirez countered. "The trouble was, you'd left the building without telling anyone where you were going. And despite what you told the garage sergeant, we weren't able to reach you by comm."

Bailey squeezed the papers tightly between his fingers, silently cursing himself. Of course they hadn't been able to contact him—he'd turned off his comm so that the background chatter wouldn't distract him from his private interrogation at the hospital and had forgotten to turn it back on. "Get a team out there now," he ordered, glancing at the rim of the sun pushing its way above the eastern horizon. "I want the cabin searched—*thoroughly*—and everyone in town questioned. On second thought, make it *two* teams. And run me up everything we have on that hermit."

"I already did that, sir," Ramirez said, indicating the papers in Bailey's hand. "But I can't send any teams without Daasaa's authorization."

"Oh, can't you?" Bailey growled, getting to his feet. It was their missing blackcollar, all right—it had to be. If he slipped through their fingers because of miscommunication or flat-out bureaucratic bumbling, heads were going to roll. Very possibly literally. "Fine. Let's go find him."

The colors of the sky to the east were fading into blue, though the sun hadn't yet appeared over the mountains, when they reached the hidden air vent. "Here we are," Jensen said, pointing to the grating at the vent's mouth as they crossed the small clearing in front of it.

"Amazing," Foxleigh said, shaking his head in wonderment. Even knowing there was something out here to find, he hadn't spotted the grating until they were practically on top of it. "You know, I actually saw the kids who were working on this, though I couldn't tell what they were doing. It wasn't until your group showed up last year that I put the pieces together."

"I'm glad Security wasn't paying you visits then," Jensen said, starting to unfasten the twisted wires that held the grating in place. "Give me a hand here, will you?"

It took them several minutes to get the grating free. After that, it took four pulls by both of them to get it off. "You were right," Jensen admitted, puffing like a distance runner. "I couldn't have done that alone."

"We're going to want to close it up behind us, aren't we?" Foxleigh asked as he peered carefully inside. Beyond the grating, a metallic tunnel stretched back about twelve meters, then seemed to turn downward.

"Absolutely," Jensen said. "Let's turn it on edge and bring it inside, see if we can wedge it into position."

Five minutes later, they had it back in position and wired again in place. "Well, that was fun," Foxleigh commented. "Any trick to the rest of it?"

"All sorts of them," Jensen assured him, pointing down the tunnel. "We start with a hundred-meter climb down a ladder, with a sonic at the bottom that'll be trying to poke holes in your balance the whole way."

"Lovely," Foxleigh said, wincing. Like he didn't have enough trouble with balance even on his better days. "You didn't think to turn it off before you left?"

"We didn't want to turn it off," Jensen said. "Anyone authorized to be in here would know about it and be mentally prepared to fight against the effects. The only others who might come in here we didn't much care about."

Foxleigh shivered. Once upon a time, he reminded himself soberly, he'd considered coming out here on his own to check the place out. It was just as well he hadn't. "Okay, consider me mentally prepared," he said. "Let's get to it."

They were at the downward curve, and Jensen was fiddling with a rope ladder that had been left behind, when

Foxleigh thought he heard the distant sound of approaching patrol boats. But it could have been his imagination.

"So they're gone," Bailey said flatly.

"Yes, sir," Ramirez said, his own voice stiff and formal. Clearly, he had no intention of taking the blame for this. "They found two ropes hanging down into a ravine from pulleys fastened beneath a trick box where Toby had mounted his toilet seat."

"Where he'd *what*?" Bailey lifted a hand before Ramirez could answer. "Never mind—I don't want to know. Did you track along this ravine to see where it goes?"

"It doesn't seem to actually *go* anywhere," Ramirez said. "The stream that Toby tapped into for his water supply joins it a little ways along, and then it just meanders its way southwest. There may be places where you can get out, though, which the team couldn't see from the air. If you'd like, I could send a couple of men to follow it on foot for a ways."

"Don't bother," Bailey growled. "Ten to one he and this Toby character left those ropes dangling as a red herring. If they're going anywhere, they'll be heading *toward* Aegis Mountain, not away from it."

"*Toward* Aegis Mountain?" Ramirez echoed, frowning.

"Certainly not away from it," Bailey said again, silently cursing his slip. Of course Ramirez didn't know the black-collars had found a secret back door into the base. "Is there anywhere else they might have gone?"

"Yes, sir, they could have gone to Denver," Ramirez said. "One of Shelter Valley's residents *and* one of the town's two cars are missing."

Bailey sat up a little straighter in his chair. "Was this resident carrying any passengers?"

"No one saw any," Ramirez said, studying Bailey's face closely. Clearly, he'd picked up on the colonel's sudden change in mood. "But there are any number of places on the road he could have stopped to pick someone up."

"And then have brought him to Denver," Bailey murmured, thinking hard. If their rogue blackcollar had gone straight into Aegis, the Ryqril were out of luck. But if he'd decided to come to town first to get the rest of the gang, there was still a chance. "Any chance of intercepting them along the way?"

Ramirez shook his head. "We've had spotters run the whole length of the road, and there's nothing's moving on it. If they started at first light, they'd be here already. Of course, we *do* have a description of the car."

"Which they probably buried the minute they hit town," Bailey said. "But there's only one road that'll take them back home?"

"Uh . . ." Ramirez sorted through his papers. "There are actually *two* possible routes, one somewhat longer than the other," he said. "But that seems to be it."

"Have both of them watched," Bailey ordered. "Spotters are to tag anything headed toward that area. High-flight only—we don't want to spook them."

"Yes, sir," Ramirez said uncertainly. "We'll have to clear it through Battle Architect Daasaa first, of course."

"I'll deal with that," Bailey promised. No matter how paranoid the Ryqril might be about attacks on Athena, they would spring for as many men and spotters as he needed once he laid all this in front of them. "You just get the spotter teams organized. I'll get you the authorization."

"Yes, sir," Ramirez said again. "Is there some reason you think he'll be going back there?"

"I guarantee he will, Lieutenant," Bailey, favoring the other with a slightly malicious smile. "If the blackcollar came to Denver, he *will* be going back. The question is how best to turn it to our advantage."

"Yes, sir," Ramirez said, his voice gone neutral. "With your permission, I'll go organize the spotter teams."

"You do that, Lieutenant," Bailey said, getting to his feet and gathering up the papers. "You do that."

"I've got the data you asked for," Poirot's voice came over the phone. "I'm afraid it's not good news."

"Let's hear it," Skyler said, his eyes sweeping the busy Denver street scene flowing around him. Security's two options were to trace the call and try to nab him, or else let Poirot continue to lead him on in hopes of setting up a trap somewhere farther down the line. So far, he couldn't tell which way they were planning to jump.

"It looks like Athena's lasers will activate if anything larger than fifteen centimeters shows a projected path over the outer fence. That's way too small for anything useful."

"Oh, I don't know," Skyler said. "You could make a serious bomb smaller than that."

"A bomb would involve explosives and probably a fair amount of metal," Poirot pointed out. "There are other sensors along the top of the fence that would tag anything like that long before the proximity and size sensors kicked in."

"I suppose," Skyler said. "I imagine small quantities of explosives might still be able to slip through the screen, though."

"Maybe, but it couldn't be very much bigger than primer cap size," Poirot warned. "Unless you know some special trick."

Skyler smiled. Poirot was so obvious when he was trolling for information. "I know a few," he said. "What about the laser emplacements themselves?"

"What about them?" Poirot asked, his voice gone suddenly cautious as the change in topic seemed to catch him by surprise.

"Are they guarded by the same sort of sensor screen?" Skyler asked.

"They're run by the Ryqril," Poirot growled. "How do you *think* they're guarded?"

Skyler chuckled. "Extremely well, I'd assume," he conceded. "Relax—it was just a thought."

"I suggest you leave it that way," Poirot growled. "You've got enough trouble with the Ryqril at the moment. You take on one of their military emplacements and you'll *really* stir them up. Trust me, you do *not* want that."

"Agreed," Skyler said. "That just leaves the prisoner transfer, then. Any changes in the schedule?"

"Not so far," Poirot said, sounding relieved to be back on ground he'd presumably already cleared with his Ryqril masters. "We're still planning a seven p.m. departure for Colorado Springs: six vans, one prisoner per."

"Anything tricky about the vans themselves?"

"They've got upgraded engines and some extra armor

in strategic places," Poirot said. "They've also got extra-wide sunroofs where someone can pop up, slap a maglock rapid-fire gun onto the roof, and spray the area with paral-darts, flechettes, or laser fire."

"And I presume you'll be planting trackers on each of the prisoners?"

"Actually, we may not bother," Poirot said. "You'll certainly have bug stompers along to block any transmissions anyway, won't you?"

"Definitely," Skyler said. "I guess that's it, then. Let's plan a call for two days from now, same time and place as our contact yesterday."

"You don't want to talk tomorrow?"

"I was thinking your office might be a little busy tomorrow," Skyler said dryly.

There was a short silence, and Skyler could practically hear the other's thoughts. If the blackcollars managed to pull this off, Athena's Security contingent would indeed be busy tomorrow. A number of them, in fact, might be facing summary execution. "Fine," Poirot said grimly. "Two days."

"Talk to you then," Skyler said, and hung up the phone.

He kept alert for trouble as he walked back to the car where Anne was waiting. But it was mostly habit. Clearly, the Ryqril had decided to feed the blackcollars rope in the hope that they would ensnare themselves with it.

Which meant that the prisoner transfer tonight would certainly be a trap. But then, Skyler had never expected it to be otherwise.

He reached the car and got in. "Well?" Anne asked.

"Athena's lasers will fire if a football goes over," he told her. "They'll also allegedly fire if *any* size explosive tries to do the same."

"So that's that?"

"Not necessarily," Skyler said. "We might still be able to do something clever."

Anne shook her head. "One of these days you're going to run out of cleverness," she warned. "I just hope you've got something else in reserve when you do."

"So do I," Skyler said with a grimace. "Let's get back and see if we can postpone that day a little."

Anne had just started the car when Skyler's tingler unexpectedly came to life. "Hold it," he said, pressing the device harder against his wrist and trying to read the dots and dashes.

"What is it?" Anne asked.

"I'm not sure," Skyler said, frowning. The message was strangely garbled, as if coming from somewhere right at the edge of the transmitter's range and critical bits were getting dropped.

Or as if the transmitting blackcollar was unable to control his fingers properly, like he'd been hit with a low-level dose of paral-dart drug. *O'Hara?* he signaled urgently.

Here, the other's signal came back. *Trouble?*

You getting any other signals?

Negative.

So it *was* apparently a distance thing. O'Hara was obviously in clear range, and at the moment Hawking and Kanai shouldn't be in range at all.

Which left Jensen and Flynn. "Get going," he ordered Anne.

"Security?" she asked, glancing back and pulling out into the traffic flow.

"No, I think it may actually be good news for a change," Skyler said, tapping his tingler again. *Jensen?*

No answer. Apparently, he'd dipped out of range again.

And if O'Hara, running backup further west, wasn't getting anything at all . . . "Head east," he told Anne, repeating his tingler message.

"What is it?" Anne persisted. "Come on, Skyler, this is no time to go all secretive on me."

"No secrecy involved," Skyler assured her, smiling tightly. "We're off to find a couple of lost sheep."

"Aegis Nountain," Daasaa repeated, his dark eyes glittering. "Yae are certain o' this?"

"I'm certain that's what the prisoner said," Bailey told him. "It is, of course, possible that he was lied to. But I don't think so."

Beside Daasaa, Halaak rumbled something. Daasaa replied, and for a minute the battle architect and *khassq* warrior conferred. Bailey waited, mentally checking over the details of the plan he had prepared. "Re nust ca'ture the 'lackcollars ali'e," Daasaa said firmly, turning back to Bailey. "Yae rill nake sure o' that."

"I intend to," Bailey said firmly. "To that end, I have an idea I'd like permission to present to you."

Daasaa inclined his head slightly. "Re rill listen."

Bailey braced himself. "We start by accepting General Poirot's plan for sending the prisoners out of Athena by convoy. Somewhere along the way, of course, I expect the blackcollars to attack it."

"And re rill ca'ture they?"

"We'll certainly try," Bailey said. "But it's always harder to capture someone alive than it is to kill him, and it may be that we'll be forced to let the rescue succeed."

"The 'risoners rill *not* esca'," Halaak snarled. "Re ha' not yet disco'ered all that they know."

"But it's the blackcollars who know what we need most, Your Eminence," Bailey reminded him.

"Yae rill *not*—"

"Yae ha' nore tae say?" Daasaa cut him off.

Halaak hissed something, his hand dropping to the hilt of his short sword. Clearly, *khassq* warriors were not used to being interrupted. But Daasaa didn't even bother to look at him, much less apologize. "Yae ha' nore tae say?" he repeated to Bailey.

"Yes, Your Eminences," Bailey said carefully, trying to make it clear he was including Halaak in the conversation. Even a *khassq* might not be authorized to take out his frustrations on a battle architect, but there was nothing to stop him from doing so on a mere human. "My suggestion is that we add a wild card to the mix, something that Poirot knows nothing about. Namely, we keep one of the prisoners here and replace him with a loyalty-conditioned substitute from Athena."

"Rill the Kheonix leaders not recognize the 'alse run?" Halaak demanded scornfully.

"Certainly, once they get a close look at him in good light," Bailey agreed. "But I'm expecting the blackcollars, not Phoenix, to be the main rescue force. Even if there are other Phoenix leaders there, they won't have time to do a close examination, particularly if we're careful in our choice of a substitute. By the time they get him to someone who realizes he's a fake, they should have arrived at either their hideout or at least a temporary rendezvous spot, places where they may not have escape plans already set up. At that point our man will ignite a cryrex flare for the spotters to lock onto, and we'll move in and grab as many of them as we can. Between the blackcollars and the Phoenix leaders, we should end up with *someone* who knows the way into Aegis."

"There rill 'e 'asswords," Halaak warned.

"We already have them, Your Eminence," Bailey said. "Our interrogators are very good at their jobs."

"It is a good 'lan," Daasaa said decisively. "Yae rill 'roceed rith it."

"Thank you, Your Eminence," Bailey said, bowing his head.

"Yae rill not 'ail," the battle architect added, an edge of warning to his voice. "Ha' yae 'ound sonerun tae act as su'stitute?"

"I have, Your Eminence," Bailey said, a brief shiver running up his back. "He's a financial analyst in the hospital administration, an extremely close match to one of the young men we have in custody upstairs. A new haircut and a couple of small moles added to his cheeks and he'll be nearly perfect."

"Yae rill sho' us," Daasaa ordered, standing up.

"As you command, Your Eminence," Bailey said, getting to his feet. "I've taken the liberty of bringing him here for your examination. If you'll follow me . . .?"

He led the way out of the conference room, ignoring the surreptitious stares of the techs at the monitor stations, a warm glow of satisfaction flowing through him. General Poirot they couldn't trust, and Ramirèz was still a question mark.

But Bailey's own loyalty was crystal clear . . . and when this scheme succeeded, he would have proved it to the Ryqril. Proved it beyond the shadow of a doubt.

Flynn finished his report, and for a long minute the room was silent. "I'm sorry," Flynn said, the words sounding wholly inadequate. "I should have tried harder to stop him."

Standing beside the door, O'Hara stirred. "You'd have gotten your face broken," he said. "Don't blame yourself, Flynn. There's nothing you could have done."

"Not with Jensen," Skyler agreed heavily. "Not once he's made up his mind."

"The question is, should *we* try to stop him?" the other blackcollar, Kanai, asked. "You said his ribs were only cracked?"

"That's what the doctor said," Flynn confirmed, eyeing him curiously. He'd heard about Kanai from Skyler on the flight from Plinry, but the man wasn't at all what he'd expected. Too quiet, maybe, as if he were still carrying some baggage from the war. Or maybe, given Skyler's story, the baggage was from the aftermath of the war. "And he did get some Calcron to help with the healing process."

"In that case, he'll probably make it all the way in," Skyler concluded. "Damn."

"It seems to me you're overreacting a little," an older man who'd been introduced to Flynn as Manx Reger commented from a corner armchair. "You make it sound like denying the Ryqril access means putting the whole mountain into orbit."

"You may not be far off," Kanai warned. "We know that at least the command level and entrance tunnel are heavily doomsdayed. Some of the other areas may be rigged as well."

"The previous owners were very determined to keep the base out of Ryqril hands," Hawking added.

"Sounds like Jensen is following right along that same line of reasoning," Reger said coolly.

"Yes," Flynn said with a grimace. "He also asked that we make as much noise and fury here in Denver as we can. I think he's hoping to make it look like a full-fledged military uprising."

"Lovely idea," Skyler growled. "Problem is, we're going to be pretty well tapped out in the noise and fury department after tonight. I doubt we'll have enough left to mount even a decent Chinese New Year."

"So what do we do?" Hawking asked.

"We seem to have two options," Kanai said. "We can either stay with the plan to free Anne's people, or we can go to Aegis and try to talk Jensen out of this lunatic plan."

"Actually, I'm not so sure it's so lunatic," Flynn said reluctantly. "That base they've got at the entrance is a *lot* bigger now than the one Caine described. They're putting forth some serious effort to get into the mountain."

"If all that's left in there are booby traps, why not let them?" Reger asked.

"Because we don't *know* that's all that's left," Skyler told him. "Regardless, it's not a decision Jensen should be making on his own."

"And he definitely shouldn't be going in there and pulling the plug personally," O'Hara added. "If we decide to wreck the base, there have to be ways of doing it by remote control."

"Perhaps that's what he intends," Kanai suggested.

"I don't think so," Skyler said with a sigh. "He's been . . . well, never mind."

"He's gotten it into his head that he owes the universe a huge debt," Hawking said. "He's spent the last two years looking for a way to pay it off."

Across the room, Anne Silcox stirred. "Then you'd better go and try to stop him, hadn't you?" she said quietly.

"What about your people?" Skyler asked.

"What about them?" she retorted, an edge of bitterness in her voice. "You said yourself the whole convoy will be one gigantic trap."

"True, but even the best traps don't always work," O'Hara pointed out. "And frankly, with the Ryqril taking a personal hand, I'm not expecting this to be one of the best."

"Besides, Jensen's not planning his move until tomorrow night," Hawking said. "We can head up there tomorrow."

"That's cutting things a little close," Flynn warned.

"No way around it," Skyler said firmly, his tone making it clear that he'd made his decision. "As Hawking said, we've got till tomorrow to get to Jensen. Anne's people are being moved tonight. Ergo, we continue the operation as planned."

"If for no other reason than to keep them thinking we still trust Poirot?" Reger asked.

"That's another reason, yes," Skyler agreed. "What's happening with the small explosives you said you could get?"

"Draper has them ready," Reger said. "He's got the tankers you wanted, too."

"Excellent," Skyler said. "Anne, you'll rendezvous with Draper and move the explosives to Site Three. The wind's still predicted to be coming from the north this evening?"

"That's what they say," O'Hara confirmed.

"Site Three it is, then," Skyler said. "And be sure to transport the explosives in small quantities—Security might make more sensor runs over the city and I don't want a collection big enough for them to zero in on. Flynn, give her a hand—she can fill you in on the plan along the way."

"Won't we need Flynn to help with the truck hijacking?" Hawking asked.

"That's been scrubbed," Skyler said. "Turns out Reger has access to enough jellied fuel for what we need."

"Ah," Hawking said. "Then it sounds like we're ready."

"Pretty much," Skyler said. "Let's tie up the last details and get to our positions."

"And hope that Security doesn't have any trump cards of their own to play," Reger warned.

"Oh, I'm sure they will," Skyler assured him with a smile. "That's what makes this so much fun."

Reger's only response was a snort.

Between the hundred-meter climb, the disorienting sonic, and Foxleigh's bad leg, the first part of the trip into

Aegis Mountain was sheer torture. Fortunately, after that it got somewhat easier.

Until, that is, they reached the final part, the narrow tunnel Torch had carved through a hundred and fifty meters of solid rock to bypass the lethal traps of the first-stage air filter system. Foxleigh kept running his knees into small outcroppings of rock as he walked, sending ripples of pain through him and draining what little strength was left in his leg. Jensen, for his part, had to duck his head through much of it, a posture that wasn't doing his injured ribs any good. "At least we don't have to worry about an attack from the rear," Foxleigh muttered when as they reached the midway point. "No Ryq over the age of five would ever fit through here."

"Torch probably designed that way on purpose," Jensen said. "Of course, that just means they'd have to stand at the far end and shoot us from there."

Foxleigh looked back along the mostly straight tunnel behind them. "Oh," he said, and kept going.

The far end of the tunnel opened up into a fifty-meter-long storage room. Foxleigh hobbled inside, panting in the stale air and gazing at the dusty crates waiting patiently to be opened by people who were long dead. All of them except him.

After thirty years, he was finally back inside Aegis Mountain.

"Sorry about the mess," Jensen said. He was breathing a little heavily himself. "Maid's day off."

"I figured," Foxleigh puffed back. "What now?"

"We'll look around a little," Jensen said, wincing as he tried to rub his side through the thincast, an exercise

Foxleigh knew from personal experience to be a complete waste of time. "Then we'll rest a while, maybe get something to eat."

"We could have done that at my cabin," Foxleigh pointed out. "What exactly are we here for?"

Jensen sent a gaze around the dusty chamber. "For thirty years the Ryqril have been the ones dealing out death and destruction," he said, his voice suddenly as dark and cold as Aegis itself. "It's about time we showed them that we can do that, too."

"And how much death and destruction exactly are we talking about?"

"Enough." For a moment Jensen just stood there, his eyes unfocused as if gazing across a long line of ghosts from the past. Foxleigh watched him, his heart thudding unpleasantly. For the first time, he realized, he was seeing past Jensen's layer of control and civilization to what lay beneath it. The man was ready to kill.

He was more than ready to die.

And as that realization sank in, Foxleigh became acutely aware of the pistol pressed against his side beneath his shirt. If he had to use it . . .

Abruptly, Jensen shook his head, a quick doglike water-shedding movement. "Sorry," he said, his voice back to normal. "Memories."

"I have a few of those myself," Foxleigh said. "So when does all this death and destruction happen?"

"Tomorrow night," Jensen told him. "But we can start the prep work right away."

"Or at least after that rest and meal you mentioned?"

"Sure," Jensen said. "Come on, I'll take you to the

medical area. The lighting's better, and there are lockers of emergency rations we can raid." He smiled, his veneer of civilization back in place. "It's a lot cleaner too."

"That's certainly the important thing," Foxleigh said, forcing a lightness into his voice that he didn't feel. "Lead the way."

Shaw's blackcollars had apparently begun arriving early that morning. By the time Lathe took Judas down to their underground staging area there were a good fifty of them present, busily uncrating and organizing various pieces of equipment.

"Looks like we're getting serious," Judas commented as they passed a pair of gray-haired men uncrating a group of flat, one-by-two-meter rectangular body shields. The staging area itself, he now recognized, was another part of the city's former subway system. "I hope this doesn't mean Shaw's taken over the planning again."

"Don't worry, he hasn't," Shaw's voice came from behind them.

Judas turned, his face warming. The tactor was striding toward them, one of the body shields hanging from his left forearm. "Sorry," he apologized. "I meant—"

"Here—try it on," Shaw interrupted, sliding his arm out of the shield's straps and offering it to Judas.

It was considerably heavier than Judas had expected. "Antilaser?"

"Alternating layers of reflective and ablative material to first scatter the light and then diffuse it," Shaw said. "The reflective parts are also highly heat-conductive, so the laser has to basically evaporate the whole layer to get to the next one."

Judas nodded. "What's this?" he asked, touching a thick metal ribbon coiled tightly against the lower left edge of the shield.

"More heat-conductive material," Shaw said. "It gets unrolled behind you to act as a heat sink."

"Must be *really* conductive," Judas said, eyeing the ribbon dubiously.

"It's the same stuff they used to layer on starfighters to protect them against Ryqril laser cannon." Shaw looked at Lathe. "But I can tell you right now that they're not going to get you across fifty meters of open ground."

"They won't have to," Lathe said. "I understand the sensors in our target fence post are pretty well gone?"

Shaw nodded. "Got the report this morning," he said. "He'll keep plugging pellets against it for the rest of the day, though, just to make sure."

"So we're going tonight?" Judas asked carefully.

"Tomorrow night," Lathe said. "We've still got some other prep work to do tonight."

"Plus a set of dress-rehearsal drills," Shaw added.

"Sounds good," Judas said, a shiver running up his back. Barely three days on the ground, and already they were nearly ready to attack a major Ryqril base. Fast, clean, and—hopefully—successful.

Of course, it was no longer the small infiltration force Galway had envisioned when he'd set this scheme in motion. Still, as long as they made it inside maybe the size of the force wouldn't matter.

"You'll be picked up at your house at four-thirty this afternoon," Shaw said. "Be ready in full combat gear."

"I will," Judas said.

"And your pickup will be at five," Shaw added, looking at Lathe.

"We'll be ready," the comsquare assured him.

Shaw nodded and moved off. "Why the different times?" Judas asked.

"Because we're going to different locations," Lathe explained. "Mordecai and I are on the initial assault team; you'll be with interior penetration group."

"Won't the assault team be coming in, too?" Judas asked, frowning.

Lathe smiled grimly. "Some of us will," he said. "Others . . . won't."

A strange sensation bubbled through the pit of Judas's stomach. Up to now, this whole thing had played through his mind almost as if it was a bizarre adventure game played on a city-sized board with living pieces. Even the carnage he'd seen in the aftermath of Security's casino trap had seemed distant and vaguely unreal.

But suddenly that unreality had evaporated. These were real men, going in against real Ryqril with extremely real weapons.

And the Ryqril would use those weapons with all the skill they possessed. Galway—and Haberdae—would make sure of that.

For many of the men assembled here, today would be their last full day alive.

"I understand," he managed. "I'll be ready."

"Good," Lathe said. "Now get over to that corner and

tell Comsquare Bhat I said to start checking you out on the special equipment you'll be using."

"All right," Judas said. "What about you?"

"I need to go talk to Shaw," Lathe said. "We still have a few details to work out." He looked across the staging area at the other blackcollars, a strangely wistful look on his face. "Because win, lose, or die, tomorrow is the night."

Earlier that day, as he had every day of his captivity, Caine had run himself through an exercise regimen consisting of some of the martial arts katas he'd been taught back on Earth during his Resistance combat training. The workout, while certainly nothing spectacular, had nevertheless run up a good sweat, necessitating a shower in his transparent stall.

But unlike the previous days, when he'd finished drying off and flipped his wet towel over the edge of the stall, this time he made sure it landed in such a way as to neatly block the spy camera hidden there.

And with that, the stage was set. It would have been nice to disable the bedpost camera as well, but Security had sneaked in last night to clear and regimmick that one as he'd hoped they would, and he couldn't keep changing the paper over the lens without them eventually getting wise to the game.

Besides, with the shower camera halfway across the room from his bed, there was a chance they'd be slightly less alert when they came in tonight to clear it.

Still, whether they were or not, the die had been tossed and was now spinning its way across the floor. He had the patterns of his prison figured out, he had the method of his escape planned, and he had the tools with which to carry it out.

All he needed now was for someone to open his cell door for him.

He settled onto bed early that night, taking his manuscript book with him as if deciding to feign his reading in bed instead of feigning it in his comfort chair. The chair itself he had already subtly relocated to the spot where he needed it to be, sitting midway between him and the blocked shower camera. That alone should help allay any suspicions; a potential escapee would certainly not be careless enough to deliberately leave a large obstacle between himself and the first enemy he would have to neutralize.

By the time they shut off his lights, he was ready. Stretched out on his foam pellet-stuffed mattress beneath his thin blanket, clothed in his orange jumpsuit and boot-slippers, he slipped his hand down and began stealthily peeling sheets of paper off the top of the manuscript stacked on the floor by his head.

Win, lose, or die, tonight was the night.

CHAPTER 14

The prisoner convoy, Poirot had said, would be leaving at seven in the evening. As it turned out, the six vans actually slipped through Athena's main gate a half hour earlier.

But that was all right. Skyler had rather expected them to try something like that anyway.

Convoy leaving, Flynn's specially boosted message came over his tingler from the empty high-rise apartment just north of Athena where he and Anne were watching the gate. *Six vans; one car front, one car rear*.

Acknowledged, Skyler signaled back. A surprisingly weak escort, even considering that the vans themselves were carrying their own collection of Security men. Clearly, General Poirot was trying to make it look like he'd manipulated the situation for the ambushers' benefit, just as he'd claimed he would. *Route?*

Primary.

The most straightforward route, in other words, for a convoy heading to Colorado Springs, and thus the route where any potential attackers would concentrate their efforts. Again, to all appearances, Poirot was doing his best to open the convoy to attack.

Unfortunately for him, the men Reger had scattered along the likely routes had already reported the extra Security vehicles that had been drifting quietly into position along that same primary route for most of the day. As Anne had predicted, and O'Hara's gut had already concluded, Poirot had indeed betrayed them.

Still, even in their attempt to be clever, the enemy was in fact being very predictable. Skyler could only hope his own plan wouldn't be equally transparent. *Air activity?*

Chatter indicates six spotters, all out of visual range.

Acknowledged, Skyler replied again, silently offering thanks to whichever it was of Anne's Whiplashed contacts who had been willing to stretch out her own neck far enough to provide them with the spotters' rolling-freq radio setup.

Leaning over the edge of his rooftop, he peered down the street. No sign of the convoy yet, but it wouldn't be much longer. Backing away from the edge, he made one last check of the small zip-line mortar he'd fastened securely to the rooftop five meters back. They hadn't had any place secure enough to do a complete test of the mortars, but the devices had come from Kanai's stock and Skyler trusted the other to have kept them in good condition. Tucking the remote for the mortar's take-up reels into his sleeve where it would be handy, he returned to the edge of the roof and slid his fingers under his sleeve to his tingler. *Flynn: launch diversion one.*

Acknowledged. Diversion one launching.

❋　❋　❋

"They've cleared the perimeter," Ramirez announced to no one in particular. "And the gate is closed. Doesn't look like there were any attempts at infiltration."

"Agreed," Bailey said, his eyes on the Denver map and the green lights that indicated the convoy vans, listening with half an ear to the quiet murmur of status reports drifting around the situation room. "Anything from the spotters?"

Ramirez looked over at the status display. "Just normal city traffic," he said.

"Yae rill 'ind nothing else," Daasaa rumbled, striding restlessly back and forth. Bailey had offered him and Halaak seats, but both Ryqril had chosen instead to stand. At the moment, the battle architect's pacing had put him directly behind Poirot, and Bailey could see the general flinching away a little from the alien's proximity. "The 'lackcollar 'ositions rill 'e rell canou'laged," Daasaa added.

"Agreed, Your Eminence," Bailey said. "Still, there's a chance that either the infrared or the microradar will—"

"Colonel?" Ramirez cut in, his forehead creasing in a frown as he leaned closer to one of the displays. "How many spotters did you order up?"

"There are supposed to be six," Poirot put in before Bailey could answer. "Are we missing someone?"

"No, sir, just the opposite," Ramirez said, pointing to the display. "Two more have just been scrambled from Boulder."

"What?" Bailey demanded, stepping to Ramirez's side. "On whose orders?"

"Major?" Ramirez prompted, nudging the spotter officer. "She identified herself as Athena Special Ops," the controller said, running his fingers across his keyboard. "Here's the playback."

He touched a final key. "Boulder spotter control, this is Athena Special Ops Command," an authoritative female voice said crisply from the speaker. "You're to scramble two spotters immediately to assist in convoy escort duty."

"Recognize the voice?" Ramirez murmured.

"No," Bailey murmured back. "You?"

Ramirez shook his head. "Authorization code?" the Boulder dispatcher asked, just as crisply.

"Alpha-nine-seven-beta-three-three," the woman replied. "This operation is under the direct jurisdiction of General Poirot."

"I gave no such order," Poirot insisted, glancing furtively at the Ryq towering over him.

"Code acknowledged and accepted," Boulder control said. "Spotters on their way."

"Acknowledged," the woman said. "They're to maintain radio silence, and to accept no signals or orders except mine or General Poirot's."

"Acknowledged."

"That's it," the major said, shutting down the recording. "Spotters' ETA to convoy, approximately three minutes."

"I gave no such order," Poirot insisted again. "It has to be the blackcollars."

"How did they o'tain the radio data?" Halaak demanded. "Colonel 'Ailey?"

"I don't know, Your Eminence," Bailey admitted. The *khassq*, he noted uneasily, had his hand resting on his laser pistol. "We could just as well ask how they got General Poirot's authorization code."

"Oh, we could, could we?" Poirot snapped back, an edge of sudden anger in his voice. "As long as we're pointing fingers, we could also ask how it is those spotters happen to come from Lieutenant Ramirez's office."

"I had nothing to do with it," Ramirez insisted.

"Neither did I," Poirot shot back. "This is all an attempt to sow confus—"

"Enou'," Daasaa said, the warning in his voice cutting off the argument. "Re know the re'els are in the extra s'otters. Re rill ratch they, and thus disco'er their 'lan."

"I'm not entirely comfortable with that idea," Bailey said, choosing his words carefully. Daasaa carried a laser and short sword, too; and if he wasn't quite as skilled with the weaponry as Halaak, he was certainly skilled enough. "Whatever they're planning, having those bandits among our own spotters could mean trouble."

"Yae rould destroy they?" Daasaa asked.

"Or try to capture them," Bailey said.

"You do that and you'll spook them for sure," Poirot warned.

"Not if we do it right," Bailey insisted. "We just have to come up with a plausible reason for bringing the spotters down."

Daasaa muttered something in Ryqrili, his dark eyes strangely distant as he thought it over. "Re rill not risk it," he said at last. "Yae rill not sto' the new s'otters."

Bailey took a deep breath. "As you command, Your Eminence. Major, inform the spotters of the newcomers from Boulder, and order them to fit them into the formation. Then order Spotters Three, Five, and Six to form up behind them."

"Yes, sir," the controller said.

Bailey looked across at Poirot, silently daring him to argue. But the general merely spared him a single, unreadable look before turning back to his own study of the monitors.

Ramirez cleared his throat. "Something you want to say, Lieutenant?" Bailey invited.

Ramirez's lip twitched. Clearly, he wasn't any happier about this than Bailey was. "No, sir," he said.

"I didn't think so," Bailey said.

No, Ramirez wasn't happy. Bailey just wished he knew exactly which part of the situation the lieutenant was unhappy about.

Convoy out of view, Flynn signaled.

Acknowledged, Skyler sent back, doing a quick mental calculation. So far, the convoy seemed to be doing the legal speed limit—no real surprise, given that it was pretending to be normal city traffic. If it maintained that pace, it ought to be coming into O'Hara's view in about two minutes.

Time to turn up the heat a little farther. *Launch diversion two*.

Acknowledged, Flynn signaled back. "Party time," he called to Anne, crossing to the window.

To the window, and the four dozen helium balloons undulating gently as they pressed against the ceiling. Somehow, Flynn couldn't help thinking that using children's balloons didn't really fit well with the blackcollar dramatic mystique.

Still, as long as they got the results, dramatic mystique could go hop.

He slid the window open and caught one of the balloons by the string hanging down beneath it, being careful not to disturb the large blasting cap that hung from the string's other end. Collecting three more balloons, he pulled the group to the window.

"Watch those bombs," Anne warned.

"I'm watching them," Flynn assured her, maneuvering the foursome out into the evening air. They floated leisurely upward, the lift of the helium almost balanced by the weight of the blasting caps hanging beneath them. "You'd better get downstairs," he added. "Once these start flying, it's not going to take them long to backtrack them here."

"Right," Anne said, scooping up her portable radio set and heading toward the door. "Don't you hang around after they're gone, either." Opening the door, she glanced both directions down the hallway and headed toward the elevator.

"No worries there," Flynn said under his breath. Getting hold of the next four, he sent them out the window behind the first group. By the time the last four balloons were away, the first ones had risen high enough over the apartment building's roof to be caught by the northerly wind. They were heading south at a brisk pace now, the later ones falling into line behind them.

All of them heading straight for the Athena perimeter fence.

Flynn grinned to himself as he headed for the door. Yes, the plan lacked dignity. Just the same, he would give a month off the far end of his life to see Security's faces when they realized just what was attacking them.

He and Anne were driving west when the brilliant flicker of laser fire began to light up the evening sky.

"Green Mountain lasers firing!" someone snapped from across the situation room.

"Where?" Bailey snapped back, pushing past Ramirez as he sprinted over to the defense station.

"North fence," the tech reported, bizarrely colored images flashing across his displays as he sorted through the various monitor images. "No speed—no metal—small explosives—"

"Got it," his neighbor said, and a full view appeared on the main monitor display.

Bailey felt his jaw drop. "*Balloons?*"

The words were barely out of his mouth when another pair drifted above the fence and vanished as the defense lasers targeted them. "Yes, sir," the tech confirmed. "They're helium-filled balloons" —a pair of small flickers of fire appeared at the top of the fence itself— "with small explosives tethered underneath."

"What in the world are they trying to do?" Ramirez muttered from Bailey's side. "They can't get explosives into Athena that way. Can they?"

"They shouldn't be able to," Bailey agreed, one of the recorded conversations between Poirot and Skyler flickering through his mind. *It couldn't be very much bigger than primer cap size, though. Unless you know some trick about that?*

These explosives were indeed primer-cap sized. But

the balloons delivering them were much larger, obviously large enough to trigger the defenses. Had Skyler thought the lack of metal or high-speed movement would let them slip over the wall? There was another multiple flicker from the lasers, and another set of small explosions from the top of the fence.

The fence.

"Security units to the north fence," he snapped toward the duty officer near the door. "Double-time it."

"What is it?" Ramirez asked, his head turning back and forth as he looked between the various displays.

"They're not trying to get those blasting caps into Athena," Bailey bit out from between clenched teeth. "They're trying to knock out the wall's targeting sensors."

"But they can't do that," Poirot protested. "Can they?"

"There!" the tech snapped, pointing to the display as something dark shot out and up from a window in one of the buildings across the wide open area outside the wall, trailing a thin rope or cable behind it. It hit the top of the fence and stuck, its trailing rope pulling taut. "Colonel?"

"I see it," Bailey gritted, turning to the two Ryqril. "It's a grappling hook, Your Eminences."

"'Rotect at runce," Halaak bellowed. The big *khassq* had his laser pistol out now, swinging it around the situation room as if looking for a target.

"Security forces on their way, Your Eminence," the duty officer called, his voice cracking a little as the Ryq's waving laser pistol waved his direction. "But it'll be several minutes before they can get there."

"Several minutes may be too late," Bailey said, staring at the image on the display. The tiny bombs were still peppering the top of the fence, wrecking or confusing or stunning the sensors there, and two more grappling hooks had joined the first in attaching themselves to the damaged section. But so far there was no sign of the blackcollars themselves. "Battle Architect, I'd like your permission to pull back some of the ambush forces."

"No," Halaak snapped. "Re nust ca'ture the 'lackcollars."

"Just the ones the convoy has already passed," Bailey told him. "They're the ones closest to the north fence anyway. We can have them surround that house, maybe hit the blackcollars or Phoenix forces before they even get over the wall."

Daasaa nodded his head sharply. "Dae it," he ordered.

Bailey caught the duty officer's eye. "You heard him," he said. "Everyone the convoy has already passed is to converge on that building."

"Yes, sir."

"And keep an eye on those two Boulder bandits," Bailey added to the spotter controller. "If they're going to make a move against Athena, this'll be the time for it."

Convoy approaching, O'Hara's signal came.

Rear guard returning to fence, Flynn added. *Spotters have been ordered to watch intruders.*

And if the spotters were keeping an eye on each other, Skyler knew, they would have that many fewer eyes focused on the drama about to unfold beneath them. So far, everything was going according to plan.

He looked across the street, where Kanai was peering at him over the edge of the taller building there. Catching his eye, Skyler gave him a thumbs-up, then turned and did the same to Hawking, twenty meters away on Skyler's same rooftop. *Alert blockers*, he signaled O'Hara.

Blockers ready.

Skyler took a deep breath and crouched down by the edge of the roof, flexing his fingers as he prepared for action. Any minute now . . .

And then, there they were, coming down the wide street toward their rooftop positions: a car followed by six unmarked vans followed by another car. Just about as obvious as it was possible to be.

He looked down at the street. One of the quiet Security vans was parked half a block away, but all the sparse civilian traffic was out of the ambush zone. There were a few pedestrians strolling the walkways, but they should have time to get out before things got messy.

Stand ready, he signaled. The lead car passed his position, then the first van, then the second— *Now*.

And in response, a large tanker truck lurched into view from an alley ahead, pulling across the street directly in front of the convoy. Even as the cars and vans screeched to a halt, a second tanker turned a corner a street back and rolled into blocking position behind them.

"You're surrounded and outgunned," O'Hara's amplified voice called, the multiple echoes from the canyon of buildings making it impossible to tell where exactly the voice was coming from. "Come out, lay down your weapons, and surrender."

For a moment nothing happened. Then, in perfect unison, the car and van doors were flung open and drivers and guards spilled out onto the pavement.

Only it wasn't the two or three guards per prisoner that

Poirot had said would be along for the ride. Instead, there were nearly three dozen Security men in full riot armor now scrambling to take up defensive positions behind doors and at the sides of their vehicles, their paral-dart and flechette rifles pointed in all directions, including up. At the same time, the vans' sunroofs slid open and more Security men popped into view, this group cradling heavy laser rifles in their arms.

Mentally, Skyler shook his head. So very predictable. *Fire*, he ordered.

And with a muffled *sploosh*, each of the two tankers began spilling a thick, viscous fluid from beneath it, fluid that began flowing slowly down the street toward the convoy.

Two seconds later, both flows burst into brilliant, yellow-white flame.

It was even more impressive than Skyler had expected. The twin walls of fire moved ponderously toward the convoy and the crouched Security men, the flows' leading edges angling toward each other along the gutter on the east side of the street. Skyler couldn't see the Security men's faces or hear their conversation, but from their body language and the way their gun barrels were dipping he guessed they were suddenly reconsidering what they'd probably thought were pretty decent defensive positions. "I suggest you move, gentlemen," O'Hara prompted, the words barely audible over the crackling of the flames. "It's not likely to stop for you."

For a long moment nothing happened. Skyler had picked this spot with its topography in mind, and as he watched, the two flows met up along the east side of the street, filling the gutter with flame and cutting off any possibility of retreat that direction. As the fuel pooled and the wall of flame widened, it began to fill the rest of the street, moving slowly but inexorably across the pavement toward the trapped vehicles.

One way or another, the Security men would very soon cease to be a problem.

"*Damn* it," Ramirez snarled under his breath. "Damn it to *hell*."

"Shut up," Bailey snarled back, his full attention on the van's-eye view of the wall of fire creeping toward his men. What were they supposed to do *now*?

For one of them, at least, the response was clearly not even open to discussion. "Get them out of there, Bailey," Poirot said urgently. "Get them *out*."

"No," Daasaa ordered. "They rill *not* run. They rill hold their ground."

"They can't, Your Eminence," Poirot protested. "If they stay, they'll die."

"They rill *not* run," Daasaa repeated.

Poirot looked at Bailey, his eyes pleading. "We have to pull them out, Battle Architect," Bailey agreed, his throat tight. Both Ryqril had that homicidal look about them again. "If they hold their positions, they'll be burned to death."

"So rill the 'risoners," Daasaa countered. "There'ore, the 'lackcollars nust ha' a 'lan to sa'e they."

"I'm sure they do," Bailey agreed, watching the fire as it inched its leisurely way forward. "But the prisoners are still inside, where they're better protected. The blackcollars can afford to wait until—"

"Colonel!" the spotter controller cut in. He twisted a control— "Boulder spotters, drop down to assist Security forces," the mysterious woman's voice came from the speaker. "Athena spotters, maintain high cover."

Halaak snarled something unintelligible. "They rill take the 'risoners!"

"No, they won't," Bailey said darkly. "Major, order the other spotters to bring them to ground immediately. They're to escort them into Athena—"

"*Not* into Athena," Daasaa cut him off.

"No, of course not," Bailey said, feeling his face flush as he belatedly realized what he'd almost done. "They're to bring them to ground outside the fence."

"Maybe by the northern fence?" Ramirez suggested.

"Yes, by the northern fence," Bailey confirmed. With two sets of Security forces already converging on that spot, they might as well try to lock all their eggs into the same basket.

"Yes, sir," the controller said.

Bailey turned back to Daasaa. "Battle Architect?" he prompted, gesturing to the wall of fire. "They can't serve the Ryqril if they're dead."

Daasaa hesitated. Then, with a derisive snort, he gestured. "Ryqril rarriors rould ne'er run," he said disdainfully. "'Ut these are only hunans. They nay retreat."

"Thank you." Bailey gestured to the duty officer. "Give the order."

For a long minute Skyler had thought the Ryqril in charge was going to cold-bloodedly allow the Security men to be burned to death for nothing. Then, to his relief, he saw them lurch to their feet and fall back before the approaching flames, making for the single alley on the street's western side that still allowed for escape. *Enemy fleeing down rabbit hole*, he signaled O'Hara as the men standing in the van sunroofs abandoned their lasers and ducked out to join their retreating comrades. *Stand ready for possible aerial move.*

Acknowledged.

Spotters turning on bandits, Flynn put in. *All ordered to ground north of fence.*

Skyler puffed a sigh of relief. And with that, they could finally get the actual rescue underway. *Hawking, Kanai: go*, he ordered. Peering down at the street, he made one final adjustment to his mortar's aim and squeezed the trigger.

With a *chuff* of compressed air, the mortar fired, sending the adhesive-tipped grappling line snaking past Skyler's head to disappear over the edge of the building across the street. Shifting aim, he fired again, sending a second line arcing over the street at a slight angle to the first. His wrist pulley was already fastened to his left forearm; peripherally noting that Kanai's and Hawking's own lines were also now crisscrossing the street, he secured his pulley over both of his lines and rolled off the edge of the roof.

He could feel the heat rising from the fire below as he slid along the slack in the lines toward the low point in the middle. He worked the remote, playing out more of the two lines as he descended. Wincing at the heat, hoping his flexarmor was up to the challenge, he dropped toward the first van in line.

And with a thunk of boots he came to a smooth landing on top of the vehicle, just in front of the gaping sunroof.

He dropped through the opening and found himself facing someone sitting in the middle of the backseat, a black bag over his head and his hands securely fastened together in front of him with a pair of mag-lock forearm shackles. "Who are you?" Skyler called over the roaring of the flames.

"Kevin Dorfman," the other said, his words muffled by the bag.

"The sky seems extra blue today," Skyler said.

There was a short pause, as if the kid couldn't believe he was being asked for a countersign at a time like this. "Probably means rain tomorrow," he said at last.

"Right," Skyler said. Reaching across, he hauled Dorfman to his feet and maneuvered him around to his side of the middle seat. With his other hand he pulled off the boy's hood, ripping it from the stubborn tape that his captors had used to fasten it to his shirt. "Oh, my God," the boy gasped, cringing back as he saw the flames bearing down on them. His face, Skyler noted, did indeed match the picture of Dorfman that Anne had showed them. "Oh, my *God*."

"Don't worry, you're out of here," Skyler assured him. Unfastening his own pulley from the two lines, he threaded a hook through Dorfman's shackles and looped it over the first line. "Just relax and enjoy the ride."

He keyed the remote, starting the mortar's take-up reel. Dorfman had just enough time for a startled yelp, and then he was pulled out and up through the sunroof. *Flynn: first sheep on the way. Position?*

Nearly to retrieval point, the other reported. *Will be ready when they are.*

Skyler was still holding the bag that had been over Dorfman's head. Giving it a quick look, he dropped it on the floor and climbed back onto the van's roof, refastening his pulley to the second line as he did so.

The fire was very definitely getting closer. He took a moment to survey the area, noting with approval that Kanai and Hawking had sent their first set of released prisoners rising upward on their lines as well. Making sure he had enough slack, he gathered his feet beneath him, ran the three steps the van's roof allowed, and leaped back to the next van.

The prisoner here was a young woman named Bryna Estrada. Skyler ran through the sign/countersign routine with her, got her hood off after the same fight that Dorfman's had put up, and secured her to his remaining line. Wrapping a protective arm around her waist, he keyed the take-up reel.

They rose together over the street, the superheated air around them cooling somewhat as they ascended over the flames now lapping against the sides of the vans. They reached the level of the roof where Skyler had set up his mortar; and as the line tightened into an uphill angle, they began to slide back down again toward safety.

Anne and Flynn were busy at the other two anchor points, helping disconnect other former prisoners from their lines, as Skyler brought himself and Bryna to a more or less soft landing in front of his mortar. "End of the line," he told her, popping them free. "Stairway's in that shed over there—wait inside until we're all assembled."

"Right," she breathed, and headed across the roof.

Skyler turned back to see Kanai and Hawking ferrying the last two released prisoners to safety. "Anything?" he called.

"No," Kanai called.

"Likewise," Hawking seconded.

"Okay," Skyler said. "Let's get to the stairs—"

And with a sudden screaming blast, a Security patrol boat dropped straight down from the sky to a hovering stop at the edge of their roof.

"Halt," a voice boomed from the fighter's loudspeaker. Moving with deceptive effortlessness, the vehicle spun horizontally around, bringing the full range of its forward weaponry to bear on the group now frozen in place on the roof. "Stand where you are—"

And then, just as the craft completed its swiveling turn, another grappling line shot out from somewhere below them. The grapple slapped firmly onto one of the stubby wings, snapping taut as the mortar's take-up reel kicked in.

The patrol boat had far too much mass and engine power for such an attack to have much effect. But in the confined space where the pilot had settled his craft, in the middle of the roiling air currents created by the fire below it, a small nudge was all it took. The boat tipped slightly forward and to the side as the take-up reel yanked at its wing, its nose dipping as it lurched a couple of meters forward. There was a brief grinding noise as it slammed into the side of the building; and then, with a surge of engine power, it snapped the cable, fatally overcorrected, and slid sideways out of their view. A second later, with a horrible crunch of tearing metal, it crashed into the flaming street below.

"Let's go," Skyler shouted to the Phoenix people still standing frozen in place, most of them staring at the spot where the patrol boat had been. "Kanai?"

"Come on," Kanai said, grabbing one of the youths by the arm and pulling him bodily across the roof. Hawking and Flynn started toward the others, but with Kanai's action the spell was apparently broken. Skyler bringing up the rear, they made it to the stairs.

With their building having presumably been identified, Skyler had expected Security to make some last-ditch attack to stop them. But apparently the disarray the black-collars had sowed was too widespread for anything like quick action. They met no opposition on the stairs, and a few minutes later were in the alleyway behind the building, where a line of four cars was waiting.

"Into the cars," Skyler ordered them. Catching up with Dorfman he grabbed the boy's arm and steered him to the vehicle at the back of the line. "Come on, come on—get in," he called to the rest as he half guided, half pushed Dorfman into the back seat. "Hawking? Get them settled and then get back here—you're driving this one."

"Give me a hand here, will you?" Hawking called back as he helped one of the others into the car. "This one's pretty woozy."

"On my way," Skyler called back. "Sit tight," he told Dorfman, closing the car door and running over to Hawking.

Dorfman was still sitting there, alone, when the other three cars roared off into the night.

❋   ❋   ❋

Bailey had very much not wanted to be the last one to arrive at the conference room. Unfortunately, he was.

"Sit," Daasaa said quietly, indicating the far side of the table from where he and Halaak were seated.

"Yes, Your Eminence," Bailey said. Poirot and Ramirez, he noted sourly, had thoughtfully left the seat between them empty, thereby putting Bailey in the middle where he could bear the brunt of Ryqril attention. "My apologies for my tardiness."

Neither Ryq replied, but merely waited in silence until he had seated himself. "Now," Daasaa said, his eyes glittering. "Ex'lain."

Bailey took a careful breath. "They outsmarted us, Your Eminence," he said reluctantly. "I wish it were otherwise. But it's not."

"That is not su'icient," Halaak growled. "There is a traitor. Who?"

"No one betrayed the mission, Your Eminence," Bailey said. "At least, no one in this room."

"Yet they identi'ied the s'y yae 'lanted," Daasaa pointed out. "How did they dae that?"

"I don't know," Bailey admitted. "Something he said or did, I suppose, or maybe something about his appearance that gave him away."

Beside Bailey, Ramirez stirred. "It seems to me that we know *one* likely candidate for traitor, Your Eminence," he said. "General Poirot is the one—"

"I did *not* betray the mission," Poirot bit out angrily. "And let me remind *you* that of all of us in this room, *I'm* the one who's been under the most complete observation.

How could I possibly have communicated anything to the blackcollars without half of Athena knowing about it?"

"There is reason to General 'Oirot's argunent," Daasaa agreed. "What o' yae, Lieutenant Ranirez?"

"I couldn't have had anything to do with this, Your Eminence," Ramirez said, his voice steady. "I didn't even know about Colonel Bailey's spy until after the black-collars left him behind."

"Those rogue spotters claimed to be from *your* office," Poirot accused.

Ramirez glared at him— "They weren't rogue," Bailey put in before he could say anything. "That was why I was late, Your Eminences. I was getting the full transcript of the pilots' interrogation."

"Yae ha' it?" Daasaa demanded.

"Yes, Your Eminence," Bailey said, pulling a set of papers from his folder and handing it across the table.

For a few minutes Daasaa and Halaak poured over the report in silence. Bailey waited, listening to his thudding heart and wondering if Poirot and Ramirez were sweating as much as he was. He rather expected they were.

At last, Daasaa looked up. "There is no sign they rere traitors," he agreed grudgingly. "'Ery rell. Let us exanine hor the 'lackcollars o'tained the s'otter 'ekencies." He looked at Poirot. "*And* General 'Oirot's authorization code."

"Actually, it wasn't General Poirot's personal code," Bailey said. "It was simply a general authorization which any of a thousand people would have access to, both here in Athena and in Boulder."

"And rich o' these thousand is the traitor?" Halaak demanded.

"I'm afraid we don't yet know," Bailey had to admit. "But we do know now that it was definitely Anne Silcox who was the one ordering them around. We've started an analysis on who in Athena or Boulder might have crossed paths with her in the past few months."

Daasaa made a strange sounding rumbling noise. "Dae yae know all o' Silcox's novenents in that 'eriod?"

Bailey winced. "No, Your Eminence, we don't."

"Then such analysis is unlikely to 'e 'ery usekhul, is it?"

"Probably not," Bailey conceded.

"Meanwhile, we also need to worry about what else this spy of theirs has told them," Ramirez said. "Isn't there some way to tell who else they've hit with this damned Whiplash?"

"We're still analyzing the tests we ran on General Poirot," Bailey said. "So far, we haven't found any detectable changes in his biochemistry."

"That's handy," Ramirez muttered.

"For someone," Bailey agreed grimly, looking back at the Ryqril. "And we can't just suspend or lock up all the possibilities, either—we don't have enough alternates to step into their places. Everyday operations would grind to a halt."

"I expect we're going to have to run everyone in the government through a second round of loyalty-conditioning," Poirot said. "Myself being first, of course," he added, looking at Ramirez.

"That rill not hel' us now," Halaak growled. "It rill take tae long."

"Actually, time may not be as short as we thought," Bailey said, bracing himself. Given the mood the Ryqril were in, there was no way to predict how they were going to react to this particular bit of news. "It appears that our missing blackcollar did indeed come to Denver this morning."

The two Ryqril exchanged looks. "Yae are certain?" Daasaa asked.

"Yes," Bailey said, on solid ground for a change. "The various recordings clearly show all five blackcollars were present during the rescue, the four from Plinry and Kanai."

"Then he is not in Aegis," Halaak rumbled.

"*Aegis*?" Poirot echoed, turning startled eyes on Bailey.

"No, Your Eminence, he's not," Bailey confirmed, throwing a warning look at Poirot as he silently cursed Halaak's careless tongue. He'd worked very hard to make sure the fact that they knew about Aegis's back door stayed strictly between the three of them. Now, Poirot and Ramirez knew it, too.

"'Erha's that neans they no longer need the 'ase," Daasaa said, his tone suggesting the kind of fate that Bailey could expect if the opportunity to get into Aegis had slipped through their fingers.

"I'm certain they'll need to go back in," Bailey said quickly. "Whatever the blackcollars came here for, this rescue couldn't have been more than just a little detour. They're still going to need whatever resources are in there."

"'Erha's," Daasaa said again. "Re shall see."

They'd found some food, and they'd had some rest; and now Foxleigh stood beside Jensen at the end of the road.

"So this is what you came all this way for?" he murmured, his voice hushed with a reverence he hadn't realized he could still feel. "This is what you hiked through the wilderness and fought bears to get to?"

"This is it," Jensen confirmed. "Why? Don't you think it'll deliver a sufficiently big bang?"

Foxleigh took a deep breath as he looked up at the sleek fighter stretched out in front of them, crouched on its landing skids like a mountain lion preparing to spring. "No, I think a functional Talus-6 interceptor will pack all the bang you could possibly want," he assured the black-collar.

And with that, Foxleigh's moment of reverence vanished. Even an advanced fighter was, after all, only a tool. A simple means to an end. "What exactly are you planning to do with it?" he asked, running a hand over the coating of dust to expose a hand-lettered word written on the underside missile rack.

"What do you think I want with it?" Jensen countered, giving him an odd look.

"There's more than one possibility." Foxleigh pointed to the word he'd uncovered. "See this?"

Jensen craned his neck. "'Gotterdammerung'?"

"It's the old Germanic version of 'doomsday,'" Foxleigh explained. "A composer named Richard Wagner wrote about fourteen hours of opera about it." He tapped the metal. "The point is that there are enough kilotons packed away in here to make sure the Ryqril never take anything out of the mountain except radioactive slag."

"I'm not destroying Aegis," Jensen said firmly. "It's resisted the Ryqril too long for us to just blow it up."

"Then what *are* you doing?" Foxleigh persisted. "You think a single fighter dodging Corsairs over North America is going to do anyone any good?"

"Depends on what you mean by *any good*," Jensen said. "What does any of this have to do with you, anyway?"

"I just want to make sure you're not going to blow up the fighter and the base with me still in it," Foxleigh said, backpedaling quickly. The last thing he wanted to do was start Jensen wondering. Not until they had the Talus prepped, anyway.

"Don't worry about it," Jensen assured him. "As soon as I'm sure I won't need extra hands, you'll be heading for home."

"I appreciate that," Foxleigh said. As if he intended to do anything of the sort. "You have any idea how to prep this thing?"

"Not really," Jensen conceded. "But I'm sure the procedural manuals are on file around here somewhere."

"Probably," Foxleigh agreed. "Let's go find them."

"So Kevin's still a prisoner?" Anne asked, her tone flat and dark and accusing.

"I'm afraid so," Skyler said, not any happier about it than Anne was. "I don't know why they picked him, unless it was because they already had a look-alike on hand."

"Instead of looking for someone to blame," Reger spoke up from his usual seat in the corner, "you might try a little gratitude that Skyler was able to identify the substitution so quickly. If he hadn't, we'd probably *all* be in Athena right now."

"I know," Anne said, lowering her eyes. "I just . . . you're sure it *wasn't* Kevin?"

"I'm positive," Skyler said. "He knew the password, and he could easily have passed as the man in the photo you showed us. Security's mistake was that they weren't as confident as they should have been and tried to hedge their bets."

"You mean the hoods?" Reger asked.

Skyler nodded. "Poirot must have thought that once we did the password check we might be too rushed to take them off, especially given how solidly the things had been taped in place. That would have postponed any close-up exam for a while, maybe even until we were back here or someplace equally vulnerable to a surprise attack."

"Only they also wouldn't want their spy traveling blind," Hawking added. "Hence, the trick hood."

"Which looked opaque from the outside but was reasonably transparent from the inside," Skyler finished. "Fortunately, we were expecting something like that and checked all the hoods. The one calling himself Dorfman was the only one who flunked."

"So how do we get him out?" Anne said, clearly not impressed by the blackcollars' on-the-spot detective work. "And Rob's still missing, too."

"I don't know how to answer that," Skyler conceded. "I doubt they'll be foolish enough to try this bait-and-raid stunt again."

"You did get into Athena once before," Flynn reminded him.

"Different time, different circumstances," Skyler said. "We'd never be able to pull off something like that again."

"So what you're saying is that they're stuck there?" Anne demanded.

"Anne," Reger said warningly, "it wasn't Skyler's fault."

Anne took a deep breath, and Skyler could see the counterargument flickering across her eyes. If the black-collars hadn't come blasting into town . . . "I know," she said at last, her voice suddenly very tired. "I'm sorry, Skyler."

"I'm sorry, too," Skyler said. "It's never easy to lose comrades."

"But don't forget that these aren't necessarily lost," O'Hara added. "As long as they're alive, there's always hope."

"Which almost makes it worse," Anne said. "If they were dead, there would at least be some closure. This way . . ." She shook her head. "Never mind. The point is that five of them *are* free. I should be content with that." She got to her feet. "I should also be helping Kanai get them settled. Good night, everyone."

"Good night," Skyler said for all of them.

Anne stepped to the doorway. There she paused, turning to touch eyes with each of them. "And thank you," she said.

Turning again, she left the room, closing the door behind her. "Some people are never satisfied," Hawking commented.

"You can add me to that list," Skyler said as he slumped tiredly in his chair. The rescue had worked, pretty much exactly the way he'd planned it. He should be content. Hell, he should be *ecstatic*.

But he wasn't.

"I wonder how Jensen's spending his evening," O'Hara murmured.

Skyler grimaced. Jensen. One more failure to chalk up to his leadership, except that this failure had the potential to blossom into a full-bore disaster. "We'll find out tomorrow," he said. "Flynn, did you get Trapper off all right?"

"He was fine when he headed out from here," Flynn confirmed. "Though of course he'll probably find Security waiting on his doorstep, who may or may not buy his story about being abducted at knifepoint."

"Maybe we can do something for him after we corral Jensen," Skyler said. Dorfman, Jensen, and now Trapper. The far end of this plan just kept throwing off loose ends.

"Assuming the whole town isn't already locked up in Athena," Flynn murmured.

"If they are, they are," O'Hara said firmly. "Focus on what can be changed, not on what can't." He lifted his eyebrows at Skyler. "Good advice for all of us," he added.

"I never said otherwise," Skyler replied evenly.

"So when are we heading out?" Hawking asked.

"About noon, I think," Skyler said. "That should get us in by midafternoon."

"Cutting it a bit thin, aren't you?" Hawking suggested. "After we get to Shelter Valley we still have to hike to the back door *and* then walk the rest of the way to the base itself."

"I know," Skyler said. "But Trapper said afternoon is when the traffic that direction is the heaviest."

"And it isn't particularly heavy even then," Flynn said. "We might want to use Trapper's secondary route, the one that meanders around through a few other small towns before getting to Shelter Valley."

"That might throw the bloodhounds off the trail a bit," O'Hara agreed. "But it'll also cost us more time."

"Command decision time, Skyler," Reger said.

Skyler looked across the room at the window, heavily curtained against the possibility of prying eyes. "We'll sleep on it," he said. "I'll make the final decision in the morning." He looked at the others, half expecting an argument. But all he got were nods of agreement. "Then let's get to it," he said. "It's been a very long day. Reger, once again our thanks for your assistance."

"Show your thanks when the Ryqril have been thrown out," Reger countered. "Until then, feel free to run a tab." Nodding to the others, he left the room.

"Opportunistic SOB, isn't he?" O'Hara commented.

"Absolutely," Hawking agreed. "I wish we could get some of that same self-interest into the people Anne wasted her Whiplash on."

"Different mind-set," O'Hara said. "Anne's pigeons were all bureaucrats. Cogs in a machine. Reger's the type who wants to run the machine."

"I suppose," Hawking said. "You think we're really going to pull this off?"

Skyler shrugged. "Depends on Lathe," he said. "If his plan works—but what am I saying? Of *course* his plan will work. His plans *always* work."

"That sounds like fatigue talking," Hawking warned, getting out of his chair with an elaborate stretch. "Lathe's had plenty of failures, and he'd be the first to admit them."

"I suppose," Skyler said, feeling a touch of shame for his guilt-driven sarcasm. "Still, I'd bet money that whatever's happening on Khala, he's got it under control."

"I'm sure he does," O'Hara agreed. "Go get some sleep, Skyler. I'll take the first watch."

CHAPTER 15

They sneaked into Caine's cell right on schedule, three hours after he'd let his breathing settle into the slow rhythm of sleep. Security was nothing, he reflected; if not predictable.

But as he opened his eyes to slits he realized that some- one had decided to alter the usual script. Instead of one man sneaking in to fix the blocked shower-stall camera while his partner covered him from the doorway, this time there were *two* men in the room, one angling toward the shower while the other came straight toward Caine's bunk. Possibly to check the second camera setup there; more likely to hold a paral-dart gun pointed at the prisoner. A third man, as usual, stood guard in the doorway.

Still, it wasn't a fatal change, but simply meant that Caine's attack pattern would have to be altered. Maintaining his slow breathing, he got a grip on the edge of his mattress and waited for just the right moment. The first guard stopped at the foot of the bunk beds as the second reached the shower, his back turning to Caine as he reached up to fix the camera.

And in that instant, Caine moved.

He slid his legs out from under the blanket and rolled off the bed onto the floor, pulling the mattress up over him as he went. The guard at the foot of the bed inhaled sharply, and before Caine had even hit the floor there was the *crack* of a paral-dart gun.

But darts whose loads had been scaled to penetrate the thin jumpsuit without tearing the underlying flesh to shreds were no match for the foam-filled mattress. A second shot got lost among the foam pellets as Caine hit the floor and rolled back onto his feet. Draping the mattress over the top of his head like an old admiral's hat gone limp, he grabbed the rear bunk support for balance and threw a blind roundhouse kick at his attacker. His foot caught the other squarely in the side of the head, slamming him into the wall and sending his gun clattering off into the darkness.

There was no time to go hunting for the weapon, but Caine didn't especially want it anyway. Throwing a second kick into the man for insurance, he headed across the room to try to cut off the other intruder, whom he could hear making a frantic break for the door. From the doorway guard came a reflexive one-two shot at Caine's torso, the tiny darts joining the others inside the flopping mattress.

And then, finally, the man woke up to the reality of the situation. His next pair of shots, aimed below the edge of the mattress, slammed squarely into Caine's legs.

Or rather, they slammed into the thick sheaves of manuscript paper he had carefully wrapped around his legs inside the jumpsuit. Caine staggered a little anyway, knowing that giving the expected response would buy him a few seconds.

Sure enough, he could hear the inside man's mad dash for the door slowing slightly as he waited for Caine to fall over. Caine staggered a little more, buying himself another two steps; and then, hurling the mattress toward the inside man, he ducked around the edge and leaped.

In the darkness the other's expression was impossible to see, but his violent twitch showed that Caine had indeed caught him by surprise. His gun, which he'd been lowering, snapped desperately up again.

But he was too late. Caine sidestepped the weapon and slammed a fist into the man's side, catching his gun arm and spinning around behind him just as the door guard fired again. A few of the darts dug into Caine's arm, burying themselves in the paper armor there, but the bulk of the blast caught the inside man squarely across his chest. He staggered the way Caine had pretended to and toppled toward the floor.

And as he did, Caine snatched the paral-dart gun from his limp fingers and fired toward the doorway.

The door guard saw it coming and dived for safety. But like his comrade, he was a fraction of a second too late. In the dim light filtering in from the hallway Caine saw his dive turn into a flounder as he collapsed to the floor.

But as Caine had noted on previous occasions, there were subtly moving shadows outside that showed the opposition was far from defeated. Keeping an eye on the doorway, he took a long step backward and grabbed the comfort chair, flipping it over and resting it on his head the way he'd earlier held the mattress. Unlike the mattress, though, this new impromptu helmet could be carried without exposing his hands. Balancing the chair with one hand, gripping his borrowed paral-dart gun in the other, he headed for the door.

They were good, all right. He was barely halfway there when a pair of heads and guns appeared simultaneously in the doorway, one on either side, one high and the other low, and opened fire.

But between the chair helmet and the rolled-paper-sheaf armor, there was nothing for them to hit. Caine leaned forward in a dead run, knowing he had to get to the door before one of them could reach inside and pull it shut.

He won the race, but just barely. The low man of the high/low combination had a grip on the handle as he came into Caine's view beneath the chair back, his other hand angled to try to shoot upward past the chair into Caine's face. Again, Caine won the race, swiveling the chair just enough to block the other's first shot. Twin kicks to the man's head and torso ensured that he never got a second.

And two steps later, Caine was outside his cell.

A volley of paral-dart fire scattered down the corridor as the momentum from his charge slammed him up against the far wall, the impact nearly knocking the comfort chair off his head. The remaining opposition would be concentrated on his left, he knew, along with whatever reinforcements they'd managed to scramble, all of them dead set on making sure he never reached the elevator and final freedom.

But that was all right, because Caine had never had any intention of making for the elevators in the first place.

Instead, turning his back to the paral-dart fire, he headed for the far end of the hallway.

Where, if his earlier analysis was correct, he would find the base's generator and electrical equipment.

"He's *what*?" Galway snarled into the phone. "Sergeant, how in *hell*—? Never mind. Where is he now?"

"In the generator room," the strongpoint duty sergeant said, his voice quavering with a hint of the terror he was undoubtedly feeling.

And rightly so. Unless they corralled Caine, and fast, Taakh might very well decide to slaughter the entire prison contingent. "I don't know why the paral-darts didn't work," the sergeant continued. "I know we hit him—"

"Where is *who* now?" Haberdae growled from across the desk, looking up from the reports on the blackcollars' evening training exercises. "Galway?"

Galway cupped his palm over the mouthpiece. "Caine's broken out of his cell," he said.

"He's *what*?" Haberdae breathed, his eyes widening in surprise. "What the—?"

Galway waved him to silence as he uncupped the phone. "So what's happening now? Have you tried to break in?"

"Yes, but he's barricaded the door," the sergeant said. "Besides, he's got one of the guns—we can't storm the place until we get our people into full armor."

Galway winced. If Taakh was here to hear excuses like that . . . "Then get them armored," he said, trying to think. If Caine was in the generator room, it must be for a very good, very logical reason.

Of course. "And while they're doing that, get another team outside," he went on. "Have them disable all the searchlights, exterior lights, and radar and sensor dishes."

"The *searchlights*?"

"He can't get out of the strongpoint on his own," Galway explained as patiently as he could. "But he might be able to get power to some of the outside lights and try to attract Lathe's attention."

"Damn," the sergeant muttered. Still, Galway thought, he sounded calmer now that he had at least the glimmerings of a plan. "Okay, I've got men on the way. What about Caine himself?"

Galway squeezed hard on the phone handset. With the heavy weapons at the guards' disposal, it would be no trick at all to storm the generator room and turn Caine into ground meat. But Galway would prefer to get him out alive if at all possible. "Barricade the corridor so he can't get out," he instructed the sergeant. "I'll be there as soon as I can."

"Understood. Thank you, sir."

Galway hung up, shutting down his reader and pulling out the magnecoded card that contained Judas's report on the evening's activities. "How in hell's name did he get out of his cell?" Haberdae demanded.

"I don't know," Galway said, dropping the card into his jacket's side pocket and checking his paral-dart gun. "But once we figure that out, I presume the Ryqril will find it another useful bit of information on how blackcollars do things."

"I'm sure they'll love it," Haberdae said stiffly. "You taking Taakh with you?"

"He's sleeping," Galway said, holstering his gun again and heading for the door. "And I don't think I want him up there right now anyway." He paused and looked back at Haberdae. "I *know* you and your men don't want him up there."

Haberdae grimaced. "Yeah," he muttered. "Well. Have fun."

"I will," Galway said. "Don't wait up."

Caine was still working on his rewiring project when a tap came at the barricaded generator room door. "Caine?" Galway's voice came. "It's Galway."

"Go away, Prefect," Caine called back. "If you or any of your trolls out there try to come in, I'll rip random limbs off you."

"No one's coming in," Galway assured him. "But be reasonable, will you? You're ten meters underground, and that room has only this one door. There's absolutely nowhere you can go."

"Maybe I like it in here."

"Or maybe you're just being stubborn," Galway countered. "You have no food, or water, or weapons. What are you expecting to accomplish?"

"I have a paral-dart gun."

"I meant no weapons that can do you any good," Galway said. "Unlike the guards out here, who have much heavier weapons available."

"Then why don't you use them?" Caine asked.

"The duty sergeant wants to," Galway told him. "He's highly upset at what you did to his men. Not to mention how this is going to look on his record."

"My heart bleeds for him," Caine said, gingerly holding back a tangle of wires as he traced his eyes along the new circuit he'd created. Almost ready. "I trust you and he both noted that I didn't damage anyone more than necessary. I can't speak for his record, though."

"Yes, I did notice," Galway assured him. "That's one reason I'm here: to try to get you out safely and peacefully."

Caine smiled. Galway wasn't half bad at this, actually. "What makes you think I have any interest in surrendering?"

Even through the thick door he thought he could hear Galway's sigh. "I already gave you my list of reasons," the other said. "I'm sure others will occur to you. Come on, Caine—you've proved your point."

Caine ignored him. One final connection . . . there. Letting the wires dangle loose again, he turned to the breaker he'd wired the circuit to and flipped it on. If he'd done it right, the concealed searchlights outside the strongpoint would now be blazing away into the sky.

Ideally, he would have liked to be able to send a message in blackcollar tingler code. But that would have required him to separately wire two different sets of the lights, and there was no way to know which of them were working and which weren't. He would have to settle instead for a simple standard Morse code SOS.

"Caine?"

"I'm still here," Caine assured him, watching the power indicators as he flipped the circuit breaker in the rhythmic three dots/three dashes/three dots pattern. There was definitely power going out, which meant at least one of the searchlights was operating. Excellent. "Sorry—I thought you were finished."

"I'm trying to keep you from getting killed, Caine," Galway said. "And I may be the only one out here who actually cares about that."

"Your humanity does you justice," Caine said, frowning at the meter as the power indicator began jumping wildly. Were Galway's people outside cutting all the wires? Grimacing, he repeated his signal, wondering if he should switch to something more specifically aimed at Lathe.

And then, without warning, there was a sizzle of blue fire around the breaker, and a tingling jolt ran through his fingers and up his arm. An instant later he was thrown backward across the tiny room to slam hard against the wall.

He slumped to the floor, his whole arm shaking violently, his numbed brain only vaguely aware of the sound of men breaking down the makeshift barricade he'd set up across the door. A minute later rough hands grabbed his arms and hauled him to his feet, ripping off his jumpsuit and scattering the pages of his paral-dart armor. Then, dressed only in his undersuit, he was hauled out into the corridor.

Galway was waiting there, along with a dozen armed and riot-armored Security men. "Are you all right?" the prefect asked.

"I'm fine," Caine said, wincing at the slurring of the words coming from his still numb mouth. "That was cute."

Galway shrugged. "A simple voltage surge across your breaker seemed the safest way to neutralize you, once we figured out what you were doing."

"Only you figured it out too late," Caine said. "Half of

Inkosi City must have seen the lights before you shut them down. Lathe's bound to hear about it."

Galway shook his head. "Lathe won't hear about it, Caine, because the lights never came on," he said. "We'd already cut the wires."

Caine stared at him. "But I saw . . ." He trailed off.

"We'd wired matching loads into a couple of them," Galway explained, confirming Caine's unspoken conclusion. "No one saw anything. No one will be coming for you."

He gestured down the corridor. "Let's get you back to your quarters," he said. "I don't know about you, but I'm ready to call it a day."

Spadafora was crouched out of sight at the center of a clump of bushes as Lathe and Mordecai slipped in to join him. "Got your signal," Lathe murmured. "We're on?"

"You ask for it, you get it," Spadafora said, pointing through the leaves at the unmarked Security car parked beside the strongpoint's door.

The *unlit* door. For that matter, Lathe noted with interest, there weren't any lights showing anywhere on or around the base. "And they were even thoughtful enough to turn off all the lights for us," he commented.

"They may be off *now*," Spadafora said. "But an hour ago there was a whole crowd out here with flashlights blazing, scurrying around like poked bugs."

"Looking for you?"

"That's what I thought at first," Spadafora said. "But they were mostly hunting around the bushes and tree stumps east of the building, doing a lot of wire cutting.

Looked like some of them might have been doing some rewiring, too."

"Interesting," Lathe murmured. "And you're sure it was Galway?"

"Positive," Spadafora said. "There were a driver and guard, too, big ones, taking up most of the front seat. But it was definitely Galway riding in back."

"Then we'd better get started." Lathe gestured toward the chest-high posts flanking the narrow weed-grown gravel drive, posts that bore a striking resemblance to the ones supporting the Khorstron fence. "They've been adequately taken care of?"

"As adequately as plutonium blobs can make them," Spadafora assured him, hefting his slingshot. "By the way, just for the record, I'm getting tired of always pulling the more mind-numbing assignments."

"Complaint noted," Lathe said, pulling out the compact tool kit he'd borrowed from one of Shaw's men. "But don't worry. Starting tonight, things are going to get much more interesting. Mordecai?"

"Ready," the other said.

Taking a deep breath, Lathe got his feet under him and sprinted down the drive, his senses alert for trouble. He passed between the posts and kept going, and a few seconds later was crouched down beside the still-warm side of Galway's government car.

A car which, according to Shaw, contained a handy transponder which would pass both car and passengers straight through a special set of gates in the government center's protective outer wall.

Of course, what was waiting in those garage areas

would be somewhat more problematic. But they'd face that challenge if and when they got there. "Anything?" he whispered as Mordecai crouched down beside him.

The other shook his head, then nodded toward the strongpoint door. Lathe nodded back; and as Mordecai slipped around the other side of the car to stand guard, Lathe dropped onto his back and wriggled his way underneath the engine.

His worst fear about this part of the plan was that Khala Security might have fiddled with their vehicle fleet over the years, altering them to the point where none of the blackcollars' bag of tricks would work. But he'd had the opportunity to check that out while he and Mordecai had been waiting to hit the subway ambush, and had found that there were no such changes, or at least nothing that would interfere with the plan. Fixing the clamp to the fuel line took ninety seconds; and then he was out and heading again for Spadafora's cozy sniper's nest. From the lack of sound behind him, he guessed that Mordecai was right on his heels.

They reached Spadafora's bushes and again ducked out of sight. "Anything?" Lathe asked.

"Nothing I could see," Spadafora reported.

"Nothing at the door, either," Mordecai added.

"Shameful security they have around here," Lathe commented, peering one last time through the bushes. "I wonder what Galway's doing in there."

"Whatever it is, I hope it was worth the trip," Spadafora said. "Are we ready to go?"

"We're ready," Lathe confirmed. "Let's see if we can find you some of that excitement you've been looking for."

* * *

The door closed with a solid *snick* of the lock, cutting off Galway's last view of Caine stretched out on his bunk. "I gather we won't be giving him any more books to read?" the duty sergeant suggested from the prefect's side as they headed back toward the elevator.

"You gather correctly," Galway agreed, noting the other's less-than-subtle effort to push the blame for the incident onto Galway instead of himself. "I gather in turn your men won't be trying any more midnight raids?"

"We were ordered to keep him under surveillance," the sergeant said stiffly. "He kept blocking the cameras."

"*All* of them?"

The sergeant's face reddened. "Well, no, there was still the fish-eye in the corner," he conceded. "But Prefect Haberdae said it didn't give enough detail. And he was right—we never even saw him stuffing all that paper down his jumpsuit."

"Didn't you?" Galway said, frowning. Haberdae had never said anything about the cameras. At least, not when he was around.

So when *had* he complained about them?

They reached the elevator, the doors opening as they approached. "No—you two stay here," Galway said as the two Security men walking in front of them started to step inside. "The sergeant and I are taking this one."

The two guards glanced at each other, then stepped to either side of the corridor. "Sergeant?" Galway invited.

The other's face had gone rigid. "Yes, sir," he managed, and stepped into the car.

Galway joined him and punched for the top floor. "So

when exactly did Prefect Haberdae tell you the fish-eye wasn't adequate?" he asked as the doors slid shut.

The sergeant was staring at the car doors, his eyes avoiding Galway's. "I don't, uh, exactly remember—"

"I left strict orders that there was to be no communication with anyone outside this facility except in an emergency," Galway reminded him. "Did you somehow miss that?"

The other's throat tightened. "Sir, I was told not to say anything about the, uh, the visit," he said, clearly flustered. "To anyone."

"And *I'm* telling you to speak up," Galway countered. "And unlike Prefect Haberdae, I have the full authority of the Ryqril behind me."

The sergeant let out a sigh. "It was two nights ago," he muttered. "Late in the evening. He—well, he had words with the prisoner."

Galway felt a wisp of anger stirring inside him. So that was the "business" Haberdae had gone off to attend to right after their failed attempt to capture Shaw. Galway remembered the look of death on Haberdae's face, and his dark promise that someone would pay for the deaths of his men. Caine was probably lucky to still be alive. "I see," he said. "Thank you for your honesty, Sergeant. If Prefect Haberdae comes here again—or anyone else, for that matter—I want to know about it immediately. Is that clear?"

"Yes, sir," the sergeant said uncertainly. "I—yes, sir."

The elevator doors slid open. Nodding to the sergeant, Galway headed for the exit.

The driver and bodyguard Haberdae had assigned to

him were waiting at the entrance guard station, sipping coffee and talking in low tones with the duty officer. "Yes, sir?" the driver said briskly as Galway approached, setting his cup on the desk.

"I'm finished here," Galway said. "Let's head back."

A minute later they were in the car, moving slowly down the entrance drive as the driver maneuvered around the worst of the ruts. They reached the main road and turned onto it, the car picking up speed as the ride settled into something more comfortable.

Galway leaned back against the seat cushions, wondering if he should head back to the Security building and finish going over the reports on the blackcollars' evening exercises. But there was still another hour of travel time to go, and the fatigue of the day was pulling hard at him. The exercises had run pretty late, which implied that Lathe and Shaw would probably be waiting until late afternoon at the earliest to begin their attack on Khorstron.

And then, without warning, the car made a sort of strangled gasp and died.

"What is it?" Galway asked.

"I don't know, sir," the driver said, frowning at his gauges as he coasted to a stop at the side of the road. "Sounds like we've lost the fuel feed."

"Wonderful," Galway muttered. Car trouble in the middle of nowhere would be the perfect cap to an already delightful evening. "Can you do anything?"

"Let me see," the driver said, popping the hood and opening his door. "If we're lucky, it'll be something simple."

"If not, we can always radio for someone to come get us," the guard added.

"Let me take a look first," the driver said, getting out and circling his open door to the front of the car. He pulled the hood all the way open and leaned down, poking and prodding with his fingers into the engine compartment.

"He is actually pretty good at this, sir," the guard assured Galway. Beside him, his door opened.

And a black-clad hand jabbed abruptly into view, slamming into the guard's neck behind his right ear.

It was so unexpected that for that first frozen second Galway just stared in disbelief as the guard slumped unconscious in his seat. Then with a rush of adrenaline, his brain caught up with him and he grabbed for his seat belt with one hand as he scrambled for his paral-dart gun with the other.

But he was too late. Before his hand could close on the gun's grip his own door was wrenched open. Another gloved hand popped his belt and grabbed the front of his jacket, and a second later he found himself being hauled bodily from the car.

And as his feet found balance on the rough pavement he found himself standing face to face with Lathe.

"Hello, Comsquare," he managed, fighting to maintain some semblance of dignity amid the disaster crumbling down on top of him. "Very good indeed."

"Like there was any trick to it," another blackcollar sniffed as he came up beside Lathe, the driver's arm held casually in a lock grip. Spadafora, Galway tentatively identified him in the starlight. "Your friend Haberdae wasn't paying enough attention to his backtrail when he came barreling up here two days ago."

Galway grimaced. He should have guessed that the

blackcollars hadn't simply fled from that failed trap. And if they also knew why Haberdae had come, then the game was over, pure and simple.

So this was what it was like, a detached part of his mind whispered, to stare death in the face. "So what now?" he asked.

"I'm afraid you're going to have to walk the rest of the way," Lathe said. "Well, you'll eventually have to walk, anyway." He gestured behind Galway. "We need the loan of your car."

Galway blinked. Caine was locked in a poorly defended strongpoint a kilometer behind them, and all they wanted was— "*My car?*"

"Don't bother," Lathe advised. "We know all about those handy little transponders that open special gates in the wall."

Galway felt his mouth drop open a few millimeters. Was *that* what all this was about? "You came all the way up here for *that?*"

"Had to," Spadafora said. "Haberdae's people usually don't let these things out at night except in convoys of three or more. That would have been a little too obvious even for him."

"Unfortunately, we weren't in position to take advantage of Haberdae's visit," Lathe added. "But we thought there was a fair chance he'd be back up here someday." He smiled. "It was just luck that we got you instead."

Galway took a deep breath, the smell of death fading away. So all they wanted was the car. They had no idea that Caine was locked up in the strongpoint, or that they had a traitor in their midst. All they wanted was the car.

"Sir, we can't let them do this," the driver murmured urgently.

"Frankly, I don't see any way to stop them," Galway said, not really interested in arguing the point. The sooner Lathe took off with his prize, the less time he'd have to wonder what was in that blacked-out strongpoint and maybe decide to go check it out. "But it won't do you any good," he added to Lathe, knowing he ought to make at least a token protest. "The garages those gates will let you into are just as secure as the wall itself."

"Oh, I doubt that," Lathe said. "With all the security focus on that new tac center, I'm guessing there are some nice juicy secrets hidden in the government offices that are just ripe for the taking."

Galway felt his stomach tighten. If Lathe was abandoning the whole Khorstron operation, then he was suddenly back to staring death in the face. "What sort of secrets?" he asked carefully.

"We'll find that out soon enough," Lathe said. "I'd love to stay and chat, but the night's getting old and we have things to do." He lifted his eyebrows at Spadafora.

Galway barely saw the other blackcollar move, but suddenly the driver was sagging unconscious in his arms. "I suppose you're going to do that to me, too?" he said, trying not to think about it.

"Sorry," Lathe said as Spadafora dragged the driver off into the trees lining the road. "For whatever it's worth, it'll only hurt a minute."

Galway braced himself. All that mattered, he reminded himself firmly, was the plan. "Fine," he said. "I'm ready."

CHAPTER 16

The Chryselli warship waiting at the rendezvous was a small one, as such things went, and considerably smaller than the *Novak* itself. But Lepkowski knew better than to judge by outward appearances, and indeed the *Novak's* sensors told the tale far better than mere human eyes. The *Rizhknoph* was packed to the gills with the most sophisticated combat systems the Chryselli had at their disposal. Small but deadly, the perfect choice for a quiet excursion into Ryqril-held space.

The alien seated in Lepkowski's bridge office was equally deceptive looking. The first humans to encounter the Chryselli had described them as giant hairballs on legs, and Commander Vivviv certainly lived up to that characterization. The flowing, dirty-white hair that covered most of his body blurred the curves and angles of the flesh and bone beneath, with the thin cranelike legs sticking out from the bottom of the mass making for a rather startling contrast.

But soft and cuddly though he might look, Vivviv was no one to be fooled with. He was a ten-year veteran of the

Ryqril war, with a string of small victories as impressive as anyone in the Chryselli war fleet could boast.

Now, with those small victories beginning to grow into larger ones, the Chryselli were beginning to detect the faint smell of ultimate victory; and it was time for the humans whose resistance efforts they'd supported to start pulling their share of the load.

[You truly believe Lathe and his blackcollars can capture this Ryqril base?] Viviviv asked doubtfully in the fluttering Chryselli language, one hand emerging from its furry concealment to accept a cup of licorice tea from Lepkowski's yeoman.

"I'm sure of it," Lepkowski said. "You may remember Lathe as the master tactician behind the recovery of these Nova-class warships a couple of years ago."

[With Chryselli assistance,] Viviviv reminded him. [A profitable adventure for us both.]

"Indeed," Lepkowski agreed, wincing as Viviviv drank deeply from the steaming mug. A hair below boiling point was exactly the way the Chryselli liked their drinks, but watching it always sent a surge of sympathetic pain through Lepkowski's own mouth and throat. "I'm hoping this one will be even more so."

Viviviv lowered his cup, a couple of stray drops rolling off the corners of his mouth to disappear into the mass of hair on his chest. [Still, it all appears too easy,] he warned. [Perhaps the tactical center is not genuine.]

"That's certainly a possibility," Lepkowski admitted. "Still, the local blackcollars have been monitoring and recording its transmissions since it came online, and there's been enough encrypted data coming in and going out for it to be the real thing. Though when Lathe and the others penetrate it, I think we'll find that much of the information they'll obtain will prove to have been deliberately falsified."

Viviviv eyed him. [In which case, it is an exercise in futility.]

"Not necessarily," Lepkowski said, permitting himself a small smile. "You'd be surprised how adept Comsquare Lathe is at turning enemy plans to his own advantage."

[Perhaps,] Viviviv said. [We shall see.]

"Yes." Lepkowski picked up a pair of magnecoded cards from his desk and handed them to his visitor. "In the meantime, here are copies of the transmissions we've picked up from the center. Heavily encrypted, of course, and our techs haven't been able to make much headway with them. Perhaps yours can do better."

[We shall see,] Viviviv said again as he took the cards. [If this center is like some the Ryqril create, you should warn your blackcollars to leave markers to guide their way out once they are inside.]

"You mean like Raakh-ree," Lepkowski said, nodding. He'd seen reconstructed floor plans of the Raakh-ree tac center, a base the Chryselli had managed to blast to rubble in a sneak raid five years ago, and it would have put the legendary Winchester House to shame. "Fortunately, they didn't have enough time here to go to that much effort. Khorstron is a simple two-story octagon design. Much cleaner."

Viviviv froze, the cards poised over the mouth of his shoulder pouch. [An octagon of two floors?] he echoed. [Have you a floor plan?]

"Nothing official," Lepkowski said, frowning at the

other's sudden reaction. Had he said something wrong? "Tactor Shaw sent us some of the work photos, though. They're on the cards I just gave you."

Viviviv held out the cards. [Show me,] he ordered.

Selecting the proper card, Lepkowski inserted it into his desk's reader. "Here it is," he said, pulling up the file and swiveling the display around to where Viviviv could see it. "Here's the control," he added, handing the page scroller across the desk.

For a minute the Chryselli gazed at the first of Shaw's photos. Then, picking up the control, he began paging through the pictures, his pace increasing until the photos seemed little more than a blur. He reached the end and, almost delicately, set the scroller back on the desk. [Have you studied these, General?]

"I looked through them, yes," Lepkowski said cautiously. "Obviously, I missed something important."

[You missed only what you could not be expected to know,] Viviviv said. [This center—this Khorstron—is a precise duplicate of the Daeliak-naa fortress on the third-tier Ryqril colony world of Saalnaka.]

One of the worlds, if Lepkowski was deciphering the alien words correctly, that the Chryselli had fought their way to a foothold on within the past two years. "All right, so they borrowed a familiar design when they built Khorstron," he said. "I'm afraid I'm still missing something."

[What you are missing,] Viviviv said, his voice suddenly taut, [is the knowledge that ten months ago we moved our own regional tactical center into Daeliak-naa.]

Lepkowski stared at the photo still on the display, the

pieces abruptly falling into place. "I'll be damned," he breathed. "They're trying to get the blackcollars to show them how to break into *your* tac center."

For a long minute neither of them spoke. [This is not good,] Viviviv said at last. [This is not the way Ryqril normally think. If they have learned how to create such tactics, all our planning and strategies must now be rethought.]

"No, they haven't learned how to think," Lepkowski said grimly. "They've just learned to hire those who can. Best guess: Plinry Prefect Jamus Galway."

[A military human?]

"Not particularly," Lepkowski said. "But he's watched and studied Lathe ever since Caine came to Plinry and got the blackcollars back on full military standing. And I suspect he had a lot of native ability to begin with."

[Then he must be eliminated,] Viviviv said firmly. [Our strategists are not set up to anticipate and counter human tactics and thinking.]

"I understand," Lepkowski said, pulling the card from the reader and handing it back to the Chryselli. "I'll head back immediately and contact Comsquare Lathe."

[And he will eliminate this threat?]

"Absolutely," Lepkowski assured him. "You can count on it."

They had laid him in the drainage ditch by the side of the road, Galway discovered as his brain finally dragged its way out of the long, turbulent blackness. *Laid* him, not *dropped* him, for which he supposed he should be grateful. But he wasn't. Not particularly. His head ached like hell, his muscles were trembling with the aftermath of their attack, and his neck was threatening to go into a painful cramp from the position his head had ended up in.

But overriding it all was the echo of Lathe's last words to him. With a breathtaking suddenness, the plan had changed.

It would take time to sort through it all. But right now, he had only one urgent job: to sound the alarm before the blackcollars reached the government center.

With a supreme effort, he dragged himself to his feet. To his mild surprise, the movement actually eased the pain and discomfort in both head and muscles. He tried waving his arms around a little, which helped even more.

The driver and guard were still unconscious, laid out on the ground as neatly as the blackcollars had left Galway himself. Both men's weapons were missing, of course, as was Galway's own paral-dart pistol. More to the immediate point, so were their comms.

Which left Galway with only one option. The strongpoint, he guessed, was no more than a kilometer away. Taking a few deep breaths to clear his lungs, he headed back along the road at the fastest jog he could manage.

"There it is," Lathe said, pointing ahead. "You see that gold crown sort of thing sticking up above the wall?"

"You mean inside the wall?" Spadafora asked, leaning over the seat between Lathe and Mordecai for a better look.

"It's not actually inside," Lathe told him. "The special-access gates are in deep indentations, set far enough back from the street that a passing government car won't accidentally trigger them when no one actually wants to go in."

"Pretty stupid design, if you ask me," Mordecai commented.

Lathe shrugged. "Shaw tells me there were a lot of riots here in the early years of the occupation. The top officials didn't want to leave their cars open to potshots from the mobs when they had to stop at guard stations for ID checks. By the time things settled down and Security got order restored, they'd gotten used to the convenience."

They drove past the gate. "Okay, yeah, I see how it works," Spadafora said as Lathe continued down the street and turned at the next corner. "Shouldn't be a problem. You want me any place in particular?"

"No, your choice," Lathe told him. "Just be ready to jump in any direction if the reaction is hotter than expected."

"Got it," the other said as Lathe turned again onto the next street, heading them back toward the gate one block away from the wall. "Anywhere here is good."

Lathe rolled the car to a halt by the walkway, and Spadafora hopped out into the deserted street. "I hope you realize how conspicuous we are," Mordecai warned as Lathe pulled away again. "I don't think we've seen ten other cars since we left the mountains."

"You don't always get to control the timing," Lathe reminded him. They continued down the street, catching another glimpse of the gate as they passed the cross street that led directly toward it. "What do you think? One block or two?"

"You think the steering can handle two?"

Lathe wiggled the wheel experimentally. "Seems pretty tight," he said. "Especially since, as you say, there's hardly any other traffic, which means we can run it straight down the middle of the street where it'll have the most wiggle room."

Mordecai nodded. "Let's make it two, then."

A few minutes and three turns later Lathe once again stopped the car, this time in the middle of the cross street with the car pointed toward the special-access gate two blocks away. Mordecai was ready with the tie rope, and together they got the steering wheel anchored securely in place. "How fast do we want?" Mordecai asked as he produced a pair of *shuriken* from his weapons pouch.

"Not very," Lathe said, pulling on his battle-hood and gloves. "They normally don't head in any faster than about thirty klicks per hour. We should probably run it a little slower than that."

"Okay." Crouching on the pavement beside the open driver's door, Mordecai pressed down experimentally on the accelerator with his hand, bringing the tachometer to the right spot and wedging one of the *shuriken* into the floor beneath the pedal. "Ready."

Lathe moved to the side and got a hand on the open door. "Go."

In a single smooth motion Mordecai shifted the car into gear, pressed the accelerator down against the *shuriken* he'd just placed, and then jabbed the other throwing star above it into the side of the center console, wedging the pedal firmly in place between them. The car leaped forward, and he just missed getting his arm slammed in the door as Lathe swung it closed. Rolling along at perhaps ten kilometers per hour, the car trundled its way down the street, heading straight for the gate.

"And away we go," Lathe murmured, pulling out a pair of *shuriken* of his own.

Keeping to the shadows, the two blackcollars set off after the vehicle, setting their pace so that the car pulled slowly but steadily ahead. The car crossed the first street without incident . . . crossed the second street, the one paralleling the wall, again without running afoul of other traffic . . . headed into the indentation on its final approach to the gate, which according to Shaw's information should even now be opening.

Only it wasn't.

"Uh-oh," Lathe muttered, holding out a warning hand to Mordecai as he slowed to a walk.

The words were barely out of his mouth when, with a muffled crunching of metal and plastic, the car rolled almost leisurely into the closed gate. An instant later all four of the open windows exploded with thick black smoke from the bomb they'd set in the backseat.

"Looks like Galway recovered fast enough to make it back to the strongpoint," Lathe commented.

"Or else they normally shut down the transponder system at night," Mordecai said. "How much effort do you want to put into this?"

"Not that much," Lathe assured him, reaching to his tingler. *Spadafora: withdraw to Point Two.* "All I care about is that they now have some evidence that we're more interested in the government center than we are in getting into Khorstron. That should help keep Haberdae's own people battening down the hatches here instead of getting in our way."

The wall's outer lights were starting to come on as the two blackcollars ran lightly down the street away from the still-smoking car. Spadafora was waiting at the agreed-upon rendezvous point, with a car already hot-wired and ready. "That has to be the shortest mission on record," he commented as he pulled away from the curb. "Can we go home now?"

"Yes, let's," Lathe said, leaning back in the seat and closing his eyes. "It's been a very long day."

To Galway's mild surprise, Haberdae himself showed up at the strongpoint to pick him up. Or at least, he was surprised until he saw who the van's other passenger was.

"Dae the 'lackcollars now know e'erything?" Taakh demanded harshly as he strode through the door, the Security men who had gathered in the entryway room backing up hastily at his approach. He came to a halt a meter away from where Galway was sitting, glaring down at him.

"No, Your Eminence, they don't," Galway assured him. "They never got into the strongpoint, and they never asked either my escort or me what we were doing up here."

A little of the stiffness went out of Taakh's posture. "Yae are certain?"

"Absolutely," Galway said. "My driver can corroborate that."

"We were lucky," Haberdae murmured.

"I suppose you could say that," Galway agreed, a touch

of cynicism coloring the pain in his still-throbbing head and stomach. Of course Haberdae had volunteered to accompany Taakh out here—it was another opportunity to subtly remind the Ryq how much more capable and competent he was than the backwoods Plinry prefect who'd been foisted on him and had then been careless enough to let himself get ambushed by their enemies.

Only in this case, though Haberdae didn't know it, his self-preening tactic was about to blow up in his face.

And in fact, Taakh's very next question was the one Galway had known he would eventually ask. "Hor did yae allor they tae 'ollow yae here?" the Ryq asked, his eyes boring into Galway's.

"They didn't follow me, Your Eminence," Galway said calmly. "The guards have examined the sensor posts guarding the driveway, and they've found the same radioactive damage that's been inflicted on the Khorstron fence post. Spadafora has to have been here for at least the last day and a half."

"S'ada'ora?" Taakh repeated. "Yae said S'ada'ora ras at Khorstron."

"Apparently, we were mistaken," Galway said, forcing himself not to flinch beneath the Ryq's glare. "It must be one or more of Shaw's men there instead."

For a few seconds Taakh glared down at Galway in silence, apparently still working it through. "All others," he said at last. "Lea'e us."

The other Security men didn't need to be told twice. They filed out quickly and silently, clearly relieved at the chance to escape the explosive atmosphere. A minute later Taakh, Haberdae, and Galway were alone. "I'

S'ada'ora ras here that long, he nust ha' 'ound it sone other ray," the Ryq continued, his gaze still on Galway. "Ex'lain."

"I don't know for certain," Galway said carefully. "But what Lathe told me was that they followed Prefect Haberdae up here two nights ago after our effort to capture Tactor Shaw."

Slowly, deliberately, Taakh turned to Haberdae. "Yae cane here?" he asked softly.

Haberdae's face had gone the color of sealant putty. "Yes, Your Eminence," he managed, his tongue stumbling over the words. "I . . . wanted to talk to Caine. I thought he might know some tricks—when a blackcollar goes to ground, I thought he might know—"

"Yae cane *here*?" Taakh repeated. His hand was resting on his holstered laser, the large fingers curled around the weapon's grip.

"They couldn't have followed me, Your Eminence," Haberdae insisted, his voice shaking, his eyes trying valiantly to tear themselves away from the holstered laser. "It's impossible. I know how to watch for—"

"'Re'ect Galray ordered that no run ras tae cone here," Taakh cut him off. "Did yae not know that?"

Haberdae took a deep breath. "Yes, Your Eminence, I did," he said. His voice had gone calm, the voice of someone whose fate was no longer even marginally in his own hands. "I have no excuse."

For a long moment Taakh stood facing him in silence, his hand still gripping his laser. Galway watched, not daring to move, hardly daring to breathe.

And then, slowly and deliberately, Taakh took his hand

off his weapon. "Yaer heart is in ny hand, 'Re'ect Ha'erdae," he said, stretching out his hand with the open palm upward. "Yaer li'e 'elongs tae ne."

Haberdae shivered. "I understand, Your Eminence," he managed.

A sympathetic shiver ran up Galway's back. Taakh had just passed a summary judgment of death for Haberdae's actions.

And though the judgment had been temporarily suspended, the prefect was living on borrowed time. From this point on, at any time, at any place, and for any infraction, real or imagined, Taakh could choose to reinstate that death sentence.

When he did, Haberdae would probably never even see it coming.

Taakh looked back at Galway. "Yae are rell?" he asked.

"I'm well enough, Your Eminence," Galway said, bracing himself. With Taakh in this mood, this might be exactly the wrong time to broach this particular subject. But on the other hand, with the Ryq's thoughts focused on Haberdae's failures—and with Galway looking that much better by comparison, especially after managing to get back to the strongpoint in time to warn about Lathe's threatened incursion into the government center—it might be precisely the *right* time. Either way, it was a risk he had to take. "Certainly well enough to be in Khorstron tomorrow for the blackcollars' attack."

For possibly the first time since they'd met, the *khassq* seemed genuinely surprised. "Khorstron? There is no reason yae need tae 'e there."

"There is every reason, Your Eminence," Galway said

firmly. "Only inside Khorstron will I have all the internal sensors and recording equipment I need to follow the blackcollars' attack from start to finish."

"Re already ha' the s'y's re'orts on the 'lan."

"Which we know are incomplete," Galway reminded him. "This evening's split exercises alone prove there are more aspects to the plan than Judas knows. Besides which, all battle plans invariably undergo changes once they're launched. We need on-spot coverage to see how they deal with the unknown and the unexpected."

Taakh looked at Haberdae, back at Galway. "Hunans are not allored into Ryqril tactical centers."

"If I can't be there, we risk this whole thing being for nothing," Galway warned.

"He's right, Your Eminence," Haberdae said, coming unexpectedly to Galway's support. "If we lose even the smallest details of their attack, the Ryqril warriors who ultimately try to use their plan to storm the Daeliak-naa fortress may very well fail." He sent a hooded look at Galway. "After all the effort and lives this operation has cost, I know we would all hate to see it fail."

"Surely a *khassq* warrior has the authority to change or modify general orders such as this when circumstances require," Galway added, gesturing at Taakh's baldric.

"O' course I dae," Taakh said, as if that were a given. "I rill consider yaer rekest. 'Ut now it is late. Re rill return tae the city."

Galway dozed off in the van as they drove, not waking until they'd reached his building. He said his good nights to the others and trudged wearily to the elevator and from there to his apartment. His whole body felt like he'd been dropped into a fodder-baling machine, and all he wanted to do was fall onto his bed and go to sleep.

But he couldn't. Not yet.

Stepping into the apartment's compact office, he lowered himself into the desk chair and turned on the computer, digging the magnecoded card from his jacket pocket and sliding it into the reader. If all went according to plan, tomorrow would be the final climactic culmination of everything he'd prepared for and worked for and hoped for for so long.

When it came, he intended to be ready.

Propping his chin on his hands on the edge of the desk, fighting against the fatigue tugging at him, he began to read.

CHAPTER 17

Bailey spent the morning at the hospital, listening with growing impatience to the interrogator's latest futile efforts to wring something more about Aegis from the wounded Phoenix boy.

It was just after one in the afternoon when the word came that the quarry was on the move.

"They left the highway half an hour ago and headed into the mountains," Ramirez reported as Bailey strode into the situation room. Beside him, General Poirot stood silently, his face settled into the same grim expression he'd been wearing ever since the blackcollars' rescue and escape the previous evening. Standing a pace behind the two men were Daasaa and Halaak, towering over the scene like brooding thunderclouds. "We weren't able to get a visual on the driver or passengers, but it has to be them."

Bailey ran his eyes down the readouts. The vehicle in question was a dark blue delivery van, the rear area fully enclosed with no windows, registered to one of Denver's longtime residents. "You've checked the ownership?"

"Stolen this morning," Ramirez told him. "Done very quietly, too—the owner hadn't even missed it."

And according to the picture being relayed from the spotter flying high overhead, the van was headed along the most direct route toward Shelter Valley. "It does look promising," he agreed cautiously, turning to the two Ryqril. "Battle Architect Daasaa, what would you have me do?"

Poirot stirred, but didn't speak. "Re rill ratch until they arri'e at their destination," Daasaa said. "Then re rill take they."

"Or re rill kill they," Halaak added darkly.

"As you command, Your Eminence," Bailey said, wincing at Halaak's almost casual comment. From what he'd seen over the past couple of days, killing blackcollars wasn't something even a Ryq should speak so confidently about. "Though we might want to keep them alive, at least for a while. They may have set up booby traps inside the base."

Halaak snorted contemptuously. "Ryqril rarriors can easily disarn any such tra's."

"Of course," Bailey said hastily. "I didn't mean to imply they couldn't."

"Assuming the warriors can actually get inside, that is," Poirot murmured.

"Yae rish t' s'eak, General 'Oirot?" Daasaa invited.

"I was simply wondering if this back door might have been designed so that only humans could pass," Poirot explained. "If I were designing such a place, I'd certainly have added choke points a Ryq wouldn't be able go get through."

"Interesting yae should suggest such a thing," Daasaa said, his tone thoughtful. "I ha' 'een rondering that nysel'."

"It seems a logical thing for them to have done," Poirot said, some of the tightness in his face easing. Bringing a Ryq potentially bad news was always dangerous unless it was something that the Ryq already knew or suspected. In that case, the human merely came off looking brilliant.

Though considering Poirot's current position, it might only mean he would look less suspicious. Under the circumstances, Bailey suspected the general would be willing to settle for that.

"In that case, we might want to bring some of our own techs and Security men along," Ramirez suggested. "That way, if there *are* choke points, we won't have to take the time to send back here for them."

"Another interesting 'oint," Daasaa said. "Ha' yae already chosen the hunans yae rish tae 'ring?"

"I—" Ramirez broke off, his expression twitching as he suddenly spotted the verbal trap. "No. No, of course not, Your Eminence."

"And yae, General 'Oirot?" Daasaa asked, looking back at Poirot. "Ha' *yae* nade a list o' hunans for this jo'?"

"Obviously, they would have to be people we can trust," Poirot said calmly. Unlike Ramirez, he'd clearly already thought it through. "With the blackcollars and Whiplash on the loose, we can't simply grab the nearest men and hope for the best."

"Yae see the 'ro'len," Daasaa said, looking pointedly at Ramirez.

"So my suggestion would be that we assemble a team out of brand-new recruits who've just completed their loyalty-conditioning," Poirot went on. "They've been in Athena for the past three weeks, with no chance that Phoenix could have gotten to them."

"Lieutenant Ranirez?" Daasaa invited.

"Yes, that should work," Ramirez said reluctantly, eyeing Poirot. "Of course, fresh recruits won't be as competent as more seasoned men."

"How competent do they have to be?" Poirot countered. "All they have to do is go in, see what condition the back door and base are in, and come back out to report."

"Unless there *are* booby traps," Ramirez countered.

"Colonel 'Ailey?" Daasaa asked

Bailey felt his throat tighten. They were his men, after all, who Poirot was talking so casually about sacrificing.

But in front of a pair of suspicious Ryqril was no time to look squeamish or hesitant. "General Poirot is right," he said firmly. "If we lose a few men, then we lose them." He looked Ramirez straight in the eye. "There are certainly more where they came from."

A flicker of surprise crossed Ramirez's face. But then his eyes went sideways to the two Ryqril, and his expression settled back into the plain-tan neutral he seemed to be wearing more and more regularly these days. "Of course," he said evenly.

Bailey looked back at Daasaa. "Does this plan meet with Your Eminences' approval?"

"It does," Daasaa said. "Yae nay 'egin 'ulling the 'iles on these new hunan recruits. Re rill rant six guards and three techs."

"Six guards and three techs, yes, Your Eminence," Bailey confirmed.

"General 'Oirot rill assist yae," Daasaa added.

Bailey grimaced before he could catch himself. "As you command, Your Eminence." He gestured to Poirot. "General?"

"Thank you, Colonel," Poirot said softly.

"Re rill stay here and ratch," Daasaa told them, his eyes drifting back to the spotter display. "Yae rill 'e ready ren the 'lackcollars reach the nountain."

"I hear," Judas said carefully, "you had a little excitement last night after the drills."

"A little," Lathe confirmed, his eyes on the kitchen table where he'd spread out his weapons in neat rows. "Not as much as we'd hoped for, unfortunately."

"I'd have thought you already had enough excitement scheduled for one week," Judas said. "Comsquare Bhat said you tried to penetrate the city government center?"

"*Tried* being the operative word," Mordecai put in as he came into the room with a flat box under his arm. "Shaw said you wanted more primer caps, Lathe?"

"Yes, thanks," Lathe said, accepting the box and setting it down in one of the few empty spots on the table. "It wasn't a big deal, as it turned out," he continued to Judas. "We borrowed a Security car up in the mountains and tried to use it to get in through one of the special-access gates. But they'd apparently figured it out and locked down the transponder system before we got there. So we ran."

"We didn't *run*," Mordecai corrected. "We vanished like ghosts into the night."

"Correction noted," Lathe said dryly. "End of story."

"Ah," Judas said, sitting down at the table and trying to

study Lathe's face without looking obvious about it. Galway and Haberdae were convinced that Lathe and the others had no idea that Caine was imprisoned inside the strongpoint where they'd carried out their carjacking. But it was Judas's life on the line here, not theirs. "So you just grabbed a car off the street?"

With a sigh, Lathe laid down the knife he'd been sharpening and turned his full attention to Judas. "I had Spadafora watch Haberdae the night they tried to grab us. Just on spec—I thought he might go into Khorstron and that we'd get to see the entry procedure. Instead, he went up to a base in the Deerline Mountains. It seemed an intriguingly out-of-the-way place, so I told him to stay put and clear the entry for us."

"You mean knock out the sensors?"

"Right," Lathe said. "There wasn't any more traffic up there until this evening, when who should show up but our old friend Galway. Mordecai and I got there before he left, gimmicked his fuel line to kill the car about a klick away, where we jumped him and his escort. Would you also like to know what all of them were wearing?"

"Security gray-green, I'd guess," Judas said, a little annoyance pushing through his relief that his cover was still secure. There was no need for Lathe to be patronizing about this. "I'm sorry if my need to know is getting in your way."

Lathe grimaced. "No, *I'm* sorry," he apologized. "With Shaw and a whole group of blackcollars to work with, I guess I've fallen back into the old routine of communication and command structure. It doesn't leave much space for outsiders, I'm afraid."

"I understand," Judas said. "I just don't like being left out of things, that's all."

"Don't worry," Lathe assured him. "From now on, you'll be completely in the loop."

"Or the noose," Mordecai murmured.

Lathe nodded heavily. "Sometimes, there's not a lot of difference."

"Right here," Bailey said, pointing to the replay of the spotter track. "You see it?"

"I don't see anything," Ramirez said, leaning a little closer. "Okay, so the van slows down a little. That's a very twisty road."

"It doesn't just slow down a *little*," Bailey countered, looking at the two Ryqril still standing their silent vigil at the status boards. "It slows down a lot. And the road isn't *that* twisty right there. More importantly, it slows down just as it passes under this nice, convenient cluster of trees."

"But why get off there?" Ramirez objected. "There's still a long way to go before the van reaches Shelter Valley."

"Only Shelter Valley isn't the target, is it?" Bailey reminded him tartly. "I'm telling you, they're gone. If we wait until the van pulls into town, we're going to come up dry."

"And if we start sending spotters swooping around with sensor disks, we're going to spook them for sure," Ramirez countered.

"Colonel 'Ailey is correct," Daasaa spoke up, his tone leaving no room for argument or appeal. "The 'lackcollars ha' le't the 'ehicle."

"But there's no IR track that shows anyone leaving that area, Your Eminences," Ramirez argued, gesturing at the sensor map.

"Because they stayed under the trees until the van had drawn the spotters' attention away from the area," Bailey said.

"Yae are tracking now?" Halaak demanded.

"We have a half-dozen spotters waiting your orders," Bailey said. "If the blackcollars are out there, we'll find them."

Daasaa and Halaak looked at each other, and it wasn't difficult for Bailey to read their thoughts. If this was just another subtly drawn blackcollar diversion, moving that many spotters into the mountains would leave Athena that much more open to attack.

But it was a risk Bailey was willing to take. The black-collars were out there. He was sure of it.

"What i' they ha' already gone underground?" Halaak asked. "'Re should nove in and take the 'an now."

"But if we do that and the driver's in contact with Skyler's team, we'll spook them," Bailey pointed out.

"Again, yae are correct," Daasaa said, looking at Halaak. "'Re rill not yet take the 'an." He turned back to Bailey. "Yae nay launch yaer s'otters."

"As you command, Your Eminence." Bailey gestured to the spotter officer. "Spotters away," he ordered.

"Yes, sir." The other touched a key. "Spotters away."

The minutes ticked slowly by. Bailey listened to the low murmur of conversation in the situation room, one hand tapping restlessly against the side of his leg. He was right about this. He knew he was right.

But if he wasn't . . .

"There," one of the techs said suddenly, pointing at the display. "Four human IR signatures moving south-south-west."

"Only four?" Ramirez asked.

"The fifth must be driving the van," Bailey said.

"Then it is tine," Daasaa declared. "Assen'le yaer tean, Colonel 'Ailey. Re nust 'e ready ren they reach their goal."

"The team is ready now, Your Eminence," Bailey said. "And I have a Groundhopper transport standing ready."

Daasaa tilted his head slightly to the side. "A Groundho'er carries only trel'e 'assengers."

"Your pardon, Your Eminence, but there are only twelve of us," Bailey said, quickly running the numbers through his head again. "There are the three techs, the six Security men, you and *Khassq* Warrior Halaak, and me."

"And General 'Oirot," Daasaa said. He shifted his gaze— "And Lieutenant Ranirez."

Bailey looked at Ramirez, seeing his own surprise mirrored in the óther's face. Poirot, for his part, merely looked thoughtful. "I was planning to leave Lieutenant Ramirez here to coordinate the operation," he said carefully. "And I thought General Poirot was still under suspicion."

"Yae are all under sus'icion," Halaak said, his eyes glittering. "That is 'recisely rhy yae are all coning."

"It is tine to 'ind out who the true traitor is," Daasaa said, his voice ominous. "Gather yaer tean, Colonel 'Ailey. It is tine tae go."

"You sure you know where we're going?" Hawking

puffed as Skyler led them to the crest of yet another wooded hill.

"Absolutely," Skyler assured him, glancing up at the drifting clouds visible between the leafy branches overhead. "Another half klick, tops."

"That's what you said half a klick ago," O'Hara murmured, just loudly enough for Skyler to hear.

"Half a klick ago I said it was a whole klick," Skyler corrected. "Try to pay attention, will you?"

O'Hara muttered something not quite seditious about the decline in the standards of blackcollar leadership. Skyler responded in equally facetious kind, and the two of them fell silent.

Flynn didn't join in the banter. He'd hardly slept last night, despite the heavy activity of the previous day, thoughts of Jensen's plans and fate swirling unpleasantly through his mind.

Which, on one level, was rather surprising to him. He'd had his share of training exercises with Jensen back on Plinry, of course, and had found the man to be a competent if somewhat distant instructor. He'd also sat in on many a late-night bull session where Jensen's state of mind had been dissected in minute and low-fact detail.

But until this mission he hadn't actually known very much about the man. Even now, after a couple of days of tromping the Rocky Mountain wilderness together, he knew he hadn't even scratched the other's paint. But at the same time, those days had created some kind of bond of understanding and respect between them, something completely intangible but just as definitely real.

Flynn didn't want to see Jensen sacrifice himself. Not

even if such a sacrifice made a point to the Ryqril. Not even if it proved the key to ultimate victory.

Back on Plinry, he'd often wondered how Jensen could have been so affected by Novak's death, especially after so many other blackcollars had died. Now, in contrast, it was perfectly understandable.

A man didn't always get to choose who his friends and kindred spirits would be. Sometimes, the universe made those decisions for him.

"Aha," Skyler said, stopping suddenly at the top of yet another short ridge. "O ye of little faith. There it is."

Flynn hurried up the ridge, trying not to jostle O'Hara and Hawking on the way. He reached Skyler's side and scanned the greenery in front of them.

Which seemed to be nothing *but* greenery. "Where?" he asked.

"There," Hawking said, pointing at the end of a hill that opened up into a small clearing. "See the grating there, just beneath the overhang?"

"I see it," O'Hara said. "Nicely done."

"Flynn?" Skyler asked.

And finally, Flynn spotted it: an irregularly patterned grille, two meters across, set back almost invisibly in the shadow beneath the overhanging rock and grass. "Got it," he said. "Man. I wouldn't have believed you could hide something that big right out in the open."

"We'd better get inside," Hawking warned. "We don't want Security swooping down on Kanai and finding the rest of the birds have flown."

"Right," Skyler said, heading down the ridge toward the clearing. "The grating's been cut free—"

"Cover!" O'Hara snapped.

For an instant Flynn continued down the ridge, muscles frozen by surprise even as the blackcollars' superior reflexes sent them diving to all sides.

But it was too late for any of them. Even as Flynn finally braked to a halt the small canisters falling from the sky slammed into the ground all around them, exploding into white clouds of cloying-sweet gas.

He was asleep before he hit the ground.

It had taken some ingenuity and several trips with the drag carts, but Foxleigh and Jensen had finally managed to fuel and prep the Talus. "Next step is to figure out how to get it into one of the aircraft lifts," Foxleigh said as they coiled the last cables and hoses clear. "There are a pair of upper-level launch bays to the east and west. Which ones were you planning to use?"

"We won't need the launch bays," Jensen told him. "Or the elevator, either."

Foxleigh stared. "You mean . . . straight out the main entrance? But isn't there a Ryqril base set up there? Adamson told me there was."

"Oh, there's a base, all right," Jensen said. "A big one, too. That's the whole point."

"What whole point?" Foxleigh retorted. "In case you haven't noticed, Ryqril bases always include large, nasty antiaircraft lasers. You won't get fifty meters before you get vaporized."

"Ah, but this base runs right up against the side of the mountain," Jensen said. "Going out through the front door will actually put me *inside* the defenses."

"Really," Foxleigh murmured. "Adamson never mentioned that part."

"He probably never got close enough to see that part," Jensen said. "The Ryqril are touchy about visitors."

"I see," Foxleigh said. Yes; it would do nicely. "Of course, they've got other weapons in there besides the antiaircraft lasers. Once you're in, you very likely won't be coming out again."

"I wasn't intending to," Jensen said quietly. "This one's for Novak and all the rest who've died at Ryqril hands."

He turned back to face the Talus . . . and as he did so, Foxleigh slipped his hand inside his jacket and drew his gun. "Actually, there's going to be a small change—"

He'd never seen a blackcollar move before. Had never dreamed that a human being could move that fast. An instant later he found his gun hand pointed toward the ceiling, his arm locked above his head between Jensen's two hands, the blackcollar facing him with their noses no more than ten centimeters apart.

And he had no idea how he'd even gotten into that position.

"I'm disappointed, Toby," Jensen said, his voice dark and cold as he gazed into Foxleigh's face. "Not surprised, really. But disappointed."

"I wasn't going to hurt you," Foxleigh insisted.

"No, of course not." Sliding his left hand along Foxleigh's right wrist, the blackcollar deftly plucked the gun from his hand and stepped back. "We wondered about this gun, Flynn and I," he said, turning the weapon over in his hand as he inspected it. "I was hoping you were just some war veteran who'd been hiding out all this time."

"I am," Foxleigh said, rubbing his elbow where Jensen had overextended it. "My name's Lieutenant Samuel Foxleigh, TDE Air Defense."

"Of course," Jensen said. "Let me guess: you flew Talus interceptors."

"As a matter of fact, I did," Foxleigh said, fighting to keep his voice steady.

"And you ended up out here how?"

"I was shot down in the final battle," Foxleigh said, his gaze drifting to the fighter looming over them. "I hurt my leg when I bailed out, but I was able to make it to Shelter Valley. Doc Adamson patched me up; but as soon as it was clear that we'd lost and the Ryqril were landing in force to set up shop, he knew I couldn't stay there."

"Why not?"

"The town was too small," Foxleigh said. "Everyone knew everyone else, and there were two or three Adamson didn't trust to keep their mouths shut under pressure. So he took me up to the cabin and asked Toby to put me up for a while."

"So there was an actual Toby?"

"Adamson's uncle," Foxleigh said. "He'd moved up to the cabin about ten years earlier to get away from what he called the irritations of civilization."

"Not much of an escape," Jensen pointed out. "He was, what, a whole two hundred meters out of town?"

"But everyone knew to leave him alone," Foxleigh said. "Actually, the cabin's location was a compromise with the rest of his family, who were adamant about him not disappearing off somewhere into the wild and maybe dying in an accident without them even knowing about it."

"And then you showed up," Jensen said. "He must have been thrilled."

"Thrilled isn't the word for it," Foxleigh said ruefully, remembering the long and heated discussions. "But Adamson promised it wouldn't be for long, just until the Ryqril and their collaborators finished the census we knew they'd be taking of the mountain areas. Once that was over, I could move back down to Shelter Valley, and eventually to Denver."

"So what went wrong?"

"What do you think?" Foxleigh retorted. "The Ryqril decided to stick that damned sensor pylon at the edge of town. That meant Security could be popping in at any time to check on the thing. Worse, it meant everyone would be on file somewhere, which killed any chance for me to slip into town and pretend I'd always been there."

"So you and Toby became permanent roommates?" Jensen suggested.

Foxleigh swallowed. "Only for a while," he said quietly. "Three months later he caught pneumonia and died."

"Leaving you his cabin and his name."

"Everyone in town already knew about old Toby the hermit," Foxleigh said. "But no one outside the Adamson family had seen him recently enough to remember what he looked like. It seemed the perfect place to hide."

"Temporarily, anyway," Jensen said. "Only you seem to have made it permanent."

Foxleigh felt his stomach tighten. "I guess I just got used to it."

Jensen shook his head. "Lie number two," he said.

Foxleigh frowned. "What?"

"That was lie number two," Jensen said. "Lie number one was in your story somewhere, though I'm not sure exactly where. But this was definitely number two. You want to try again?"

Foxleigh sighed. "All right," he said. "The fact is that I wanted to stay near the mountain. I knew it was locked down, but I thought someday I might be able to find a way back in."

"To do what?"

"Basically, to do exactly what you're planning," Foxleigh said. "I wanted to take a fighter and do as much damage as I could to the Ryqril before they caught up with me." He squared his shoulders. "And I'll guarantee I'm a better pilot than you are."

"No doubt," Jensen agreed. "So what exactly do you want?"

"What I just said," Foxleigh told him. "Let me take the Talus out into the Ryqril base."

"Sounds reasonable," Jensen said. "The answer's no."

He said it so calmly that for a second the word didn't register. When it finally did, it hit Foxleigh like a slap in the face. "What do you mean, no?" he demanded.

"I mean that before you pulled this I might have been interested," Jensen said, hefting the gun. "Now, your currency's all been burned."

"I wasn't going to shoot you," Foxleigh insisted again, his stomach churning. This was his last, his very last chance. "I just wanted to make sure you'd listen."

"And if I didn't, you had the final argument?" Jensen shook his head. "Sorry, Toby. Or Foxleigh, or whatever your real name is."

"It's Foxleigh."

"Whatever." Jensen gestured back toward the elevator. "Come on. You're going home."

Silently, they made their way back down to the Level Nine storage room where they'd first entered Aegis Mountain. Sitting Foxleigh down on one of the crates, Jensen poked around for a few minutes and came up with a short length of thin cord. "I'm going to tie your hands together," he told Foxleigh as he set to work. "It'll make some parts of the trip a little tricky, I'm afraid, but a former fighter pilot should be able to make do."

"What about the rope ladder?" Foxleigh asked. "I can't climb it this way."

"The housing on the sonic Torch set up at the base of the shaft has a couple of sharp edges on it," Jensen told him. "I damn near sliced my hand open on one of them on our way out last time. A little work and you should be able to cut yourself free."

"And meanwhile you'll be committing suicide?"

"I'll be avenging fallen comrades," Jensen corrected. "And, with luck, I'll be helping bring all this to an end. Okay; on your feet."

"Wait a second," Foxleigh said as Jensen took his arm and helped him up. "What do you mean, bring it to an end? Bring *what* to an end?"

"The Ryqril domination, of course," Jensen said. "What else is there?"

"No—hold it," Foxleigh protested as Jensen started pulling him toward the tunnel. "How is shooting up one Ryqril base going to do *that*?"

"Just part of the larger whole," Jensen said. "I'd love to

chat about it, but I've got work to do." Gently but firmly he pushed Foxleigh through the opening. "Get going."

"Jensen, I want to be a part of what you're doing," Foxleigh said, trying one final time. "I *need* to be a part of it."

"And don't try to come back," Jensen added, shoving Foxleigh's gun into his own belt. "If you do, I'll kill you." Turning, he strode back across the room.

Foxleigh watched him go, his heart feeling like a chunk of lead. It had been his absolute last chance.

And he'd blown it.

Jensen disappeared out the door. Foxleigh stood there a little longer, wondering if he should follow the other and try again. All the blackcollar could do would be to follow through on his warning and kill him. And one way or another, Foxleigh was already dead.

With a sigh, he turned his back on the base. Yes, he was dead, but even a dead man had obligations. At the very least, Adamson deserved to hear the whole story, and to finally know what kind of person he'd spent all these years protecting.

When he did, maybe the old medic would kill him himself.

Lowering his head, balancing himself with his tied hands, he headed for home.

Skyler drifted back to consciousness with a sense that he was sitting up, his chin lolling against his chest, his arms pinioned together in front of him. Carefully, expecting to find himself in a Security interrogation cell, he opened his eyes.

He wasn't inside a cell, or even indoors. He was seated on the ground not five meters from where they'd been attacked, his back braced against the trunk of a tree at the edge of the small clearing. His feet were free, but his forearms were pinned securely together by a pair of heavy-duty mag-lock shackles, the sort that couldn't be removed without special equipment. His *nunchaku* had been taken, as had his slingshot and the knives and *shuriken* from his various pouches and sheaths.

He turned his head a couple of degrees to his left. Flynn was sitting against the next tree over, his head still bowed against his chest but his eyes half open as he worked his way awake. Beyond him at successive trees were O'Hara and Hawking, similarly trussed up, similarly coming awake.

"Yae are arake," a Ryqril voice said.

There didn't seem much point in pretending he wasn't. Opening his eyes all the way, Skyler lifted his head.

A half dozen Security men were standing across the small clearing, some of them watching the four prisoners, the others peering into the now open air vent grating. Standing a few feet to the side were General Poirot, Colonel Bailey, and an unfamiliar man wearing lieutenant's insignia. Thirty meters above the clearing a Corsair hovered like a vulture waiting for its prey to die.

And standing directly in front of Skyler, three meters away, were a pair of armed Ryqril.

"Good day to you, *khassq* warrior," Skyler greeted the nearer of the two aliens, forcing his voice to remain calm as he eyed the other's distinctive baldric. He'd faced a few *khassq* during the war, and even with all his weapons and faculties to call on, those contests had been tricky. Here, weaponless and with his hands pinioned, he wouldn't have wanted to face even a regular Ryqril warrior. "I'm Commando Rafe Skyler."

"*Khassq* rarrior Halaak," the other rumbled, and Skyler found himself breathing a little easier. A *khassq* wouldn't bother giving his name if was planning a quick and simple kill. Exchanging names implied he intended to at least wait a while before dealing with the prisoners, and any extra time was to the blackcollars' advantage.

He shifted his attention to the second Ryq. This one wore the less elaborate but equally distinctive baldric of a battle architect, the Ryqril equivalent of a senior tactical officer. "And good day to you as well, Battle Architect," he added.

"And tae yae, Connando Skyler," the other said, his grating voice almost courteous. "I an 'Attle Architect Daasaa. Yae ha' 'ought rell and rith courage."

"Thank you," Skyler said, not about to be out-courteoused by a mere Ryq. "General Poirot told me the Ryqril military had taken an interest in this operation. I had no idea just how serious that interest was, though." He looked past the Ryqril at Poirot. "You might have warned me, General."

"And I might have betrayed my people and position," Poirot countered, his voice stiff. "Unfortunately for you, I did neither."

"So I see," Skyler agreed, taking a moment to study Colonel Bailey and the unidentified lieutenant. Both of them were showing the same tension he could see in Poirot's face. "Your force seems rather heavy with senior officers, General. Is this some sort of refresher field trip?"

"We just wanted to be in on the victory," Bailey said before Poirot could answer.

"Or more likely, this just happens to be where your Ryqril masters told you to stand," O'Hara put in.

Poirot's face went rigid. "Listen, *blackcollar*—"

"Enou'," Daasaa cut him off tartly. "Yae rill now tell us, Connando, what tra's there are inside Aegis Nountain."

"I don't know anything about any traps," Skyler said. "But if you're worried, I'd be more than happy to go in and check."

"Yae rill not no'e 'ron that s'ot," Halaak growled.

Daasaa murmured something to him in Ryqrili. Probably explaining the concept of sarcasm, Skyler guessed. "There is no need 'or that," the battle architect said. "Yaer 'ellow hunans rill disco'er any such dangers."

There was a small flurry of commotion by the air vent, and a pair of techs in slightly dirty uniforms emerged through the opening into the late afternoon sunlight. Poirot and Bailey stepped over to them, and for a minute they talked together in low tones.

"Skyler?" Flynn murmured from Skyler's side.

"Yes, I'm here," Skyler said sourly, watching the two Ryqril. Halaak still had his eye on the prisoners, but Daasaa had half turned to face the conversation going on by the grating.

"That trick throw of Mordecai's," Flynn said. "The spinning throw? He invented it to be used by a man in forearm shackles."

"Really," Skyler said thoughtfully. Now that he thought about that, he could see that Flynn was right. Leave it to Mordecai. "You have anything left to throw?"

"No," Flynn said. "But you do."

Skyler's eyes dropped to the silver dragonhead ring on his right hand. "Understood," he murmured. "Let me pick the timing."

Daasaa turned back. "So," he said. "Again General 'Oirot ras correct. The 'assage'ay is not large enou' 'or Ryqril tae 'ass. The hunans rill go in alone."

Skyler suppressed a grimace. Into Aegis Mountain, where Jensen almost certainly had his own plan well underway. Unknowingly, probably uncaringly, the Ryqril were sending those men to their deaths. "I suppose they will," he murmured.

For a moment Daasaa gazed at him, as if trying to read the alien human face. Then, with a snort, he turned away, pushing aside one of the long branches that hung just low enough for its leaves to brush the top of his head. "General 'Oirot, yae rill send yaer nen into the nountain," he ordered. "They rill 'ind the control 'or the nain door and o'en it."

"As you command, Your Eminence," Poirot said. "I'd like permission to accompany them."

"Denied," Daasaa said. "Yae and the other o'icers rill stay here."

Poirot's lips compressed briefly. "As you command, Your Eminence," he said again.

Halaak took a step closer to the prisoners. "Yae rill renain here, too," he added, his eyes glittering, his hand resting on the hilt of his short sword. "Unless yae rish tae try tae escape."

So that was why they'd left the blackcollars' legs unshackled. "Looking to add a few blackcollars to your trophy wall?" he asked.

"One o' yae killed a Ryqril rarrior outside the Aegis Nountain 'ase," Halaak said, his voice dark. "I rould relcone the chance tae a'enge his death."

"I'm sure you would," Skyler said quietly. "Maybe you'll get your chance."

CHAPTER 18

The sun had disappeared behind the buildings of Inkosi City as Judas and the three Plinry blackcollars sat in a car at the town's southeastern edge. Visible through the sparse woodland to their right was the Khorstron Tactical Center. An hour or so until sundown, Judas estimated, plus another hour to allow dusk to turn into night, and the attack would finally begin.

Seated beside him behind the steering wheel, Lathe stirred. "Almost time," he said.

Judas frowned past him at the clear blue sky. "We're not waiting until full dark?"

"With modern sensors there's not a lot of difference between day and night," Mordecai reminded him from the backseat.

"Except that they'll also probably assume we'll wait until dark," Spadafora added from behind Judas. "The first rule of warfare is to try not to play to the enemy's expectations."

"Of course," Judas murmured, wondering briefly if Galway and Haberdae would be caught by surprise by the

387

schedule. If they weren't inside Khorstron already, he suspected, they weren't going to get there in time. "So how exactly is Shaw handling the initial attack?" he asked. "You're not all going to try to climb the fence at that one spot where the sensors got fried, are you?"

"With the Ryqril in the bunkers shooting leisurely at us as we popped over?" Lathe pointed out. "No, we have some nice camouflage all prepared." He pointed. "Here it comes now."

Judas peered out the windshield, shading his eyes with his hand. An unmarked panel truck was driving slowly down the access road leading to Khorstron's western fence gate. "I don't remember any truck bombs in the original planning," he said uneasily.

"A truck bomb wouldn't work here," Spadafora told him. "The fence's sensor array includes explosives detectors. A load that big couldn't get within three blocks without setting them off."

"Just stick with us, Caine," Lathe added. "We'll try to get you through what's ahead."

"Wait a second," Judas said, his skin starting to crawl. "I thought I was supposed to be on the penetration team."

"You are," Lathe said, smiling tightly as he gestured to the four of them. "We're it."

Judas stared at him . . . and before he could think of anything to say the truck blew up into a cloud of heavy, dense, white smoke.

"Here we go," Lathe muttered as he started the car. "Filters."

"What is that?" Judas asked as he fumbled for his gas filter.

"It's your standard high-tech smoke screen," Spadafora said, his voice muffled by his own filter. "Shaw had a few left over from the war. Basically, it's a heavy chemical fog rich in suspended metallic particulates, which—well, there you go."

The Ryqril in the two guard bunkers flanking the gate had opened fire on the truck now, its outline barely visible through the fog rolling its leisurely way toward the tac center on a stiff westerly breeze. With each laser shot, the entire cloud lit up like a brilliant green strobe light. "Not only does it scatter some of the laser light, thereby reducing its effectiveness," Spadafora went on, "but as an extra bonus, it bounces that light all around and right back into everyone's eyes."

"Makes it very hard to see unless your goggles include a special polarized layer," Lathe added as he settled his own goggles into place. "Which ours do, of course."

He'd barely finished when the laser barrage apparently hit a sensitive spot and the truck disintegrated into a burst of flame that lit up the billowing cloud even more brilliantly than the lasers had. "Phase One complete," Spadafora commented as a fresh surge of white smoke boiled upward like a volcanic plume and started falling leisurely over toward the tac center grounds.

"Phase Two begun," Lathe said, pointing across Judas's chest. A dozen vehicles had suddenly appeared from various areas around the southern and western sides of the center, bouncing wildly as they drove at high speed through the trees. "They're coming in on the east and north sides, too," the comsquare added.

All of them heading straight for the sensor fence, Judas

saw, and the sonic trap Shaw had warned was built into the posts. "And what exactly is this supposed to accomplish?"

"Just watch," Spadafora advised, an edge of malicious amusement in his voice. "Watch, and learn."

Taakh snarled something, and the half-dozen Ryqril techs seated at the security monitor room's wraparound console bent feverishly to work. "What did he say?" Haberdae muttered.

"I don't know," Galway murmured back. In the year he'd spent with Taakh he'd managed to pick up a little bit of Ryqrili, but not nearly enough for a situation like this. And the conquerors had been very careful not to give any formal language instruction to their human slaves. "Best guess is that he wants them to analyze the smoke screen."

Haberdae grunted and fell silent. Shifting his attention away from the approaching smoke, Galway concentrated instead on the monitors showing the views to north and south.

One of the techs was giving a short speech now. Taakh listened in silence, then turned to the two humans. "It is a chenical cloud designed tae con'use sensors," he told them. "It also scatters sone o' the strength o' laser 'ire." He jabbed a finger at Galway. "Yae rill nake a note o' it."

Galway nodded. "As you command, Your Eminence."

The Ryq turned back to the monitors. The smoke had passed the fence, Galway saw, and was starting to roll around the building itself.

And there they were, right on cue: fifty cars appearing suddenly from streets and driveways and from beneath camo nets, all of them charging at full speed straight toward the Khorstron fence.

One of the techs had obviously seen them, too. He snapped something at Taakh, and the big *khassq* stepped to his side. "Are they 'ools tae think re rill 'e caught un're'ared?" he growled contemptuously.

"Maybe they're a diversion while the real infiltration team sneaks over the fence where they fried the sensors," Haberdae suggested. "Without sensors, you'll never spot them in this damn smoke."

"Somehow, I don't think sneaking is the plan," Galway said.

"I thought that's what blackcollars did best," Haberdae growled.

Galway nodded at the monitors. "Let's find out."

The smoke screen was filling the entire grounds now, and the techs had switched the displays from straight visual to the false-color images of sensor scans. Galway had never found such scans to be very clear, and even the best of the images were now being hampered further by snowlike flickers. The worst of them showed nothing but multicolored static. "Those must be the pictures coming from the sensors on the building," Haberdae said, gesturing toward the latter group.

"With the ones where you can actually see something coming from the sensors in the fence posts," Galway agreed, nodding. "Whatever they've got in that smoke, it's damn good."

Haberdae grunted. "I just hope they don't realize how blind we really are."

Around the perimeter, the cars were braking to a halt,

stopping ten to fifteen meters back from the fence. The doors swung open and blackcollars emerged into the smoke in groups of three, each group huddling close together as they hurried across the remaining distance. "What are they *doing*?" Haberdae demanded, starting to sound uneasy. "I thought they knew about the sonics in the fence posts."

"That's what Judas said," Galway agreed. The groups reached the fence, and in near-perfect unison the two end men in each set reached down to grab the feet of the man in the middle and hurl him up and over the fence.

Haberdae inhaled sharply. "What the *hell*—?"

"Relax," Galway said, pointing to the monitors as the flying blackcollars hit the ground and toppled over to lie flat and unmoving. "They're down. The sonic must have gotten them."

"The sonic and the mines," Haberdae corrected, pointing to the grounds schematic where five orange lights were flashing at various points just inside the fence. "I wonder whether that flexarmor is good enough to block scud grenade needles."

Across the room, one of the techs spat something. "So that is their 'lan," Taakh rumbled. "The in'iltrators carry large quantities o' ex'losi'es."

"You think they're trying to blast the fence?" Haberdae asked.

"They could have done that from the outside and stayed away from the sonic and mines," Galway reminded him. On the displays, the shadowy images of the blackcollars still outside were drifting away, heading back toward their cars.

"'Re'ect Galray is correct," Taakh agreed. "They think tae wait until the sur'i'ing in'iltrators are reco'ered, then use their ex'losi'es tae 'last down the doors."

"While meanwhile the blackcollars still outside drive the cars through the fence?" Haberdae suggested.

"I' that is their 'lan, they rill 'e disa'ointed," Taakh said with malicious satisfaction. "The 'ence is 'ar tae strong tae crash through."

"Meanwhile, we have the inside group to deal with," Haberdae reminded him.

"That rill not 'e a 'ro'len," Taakh assured him. He snapped an order, and on the edge of the building monitor displays, just barely visible through the smoke, Galway saw the tips of laser rifle muzzles emerge from the firing slits in the bunkers flanking the building's doors, tracking downward toward the figures still lying motionless on the ground. "I don't like this," Galway warned. "There's some catch here."

"The catch rill 'e 'or they," Taakh said. Gesturing imperiously to one of the techs, he snapped an order.

Lathe had maneuvered their car through a line of trees toward the southwestern part of the fence as the smoke screen spread out over the base, heading for the section where Shaw had said the radiation-wrecked sensor post was located. The last thirty meters were done in near-total blindness as the fog settled down around the grounds. "Everyone out," the comsquare called as he shut off the engine. "Spadafora, get the shields. Caine, come with me."

"Sure," Judas muttered, grimacing behind his filter and

goggles as Lathe led the way through the smoke. He had always hated blindfold games, hated them with a passion. "What exactly are we doing?"

"We're going over the fence," Lathe said. "Hold up here."

"You know, you promised I'd be kept in the loop," Judas said as he stopped. "This hardly qualifies."

"Events are moving faster than expected," Spadafora said, coming up behind him and handing over one of the body shields. "If you'd rather, you can wait for us in the car."

Judas swallowed a curse. In full honesty he would like nothing better than to sit this one out. The Ryqril in there would be playing for keeps, and the flexarmor he was wearing wasn't guaranteed against anything but the first laser shot. Maybe not even that much.

But Galway needed someone on this end of the attack to pick up on any details they might miss from inside the tac center. "Thanks, but I'm going," he growled.

"Good," Lathe said. "You can start by hooking your shield over your back to keep your hands free." He demonstrated.

Judas had just gotten the shield in position when his tingler came to life: *all blackcollars, stand ready; launch in five.*

"What are we launching?" Judas asked as Mordecai grabbed his arm and pulled him down into a crouch. "We're not using missiles, are we?"

"Of a sort," Lathe said. "We're tossing a few bodies over the fence."

In the distance, Judas heard a series of muffled thuds.

"That didn't sound like bodies hitting the ground," he said apprehensively.

"Scud grenades," Spadafora identified the sounds. "Some of them must have landed on the mines."

Judas grimaced. "Are they all right?"

"As all right as the rest of them," Lathe said. "Turn your eyes away from the fence a moment."

Judas had barely complied when the inside of the cloud abruptly lit up with brilliant green light as a dozen or more lasers all fired at once.

And an instant later he was thrown to the ground as the whole cloud seemed to erupt in a single, violent explosion.

Even at the very center of the base, Galway felt the vibration of the multiple blasts. "Good *God*," Haberdae gasped as every sensor screen went solid white and then turned to static. "What the hell kind of explosives have they *got*?"

"It wasn't the quality," Galway said grimly. "It was the quantity."

"The *what*?"

"Don't you see?" Galway said, pointing to the fence sensor monitors. "Those weren't real people they tossed over the fence. They were more of those same sensor dummies they had riding their decoy hang gliders when they first arrived. Only this batch were loaded with explosives."

Taakh was snarling at the techs, who were in turn pounding frantically at their keyboards. "And they were lying right by the fence," Haberdae murmured, his voice suddenly graveyard quiet as he pointed to the grounds schematic. The entire fence line was flashing orange now, Galway saw. "Shaped charges designed to send a pressure wave through the ground when they blew," the prefect added. "Probably took out the whole minefield."

"And the whole fence sensor system, too," Galway said grimly. "Ready or not, here they come."

The hammering in Judas's ears faded away, leaving only a persistent ringing behind. Cautiously, he opened his eyes.

To find to his shock and dismay that the smoke screen was gone. On the far side of the fence, fifty meters away, he could see Khorstron's western entrance with its two flanking guard bunkers.

Both bunkers in full targeting view of them.

"Don't worry, they're probably still too blinded or dazed to shoot straight," Mordecai assured him, getting a grip on his upper arm. "Time to go."

"Right," Judas said, his explosion-dazed brain starting to put the pieces together. Obviously, the smoke screen was gone because the concussion of the multiple blasts had blown the smoke up and away.

Fortunately, the wrecked truck was apparently still churning out more of the fog. Even as they again moved toward the fence a fresh cloudbank began to flow in from the west.

Lathe was the first to reach the fence. "Up and over," he said, and started up.

Judas followed, the shield on his back bouncing awkwardly as he climbed. Half a minute later, with the fog thickening comfortably around them, they were back on the ground and moving cautiously toward the building. "What now?" he asked, wincing as he walked past sections of torn ground where hedge mines had been.

Right on cue, his tingler signaled. *Commence shutout.*

"We start Phase Three," Lathe said. "Spadafora?"

"I'm on it," Spadafora said, dropping into a sniper's kneeling posture, his slingshot ready. Setting a small object into the weapon's pouch, he drew it back a few centimeters. "Ready."

Lathe nodded and reached under his sleeve. *Lathe: ready*, the message tingled against Judas's wrist.

In the near distance, Judas could now hear a crackle of small, oddly muffled explosions. "Primer caps being shot into the guard bunkers at the other three entrances," Lathe identified the sound. "The goal is to kill or otherwise incapacitate the Ryqril inside and keep others from replacing them."

Judas nodded. With the sensors in the fence gone and those on the building of limited range in the smoke screen, the warriors in the bunkers were about the only eyes Galway and Taakh had left. If Shaw could eliminate them, the blackcollars would have nearly free run of the Khorstron grounds.

The question was, what did he and Lathe intend to do with that freedom of movement?

He frowned, belatedly noting that Spadafora himself hadn't joined the slingshot barrage. "What about the bunkers on the western door?"

"Patience," Lathe said. "We have something special planned for them."

Judas shook his head. "I'm sorry, but I don't get any of

this," he growled. "If we were going to blow the sensors on the fence anyway, why did we bother nuking the ones on that one particular fencepost? Just to give the Ryqril a little misdirection?"

"Partly," Lathe said. "For the past couple of days, ever since we assume they spotted the pellet barrage, they've probably been expecting a quiet infiltration from that one single direction and have been setting their plans accordingly." He gestured toward the building, rapidly growing less distinct as the smoke screen continued to roll in. "But more importantly, the fence sensors spot explosives and fast-burning fuels. We needed a gap we could use to send in some extra surprises."

"Such as?"

"Patience," Lathe said. "As soon as Shaw gives us the okay—"

Shaw: go.

"And here we go," Lathe said. Spadafora's slingshot snapped—

And somewhere in the direction of the western door the white smoke erupted in flame.

Judas caught his breath. Spadafora fired again; and as a second sheet of flame burst into existence, he realized the fires were situated at the bases of the two guard bunkers. "Surprises, you say," he managed.

"They're called burn pellets," Lathe told him. "Jellied aviation fuel inside a thin and highly flammable shell. Once the snipers had fried that fence post, they could lob over enough of them to make a pile against each of the bunkers' bases."

"And now if the gunners try sticking their lasers out

the firing slits they'll get their faces burned off?" Judas
suggested.

"Something like that," Lathe said, digging again for his
tingler. *Lathe: flame on.* "And whether they stick their
noses out or not, it's going to be getting very hot in there."

Acknowledged, Judas's tingler signaled. *All blackcollars,
deploy around Point One.*

"And you had all this set up two *days* ago?" Judas asked.

"First rule of magic, kiddo," Spadafora said. "When the
magician says 'Watch very closely,' the trick's already been
done."

"Exactly," Lathe agreed, and Judas could hear the tight
smile in his voice. "Here we go, Caine. And watch very
closely."

The quiet intensity in the monitor room had dissolved
into barely controlled chaos. Taakh strode back and forth
behind the techs, barking orders and commands and
demands as warning lights and displays began flashing all
across the boards. "What the *hell* is happening out there?"
Haberdae gritted.

"I don't know," Galway said, studying the flashing
orange lights on the status displays. "It almost looks like
there are fires in some of the guard bunkers."

"The 'lackcollars are shooting intae the 'unkers," Taakh
said, his voice tight. "They seek tae silence the gunners
there."

He had barely finished when a new pair of orange
lights, much larger than the other indicators, began flashing
on either side of the western door. Taakh barked a taut
question; was barked an equally taut answer. "They ha' set

'ires 'eneath the guard 'unkers at the restern entrance," he bit out. "They had no 'uel or extra ex'losi'es. How did they dae this?"

"I don't know," Galway said. "We'll have to ask Judas when it's all over."

"Rhy did he not already tell us?" the *khassq* demanded.

"I don't know that, either." Galway studied Taakh's face, a sudden revelation striking him. "You never really believed they could get in here, did you, Your Eminence?"

"Rhat I 'elie'e is not in'ortant," Taakh ground out. "And they rill not 'enetrate this tactical center."

Despite the danger, Galway had to smile. The goal of the mission had abruptly run squarely into Taakh's personal pride, and the *khassq* wasn't at all happy about it. "If they don't, then it'll all have been for nothing," he again reminded the Ryq. "And not just into the building—they have to penetrate all the way to the core. Otherwise when your warriors get into Daeliak-naa they may find themselves stopped by the Chryselli's interior defenses with no idea how to get through."

"And if those guards in the western bunkers get burned out, the blackcollars will have a clear shot at that door," Haberdae put in, an edge of nervous impatience in his voice.

"So it rould seen," Taakh said, his dark eyes flicking to the status boards and then back to Galway. "Yaer s'y has said nothing a'out *this*, either."

"No, he hasn't," Galway said, forcing his voice to remain steady. "My guess is that at the last minute Shaw took over planning and froze Judas out."

"Shouldn't we be getting warriors into position in the

western entrance foyer?" Haberdae put in, his impatience taking on an edge of urgency. "They could be stacking explosives against the door right now for all we know."

"I dae not 'elie'e it is that sin'le," Taakh said, gazing hard at the displays, most of which still showed little more than fuzzy images. "There is sone trick."

"I think you're right, Your Eminence," Galway said, moving beside him and studying the displays. "Setting big, ostentations fires outside the western bunkers is exactly the sort of thing they'd do to try and draw our attention that direction."

"'Or rhat 'ur'ose?" Taakh demanded.

"Something clever, no doubt," Galway said slowly, turning to the tactical schematic with its multitude of flashing orange lights. "I also noticed that when they were throwing their dummies across the fence, all but one of them was sent straight over. Only *this* one—" he pointed to a spot just east of the southern road "—was thrown in at an angle."

"And it was thrown farther in than the others," Haberdae murmured.

"Yes," Galway said. "And unless I'm remembering the schematics incorrectly, it landed right over the tunnel that leads out to the southern guard bunkers."

"And its explosion has now torn up the ground there," Haberdae said, his uneasiness vanishing into cautious excitement as he caught Galway's line of reasoning. "You think they're going to try to blast their way in through the tunnels?"

"I don't think we'd better give them the chance to find out," Galway said. "Your Eminence, I expect you want to keep the warriors inside where it's safe—"

"Ryqril rarriors dae not stay rhere it is *sa'*," Taakh cut him off sharply. "Re rill take the 'attle tae they."

"Do you think that's wise, Your Eminence?" Haberdae asked. "Couldn't you just set up something right at the tunnel entrance?"

"Prefect Haberdae is right, Your Eminence," Galway seconded. "In all that smoke the blackcollars are going to have the advantage, certainly over ordinary Ryqril warriors."

"No run has the ad'antage o'er Ryqril rarriors," Taakh snapped.

"I understand that," Galway hastened to assure him. "But I've seen blackcollars in action. It would take a battalion of *khassq*-class warriors to stop them."

Taakh drew himself up to his full height. "It rill not take a 'attalion o' *khassq*," he said, his voice all but ringing with pride. "It rill take only run. I rill lead they."

"You're going to go out there and leave us?" Galway asked, his eyes flicking to Haberdae. "But what happens if some of them get inside?"

"They rill not," Taakh said firmly.

"No, of course they won't," Galway said. "But if they do, we'll have no way to protect ourselves. If you could leave us a couple of warriors, maybe ones you don't think can handle blackcollars anyway—"

"*Enou'!*" Taakh barked. Snatching out his laser, he thrust it into Galway's hands. "There. *Yae* rill now dekhend." Barking a final order at the techs, he strode from the room.

"Feel safer now?" Haberdae asked sarcastically.

Galway hefted the laser in his hands. "A little, yes," he

said. "He couldn't have used it out there anyway. Not in all that smoke."

"No, of course not," Haberdae said, heading for the door. "You just go ahead and play soldier. I'll be right back."

"Where are you going?" Galway asked, frowning.

Haberdae sent a tight smile over his shoulder. "To help you feel even safer."

Ten Ryqril advancing from east door; turning south toward Point One, the terse report came from one of the comsquares on the eastern side of the Khorstron grounds.

Eight Ryqril advancing from south door, another comsquare added. *Second group, silent: six Ryqril.*

Acknowledged, Shaw's reply came. *All blackcollars defend. Lathe—go.*

"And here we go," Lathe muttered, getting a grip on Judas's arm and pulling him toward the blazing fires. "Shields ready."

"We're heading to the *bunkers*?" Judas asked as he fumbled his shield into position on his arm. "Shaw said the Ryqril were heading south."

"Because that's where they think the main attack is coming," Lathe said. "Shaw's made it look like—*hsss!*"

He yanked Judas down into a crouch, the other blackcollars dropping down beside them. There they all squatted, motionless, while around them the shadowy figures of a Ryqril warrior squad hurried past through the smoke. The sound of their footsteps faded away, and Lathe pulled Judas back to his feet.

The fires were still blazing when they reached the

nearer of the bunkers. Even as the structures themselves began to appear through the smoke Judas heard the *twang* and muffled cracks as Spadafora began to lob primer caps through the firing slits. "Breaking into the bunker won't do us any good, you know," he warned as they continued forward. "The door leading from it into the tac center is just as strong as the main ones."

"True," Lathe said. "But only if—watch it."

He snapped his shield up as a laser poked through the slit and a green bolt shot through the writhing flames. The shot hit the shield dead center, and Judas heard the crackle of heat stress as some of the metal and ablative material burned away.

The gunner never got a second shot. Spadafora's slingshot snapped again, and through the flames Judas saw a tiny explosion inside the bunker directly behind the muzzle. The weapon tilted sharply upward and slid back out of sight.

And then, deep in the bunker's darkness, Judas saw a faint glow suddenly appear.

"It's open!" Lathe snapped. "Mordecai?"

"Got it," Mordecai said. He stepped through the flames right up to the side of the bunker, his shield with its trailing heat-sink metal ribbon gripped horizontally in his hands. Slipping the edge of the shield into the firing slit, he ducked his head and peered around its side into the interior. Then, with a precise, sharp movement, he shoved the shield into the bunker.

"Half a meter back," Spadafora said, also ignoring the flames as he peered through the slit on the bunker's other side.

"Half a meter back," Mordecai repeated, taking hold of the end of the metal ribbon now trailing out the slit. Carefully, he pulled a half meter of it back toward him.

"That's it," Spadafora said. Stepping back away from the fire, he raised his slingshot, crouching a little as he continued to peer into the bunker.

"Let's move it," Lathe said. He had pulled a soft-looking pouch from his pack and was busily stuffing it into one end of Spadafora's firing slit. "Caine, you want a look?"

"Already figured this one out, thanks," Judas assured him as he nevertheless stooped for a quick look. Between the fire and the primer caps, the blackcollars had succeeded in driving the Ryqril gunners in from their bunker . . . and when they'd opened their door to retreat, Mordecai had shoved his shield in across the floor to block it open.

Sure enough, through the smoke he could see the half-open door and the ready room beyond it. A couple of Ryqril were also visible, frantically working at a small control box on the wall just inside the door. Spadafora's slingshot snapped, and the aliens shied back as the box exploded in a shower of sparks.

"I got the controls," Spadafora reported, returning the slingshot to his belt and pulling out a soft pouch of his own.

"There'll be a backup system," Judas warned as he stepped back out of the flames.

"Right, but now they'll have to go and find it," Lathe pointed out as he pulled a small igniter from his belt and flipped it open. "By the time they do, we'll hopefully be inside. Spadafora?"

"Clear," Spadafora said, stepping back from the bunker.

"Clear," Mordecai added, his *nunchaku* ready in his hand.

"Clear, and fire," Lathe said. Turning half away, he squeezed the igniter.

There were a pair of muffled explosions; and the entire front of the bunker shattered and collapsed into the flames. Mordecai was through the gaping hole even before the wall had finished coming down, darting across the bunker and ducking through the half-open door into the ready room. Lathe was right behind him, half pulling Judas along.

There was, as it turned out, no need for haste. By the time Judas squeezed through the door, the fight was already over.

"Hell," he murmured, looking around at the five crumpled Ryqril bodies sprawled on the ready room floor. Mordecai, standing over them with his *nunchaku* cocked under his arm, wasn't even breathing hard.

"Very much so," Lathe agreed. "Anyone get out?"

Mordecai shook his head. "Sounds like most of them are waiting for us outside the mantrap foyer," he said. "I guess they were expecting us to come in the front door."

"We'd better clear them out," Lathe decided. "We don't want to leave them at our back while we're trying to get into the monitor room."

Judas felt his chest tighten. Galway, Haberdae, and Taakh were supposed to be watching the operation from the monitor room. "I thought we were going to the main core," he said.

"We'll get there soon enough," Lathe assured him. "But first things first. Let's go clear out the backtrail."

* * *

Behind Galway, the door slid open. He spun around, tensing; but it was only Haberdae. "Where have you been?" he demanded as the door slid shut again. "There's some kind of alarm going off."

"I know," Haberdae said calmly, glancing up at the silently flashing warning lights as he crossed the room. "From the commotion down the western corridor, I'd say your blackcollars have entered the building."

Galway glanced at the displays, most of them still showing nothing but static. "Did you see them?"

"Fortunately, that wasn't the direction I was coming from," Haberdae said. Leaning over one of the techs, he flipped up an orange safety cover and turned a knob over. "I was down near the south door, talking with Taakh."

"About what?" Galway asked, frowning at the knob Haberdae had just turned. "What did you just do?"

"Like I said, I'm making us all safer," Haberdae said. "Taakh and I had a quick discussion while he was getting his warriors ready, and we agreed that letting Lathe find a way into the building was all we really needed. We don't actually need him to get all the way to the core."

Abruptly, his face hardened. "Did you really think this was your ticket to fame and fortune?" he bit out. "Hitching your future to a group of *blackcollars*?"

Galway's throat felt suddenly tight. "Prefect, what did you do?" he asked carefully.

"You're a very little man, Galway, from a very little world," Haberdae went on, ignoring the question. "How you sold the Ryqril on this piece of froth I'll never know. But the only thing it's going to get you is a one-way ticket back to your private dirtball."

"What did you *do*?" Galway demanded.

"I activated the autotarget defense lasers in the corridor out there," Haberdae said, waving behind him. "Your buddy Lathe gets five meters from that door and he's a cinder. Oh, put that down—we both know you can't use it on me."

Galway hadn't even realized he'd lifted Taakh's laser into firing position. "Taakh agreed to let them get to the core," he said, lowering the laser.

"And now he's changed his mind," Haberdae said. "He's a *khassq*, remember? He has the authority to change or modify general orders when circumstances require."

Galway felt his stomach tighten. "So that's why you supported me last night when I asked Taakh to let me be here today."

Haberdae shrugged. "I thought that in the heat of combat it might be easier to get him to see things my way."

"Your way being a little private vengeance?"

"Private?" Haberdae shook his head. "Hardly. These blackcollars aren't some advanced weapons system for us to use, something you can simply point and shoot. They're unpredictable, they're *damned* dangerous, and the sooner they're eliminated the better it'll be for the Ryqril and everyone else in the universe."

"They're a valuable resource," Galway insisted. "Haven't you been paying attention? I've proved I can maneuver Lathe into doing a job without him ever knowing he's actually working for the Ryqril. If you and Taakh get him killed, any chance of doing that again will be gone."

"There are other blackcollars around the TDE," Haberdae said. "I'm sure the high command can find someone else for you to play your mind games with if they really want to continue this insanity."

"But Lathe's the best."

Haberdae's face settled into a mask. "He made me look bad, Galway," he ground out. "In front of my men, and in front of the Ryqril. No one does that and gets away with it. No one."

"Prefect—"

"And don't even think about going near that control," Haberdae added. "I have direct orders from the ranking Ryq warrior on the scene. I can flatten you if you try to go against me."

Stepping to the monitor board, he snagged a spare chair and pulled it to a spot behind the row of techs. "Relax, Galway—your blackcollars are coming." He smiled tightly. "Let's enjoy the show."

CHAPTER 19

The passage through the tunnel had been tricky enough when Foxleigh's hands had been available to help protect him from the multitude of protrusions that reached out toward head and feet and hips. This time, with his hands tied together, was far worse. He'd made it only halfway through, and had already given up trying to count the bruises he'd collected, when he heard the sounds of footsteps ahead.

He froze, holding his breath as he listened. It was footsteps, all right. At least a half-dozen sets of them, possibly more.

His first, hopeful thought was that Flynn had returned with the rest of the blackcollars. Surely between Flynn and Skyler he would find someone who would be willing to help plead his case to Jensen.

But the whisper of hope was barely formed before it evaporated in the cold light of reality. He'd traveled this tunnel with Jensen, and he knew how the other moved. There was no way a group of blackcollars would make the kind of noise he was hearing.

And if it wasn't the blackcollars, there was only one other possibility.

He collected another set of bruises as he retraced his steps back toward the base. But this time he hardly noticed, his full attention focused on making the trip with as much speed and stealth as he could manage.

Finally, after a short eternity, he arrived and set off across the storage room as fast as his leg would let him. Hopefully, Jensen had gone back to the Talus. If he hadn't, if he was somewhere else in the base, Foxleigh could search for hours without finding him.

And neither he nor Jensen had nearly that much time to work with. Clenching his teeth, pushing his leg as hard as he could, he reached the corridor and turned toward the elevator.

And gasped as something whipped across his vision to settle firmly against his throat. "It's me—it's me," he gasped.

"Yes, I see it's you," Jensen growled into his ear, the pressure of the *nunchaku* sticks against his throat not letting up even a little. "You have got to be the *noisiest* infiltrator—"

"They're coming," Foxleigh cut him off. "Footsteps in the tunnel. Lots of them."

The *nunchaku* sticks stayed against his throat, but the pressure eased slightly. "It's probably Flynn and Skyler," Jensen said.

"No." Foxleigh tried to shake his head, discovered he couldn't. "They're way too loud to be blackcollars."

Jensen hissed, an coldly ominous sound. "So Security's found the back door. Too bad."

"It sounded like a lot of them," Foxleigh said. "Let me help you."

"Thanks, but I can handle it myself."

"Your ribs are going to limit what you can do," Foxleigh persisted. "Besides, I learned enough tactics to know that a situation like this requires a double-flank trap. I can be the other flank."

"No."

"I have to help you," Foxleigh begged. "Please."

For a long moment Jensen remained silent. "You lied to me earlier," he said at last. "Tell me what you lied about."

Foxleigh closed his eyes, tears of ancient shame welling up behind his eyelids. So here it was at last. "I told you I was shot down in the final battle," he said, the words feeling like hot embers in his mouth. "I wasn't. I was driving back to the base when the Ryqril attacked."

"You were AWOL?"

"Not on purpose," Foxleigh said, wincing at the pleading defensiveness in his voice. "There was a girl I knew in Central City, and—I didn't expect the Ryqril to attack so soon. I swear."

Jensen sighed. "Yeah, that happened a lot in that war," he conceded. "What happened then?"

"What happened is that I never made it," Foxleigh said bitterly. "I saw them coming in and pushed my speed and took a curve too fast. I tried to keep going on foot, but I'd wrecked my leg the same time I wrecked the car. After that . . . well, the rest of it goes pretty much the way I told you."

"Except for why you stayed in Shelter Valley," Jensen

said. "You didn't just get used to it, did you? You were hoping for another crack at the Ryqril."

Foxleigh snorted. "Fine—so it's been an obsession. Haven't you ever obsessed over something?"

"No," Jensen said flatly. He hesitated. "Nothing that interfered with my duty, anyway."

"Your *duty*?" Foxleigh countered. "This is *my* duty, Commando. This is—" He broke off, blinking back another pair of tears. "That Talus we prepped, the one named *Gotterdammerung*?" he said quietly. "That's my fighter, Jensen. The one I should have been flying in that battle. The one I should have died in."

For a minute Jensen didn't reply. Foxleigh waited, his mind wrapped in a strange sense of peace, as if thirty years of accumulated dread and anticipation and forlorn hope had been flushed away in the catharsis of his long overdue confession. Whatever happened now, it would simply happen.

And then, as the internal pressure of his emotional turmoil faded, so did the external pressure against his throat. "We'll take them in the storage room," Jensen said, stepping out from behind him. A knife flashed, and with a quick slash Foxleigh's hands were free. "I trust you remember how to use this?" he added as he handed Foxleigh the pistol he'd taken from him.

"Oh, yes," Foxleigh said softly as the familiar weight of his issue sidearm settled into his hand. At least once a day for the first five years of his self-imposed exile, he'd cleaned the gun, loaded it, and held the muzzle to his own head as he decided whether or not to pass judgment upon himself for his failures.

Now, after thirty years, he would finally have the chance to give his life for something more useful and fitting than simple punishment. "I remember very well."

There were more Ryqril waiting at the west door than Judas had expected. But their numbers actually ended up working against them, denying them the maneuverability that might otherwise have made the battle more even.

As it was, the fight was over very quickly. Taking on their enemies' lasers and short swords with nothing but hands, feet, *shuriken*, and *nunchaku*, Lathe and the others waded systematically through the crowd until every one of the Ryqril were incapacitated, unconscious, or dead.

"Everyone all right?" Lathe asked as he crouched over one of the bodies. "Caine?"

"I'm fine," Judas assured him, looking around the room with the sense of unreality he always seemed to experience when watching blackcollars in action.

"Nothing here," Spadafora said. He was crouched over another of the bodies, his hands darting deftly through the various pockets and pouches in his baldric and pants.

"Or here," Lathe agreed, standing back up. "That could be good *or* bad."

"What are you looking for?" Judas asked.

"Immunity transponder," Spadafora explained, crossing to where Mordecai was peering out the half-open door leading into the inner corridor. "Something to shut down those autotarget lasers Shaw warned they probably have installed around the core." He nodded toward the bodies. "Only none of our friends here seems to be carrying one."

"Which either means they've shut down the interior defenses, or that this particular crowd was considered expendable," Lathe said.

"Or else that none of these particular warriors were authorized to leave this area," Judas pointed out, some of the tension between his shoulders easing. This one, at least, he knew the answer to—Galway had told him they would be leaving the lasers off.

"Maybe," Lathe said, picking up two of the short swords that lay scattered across the floor and sliding them into his belt at the small of his back where they'd be out of the way. "Let's find out. Mordecai, take point."

Mordecai nodded and opened the door the rest of the way.

And dropped into a crouch as a laser bolt sizzled past where his head had just been. Judas caught a glimpse of a Ryq crouched in partial concealment around the corner of the next cross corridor, dropping the muzzle of his laser as he tried to line up his second shot.

The shot never came. Mordecai's *shuriken* flashed across the distance and the Ryq toppled over, the throwing star buried in his forehead. Another alien started to lean out, ducked quickly back as Spadafora sent a primer cap past the corner to explode against the cross corridor's far wall.

And as he fired off a second cap to the other side of the intersection, Mordecai and Lathe were on the move, running silently toward the concealed defenders. They reached the intersection simultaneously, one turning to each side of the cross corridor and charging in among the hidden aliens. There was a single surprised squawk from someone; and then Lathe flashed a hand signal, and Judas and Spadafora ran up to join them.

By the time they arrived it was over. Five armed Ryqril lay scattered on the floor on Lathe's side, while six bodies decorated Mordecai's. The rest of the cross corridor, on both sides, was deserted. "One down, four to go," Lathe said, peering at the four cross corridors cutting across their path ahead. "Spadafora, watch the backtrail; Caine, stay close to him."

Shifting his *nunchaku* to his left hand and pulling out a fresh pair of *shuriken* with his right, he started forward.

There were nine of them in all: six heavily armed Security types followed by three lightly armed men carrying tech-type equipment boxes. All were young, all were clearly nervous, and as they filed one by one through the scorched entrance they formed themselves into a parade-ground-perfect semicircle perimeter until the three techs had negotiated the last part of the passage and joined them.

The whole spectacle was so training-school fresh that it made Foxleigh wince. Clearly, these were brand-new recruits to the Ryqril cause, chosen for their courage and stamina.

And, no doubt, their expendability.

He grimaced, fingering his pistol as the group reformed itself into a standard boxed-centipede formation and started moving toward the door. He couldn't afford to think of them as people, he reminded himself firmly. They were the enemy, their presence an obstacle to his own redemption.

Lifting his gun, bracing his wrist on the edge of the box he was hiding behind, he lined up the muzzle on the lead Security man and squeezed the trigger.

His aim was every bit as good as he'd promised Jensen it would be. The leader toppled over, and the rest of the group behind him erupted in instant chaos. For a few precious seconds they looked around in panicked bewilderment, the echoes from walls and ceiling apparently having confused the direction the shot had come from. Foxleigh lined up his gun on the next man in line; and as he did so one of the armed men in back twitched violently and similarly collapsed to the floor. Foxleigh fired his second shot, and one more of the enemy was eliminated.

But this time one of the others had apparently spotted his muzzle flash. There was a hoarse shout over the echoes, a pointed finger—

And suddenly Foxleigh's hiding place was the center of a hailstorm of return fire.

He ducked back as a horizontal hail of paral-darts thudded into his box or burned past to clatter against the far wall. He stuck his hand around the side, exposing as little flesh as possible, and blindly fired two quick shots before yanking his hand back. As he did so, the soft *chuff-chuff* of paral-dart fire was joined by the sharper cracks as some of the Security men switched over to flechette guns. Foxleigh could hear tearing sounds as the tough plastic of his refuge began to disintegrate under the assault. He started to stick his hand out for another shot, jerked it back as a stray flechette sliced a thin line of pain across his wrist. The barrage seemed to waver. . . .

And then, abruptly, all was silence.

Foxleigh waited another handful of seconds, then eased a cautious eye around the corner of his box.

They were all down. All of them. Two of the three techs were still twitching, clearly still alive. None of the others was moving at all. Gathering himself back to his feet, Foxleigh limped over for a closer look.

He and Jensen reached them at the same time, the blackcollar pressing a hand to his thincast above his injured ribs. "Thanks for your help," he said, his voice strained a little.

"You're welcome." Foxleigh looked around at the bodies, feeling more than a little sick. "I wish to God we hadn't had to do that."

Jensen sighed. "So do I," he said. "This war was never supposed to be against our own people. Damn the Ryqril to hell for doing this to them."

"And to us." Foxleigh took a deep breath. "Speaking of hell, it's time for us to deliver some." He looked up from the bodies and locked eyes with Jensen. "I presume we're not going to have any more nonsense about who's going to fly my plane?"

"No," Jensen said quietly. "Under the circumstances, I think you deserve a final crack."

"Thank you." Foxleigh hesitated, then turned his gun around and offered it to Jensen. "Here—I won't be needing this anymore. Tie up the survivors and meet me back at the Talus."

He started to turn away, but Jensen caught his arm. "I was willing to fly the fighter into that hell, you know," the blackcollar said quietly.

"I know," Foxleigh assured him. "And I'm sure the

ghosts of your past appreciate the thought. But this is my world, and my duty."

"And you have your own ghosts to deal with?"

"Actually, I've been able to mostly put them to rest over the years," Foxleigh said, eyeing him. The man still wasn't completely convinced, he sensed. "You mentioned someone named Novak just before I pulled my gun on you. A friend of yours?"

"The best," Jensen said, a flicker of old pain crossing his face. "Two years ago, on Argent, he died in my place."

"I'm sorry," Foxleigh said. "But look at it this way. If I'd been in *Gotterdammerung* that day like I should have been, I'd probably have died very quickly, certainly without making any real difference. Was Novak a pilot?"

Jensen shook his head. "He couldn't have found the throttle with a map."

"So if he'd been here instead of you, he probably wouldn't have had any reason to want to get into Aegis," Foxleigh said. "And without someone to help me, *I* wouldn't have been able to get in. I trust you see where I'm going with this."

Jensen rolled his eyes. "By surviving the way we did, we're now going to get a better shot at hurting the Ryqril than we would have had otherwise?"

"Basically," Foxleigh said. "Don't you love it when the universe gives you object lessons?"

"Not really," Jensen said candidly. "But I guess it's better than no lessons at all."

"Agreed," Foxleigh said. "So tie them up and let's get to it. We've got a final checklist to run. And odds are I'm going to need your help getting into the cockpit."

* * *

The last cross corridor had been cleared, with another half-dozen Ryqril bodies to add to the afternoon's toll, and Spadafora had spotted and driven back two attempted sorties from behind.

It had been a good assault, Lathe knew, as such things went. All four of them had collected a number of laser burns across their flexarmor, but so far none of the enemy had been lucky enough to get that crucial second shot that would burn all the way through to the fragile skin and bone and blood underneath.

Eventually, they would, he knew. Certainly for many of the blackcollars embroiled in the battle outside their skill and luck had already run out. The tingler messages flashing back and forth between Shaw's men was a bitter reminder of what it was costing to keep the bulk of Taakh's troops pinned down and out of the inside team's way.

It was up to Lathe to make sure those men hadn't given their lives for nothing.

"Is that it?" Spadafora asked, coming up behind him and pointing to the door directly ahead.

"Should be," Lathe agreed, reaching behind him and sliding one of the appropriated Ryqril short swords from his belt. "Let's see what's happening with those lasers." Holding the sword like a spear, he threw it toward the door.

And flinched back as the acrid green flash of a laser slashed out, slicing across the flying blade and sending a spray of liquid metal droplets in all directions. By the time the sword completed its arc, barely half of the hilt was left to bounce off the door.

"That answers *that* question," Spadafora said conversationally.

Lathe nodded grimly. "I guess it does."

From the other side of the monitor room door came a soft thunk. "What was that?" Haberdae demanded, half turning in his seat to look at the door.

"Something hit the door," Galway told him. "Something thrown, probably, that your defense lasers weren't able to completely disintegrate."

"Maybe it was a spare arm bone," Haberdae said with a sniff.

"I doubt it," Galway said. He drew a deep breath. "They didn't follow you to the strongpoint, you know."

Haberdae frowned. "What?"

"They didn't follow you to the strongpoint the night of the casino attack," Galway repeated. "They already knew that was where Caine was being held."

Haberdae's face was a surging sea of bewilderment. "What the bloody hell are you talking about?" he demanded.

Lifting Taakh's laser, Galway shot him in the leg.

The bewilderment vanished into utter disbelief as Haberdae bellowed in pain. Ignoring him, Galway shifted his aim to the row of Ryqril techs, shooting his way systematically down the line of suddenly panicked aliens until all of them were dead. Then, stepping to the control board, he lifted the orange cover and turned off the defense lasers.

He'd just closed the cover again when a much louder thud came from the door. "Galway!" Haberdae hissed between clenched teeth, his hands gripping his injured thigh. "What the hell are you *doing*?"

"Don't you really mean how the hell am I doing it?" Galway countered.

Haberdae's eyes widened as the deeper question finally sank in—

And then the door slid open, and Lathe and the others strode into the room. "You made it," Galway greeted them soberly, gesturing toward Haberdae. "I've got mine."

"And we've got ours," Lathe said. Turning to a clearly stunned Judas, he took the spy's wrist and twisted it suddenly behind him.

"Lathe!" Judas yelped. "What are you—?"

"Clear me a chair," Lathe told Galway as he deftly snapped off Judas's belt, letting it and its attached weapons clatter to the floor.

Galway stepped over to the closest chair and pulled the dead Ryq out of it, swiveling it around to face the black-collars as Lathe walked a still protesting Judas over and sat him down. Spadafora produced a pair of quick-ties, and a moment later the boy's wrists were fastened securely to the armrests. "There we go," Lathe said as he began removing Judas's other weapons from the various pouches on his flexarmor. "Sorry about this—what's his name, Galway?"

"Karl Judas," Galway said, watching the blood drain from Judas's face.

"*Judas*?" Lathe echoed, looking at Judas with fresh interest. "You're joking."

"Not at all," Galway assured him. "Caine's Resistance friends have a very warped sense of humor."

"I think it's more irony than humor, actually," Spadafora put in as he similarly secured Haberdae's wrists.

"Whatever," Galway said. "For what it's worth, he didn't really want to do this. His whole town's essentially being held hostage for his good behavior."

"We'll have to bring that up with the command half-circle when we talk to them," Lathe said, stowing Judas's weapons in his own pouches. "They in the central core?"

"Either there or in the lounge just off the core," Galway said. "Watch yourselves—they probably have a full guard in there with them."

"Understood," Lathe said, collecting Judas's weapons belt from the floor and tossing it to Spadafora. "You want one of us to stay here with you?"

Galway shook his head. "I can handle them."

"We'll be back soon," Lathe said, motioning the others to the door. Mordecai opened it and glanced out, and the three blackcollars disappeared outside.

"This is insane," Haberdae said mechanically, his eyes locked in disbelief on Galway. "Insane."

"Perhaps," Galway said, looking over at Judas. Some of the color had come back into the younger man's face, but he had much the same look as Haberdae. "It's called Whiplash, Judas," he said. "I don't know where it came from, but its sole function in life is to release people from Ryqril loyalty-conditioning."

Haberdae sucked in his breath. "That's impossible," he said.

"Impossible and insane both," Galway agreed. "But it works." He took a deep breath, let it go in a tired sigh. "It works."

Judas's tongue swiped at his lips. "How long?" he asked.

"Since I was turned?" Galway shook his head.

"Actually, only since last night. Lathe ambushed me on the road, knocked out my guard and driver . . ." He hefted the laser. "And gave me a whole new purpose in life."

"A purpose of—" Judas broke off, an odd look flashing briefly across his face. "A purpose of treason," he continued, a subtle new tone in his voice. "How can you do this to your people?"

"What my people need is freedom," Galway said, frowning. Something was wrong here. But what? He looked down at Judas's wrists, still fastened to the armrests, confirmed that Haberdae was also still restrained.

So where was Judas's sudden new courage coming from?

"And you think this will get it for them?" Judas demanded. "Well, you're wrong. All it'll do is get you killed and bring reprisals down on the whole TDE."

"Lathe has a plan," Galway said firmly, trying to conceal his own misgivings. He wasn't at all sure that this was going to work, that the Ryqril wouldn't react in exactly the way Judas was suggesting. But the plan was already in motion, and he could either help or watch it go down in flames.

If Lathe was wrong, God help them all.

Across the room, the door slid open. "That was fast," Galway commented, turning toward it.

But it wasn't Lathe.

It was Taakh.

For a suspended fraction of a second, man and Ryq stared at each other in mutual disbelief. Then, Galway broke free of his paralysis and swung his laser around, trying desperately to get in the first shot.

But if *khassq* warriors weren't as fast as blackcollars, they were far faster than ordinary humans. Even as Galway tried to bring his weapon to bear Taakh snatched out his short sword, flipped it into a throwing grip, and hurled it across the room. The sword slammed crossways into the laser's trigger guard, slicing two of Galway's fingers and knocking the weapon out of his grip. It caromed off the monitor board and skittered away into the far corner of the room.

"I could ha' killed yae," Taakh said, his voice quietly dark, his eyes flicking once to the dead techs.

Galway clenched his hand over the blood welling from his fingers. "Why didn't you?" he heard himself ask.

"'Ecause I rould rather kill yae rith ny own hands," the Ryq said. Stepping away from the door, he started toward Galway. "'Re'are yaersel' 'or death."

The sky was beginning to darken over the mountains when, in the distance, Skyler heard a faint explosion.

He looked at the two Ryqril, standing over by the air vent with Poirot, Bailey, and the lieutenant. Both aliens had turned toward the southeast, their postures unnaturally stiff as they listened intently. There was a second explosion, and a third—

Abruptly Halaak snatched a small comm from his belt and snarled into it. Even as a fourth explosion echoed through the mountains the Corsair hovering overhead stirred and lifted into the sky, picking up speed as it headed toward the sound. Putting away the comm, Halaak turned and strode across the clearing toward the prisoners, his hand clenching the grip of his holstered laser. "This may be it," Skyler warned the others quietly.

Out of the corner of his eye, he saw Hawking and O'Hara exchange glances. "We're ready," Hawking said.

Halaak came to a halt three meters from Skyler, his dark eyes glaring down at the blackcollar. "Who is in the nountain?" he demanded.

Skyler gazed up at him, a sudden whisper of hope floating through him. He'd been improvising on the mission plan ever since they'd arrived on Earth without ever really getting back onto Lathe's original track. Now, with Halaak demanding answers and Battle Architect Daasaa listening from across the clearing, maybe there was one last chance to do so. "There's no one else," he said mildly. "We're all here. You counted us yourself."

"A traitor 'ron Khoenix, then," Halaak persisted. "Who?"

Skyler shook his head. "There's no one in Aegis," he said. "No one but the nine men you just sent in."

"That's impossible," Poirot insisted, taking a step toward them. "They were fresh recruits who'd been in Athena since their loyalty-conditioning. You couldn't possibly have gotten to them with your damned Whiplash."

"No, we couldn't," Skyler agreed. "But then, *we* didn't have to."

Deliberately, Halaak drew his laser. "Traitor," he said, very softly. He lifted the weapon—

And turning, he pointed the weapon at Poirot and fired.

There was a brilliant green flash, and without even a gasp Poirot fell to the ground. "Traitor!" Halaak shouted again at the limp body. Shifting aim, he fired again, this time at the Security lieutenant standing beside Daasaa. "Traitor!" he said. He swung the weapon toward Colonel Bailey—

And in that instant, with the *khassq*'s back to them and his weapon pointed the wrong way, the blackcollars moved.

Shoving off the ground and the tree trunk behind him, Skyler leaped to his feet. Flynn was right with him, bringing his shackled arms around as Skyler tossed his dragonhead ring into the boy's hand.

Halaak spun back around at the commotion, his weapon swinging around with him. But he was too late. Dropping into a half crouch, Flynn twisted his torso and legs into the spinning kick that Skyler had seen him and Mordecai practicing for so many long hours back at the Hamner Lodge training center.

And as his leg and arms windmilled around toward the front, Flynn sent the ring spinning straight at Halaak.

The *khassq*, stepping casually back from a spinning kick he saw would be short, was caught completely off guard. Before he could do more than jerk in surprise, the ring's bat-wing crest buried itself in his throat.

The impact staggered him back, his reflexive shot going wild. He bellowed, a strange gurgling sound, as he tried to bring his laser back onto target.

But even as he lined up the weapon, O'Hara half leaped up into Hawking's cupped hands and was hurled into the tree branches above them, his weight pulling one of the branches straight down to slash down across Halaak's face.

The *khassq* bellowed again, swinging a hand up to push the branch aside, trying desperately to dodge out of its way to where he would be able to see again.

But once again, and for the last time in his life, he was a fraction of a second too late. Charging toward him at full speed, Skyler threw himself sideways at the Ryq's legs, catching him just below the knees and throwing his head and torso violently forward.

Just in time for Flynn's sideways door-clearer leap to catch him squarely in the face. There was a muffled snap of breaking spinal bone, and Halaak slammed onto the ground and lay still.

"Hold it!" Hawking snapped. "You hear me, Ryq? Stand down."

Skyler rolled out from beneath Halaak's legs and up into a crouch. Hawking had retrieved the *khassq's* laser, his manacled hands holding it pointed toward Daasaa and Bailey. O'Hara was kneeling in front of him, his shoulder providing a rest for the laser barrel, making it dead certain that the other wouldn't miss his shot.

And Daasaa clearly knew it. His own laser was half drawn, but still pointed at the ground, and he was making no attempt to draw it out any farther. "Rhy?" he shouted back.

"Because we don't particularly want to kill you," Skyler said. "On the contrary, we have a message we want you to deliver to the high command."

Daasaa looked at Bailey, then back at Hawking. Then, slowly, he lowered the laser the rest of the way into its holster and let his hand fall to his side. "I rill listen."

Skyler looked over at Hawking and O'Hara, caught the latter's eye and nodded toward Halaak. O'Hara nodded back in understanding. The *khassq* was almost certainly dead, but O'Hara would make sure. "You okay?" Skyler asked, turning to Flynn.

The boy nodded, his eyes on Halaak. "It worked," he

murmured. "It actually *worked*." He looked up at Skyler, the ghost of an uncertain smile touching his lips.

"It sure did," Skyler agreed.

And now this was it. His improvised tactics had gotten him here; but it was Lathe's message that would or would not carry the day. Taking a deep breath, he gestured Flynn toward Daasaa. "Come on," he said. "Let's go end a war."

"You don't want to kill me," Galway said as Taakh took another step forward, a small part of his mind noting the insane irony of the words. Of course Taakh wanted to kill him.

And he would, too. Without a weapon, Galway had no chance in the universe of surviving a confrontation with a *khassq*-class warrior.

And then, from nowhere, came a small, desperate flicker of an idea. "Because if you do," he added, "you'll never know what happened here."

"Yae are a traitor," Taakh said. "There is nothing else tae know."

"Don't you at least want to know Lathe's plan?" Galway persisted.

Almost reluctantly, Taakh slowed to a halt. "What ha' yae tae say?"

"Be careful, Your Eminence," Judas put in urgently. "He's stalling for time. The other blackcollars are here somewhere."

"I dae not 'ear the 'lackcollars," Taakh said contemptuously. "'Ery rell, traitor. S'eak."

Galway took a deep breath. He'd bought himself some time. Now all he had to do was figure out what to do with it. "We never fooled him," he told Taakh. "Not for a minute. He was on to our replacement of Caine from the very beginning."

"I knew it," Haberdae growled, glaring at Judas. "I *knew* he'd foul up somewhere."

"It wasn't anything Judas did," Galway told him. "Lathe's been expecting someone to try this trick ever since he found out that Caine was himself a clone. He followed the same logic we did—that the Resistance would have created more than just one—and knew we'd eventually track down one of the others and try a substitution."

"So he had some kind of private recognition signal set up," Judas murmured, wincing.

"Exactly," Galway said. "I don't know what it was. Not that it really matters."

"So Lathe knew o' the su'stitaetion," Taakh said.

"Yes," Galway said. "But he also knew we'd have to wait until the team reached Khala to make the switch. That's why he went to so much trouble to decoy us with those fake drop pods and sneak in another way. He needed a few minutes while they weren't under surveillance to call Shaw and arrange for someone to tail Caine once they made the switch."

"That tavern they first stopped at," Haberdae growled.

"Right," Galway said, nodding. "Shaw's people got there first and set up surveillance. When we took off with Caine, they just followed us up to the strongpoint." He looked at Judas. "And from that point on, everything that was said and done in your presence was designed to throw you—and us—off their real plan."

"All the backbiting between Lathe and Shaw," Judas

murmured, his face looking suddenly old. "The changed plans, the fake hints—all of it."

"All of it," Galway said mechanically, his thoughts freezing. Judas—the blackcollars—

"Rhat then ras their 'lan?" Taakh demanded.

"Their plan was me," Galway said, turning back to the Ryq. "Everything they did from the moment they landed was aimed toward one of two goals: to get them into Khorstron, and to get me alone for a few minutes."

"Rich they did last night."

"Exactly," Galway said, taking a casual step toward Judas. "Caine was running on his own timetable, with orders to make some kind of escape attempt after a couple of days that would hopefully lure me out of Inkosi City and up into the mountains to check on him. They already had Spadafora in position to fry the entryway sensors so that they could get in and gimmick my car while I was inside."

"Yet yae are loyalty-conditioned," Taakh said.

"I was," Galway corrected. "I just learned last night that they have a drug called Whiplash that breaks loyalty-conditioning."

"That is not 'ossi'le," Taakh said flatly.

Galway spread his hands to the sides. "I'm proof that it works," he pointed out, taking another step to his side. One more step, and he would be beside Judas's chair.

"But why?" Judas asked, clearly still not understanding. "They were already running rings around us. What did they need you for?"

"Many things," Galway told him. "Because they *weren't* running rings around us, not really. Not until this afternoon.

If you think back, Your Eminence, I was the one who suggested that the bunker fire was probably a diversion. I also pointed out that one of the dummies had been tossed on top of the south tunnel and suggested Shaw's men might be trying for a breach there." He looked at Haberdae. "And of course, I'm the one who turned off the corridor lasers after Haberdae turned them on."

"Fine," Haberdae said. "So they get into Khorstron. So what? There's nothing useful in here for them to steal."

"It was never about stealing anything," Galway said, taking the step that put him at Judas's side. "Khorstron was just a means to an end. The real point of the plan is much more subtle." He turned back to face Taakh, letting his hand drop casually to Judas's left wrist.

And as he did so, his fingertips pressed against the tingler beneath the other's flexarmor sleeve.

He didn't know blackcollar tingler code. But he didn't have to. Hopefully, a long, sustained signal would be properly interpreted as a cry for help. "You see, Your Eminence, what this little exercise has demonstrated is that your universe has abruptly changed," he told Taakh. "If we can penetrate right to the center of a Ryqril base—"

"Your Eminence!" Judas barked, his eyes suddenly wide. "He's signaling with my tingler!"

"Stand aray," Taakh snarled, taking a long step forward, his hand lifted to strike.

Galway dived to his left, trying to get out of the other's reach. But the *khassq* was too big and too fast. His hand slapped across the side of Galway's head hard enough to spin him halfway around.

The prefect tumbled to the floor, a stab of pain knifing

through his head and neck as he scrabbled back up into a sitting position. Shoving against the floor with his feet, his bloody hands raised in front of his face, he slithered backward, trying to get away from the killing blow that would certainly be coming next.

But the blow didn't come. His back bumped up against the wall, and still the blow didn't come. Carefully, hesitantly, he lowered his hands.

Taakh wasn't looking at him. He was turned to face the door, his hands curled into claws at his sides.

And standing facing him just inside the doorway was Mordecai.

For a moment they just stood there, gazing silently across the gap between them, each warrior apparently sizing up the other. Then, abruptly, Taakh leaped sideways, grabbed Judas's chair, and heaved it and Judas straight at Mordecai.

The blackcollar was far too quick to be caught that easily. He sidestepped effortlessly, leaving Judas to continue on to crash with a yelp onto the floor beside the door.

But Taakh hadn't really cared whether Mordecai was caught by the chair or not. Even as the blackcollar dodged, the *khassq* dived across the room behind the rest of the chairs, his outstretched hands reaching for the laser he'd knocked earlier from Galway's grip.

But if Mordecai was too fast to be caught by a thrown chair, he was also too smart to be taken in by such an obvious diversion. Taakh was still two meters from the laser when a *shuriken* flashed across the room to bury itself into the weapon's side. There was a flicker of light and a brief cloud of sparks, and the weapon was dead.

Taakh scooped it up anyway, squeezed the trigger once to make sure, then spun and hurled it at Mordecai's head. Again Mordecai managed to evade the missile, but this time it cost him the accuracy of his next *shuriken*. The throwing star flashed past Taakh's head without connecting as the Ryq dodged out of the way and again threw himself across the room, this time aiming for his short sword. Another *shuriken* caught him in the upper arm as he hit the floor and rolled back to his feet with the sword ready in his hand. Spinning around to face Mordecai, he pulled the *shuriken* from his arm and charged.

The blackcollar leaped to the side, whipping out his *nunchaku* and spinning it in a blinding arc toward Taakh's head. The Ryq swung his sword up to meet the flail, and the weapons met with an earsplitting crash and a brief shower of hardwood splinters. Taakh let the impact bounce the sword back, riding its altered momentum around in a tight circle and stabbing up toward Mordecai's side. The blackcollar danced back out of its way, and as the tip burned bare millimeters past his ribs he snapped his left arm down and around, catching the back of Taakh's sword hand with his own forearm and adding a little extra momentum to his thrust. Taakh seemed to stumble as his center of balance was thrown off; twisting around, Mordecai threw a spinning kick at the Ryq's torso as he simultaneously swung the *nunchaku* at his head.

The flail missed, but the kick connected. With a grunt, Taakh swung his sword again, a pair of quick, downward blows toward Mordecai's shoulders and head. The blackcollar dodged both attacks and leaped back out of range, his back bouncing against the wall as he suddenly ran out of maneuvering room. With a roar, Taakh leaped forward, this time swinging his sword horizontally at Mordecai's torso. Ducking under the blow, Mordecai braced one hand against the wall and snapped a side kick into the alien's abdomen.

It was a solid, powerful blow, the sheer impact of it sending Taakh staggering back. Shoving off the wall, Mordecai followed it up with another *nunchaku* attack, but the Ryq managed to get his sword back up in time to block the swinging flail. But the impact threw him a little farther off balance, allowing Mordecai to duck past him away from the wall and back into the center of the room. Taakh spun to face him, and for another moment the two opponents seemed to pause, sword and *nunchaku* poised and ready.

For Galway, his head and neck and fingers throbbing as he gazed at the tableau, it was a moment of unrelieved blackness. Taakh, *khassq*-class warrior of the Ryq, stood strong and tall and muscular, hardly affected by the blows his opponent had managed to land. Mordecai, human blackcollar, was unmarked, but in the confined space of the monitor room he could hardly avoid his enemy forever.

And with the Ryq standing nearly twice his height and pulling perhaps three times his weight, it wouldn't take more than a single solid punch or sword slash to bring the fight to an end.

Galway looked desperately around the room, searching for something—anything—he could use as a weapon. Something he could use to tip the odds even a little in Mordecai's direction.

He was still looking when Taakh, his moment of combat meditation apparently over, leaped again to the attack.

Once again, he slashed his sword down toward Mordecai's head. This time, though, Mordecai didn't simply dodge away, but instead lifted his *nunchaku* upright, one stick gripped in each hand with the connecting plastic chain stretched horizontally above him, ready to receive the blow. The blade slammed into the chain, its momentum pressing it downward toward Mordecai's head. Turning his body out from under the descending weapon, Mordecai swiveled one of the *nunchaku* sticks around, letting the sword's momentum carry the weapon down past his shoulder. Before Taakh could recover his balance, the blackcollar swung his left arm around the sword point, looping the *nunchaku* around the weapon. The chain wrapped solidly around the base of the blade, trapping it in place.

Taakh's roar of anger changed to a grunt of pain as Mordecai slammed his right elbow across the other's forearm, clearly trying to shake the sword loose from his grip. He slammed the Ryq's arm again; and then Taakh took a long step backward, gripped the sword with both hands, and pulled up and back.

Mordecai tried to hold on, but the Ryq's size and weight were far more than he could handle. Even as he was lifted bodily off the floor he let go with his left hand and allowed the *nunchaku* to swing around and away from the blade as Taakh continued to yank the sword upward. Both of them raced to get their weapons back under firm control; Mordecai won by a fraction of a second, swinging a stinging *nunchaku* blow across Taakh's face before being forced to leap away from the sword's whistling slash.

Lifting the weapon again, the Ryq leaped forward,

pressing his attack as he tried once again to push Mordecai to the wall. But he was finally starting to show some fatigue, and his swinging weapon was moving marginally but noticeably slower. Mordecai dodged with relative ease, and again managed to slip out of the potential trap and back to the center of the room.

But Mordecai was slowing down, too, missing two of his blocks as he fended off the flashing sword, only reflex and luck keeping the blows from taking him out of the fight permanently. He was in trouble; and as Galway watched helplessly, he realized suddenly that Mordecai was trying to work his way back to the door and escape.

Taakh saw it, too. With every step toward the door that Mordecai tried to take, the Ryq countered with one that forced him back toward the center of the room.

And then, as Taakh continued to press him back, Mordecai's foot caught the edge of the laser Taakh had thrown at him earlier, and he jerked slightly as he tried to regain his balance.

It was all the opening Taakh needed. Leaping forward, he slashed his sword downward again toward Mordecai's head. With his feet still tangled beneath him, Mordecai had no option but to once again swing his *nunchaku* up in a two-handed grip and catch the descending blade on the chain. Twisting to the side, barely making it in time, he again whipped the left-hand stick around the sword, twisting the chain around the hilt.

Only this time, Taakh was ready. Instead of simply pulling back and trying to free his sword, he reached over with his free hand and wrapped his hand around Mordecai's in an unbreakable grip.

And with that, Galway knew, it was all over. In his mind's eye he could see the inevitable outcome: Mordecai hauled off his feet, dangling helplessly in midair from his own *nunchaku* while the Ryq kicked him into a bloody, broken puppet. With a triumphant bellow, Taakh planted his feet and heaved himself backward, his massive shoulder and arm and back muscles bulging as he pulled the puny human off the floor.

Only to Galway's astonishment, Mordecai didn't resist the maneuver. Instead, he moved with it, leaping upward as he pulled down on his *nunchaku* for extra power, his efforts combining with Taakh's to send him flying toward the ceiling. Tucking his knees to his chest, rotating around the pivot point like an athlete around a high bar, he swung completely over the startled *khassq*'s shoulder, straightening out his legs again as his body slammed hard against Taakh's back. Arching his own back, he pulled with all his strength on the *nunchaku* still wrapped around the base of the sword blade.

And with Ryqril muscles still pulling the sword up, and human ones pulling it down and back, the sword tip was driven solidly into Taakh's forehead.

Some trick of balance and locked muscles held the Ryq upright for another half second. Then, without a sound, his legs collapsed beneath him, and he toppled over onto the floor.

Slowly, Galway tore his eyes away from the dead *khassq* and looked at Mordecai. "You killed him," he heard himself say.

"Yeah," Mordecai said, breathing hard. "It seemed the thing to do."

"What happens now?" Judas asked, his voice shaking.

Galway looked down again at Taakh. "Nothing," he said. "It's all over."

"The bottom line," Skyler said, "is that it's all over."

Daasaa's eyes flicked to Bailey, standing under Flynn's watchful eye, then back to Skyler. "I dae not understand."

"I think you do," Skyler said. "In fact, as a battle architect, you probably understand better than any Ryq on the planet." He nodded back at Halaak's body. "Certainly better than he would have."

Daasaa shook his head. "Yae cannot 'ight us," he insisted. "There are not enou' o' yae tae rin."

"But that's just the problem—you don't know how many of us there are," Skyler said. "Worse than that, you don't know *who* we are." He pointed at the crumpled bodies of Poirot and the lieutenant. "You see, you don't have just a single Judas in your governmental ranks, or even just two or three. You have a whole army of them. And there's no way to identify them. Not until it's too late."

"Then re rill sin'ly reno'e *all* o' they," Daasaa countered.

"You can't do that, either," Skyler countered right back. "There aren't nearly enough of you in the TDE to control us without the collaborationist bureaucracy you've set in place. Your only option would be to bring in a bunch of troops to take their place. Only you can't, because if you do you won't have enough forces to keep back the Chryselli."

"You see, friend, you've suddenly run into military doctrine's number one blunder," Hawking put in. "You've got yourselves a two-front war."

"Yae cannot 'ight us," Daasaa insisted again. "Re can destroy yaer cities rhene'er re rish."

"Can you?" Skyler asked pointedly. "Can you really? Aside from the defenses around your private enclaves and maybe a few hundred Corsairs, you have practically nothing in the TDE under your direct control. Most of the weaponry is handled by your tame Security forces . . . who aren't going to be tame much longer."

For a long minute Daasaa didn't reply. Skyler listened to the distant chirping of the evening insects, mentally crossing his fingers. If Daasaa didn't go for this, the TDE was going to be in for a long, bloody nightmare of attrition that could end up being worse than anything they'd seen during the actual war itself. "Re rill not gi' u' rithout 'attle," the Ryq said at last.

"But it's a battle you can't win," Skyler told him. "Oh, you can certainly kill a lot of humans, if that's what matters to you. But we have the numbers, and with Whiplash we'll have access to the weaponry, and the people, and the inner fortresses. Eventually, inevitably, you'll lose." He paused. "But there is an alternative."

Daasaa's dark eyes were steady on him. "I an listening."

"You leave," Skyler said flatly. "All of you—tonight, tomorrow, next week, but you all leave. You pull out your people and your troops—hell, take all the weapons you can stuff aboard your ships if you want to. But you pull out."

Daasaa barked a short, derisive laugh. "And this gains us rhat?"

"It gains you breathing space," Skyler said. "You see, if you pull out slowly, scorching the ground as you go, you'll give humanity time to organize and build back the political control systems we need to function as a cohesive society. But if you leave now—" he grimaced "—I guarantee months or years of chaos as your government flunkies try to hold onto power and the various Resistance groups try to seize it and everyone else just tries to figure out how the hell this freedom thing works. We've seen it happen time and time again when a nation or region is suddenly freed from tyranny. Trust me, it'll happen this time, too."

Daasaa snorted, his gaze drifting to the bodies of the two Security officers Halaak had killed. "Sone 'eo'les rere not neant to 'e 'ree," he said contemptuously.

"Sometimes I wonder about that myself," Skyler conceded. "And you're welcome to think that we're not fit to be anything but Ryqril slaves if that makes you feel better. Only believe me when I tell you it's the only way."

Daasaa shook his head. "The high connand rill not acce't this," he said. "Re need the 'actories and rea'ons 'roduction lines."

"They're gone, Battle Architect," Skyler said. "Your weapons plants will be the first things we go after. We'll infiltrate Whiplashed people and either take the plants over or blow them up."

"Thousands o' yaer 'eo'le rill die."

"So will dozens of yours," Skyler countered. "I've already said that you can hold on for a while if you really want to. But it'll cost you time and energy and people, none of which you can spare. And in the end you'll be forced out anyway."

He gestured up toward the sky. "Maybe you can win against the Chryselli while we're fumbling around trying to figure out who the mayor and governor and dogcatcher should be. Maybe you can't. But it's your only hope of avoiding a two-front war that you absolutely cannot win."

Daasaa snorted again, but this time it was a softer, more contemplative sound. "I rill take yaer 'ro'osal tae the high connand," he said. "They rill decide."

"Just tell them to decide quickly," Skyler warned.

"I rill take that nessage." Daasaa hesitated. "It rill take nearly a nonth tae recei'e a decision," he said. "Rill yae halt yaer attacks until then?"

Skyler thought it over. Considering how miniscule an army they actually had at the moment, it would be a ridiculously easy promise to make. "Agreed, provided you take no action against us in the meantime," he said. "*And* provided you release the two Phoenix members you still have in custody."

"They rill 'e 'rought tae the western Athena gate taenorror norning," Daasaa promised without hesitation. "Run o' they is injured and rill rekire an a'ulance."

"We'll have something ready." Skyler looked over at Flynn. "And tell the high command one other thing," he said. "There aren't too many of us left who lived through the war and remember what Ryqril are truly like. The younger generation doesn't, and their overall attitude toward you is probably pretty casual."

He lifted a warning finger. "But if you try destroying cities and slaughtering our people on your way out, they'll find out about you . . . and when we and the Chryselli finally have you broken on the ground—and we will— you'll find out how vengeful we humans can be. Trust me; you do *not* want to see that."

Daasaa held his gaze without flinching. "I ha' said I rill take yaer 'ro'osal tae the high connand," he said evenly. "I can 'ronise nothing else."

"Then go," Skyler said. "Call a spotter from Athena and go."

For a moment Daasaa didn't move. Then, pulling a comm from his belt, he keyed it on and spoke a few words in Ryqrili. He was answered, said something else, then turned off the device and put it away. "They rill cone," he said. He drew himself up to his full height, one last show of pride, and stared down into Skyler's eyes. "Re rill not neet again, hunan."

"No," Skyler agreed quietly. "We had better not."

Skyler had half expected a last-minute attempt at an ambush, either while Daasaa was still in their hands or just after he was taken away. But twenty minutes later, with the departing spotter a fading speck in the sky, there had still been no such move.

Perhaps the plumes of glowing smoke drifting across the darkening mass of Aegis Mountain had something to do with it. The Ryqril were rattled, straight down to the soles of their rubbery feet.

And Daasaa, battle architect, held the key to their only way out.

"When did you get to Ramirez?" Bailey asked.

Skyler turned from his contemplation of the distant smoke. "Excuse me?"

"I know when you treated General Poirot," Bailey said. "I want to know when you turned Lieutenant Ramirez."

Skyler shook his head. "We didn't."

Bailey's eyes widened. "But Halaak called him a traitor. He *killed* him, for God's sake."

"He killed Poirot, too," Skyler said. "But the general wasn't a traitor, either. Despite the Whiplash treatment, he was never actually working with us. On the contrary, he was working just as hard as he could to nail us to the wall."

"That's impossible," Bailey insisted, his disbelief turning to anger. "Your plan was too neat to have happened by accident. The rescue, and then—wait a minute. If Ramirez and the general weren't working for you, how did you get to the team we sent into Aegis Mountain?"

"We didn't," Skyler said, his heart tightening as his eyes drifted back to the smoke. "We had a man already in the mountain. Jensen—you might remember him from the last time. He's the one who wrecked the Ryqril base."

Bailey's face tightened as he looked across the clearing to where Hawking and O'Hara had moved the bodies of his fellow officers. "So it was all smoke and mirrors," he said bitterly. "You don't have any secret army waiting to rise up and take Earth back from the Ryqril."

"No, but we could," Skyler said. "We do have Whiplash, and it does work as advertised. But at the moment, no, we don't have more than a few people, and they're in very lowly places. The best we could get out of any of them was the spotters' radio system for us to use during the rescue."

"So Halaak killed Poirot and Ramirez for nothing."

"For absolutely nothing," Skyler agreed. "Which is really the final irony of this whole thing. Once we've proved we *have* Whiplash, and proved that it works, we almost don't even need to use it on anyone. The Ryqril will shoot at every shadow, real or not, until they've torn down their command structure and their rule all by themselves."

"Only you *haven't* proved it," Bailey countered. "Stolen radio frequencies apart, you haven't proved Whiplash's abilities at all."

"We haven't proved it here, no," Skyler said. "But with a little luck, Lathe and his team should have just finished proving it in a much more spectacular fashion on Khala."

Bailey frowned. "On *Khala*?"

"Don't worry about it," Skyler advised. "The point is that, one way or the other, this is the beginning of the end for Ryqril rule in the TDE." He raised his eyebrows. "The question you have to ask yourself is where you want to be standing when that happens."

Bailey's lip twisted. "What do you expect me to say?" he demanded. "I'm a loyal servant of the Ryqril and the TDE government. I could never even think of betraying them."

"Of course not," Skyler said. "Do you remember, Colonel, back at Reger's house when I said you and General Poirot were about to graduate from the third type of person to the fourth?"

"Yes," Bailey said, nodding. "I wondered what you meant by that."

"It's from something my high school physics teacher wrote in my yearbook," Skyler said, his mind drifting back to a distant, simpler past. A past before war and conquering Ryqril and blackcollars. "It goes this way: 'There are four types of people in the world:

"'He who knows not, and knows not that he knows not. He is a fool; shun him.

"'He who knows not, and knows that he knows not. He is simple; teach him.

"'He who knows, and knows not that he knows. He is asleep; wake him.

"'And he who knows, and knows that he knows. He is wise; follow him.'"

For a long minute Bailey was silent. "And what is it you think I know?"

"I don't know," Skyler said. "Life, maybe, or loyalty, or service, or sacrifice. The question is, how interested are you in finding out?"

Bailey shook his head. "You know I can't make a decision like that." He took a deep breath. "But then, I'm your prisoner, aren't I? Prisoners never get to make their own decisions."

"I understand," Skyler said quietly. Reaching into his belt, he withdrew a hypospray from his medkit. "'He is asleep.'"

Bailey's gaze drifted again toward where the bodies of Poirot and Ramirez lay. "'Wake him,'" he murmured.

Mordecai had a pair of patches from his medkit on Galway's bleeding fingers by the time Lathe and Spadafora returned. "You all right?" Lathe asked, his eyes flicking to Taakh and then back to Galway.

"I can travel," Galway said, wincing as Mordecai helped him to his feet. "I'm just glad you got my message."

"Actually, Mordecai was already on his way back," Lathe told him. "We'd gotten a warning that no one outside could find Taakh anywhere."

So that was what had sparked Judas's sudden burst of courage. "Ah."

"I *did* make it a point to hurry when you leaned on the tingler, though," Mordecai added. "Speaking of which, are we taking him with us?"

"I don't know," Galway said, looking at Judas. "Karl? You want to be able to go back to what you were a year ago?"

"I don't know," the young man admitted. "It seems so utterly unthinkable." He hesitated. "But I *do* know I'd like to see my family again."

"Close enough," Lathe said. "I don't suppose you'd be interested in sampling freedom, Prefect Haberdae?"

"Go to hell," Haberdae snarled. "All of you can go straight to hell."

"I'd say that's a no," Spadafora murmured.

"Maybe some day," Lathe said, springing a knife and cutting Judas free from his chair. "Come on. Let's get out of here."

Full night had fallen by the time Jensen finally pulled himself up the last few rungs of the rope ladder and reached the tunnel leading out into the forest. For a minute he stood there, gazing out the air vent a dozen meters away, wondering what kind of reception Security might have left for him.

"You're late," a voice said from just inside the grating.

Jensen had a *shuriken* in his hand before his fatigued mind caught up with the voice. "*Flynn?*" he asked disbelievingly.

"You were expecting the Ryqril high command?" A long dark bundle lying at the entrance pulled itself out of the shadows and reformed itself into a human being. "Or did you just think we'd all pack up and take off without you?"

"Frankly, I'd have put the high command higher on my probabilities list than you," Jensen said, crossing to him. "You didn't come out here all alone, did you?"

"Oh, no, the whole gang was here for a while," Flynn said. He whipped something up and around, and Jensen found a blanket settling down around his shoulders. "You missed a fun party, too—Security officers, blackcollars, even a couple of Ryqril stopped by."

"Ryqril?"

"Don't worry, we dealt with them," Flynn assured him. "The *khassq* is dead, and the battle architect went off to deliver Lathe's ultimatum. No casualties on our side, either, now that you're here." His silhouette cocked its head slightly. "It was Toby, wasn't it?"

"You mean who wrecked the Ryqril base?" Jensen nodded. "He insisted on taking that honor for himself."

"Probably the right thing to do," Flynn said. "He was a pilot, then?"

"Lieutenant Sam Foxleigh, TDE Air Defense," Jensen confirmed. "How did you know?"

Flynn shrugged. "There was just something about him that reminded me of you."

Jensen snorted. "Bullheadedness is hardly a quality unique to pilots," he pointed out. "What did you mean, it was the right thing to do?"

"I meant that if he was a pilot, it was right for him to take on the job." Flynn hesitated. "And that it was right for you to let him take it."

Jensen grimaced. "Look, Flynn, I know some of you

have been a little worried about me. When Novak died . . . well, they teach soldiers to watch out for the trap of survivor's guilt, but I guess I wasn't paying enough attention that day."

He nodded back toward the mountain behind him. "But I think maybe talking with Foxleigh put it into a little better perspective. In warfare you do what you can, and you play out the hand that's been dealt you, and you don't look back. The only purpose for second-guessing is to find the mistakes you made so that you don't make them again."

"Sounds like the wise advice of a grizzled old warrior," Flynn said.

Jensen nodded. "Foxleigh was all that," he agreed.

"I meant you," Flynn said, a touch of humor coloring his voice. "I mean, it took you *forever* to get up that ladder."

"Watch your mouth, kid," Jensen growled, mock-warningly. "I'm not so tired I can't run you through a couple of sparring sessions."

"I'll pass," Flynn said. "Anyway, the others had to head back to Denver, but someone will be back to get us in the morning."

"Or at least to get you?"

Flynn shrugged. "I'll admit they're still mostly convinced you died in the attack," he said. "And Skyler wasn't particularly enthusiastic about letting me stick around to wait for you. But like you said, bullheadedness isn't just for pilots."

"Neither is stamina," Jensen said. "Which is just as well. Two of the techs Security sent in are still alive, but with my ribs the way they are I knew I'd never get them back here on my own."

"I can go do that now," Flynn offered. "At least get them to the bottom of the shaft so we can take them out in the morning."

"We'll go together," Jensen said, peering out into the darkness. "And before we leave this place entirely I need to stop back at Shelter Valley. I think that Doc Adamson and his son would appreciate knowing how Foxleigh died."

"Sounds good," Flynn said. "Just bear in mind you'll probably end up telling them his whole life story along with it."

The story of the man who'd lived in secret shame for thirty years . . . "Not to worry," he murmured. "They already know all the rest of it."

Shaw and Caine were waiting at the rendezvous point when Galway and the others arrived. "Caine," Galway said, watching the younger man warily as they walked over. The last time he'd seen Caine the two of them had been enemies, and Galway had treated him accordingly.

But if Caine was holding a grudge, it didn't show in his face. "Galway," he greeted the prefect in turn. "Welcome back to our side."

"It has been a while," Galway admitted, turning to Shaw. "Tactor," he said, nodding.

"It's good to meet you at last, Prefect," the other said. "And for you to truly meet me, as well."

Galway had to smile. The quiet, confident man standing in front of him was so very different from the picture Judas's reports had painted. "Indeed," he said.

"You have any trouble getting Caine out?" Lathe asked, stepping up beside Galway.

Shaw shook his head. "They were about as unready for trouble as it's possible for military men to be." He nodded past Lathe's shoulder. "I see you brought his evil twin with you."

"Not evil any more," Lathe assured him. "He's had his Whiplash, and is busy regaling Mordecai and Spadafora with the details of the government center security layout. If you're interested in hitting it sometime, that is."

"I might," Shaw said, a touch of quiet pain coloring his voice. "But I lost a third of my men at Khorstron tonight, killed and wounded. I'll have to wait to see what kind of force I can put together."

"You should have Whiplashed the guards at the strong-point after you got Caine out," Galway said.

"Oh, I did," Shaw assured him. "That should help." He looked at Lathe. "Did you deliver your message?"

Lathe nodded. "We found the half circle hiding in their lounge, behind about a dozen warriors. Between them and the Denver Security people Skyler should have talked to tonight, I think the high command will take the suggestion seriously."

"If they don't, we're in for a long, hard battle," Shaw warned.

"But at least it's a battle we know we'll ultimately win," Lathe said. "It's amazing what a difference hope can make in a person."

Galway's eyes drifted upward to the stars overhead. Hope. For most of his professional life, he reflected, all he'd ever hoped for for the people of Plinry was a little safety, a little security, and a fighting chance to live out their lives without unnecessary interference from their alien conquerors. He'd schemed and argued and fought to provide them that chance, straining against the small degrees of latitude his loyalty-conditioning provided in order to do so. He would have done anything he could toward that end, up to and including sacrificing Lathe and the other blackcollars if that was what it took.

It was only in the past twenty-four hours, when the loyalty-conditioning had been stripped away from his mind, that he recognized how low his goals had actually been.

He'd had his own small taste of freedom. Now, he had the chance to help bring that same gift to his people.

Someone was calling his name. "Sorry?" he said, lowering his eyes back to the others.

"I asked if you wanted to get some rest," Shaw said. "Maybe have your hand and face looked at. I have someone ready to take you to a safe house."

Galway snorted. "Rest? Now? You've got to be kidding. With all the chaos still going on at Khorstron, we have a golden opportunity to hit the government center before they can get themselves reorganized. I can let you inside—"

"Whoa," Shaw said, frowning as he held up a hand. "How are you going to do *that*? Haberdae knows you got us into Khorstron, doesn't he?"

"Sure," Galway said. "But he's the only one who does. Why couldn't it have been *him* who betrayed the base instead of me, with him having been left tied up to confuse everyone? It's exactly the sort of thing Lathe would do." He looked at Lathe. "Comsquare? There must be a way to pull this off."

Lathe was staring into space, a faint smile touching the corners of his lips. "I think there probably is," he agreed. "Okay, Galway. Let's try this . . ."

EPILOGUE

The blackened pieces of burned wood crunched beneath Caine's feet as he walked through the block-wide path of destruction that had been cut across the city of Capstone. "They did this on their way out?" he asked, a shiver running through him as he looked around at the still-smoldering ruins that had once been homes and businesses.

"Yes," Lathe said, an edge of contempt in his voice. "Apparently the Ryq commanding the troop carriers' escort decided Plinry in general and Galway in particular needed a parting lesson in what it costs to cross the mighty Ryqril. Or something like that."

"As if any of these people had anything to do with that," Caine growled. "If they wanted to send messages, they should have hit Hamner Lodge instead."

"I'm sure they would have if there'd been any actual military reason to it," Lathe agreed. "But as I said, it was nothing but a final symbolic slap in the face." He gestured around them. "Fortunately, De Vries anticipated they might do something like this on their way out, and he and

Haven were able to figure the likely target zone from their probable lift vector. He got emergency gear in place and was able to slip a lot of the residents out before the attack came. We could have lost a thousand or more, but we actually only lost twenty."

Caine sighed. "That's still twenty civilian deaths too many."

"Agreed," Lathe said. "Let's hope they're the last. Anyway, he's got a bunch of the refugees temporarily settled in the tube between the city and Hamner. That's where Galway disappeared to, by the way—Haven took him up there to assess the situation."

Caine looked up at the Greenheart Mountains rising majestically into the sky. "You really think they're gone for good?"

Lathe shrugged. "The logic of the situation is certainly unarguable," he said. "Their only choices are total war against humanity—which they can't afford with the Chryselli breathing down their necks—or a slow, bloody, fighting withdrawal—ditto—or accepting the TDE-in-chaos scenario Skyler and I pitched them. And of course, wrecking all their TDE armaments factories on their way out was a fairly significant bridge-burning move all by itself. No, I think they really have decided that option three was their best bet."

"Unless they've just pulled back to regroup."

"That would be the worst choice of all," Lathe said grimly. "Because I think we're going to bounce back a lot faster than the Ryqril expect. Now that they've left, if they try to come in again they'll lose big time."

"Maybe," Caine said, a little doubtfully. "Though we're

hardly going to be fielding any serious armies anytime soon."

"Which is fine, since that's mostly what we promised them anyway," Lathe said. "Still, not fielding soldiers doesn't mean we won't be doing our part for the war effort. I understand Lepkowski's already talking to some of the TDE's freshly Whiplashed industrialists about retooling their factories to produce war materiel for the Chryselli. And of course, without Ryqril warships prowling around TDE space, we can turn normal transportation duty over to civilian starships, which will free up the *Novak*, *Defiant*, and *Karachi* for direct battle-line operations."

Caine nodded. It might work. It might actually work. "And what about you?" he asked. "You're going to be taking a role in the new government, aren't you?"

Lathe snorted. "Don't be ridiculous. We're not statesmen, Caine. Most of us aren't even politicians. All we are is soldiers."

"The best soldiers."

"Best is a slippery concept," Lathe warned. "But it doesn't matter. We're still just soldiers . . . and our war is finally over. It's in the hands of people like Lepkowski and Galway and Anne Silcox and Colonel Bailey now."

He gestured toward the mountains. "Me, I'm thinking about building myself a little cabin, sort of like the one Jensen told us about where Foxleigh lived. Near the lodge, of course, so I can keep on teaching Plinry's eager youth the art of combat. Assuming any of them will still want to learn, of course."

"They will," Caine said. "They do."

"We'll see," Lathe said. "And after that . . ." He turned toward the mountains, his eyes taking on a faraway look. "There's no Backlash left, Caine," he said quietly. "And without it, this first generation of blackcollars is also the last. It's time for us to start our graceful fade into the history books."

Caine swallowed around a sudden lump in his throat. "You saved humanity," he said quietly.

"We helped," Lathe agreed. "But it was hardly our show alone. There were Lepkowski and the Chryselli, Shaw and the Khala blackcollars, Anne and Kanai and the old Torch people who created Whiplash—the list goes on and on."

"And Galway, of course," Caine said, nodding. "Risking his neck to try to do right by his people."

"And don't forget yourself," Lathe added. "You're the one who started the ball rolling, after all."

"Maybe," Caine said. "But no matter how you slice it, you and the other blackcollars carried the heaviest load. We're never going to forget that."

"Never is a long time, Caine," Lathe said, a small smile on his lined face. "But we'll see. We'll see."

The End

ABOUT THE AUTHOR

Timothy Zahn is the winner of the coveted Hugo Award for his novella "Cascade Point" and is author of the *New York Times* best-selling Star Wars novel *Heir to the Empire*. Born in Chicago, he earned a B.S. in physics from Michigan State University and an M.S. in physics from the University of Illinois. Selling his first story to Analog in 1978, he quickly attracted attention as a new writer of "hard" science fiction, based on real, cutting-edge science. In addition to his novels for Baen set in the Cobra universe, he has also written such popular series as the "Blackcollar," "Conqueror," and "Dragonback" novels. Other recent novels include *Angelmass* and *Manta's Gift*. He and his family currently live in Oregon.